THE TROUBLE WITH
JACK IRELAND

D1714313

THE TROUBLE WITH
JACK IRELAND

Terry Crawford

Copyright © 2015 by Terry Crawford.

Library of Congress Control Number:		2015900046
ISBN:	Hardcover	978-1-5035-3194-9
	Softcover	978-1-5035-3196-3
	eBook	978-1-5035-3195-6

This book was printed in the United States of America.

Rev. date: 01/19/2015

Author photo by Andrew Langille
Cover design by Randy Kee

To order additional copies of this book, contact:
Xlibris
1-888-795-4274
www.Xlibris.com
Orders@Xlibris.com
699370

FOR VERONICA LEE FENWICK

Good men must not obey the laws too well.

Ralph Waldo Emerson

CHAPTER ONE

VALENTINE'S DAY, 1939. I'd been doing a ton of extra duty lately so, as a reward, I didn't have to show up at the station until around eleven. When the telephone rang at seven o'clock I almost didn't bother to get up. It was probably the desk sergeant forgetting that I didn't need a wake-up call today. By the time I crawled out of bed and padded in bare feet to the kitchen I was ready to toss Mr. Bell's invention into the nearest trash can.

"Yeah, what is it?" I said, gazing out the window. Snow had blanketed the bare ground sometime during the night.

"Detective Ireland?"

I gave my head a shake and straightened up. "Alive and kickin'."

"Sorry to phone you so early but this is Constable Waterman."

I liked Waterman. He was a young cop but very smart. "It's okay, Waterman. What's the trouble?"

Waterman sounded nervous.

"Perhaps nothing, and I might be way off base phoning you, but I'm over on the West Side close to the waterfront," he said, and then went silent.

"That's nice," I cracked. "Getting some fresh air?"

Waterman's nervousness evaporated. "There's been a man murdered here. A Eugene Robichaud."

"Murdered?"

"He was found about forty minutes ago in the bottom of the empty hold of a Norwegian steamship – the *Bergensfjord*."

"Constable, once in a while men do fall, especially if the ladders are wet or icy."

"I know. There have been three similar deaths in the past two years but this is different, Detective Ireland."

"Yeah, how so?"

"My brother-in-law is a stevedore over here. He's worked the winter port for thirteen years. Him and Robichaud were best pals so he was naturally shook up when he heard. Anyway, I was talking to him a few minutes ago and he told me that Robichaud hasn't worked on the ships for three years."

"What's that?" I reached over to plug in the electric kettle my father had given me for Christmas. I still didn't trust it but I suddenly needed a pot of tea.

"Robichaud's been manning a desk in the shipping and receiving office in Shed 7 ever since he shattered one of his kneecaps three years ago."

A blue spark flew from the wall receptacle to the plug. I mumbled, "Grand," at the kettle. "That's interesting, Constable. There could, of course, be a perfectly logical explanation, especially if the guy had a bum leg. Maybe he was invited on board for a drink. Sailors can get hard-up for company when they're standing nightwatch in port."

Waterman lost his temper. "This business is being treated like a standard industrial accident. The Deputy Chief just blasted me for walking past the cordoned-off area. This neighbourhood's my beat and even if the waterfront along here usually comes under C.P.R. Police jurisdiction, I think this is something beyond what they can handle."

"You're right, Waterman. Dead right. Where are you now?"

"In a phone booth on Ludlow Street."

"All right. You hang around there and keep an eye peeled in case an ambulance tries to cross the railyard. If one comes for the body before I arrive, stall it. On my orders if you have to. Got that?"

"Yes Sir, thanks."

I took a deep breath. The Deputy Chief. If ever there was a self-important crud placed on the face of the earth for the annoyance of mankind – he was it. After I shaved and dressed, I sat down for a minute to ponder the situation.

A couple of noisy altarboys disrupted my not-so-idle speculations. They were horsing around on the church sidewalk next to the house. One of them was tossing little red hearts high up into the air and catching them in his mouth. Tiring of the game, he fired up a handful of hearts that bounced around him like red hailstones on the freshly plowed snow. A few elderly people hurried by on the way to 7:30 Mass, their breath visible in the cold.

TERRY CRAWFORD

Before I went out to warm up the Studebaker I switched my shirt and tie for a turtleneck sweater. It might also be wise to wear my pea jacket and stocking hat. If I was going to be on the wharf or rooting around in the hold of a ship I didn't want to come down with laryngitis for the second time this winter.

In the yard I wasn't surprised to see that some moron had written "Nix on Dicks" in the snow on my windshield. Looking over the fence at the statue of St. Joseph, I offered that one up to the little guy he held in his arms.

CHAPTER TWO

B Y THE TIME I drove the car to the Reversing Falls Bridge the sun had come out from behind the clouds. No matter what a lot of people thought, mostly outsiders, Saint John could be one beautiful city. I glanced through the bridge railing into the gorge below at the phenomenon of the rapids in full reverse. Ahead, on a promontory overlooking the river and the harbour, the Provincial Asylum presented a forbidding mass of red brick and barred windows. The location possessed one of the best views in the city. Maybe the founders chose the site for therapeutic purposes. I figured it was for maximum lunar exposure during periods of the full moon.

I wheeled the car off the bridge and headed for Simms Corner, named after the brush and broom factory which dominated the intersection. A freight train was crawling through one arm of the intersection but I was headed in the other direction. If I had been going up into Lancaster – Saint John's twin city – it would've meant sitting in traffic for twenty minutes or more. Both cities were cursed with railway lines that ran across some of the busiest arteries going in and out of town.

Waterman was anxiously pacing in front of a news-stand on Ludlow. Every so often he would step off the curb and peer up the street.

I hauled up in front of him and told him to simmer down and get me a copy of *The Telegraph Journal*. While he was inside the store I noticed an ambulance parked at the cafe on the next block.

Waterman climbed in the front seat and pointed. "There's our ambulance. Can you believe it? The driver and the attendant stopped for breakfast."

"These boys have seen it all, Constable. They're not a bit squeamish. Are you?" I said, pulling the car into the road and heading for the pier.

"A little."

"Good. Me too. How'd the Bruins do last night?"

"The Rangers beat them one-nothing," Waterman said, eyes fixed on the front page of the newspaper.

"What's so interesting, Constable?"

"Oh, sorry, Sir. This European stuff is hard to believe."

"What? Adolf Hitler at it again?" I turned the Studebaker onto the railway crossing after I'd made sure the ambulance wasn't behind us in the rearview mirror.

"Yes. Hitler changed the head of the German Bank and the British are afraid that's curtains for the forty million pounds they've got in Germany. When are the Nazis going to stop?"

Waterman's concern seemed genuine. I wondered how serious he was about politics in general. "Who knows? Not even The Shadow knows. I think we should never have let Germany re-arm. Cripes, now we've got a full-blown arms race on our hands. F.D.R. just deep-sixed the U.S. neutrality act by selling six-hundred planes to France and five-hundred to England. But hey, it's estimated Germany's got about ten-thousand."

"Here we are, Sir. Looks like we've got a bit of a crowd gathering."

I braked the car behind a pallet of cedar shingles and stepped out after I yanked on my stocking hat. A bitterly cold wind was whipping in off the Bay of Fundy.

There appeared to be a fair amount of confusion on the dock. About a dozen men in pea jackets and watchcaps were milling around in front of the roped-off gangplank of the *Bergensfjord*. All I could see was one C.P.R. cop trying to control the whole bunch. He kept yelling for them to come back in an hour but they didn't seem to understand a word he was saying.

"Hello, McManus," I said to the railway cop.

"Hell, Ireland, am I ever glad to see you. Dressed in that get-up I thought you were another longshoreman."

"I despise the cold with undying passion. What's all this flap about?"

One of the sailors started yapping to me in Norwegian. To my great surprise Waterman began talking to him in his native tongue.

"I'd like to go aboard, McManus. Constable Waterman will give you a hand with this mob," I said, ducking under the rope.

The seaman Waterman was gabbing to grabbed me by the arm. I shook him off and showed him my I.D. All that did was get him really agitated.

"Why's he so hot under the collar?" I asked Waterman.

"He claims, as near as I can tell, that you can't go on the ship without the captain's permission and he's not due back until noon."

"Is that so? Well, tell him to hightail it to Station Street and drag the captain out of whatever cathouse he's shacked up in. Meanwhile, I'm going to have a look around whether he likes it or not."

I went up the slippery gangplank trying my damnedest not to look down between the ship and the dock to the dark water below. Besides hating the cold I was a Grade A chicken about heights.

There was a solitary seaman standing watch on the bridge. The cargo hold was completely covered except for one hatch on the starboard side. Because of the footprints in the snow leading to it, I guessed this was where the man had fallen to his death. I held up my badge and indicated that I wanted to go down and view the corpse. The seaman nodded then reached for a switch that turned a light on in the recesses of the hold. When I peered inside I almost lost my breath. It was easily a thirty-foot drop. The deceased lay in a crumpled position a few yards from the foot of the ladder. From a distance he appeared to be a poorly drawn small "h". This part of my job was always terrible. If I had wanted to spend time viewing human remains I would've become an undertaker. I had that old flat taste of tin in my mouth as I descended the ladder, rung by careful rung.

For some unknown reason whenever I'm alone with dead people I think they're suddenly going to do something unexpected. Like sit up and point to heaven or hell. Or even worse, speak to me. Despite this apprehension I knelt down to look at the man's face. He was a handsome guy in his mid-thirties with a splotch of premature gray hair at the temples. Like a red tear, there was a tiny drop of blood congealed at the corner of each eye. When he died his face had been scrunched in a grimace as if he'd swallowed something sour.

I've seen stranger expressions on people who died violently. During my rookie year I found the head of a woman decapitated in an automobile accident. She had the calmest face I'd ever seen – the kind of resignation martyrs' faces have in holy pictures.

The mercury had dipped well below the freezing mark the night before and yet this fellow was dressed more for moving around a chilly warehouse than the out of doors. There was a strong smell of whiskey on his clothes, not the usual rotgut longshoremen drink to fortify themselves against the sea wind, but something expensive. I lifted him up slightly and caught sight of the label of a broken bottle – Chivas Regal – ritzy hootch for a working man. I laid him down gently, then I started up the ladder, rushing the last dozen rungs in sheer panic. Nothing on earth gives me the heebie-jeebies like the fear of falling.

While I was clambering up the stairs to the bridge the ambulance screamed along the wharf, siren going full volume. Waterman yelled to me that he had to get back to his beat. I knew that if he didn't phone in from certain call-boxes within a reasonable amount of time the boys across town at the station might get worried and dispatch a squad car to find him. I didn't want him getting into trouble on my account.

"Hey, Ireland. How's she going?" the ambulance driver said when he and the attendant cleared the gangplank, a stretcher held under their arms like an immense book.

"Fine, Joey. How's the coffee at Hilda's Cafe?"

"Just fair. Still don't miss a trick, eh, Jack? Seriously, don't squeal on us. We just cruised back from a long run to Sussex when the call came in to pick up this poor bastard. A guy's gotta eat, you know?"

"Sure, Joey. As long as you don't stop for dessert on the way back to the morgue."

While we were talking the irate seaman Waterman had spoken with was throwing a minor fit. There was always one in every crowd. The loudmouth anti-police type.

"Where's the stiff, Jack?" Joey asked.

I heaved a loud sigh. "The deceased, Joey, the deceased. And you could address me as Detective Ireland once in a blue moon," I said sternly. "He's at the bottom of the hold. Get him out and into the Cadillac with as little fuss as possible."

"Aye, aye. You're the boss."

I turned away and walked along the foredeck but not before giving the loudmouth sailor the hairy eyeball for a couple of seconds.

"Speak English?" I said to the man standing watch on the bridge.

"Yah, little," he said, fidgeting from side to side.

I noticed he had a pot of coffee simmering on a portable gas stove nearby. "Do you mind?" I said, helping myself to a mug.

He handed me a can of Borden's milk."Are you Royal Canadian Mounted Police?" he asked as if reading from an elementary grammar.

"No. Saint John City."

"Ah," he nodded.

I laughed. "Are you disappointed?"

"No, Sir."

Now that he was at ease, I asked, "Did you find the man who died?"

"Yah," he said sadly.

"Did you know him?"

"Yah. Gene come on boat to get stamps for collection."

"I see. How did he get on the ship last night without you seeing him?"

"I take coffee to engineer down below. When I return, hatch lid open, he down in hole."

"How long were you gone from the bridge?"

"Bridge?"

"Here," I said, knocking on the instrument panel.

"We play three, maybe four games cards," he replied, casting his eyes downward. "Please, not tell captain."

"No, I won't. What game?"

"With matchsticks and board with holes."

"Cribbage?"

"Yah, yah," he said, as if delighted with what he thought must have been my brilliant deductive powers.

"When did it snow last night?"

"I go below, it start. I come up, lot of snow blowing hard."

"And the body?"

"I come here, not see hatch open till sun come up," he said, raising the sun with his hands.

"Was it still snowing then?"

"Yah, little."

"Footprints," I said, raising a foot and grasping it. "In the snow?"

Puzzled, the man removed his hat and ran a hand through his blonder than blonde hair. All of a sudden, he understood. "Yah?"

"Were-there-footprints-in-the-snow?" I said.

"No."

I had what I thought was a pertinent idea but with his answer it fizzled into nothing.

Ushering the fellow to a porthole, I singled out the seaman who had grabbed me by the arm. "Please, tell me about him."

"He first mate. Nobody like. He always shoot… shooot…" At this point the man mimicked someone using a camera.

"Pictures. Photographs."

"Yah. He have many pictures in berth. Use red lights. Pictures all over. He get mad, madder if anyone go in."

"Pictures of what?"

"Everything. Ships, people, places we go. I know, I know," he said, pleased with himself. "It his hobby."

I nodded. I suppose whiling away the time in a darkroom would relieve the monotony of life at sea. "Thank you," I said, shaking hands. "Your coffee is great and so is your English."

"Yah, thanks. I try learn English."

Joey and his burly assistant struggled onto the deck, cursing magnificently at the difficulty of manoeuvring the deceased up the ladder. They had the small man's body covered in canvas and strapped to the stretcher. The men on the dock fell silent, some removing their watchcaps as Joey led the way down the gangplank and into the ambulance.

I waited amidships until the Cadillac disappeared and the seamen filed slowly back on board, then I went ashore. The intense cold had worked up my appetite. I needed a hearty breakfast and somewhere to read the newspaper. All in all, it had not been an auspicious way to start the day.

CHAPTER THREE

THE WAITRESS ACCIDENTALLY dumped an overloaded tray of dirty dishes into the sink, muttered something unrepeatable, threw a dishrag at the laughing short-order cook, then pulled my newspaper down out of the way and poured me a second cup of coffee.

"Thanks," I said. "Must be one of those days."

"You said it, Buster. And here I thought Valentine's Day was supposed to be romantic."

"Give it time, it's not even nine o'clock yet."

"Got something in mind?"

"Wait till spring," I suggested. "I'll be more in the mood."

She sashayed sweetly away. I'd seen her before and knew she liked to kid around with the customers. "You've got a date, killer. Don't forget."

"I'll write it down," I said, frowning at *The Telegraph Journal*. If the reports from overseas got any more ominous I vowed to give up reading the news altogether.

The buzzing neon sign in the window was drilling a hole in my forehead so I moved from the fountain to a booth in the far corner. The coffee at Pepper's Diner was five-star. The food was only okay but came in such quantity you never left hungry.

Fishing into my shirt pocket, I retrieved a note Waterman had tucked under my windshield wiper. It was his brother-in-law's address. The fellow was the late Eugene Robichaud's best friend. Like an unwanted visitor, an ugly image came into my mind – the deceased naked and split open in the autopsy room. I was becoming morbid lately. Maybe it was the horror movies I'd been dragged into by my nephew, or maybe it was not feeling comfortable around dead bodies. Mostly though, I think it was the war fever going the rounds. I was getting visions of dead bodies all right, bodies piled up higher than the pulpwood at the woodyard across the street.

The waitress slipped me the check and refilled my cup.

"Is that all?"

"Yeah, thanks. Tell me, this place is open all night, do you get many seamen in here?"

"Sure. Why?"

"Any trouble?"

"I got a kid in school so I don't work the graveyard shift but, come to think of it, the night cook told me there was quite the fracas in here last night involving some foreigners," she said, sitting down opposite me. Her manner had become softer, less flirtatious.

"A fracas? How come?"

"I guess it was a big argument about A-Dolf Hitler. That was the only word the cook could understand. You a sailor?"

"Me? I get seasick in elevators. I was just curious about the late-night clientele," I said, rising to leave.

"Late night? H'mm, railway workers, sailors, coppers, the odd bum – God bless 'em – with no place else to go."

I glanced at the check – 65¢ – and laid a two-dollar bill down. "Keep the change," I said. "Happy Valentine's. See you around."

While the car warmed up, my thoughts kept circling like vultures around the dead man. His friend's address was in the East End, 56 Erin Street, a few blocks from the station. But since I was already on the West Side my best move would be to visit Shed 7 now, especially since the morning shift was in full gear and I wouldn't be so conspicuous. It bothered me that the Deputy Chief had been at the scene but had not ordered even a routine investigation. He was an inefficient boob, but this whole business was stranger than fiction.

The bells on the railway crossing behind me began dinging so I pulled the car around and gunned it across the tracks. Before I'd driven half a block a locomotive chugged into the rearview mirror. I also glimpsed an unmarked car but I stupidly didn't pay any attention to it.

I parked the Studebaker where I'd hidden it earlier and put on my stocking hat. If I could pass for a stevedore then maybe I wouldn't attract any unnecessary attention. All I wanted to do was have a quick sneak around Shed 7.

When I reached the wharf the sight of the *Bergensfjord* backing toward mid-harbour gave me a jolt. But not nearly as much as spying a certain guy on deck with a camera. He had a tripod set up on the poop and appeared to be getting a fistful of portraits of yours truly. So much for the line about the captain not being due back until noon. Mr. Bigmouth the Liar was hunched over the camera's viewfinder.

I grinned and gestured obscenely. Certain bits of sign language are recognized internationally. The way Bigmouth jerked his head back, I'd say he got the message. Some actions do speak louder than words.

CHAPTER FOUR

I F YOU TRAVELLED by way of the wharf, Shed 7 was about a thousand feet from where the *Bergensfjord* had been moored. I decided to take a shortcut through Shed 7 and then 6. The big rectangular sheds had sliding doors on their long sides, which faced the railway tracks to the west and the waterfront to the east. I eased open a door and peered into the murky interior of Shed 7. It was three-quarters empty with only five workmen visible at the far end. They were busy loading tires into boxcars and didn't see me when I walked quietly to the cramped pen that passed for an office.

"Gene Robichaud" was stencilled in red across the window of the work-space door. I tried to get in but the knob wouldn't budge. I felt along the top edge of the door frame and, sure enough, knocked a key onto the asphalt floor.

After I gained entry and replaced the key, I sat down at Robichaud's desk and looked the place over. It was tidy enough even if it did reek of whiskey. Everything in the office could be reached from the chair. The usual pigeonholes occupied three walls and a huge calendar hung on the door. On the wall to my right a photograph in a polished brass frame of a man, woman, and child gleamed in the overall drabness. Beside it, on a plain sheet of paper tacked to a bulletin board the word *tires* was written in inch-high letters in a childlike script. I took a hurried inventory of the desk's contents and clicked off the overhead light.

As I started to leave I knocked over the wastebasket. A partially eaten sugared doughnut rolled onto the floor. Handling it made me nauseated. It was likely the deceased's last food. Something about the way the simple office was personalized inclined me to like Eugene Robichaud without ever having met the man.

I left to trace the route as the crow flies from Robichaud's desk to the location of his death. After making sure the office door was locked, I turned around and ran headlong into a hulk who could have been Bluto in human form.

He grabbed me by the throat before I could utter a syllable. "And who are you?" he bellowed like a foghorn. "Nobody but his sister's allowed in Gene's office."

About to mash my oft-abused nose with a fist the size of a pile-driver, the not-so-gentle giant stopped at the sight of my I.D.

"Cops. Youse were already snoopin' around here," he said, releasing me with a shove.

I massaged my throat. His grip had all but shut off my windpipe. Unable to talk, I stared at him as calmly as possible.

"Beat it," he said. "Take a powder."

I wasn't about to argue with someone that a fast freight wouldn't stop. "Take it easy," I stammered.

He swiped a number 14 boot at me as if I were a troublesome dog. "Beat it," he repeated.

I beat it. As fast as I could march toward the *Bergensfjord's* mooring. In my haste to slide the door open I whacked my cheek hard. The damn thing had stuck only partway open. I slipped sideways through the slit and out into the daylight. Blinded by the sun glaring off the snow, I fell back into the shade under the eaves. While my eyes were adjusting to the light I thought I could see a handful of those candy valentine hearts strewn along the ground. But when my vision cleared I stooped down and realized that I was looking at a trail of blood splattered on the undisturbed snow under the shelter of the overhang. It could be that someone smacked their nose like I had just struck my cheek but then again...

I scraped a sample of the red stuff into an envelope. Sometime in the afternoon I could take it to a lady-friend who worked at the General Hospital for a confidential analysis.

My cheek was throbbing in the cold so I continued on to Shed 6. Unlike 7, it was jammed to the rafters with cargo, mostly canned goods that had to be protected from freezing. The place was positively tropical compared to most of the other sheds. It was also dark as a dungeon.

As I felt my way along between the stacks something peculiar occurred to me about Robichaud's office. It was excessively neat whereas the contents of the desk drawers were a mess – a kind of orderly mess but a jumble all the same.

A straight path from Robichaud's desk would have led directly to the *Bergensfjord*. Providing the tide-level was right it would be easy for someone in Shed 6 to observe the deck of a ship tied up alongside through the small panes in the doors.

Earlier, when I drove over the Reversing Falls Bridge, the rapids were in full reverse, which meant it was low tide during the night. Robichaud could have wandered drunkenly through the sheds and walked onto the *Bergensfjord's* deck without having to climb the gangplank.

A simple enough theory – the best kind. But what nagged me like a toothache was how a man about five-four who might have tipped the scales at a hundred pounds soaking wet managed to pry off a hatch cover that weighed almost as much as he did. And he was probably knowledgeable about ships – why go into the hold? What could he possibly have been looking for? Surely he knew it was empty?

I submitted myself to the first Philip Morris of the day. The nicotine hit my brain like a slow, stimulating poison. Was I too suspicious? It was one of the hazards of the trade. Eugene Robichaud could be yet another dockside case of death by misadventure. Sad but true. These things happen. As I'd reminded Constable Waterman – men *do* fall.

I went outside into the brutal wind and surveyed the harbour for a minute while I thought about the little man who died violently sometime before dawn. Violently and horribly. And now he was being transformed into a handful of papers shuffled from one desk to another. It somehow seemed too abrupt and too final.

I silently cursed my bad luck after I ambled back to the Studebaker. The long freight train I beat through the crossing at Pepper's Diner had me stranded between the waterfront and the city. A gang of stevedores was busy unloading boxcars down the line. A passing brakeman informed me that they were going to be at least an hour.

I crawled under an Indian blanket in the back seat of the Studebaker and drifted off to sleep.

About an hour later I sat bolt upright, undershirt glued to my back with sweat. I scrambled behind the wheel and sped home. I had dreamed a terrible dream. A dream where it was snowing fat drops of blood which turned into tiny hearts when they hit the soft ground. Ground bandaged with thick white gauze.

CHAPTER FIVE

I PUT SYDNEY Bechet's *Chant in the Night* on the record player for something to listen to while I changed out of my longshoreman's disguise and into my detective's costume. Yes, costume. Because that's what I think pin-striped suits and neckties are – detective outfits. If the Chief wanted to earmark us as dicks he should have gone all the way and forced us to wear deerstalkers and capes. The first time I wore a necktie was thirty-two years ago at my Confirmation. I hated them then and I hate them now.

Sydney hit a high note on the soprano, knocking me out before I worked myself into a lather about dress regulations. In the bureau mirror I was frowning my best dissatisfied-with-the-world frown, always a dead giveaway for anyone trying to gauge my mood. I smiled goofily at my reflection. Good jazz always made me feel better even if the gray hair prematurely dusting my temples didn't.

The telephone rang at the same moment the kettle started whistling. The two alarms in shrill harmony. I took my time getting into the kitchen. Lifting my tried-and-true kettle off the stove – I'd decided to stow the new electric in the cupboard until I was feeling more adventurous – I fixed a pot of tea and picked up the phone on its eighth ring.

"Detective Ireland?"

"Constable Waterman. How goes it?" I said, maybe too breezily. Even with the bad dream, the sleep in the Studebaker had recharged my batteries.

"Not bad, Sir. What did you think?"

I could hear traffic roaring behind him. "About?"

"Eugene Robichaud."

"His death should be investigated but if the Deputy Chief says accident – that's that."

"Sorry, Sir. What do you mean?"

"If Robichaud's death is declared an accident then any action we might undertake as policemen would be looked upon as redundant and a waste of the taxpayer's hard-earned cash," I stated, testing Waterman to see how far he would commit himself. The last thing I wanted was to embark on an unauthorized investigation with someone who'd get cold feet once we started.

Waterman hesitated, probably uncertain of my meaning. "Are you saying that you suspect foul play?"

"Perhaps."

"But that we can't do anything official to try and find out?" Waterman said. The traffic noise behind him diminished so that he virtually shouted "find out."

"Precisely."

"I'm at your service, Sir," he said, sounding almost British.

"Hold your horses, Waterman," I cautioned. "This will have to be done on the sly. *On the sly*, understand?"

"Yes, Sir. Thank you."

"Don't thank me yet. And remember that, in the end, we likely will discover that it was an accident. Or, barring that, we'll be unable to prove that it wasn't. We'll have to walk on eggs, Waterman. If we're caught poking around, stirring up rumours of homicide, we'll get more than a reprimand for our troubles."

"Fair enough. I only want the opportunity to prove that it wasn't just an accident."

"Fine, Waterman. I appreciate that but don't let it interfere with the performance of your duties as a constable on patrol."

"No Sir, I won't."

I carried the phone from the counter to the table by the window. The snow was beginning to melt on the shoulders of the statues in the churchyard. "By the way," I said, "I didn't know you spoke Norwegian. You weren't born in Norway were you?"

"No. My parents came from Germany. They legally changed their name from Himmelmann to Waterman the year I was born."

"Germany? Then the guy you talked to was German?"

"Yes."

"What was he beefing about?"

"Since Mom and Dad passed away my German's gone downhill," Waterman explained. "As far as I could tell he was in a panic because he thought you'd upset his darkroom during a search of the ship. Something about pictures he was developing."

"Which strikes me as very curious, Waterman. What else did he say?"

"Nothing much. He was so excited I couldn't understand everything."

"Excited? His hair was damn near on fire. Well, I'm going to let you get back to pounding your beat. Thanks for your brother-in-law's address. I'll keep in touch. It's best if we talk about this Robichaud business away from the station, all right?"

"Yes, Sir. Good-bye."

"Constable?"

"Yes?"

"Walk softly."

I propped my feet up on the windowsill, leaned back in the chair, and contemplated the outline of St. Peter's Church roof etched against the clear blue sky. It was a beautiful winter day with the sun betraying a hint of spring. Having to go to work was about as enticing as spending a weekend in the dentist's clutches. Before I got too comfortable basking in the sunlight, I poured another cup of tea and went into the living room.

I listened to Benny Goodman's ride and sock arrangement of *Sing, Sing, Sing*. Krupa's drum solo never failed to get me up and out the door with an extra dose of pep in my stride.

CHAPTER SIX

TRAFFIC AROUND KING Square was pandemonium. I nearly side-swiped a streetcar and almost rammed into the rear of a stalled Model A. If I'd been smart I would've avoided the shopping district and gone the long way around to the station. But I hadn't been very smart today. By the time I got the Studebaker out of the snarl my nerves were worn to a frazzle. Instead of parking in the area reserved for police vehicles, I wheeled past the Courthouse then swerved around the corner and onto Union Street.

I left the car beside the Red Ball Brewery across the road from old man Breen's blacksmith's shop and walked from there to work. It was only a short distance up the hill through the Loyalist Burial Grounds. A firehall, the police station, jail, and courthouse looked out over the graveyard. Unlike a lot of the younger crowd I enjoyed the 19th century atmosphere of this part of the city. And I had no qualms about advocating preservation. It exuded what the tourist brochures liked to call local colour.

The front desk was surrounded by a bunch of winos rounded-up from one of the South End railyards. They had set up housekeeping in an abandoned caboose on a neglected siding and were rousted out because of a complaint from a couple of ten-year-olds who liked to play Junior G-Men on the disused trains. I recognized a trio of the older derelicts so I slinked by before they could collar me into sticking up for them. They were harmless victims of the Depression. Live and let live, I say. But there were always a few busybodies concerned with running them out of whatever place they could find to squat.

When I entered my office my former and still occasional partner, Sully Sullivan, was idly studying the paperwork on my desk.

"Looking for something, Sweets," I said, stuffing what little he hadn't seen into a drawer.

He pushed a lemon tart into his mouth. "M'mnph," he said, shaking his curly red mop.

I noticed for the first time that Sullivan was going bald on the crown. There was a shiny spot the size of a silver dollar showing through the red. He habitually wore a hat indoors and was addicted to pastries and doughnuts. I swept a sprinkling of crumbs off the desktop with the back of my hand, sat down, and put my feet up.

"What happened to your cheek, Jack? Stick your face someplace where it wasn't welcome?"

I bared my teeth and said, "Ran into a door."

"Oh sure, sure. By the way, did you get my message, Jackie boy?" Sullivan said, slurping coffee out of a beer stein. It was one of those German rigs with a lid and reminded me of the bigmouth photographer.

"Message? What message?" Sullivan was in my bad books these days. Once upon a time he was a good policeman. Nowadays he was the kind of self-serving, narrow-minded bigot who gave cops a bad reputation. Corrupt in a petty way, he could no longer be trusted when it came to anything confidential. Most of the department knew he was the Deputy Chief's in-house spy.

"Inscribed in snow," he smirked. "Nix on Dicks."

"Yeah, lovely. Remind me to nominate you for jerk-of-the-month."

He rolled his walrus-like bulk off the corner of the desk and waddled out of the office. A second later he reappeared. "Before I forget, the Deputy Chief wants to see you, and I'm quoting, 'The second he arrives.' Toodle-loo, Jack."

The Deputy Chief. Hell. What could he want with me? Always hostile towards the more independent members of the force, he barely contained his contempt for me and a handful of other officers. Deputy Chief Hardfield – Hardy to his friends – was a former Army Major who served overseas in France from '16-'18 without distinction. In fact, the scuttlebutt claimed he was a notorious dunderhead who was continuously reassigned just to keep him from doing any harm. Following the armistice Hardfield served out his commission in obscurity. Shortly after retirement from His Majesty's Service he was handed a couple of positions out west and in Ontario until he arrived in our foggy city.

I picked up the phone and called the front desk. "Sergeant Devlin, are you still getting serenaded by the Wino's Choir?"

"Yes, Ireland. What am I going to do with these heathens?" Devlin said sleepily. "They spent the last two nights in the lock-up for vagrancy and they're free to go but they'll be back before nightfall."

"Tell Jimmy Feran, he's the jittery one with the hooked nose, to take his buddies down to the Salvation Army H.Q. on Saint James Street and talk to Captain Gibbons. He's got some clean-up work for them and a bed if they stay sober. If Feran gives you any guff tell him it's Ireland on the line."

"Right-O, thanks, Jack."

I knew every derelict and rummy in Saint John. Apart from growing up in the same neighbourhood with many of them, I had met the rest when I used to pound a beat. They were the dregs of society – most of them weren't even allowed inside a church – but they were one of the best sources of reliable information anywhere.

CHAPTER SEVEN

I RAPPED ON Hardfield's door and waited for the customary drill instructor's bark he affected as a signal for subordinates to enter. When I heard "Entah!" I exhaled and stepped into the great man's inner sanctum.

Hardfield stood with his back to me but was scrutinizing my face through a shaving mirror propped up on a filing cabinet. Without turning he told me to sit down. Adjusting the mirror so he could watch me, he continued clipping his handlebar moustache with a pair of small gold-plated scissors. Hardfield had black bushy eyebrows and the most penetrating stare I'd ever seen. All of which annoyed me to no end. It was his one big trick and he never failed to use it. During inspection I'd witnessed young constables actually tremble when Hardfield halted and, eyeball to eyeball, fixed them with that accusatory glare.

Even through the mirror Hardfield's stare was beginning to make me squirm. I surrendered and looked out the window at the pedestrians on their way to the City Market and the stores around King Square. A flock of seagulls kited high over the trees in the Loyalist Burial Ground.

Hardfield dribbled a few drops of brilliantine on his pink hands and slicked back his short hair. With a barber's comb he parted it in the middle then quickly stroked it into place. He gave his moustache a final appraisal and turned on his heels.

"Now then, Ireland."

At this point I was supposed to snap to attention. Instead, I stifled a yawn. "Yes, Sir."

Hardfield was staring daggers at me. Ten, twelve seconds passed. Finally I said, "Sullivan informed me you wanted to see me."

He kept staring like a captive hawk. His moustache glistened with hair oil. Motionless, he uttered icily, "What were you doing on the *Bergensfjord* this morning?"

I played dumb. "The *Bergensfjord*?"

Hardfield leaned across his desk. "Detective Ireland, answer my question."

I was thinking about the unmarked car I'd spotted behind me in Lancaster. Later on I would make a big point of finding out who tailed me. "Nothing much."

Hardfield exploded. "Nothing much? Nothing much? I'll have you know that I was at the scene long before you arrived. The situation was well in hand. There was absolutely – absolutely, Ireland – no need for you to countermand my orders. I've got half a mind to cite you for insubordination."

I agreed that he had half a mind but I wasn't about to tell him so. I'd been careless but I wasn't reckless. "No offense intended, Sir. Please accept my apologies," I said, smoothly as a snake.

Hardfield picked up his ever-present swagger stick and strode to the window. Addressing the outdoors, he muttered between clenched teeth, "I understand you had most of the morning off because of extra duty."

"Yes, Sir."

"So how did you come to hear of this accident?"

He said accident with a condescending twist that I didn't like one damn bit. I took a chance and replied, "An anonymous telephone call."

I couldn't see his face reflected in the window but I'd swear on a stack of Bibles that he winced. I was getting curiouser and curiouser.

Hardfield turned his profile to me and struck a gallant pose. "You are a consummate liar, Ireland," he said. "However, be that as it may, since you are so interested in the demise of a drunken port worker," he faced me squarely, "yours is the odious task of offering condolences to the bereaved on behalf of the department."

I started to object.

"Yes, Ireland?"

"Nothing, Sir." Damn his stuffed shirt, he knew how I dreaded that kind of duty.

"And for the love of all that's good and holy, wear a suitable necktie."

I glanced down. I didn't think a ruffed grouse taking wing above its Latin name on a copper background looked all that bad. I grinned, "This is my most expensive cravat."

"Don't be insolent, Ireland. Mark my words: This cavalier attitude of yours will land you in deep trouble someday."

I kept grinning. Hardfield had lost his much-vaunted composure and I was revelling in every second of his discomfort.

He regarded me with disdain. "What is the world coming to?" he said, wagging his head profoundly.

"That's exactly what I hear, Sir. Everywhere on the streets. 'What's the world coming to?' It's the question of the year."

Hardfield twisted the ends of his moustache and issued an exasperated moan. "Oh, get out, Ireland. Leave. And don't let me see your sarcastic face in here again. You seem to take particular pride in imitating a Tinseltown detective. Well, I'm serving you final notice that I'll not tolerate cheap behaviour on my force."

I wondered what expensive behaviour might be like. "Yes, Sir." I left as slowly as I could without appearing to drag my feet.

In the corridor I almost laughed out loud like a deranged leprechaun. It felt nice to win a round once in a while.

Back in the office I telephoned Peacock's Flower Shop. "Hello, I'd like to send a Valentine bouquet, sweetheart roses would be the answer, to Roxanne at Pepper's Diner. Bill them to Jack Ireland, sixty-five Douglas Avenue. A card? Yeah…yes. No, don't put my name on it. Lemme see, put – Cheers, from Killer – okay? Thanks a lot. Bye."

I sat back, a little drunk with glee. I'd gotten off easy. But I sobered instantly at the thought of the black-tie affair ahead.

CHAPTER EIGHT

IT WOULDN'T TAKE a genius to figure out which flat Eugene Robichaud used to live in. It was the middle of the day and the blinds were drawn all the way down; the traditional indication of a death in the family.

I grew up on the next block so I knew the neighbourhood better than the back of my hand. Funny. It was smaller than a small world. When I was a kid I used to short cut through Robichaud's alley on Saint Patrick Street to get to our house on Saint David.

Most of the houses were crammed together along the sidewalk. It gave the street a closed-in, claustrophobic feel. Fire was a constant fear because it could sweep through the wooden structures in no time. The vicinity was mostly working class with woeful pockets of poverty.

I'd left the Studebaker parked where it was on Union and walked the two blocks. It was snowing again; fine, powdery flakes that hushed the afternoon. The only signs of life were a few customers going in and out of the corner store. I crossed the street and entered the house. The hall was unlit and emitted a strong odour of tomcat. Hanging onto the banister, I felt my way upstairs in the dark. At the first landing I stumbled over a congestion of overshoes and rubbers.

Someone opened the door in response to the commotion. Embarrassed and squinting into the light, I said, "Mrs. Robichaud?"

A petite, round-shouldered woman in her late forties, wearing a faded house dress, tried to smile. "No, I'm Gene's sister, Marie," she said in a thick Acadian accent. "Come in, please."

"Thank you," I said, removing my fedora. The front room was packed with men and women standing around drinking tea and eating sandwiches. Most of them still wore their coats. I quietly introduced myself to Marie and offered my condolences. She thanked me graciously, insisting that I have some tea. Her eyes were completely rimmed in red – she looked cried out. I didn't feel I should stay but I couldn't very well say no.

The place was a typical cold-water flat with that strange kind of immaculate cleanliness you often find in slum dwellings.

On a shelf over the kitchen table two votive candles flickered in front of a picture of the Blessed Virgin. I got a bit choked up. My wife had been killed by a hit-and-run driver four years before and something in that simple altar reminded me of her funeral. Sometimes certain memories lurk in the shadows waiting for something to lure them out.

Robichaud's sister passed me a cup of strong tea. Her hands were steady.

"Was Gene married?" I asked.

"Once, a long time past, home in Madawaska," she said in a daze.

I suspected the poor woman hadn't a moment's peace all day. When I pulled a chair around she sat down without thinking it was for me. It was easy to tell she wanted to be alone.

I went and joined the crowd. Everyone was speaking French. They all fell silent when I walked into the room. A guy I went to school with recognized me and said hello. The chatter immediately started up again.

"Eh, Jack, *comment ca va?*"

"*Tres bien*, Andre, *et vous?*" I replied awkwardly.

"Fine, thanks. This is a sad thing, eh?"

I wordlessly agreed.

"Marie is taking it hard," Andre said. "Gene phoned her from work late last night."

"Oh?" I said, trying not to appear too interested.

"Yes. He was loaded and guilty about something."

"Guilty?" I queried in the direction of a wall decorated with religious pictures and mementos. A large plaster crucifix painted in Disney colours seemed suspended in the gloom over the chesterfield.

"Well, you know, Gene was real religious and always got blubbery about his sins whenever he was drunk," Andre explained, a bit tipsy himself. His teacup was filled to overflowing with cheap sherry.

I conversed in English with several other mourners for a while then bowed out after saying good-bye to Robichaud's sister.

On the sidewalk I looked up and down the street just in case I was being followed. Call it intuition, or an experienced cop's sixth sense, but since my dressing-down by Deputy Chief Hardfield I had the distinct feeling I'd best keep one eye over my shoulder. By and large, it was somewhat like operating on both sides of the law at the same time. More than somewhat. But there was something rotten about the Robichaud business – and it stank worse than Andre's breath.

CHAPTER NINE

CONSTABLE WATERMAN'S BROTHER-IN-LAW lived a stone's throw away from Robichaud's place. I nipped into the corner store for a pack of Philip Morris and a Coca-Cola. The proprietor was listening to one of those obnoxious game shows that polluted the airwaves. It seemed half the human race was on the radio trying to win a prize.

I stood in the warmth of the stove and smoked a cigarette. A mousey, jug-eared kid sat at my feet reading superhero comics. A masked man in green and yellow tights was battling criminals on a runaway train. The kid's mouth hung open. His eyes didn't blink. I lowered the rest of the Coca-Cola to him and left the store. He slugged back the pop without taking his eyes off the comic book.

Erin Street was an extension, at a dog-leg, of Saint Patrick. A fair number of its residents worked at the York Cotton Mill in back of the street on the shore of Courtenay Bay. When the tide was out the innermost part of the bay emptied, exposing a mudflat that often smelled of sewage, a stench usually offset by the salty ocean breeze and the woodsy scent of the neighbourhood lumberyards.

I double-checked the address and name on Waterman's note. His brother-in-law's flat was next to Christie's Woodworkers. When I went into the alley and up the stairs attached to the side of the house, a saw periodically whined in the air.

The Moffats' and their two kids' names were printed in crayon on a bristol-board card tacked to the door. Upstairs on the third floor someone was playing Artie Shaw records loud enough to deafen Helen Keller.

I knocked and waited. A woman who had the same sharp jawline, thin lips, blue eyes, and dark brown hair as Constable Waterman answered.

"Mrs. Moffat?" I said. "Thomas Waterman's sister?"

She was no more than twenty-eight or twenty-nine but looked haggard and spent.

"Yes."

"Detective Ireland. I work with Tom." I barely knew Waterman and shouldn't have pretended familiarity but I figured it would relax her somewhat. "Tom asked me to drop by and talk to your husband."

"Oh, Gawd. Billy isn't in trouble?" she said, taking off her apron and unconsciously fixing her hair.

"No. It's about Gene Robichaud."

"Poor Gene. He was such a sweetheart. Come in, please."

I tugged off my toe-rubbers.

She ushered me through a sparkling blue and white kitchen that had just been scrubbed with Dutch Cleanser and Sunlight soap. In the front room Billy Moffat sat disconsolately staring at the wallpaper, white and pink striped wallpaper with big yellow roses that would've driven me bonkers.

He stood and thrust out a hand. Moffat was sturdily built and, to my eyes, old before his time. With him it might have been the sorrow of the day but I'd always noticed that a lot of labourers and factory workers tended to age prematurely. Including my father.

Mrs. Moffat introduced us to one another then went away.

"I'm sorry about your friend, Mr. Moffat," I said.

"Bill, call me Bill. Thanks, he was one of the best. Have a seat."

I sat down on the sofa, momentarily taken off-guard by its softness. My knees almost hit me on the chin. When I stretched my legs they stuck out into the room like oars but I was comfortable.

Bill Moffat found the rose he'd been staring at and continued boring a hole through it. His grief was tangible.

In the uneasy silence I scanned the room. Magazines sorted into his and her piles were stacked on top of a bookcase full of Zane Grey westerns and children's books. Her pile was comprised of *Modern Screen*, *McCall's*, and *Ladies' Home Journal*. His stack was all outdoors: *Field and Stream*, *Argosy*, and *Rod and Gun*. The stuff dreams are made on.

I was looking at a photograph of Gene Robichaud and Bill Moffat holding a string of trout between them when I heard Mrs. Moffat say, "Is there anything you want, Billy?"

He took a long time to answer. "Bring us a couple of Moosehead, honey."

I listened as she unlatched an icebox in the hall and returned a few seconds later with two quarts and a beer opener.

Moffat snapped the caps off the ale and handed me one.

"Here's to Gene. May he rest in peace," he said, raising a toast to the photograph.

We clinked bottles and drank the brew slowly. Finally, I asked, "Did you know Gene for a long time?"

Without looking at me, Moffat said, "Since he came to Saint John in '34. He didn't have more than fifty words of English. I taught him, though. He picked it up fast."

I took a long swallow then set the Moosehead down on an end table. "Mind if I ask you a few questions about Gene?"

"No. Go ahead."

"How much of a drinker was he?"

Moffat swung his head my way then back at the wallpaper. All the while we were sitting, one Artie Shaw record after another had been blaring upstairs. I'd been tapping my toes without realizing. Moffat abruptly got to his feet and angrily rushed into the kitchen where he grabbed a broom and pounded the ceiling with the handle. The music's volume dropped by half but was still loud.

Moffat came back and sat in his chair. "Gene was an alcoholic."

"When he came to S.J. or later?" I had another swig of beer and lit a smoke after giving Moffat one.

"His relatives bootlegged booze during Prohibition. He grew up on the Maine/New Brunswick border in Madawaska. Gene told me he was hooked before he was fifteen, if that's possible."

"I suppose it is," I said. "Did he like expensive liquor?"

"Gene? Naw, he said his liver couldn't tell the difference. I always bought him a good bottle of the hard stuff at Christmas, though."

"Chivas Regal, maybe?"

"Never heard of that. He liked Canadian Club. That's what his folks trucked into the States."

"How come he landed in Saint John? Quite a lot of people got wealthy off the Volstead Act."

"Some of his relatives did all right for themselves. Gene was a trucker's helper, then a driver, that's all. His money went on a wife who skipped to Montreal when Prohibition ended. That hit him like a ton of bricks. He escaped, as he put it, to Saint John. His wife's disappearance turned him religious but no matter how many times he took the Pledge he kept falling off the wagon."

"H'mm," I said. Certain pillars of the community who had built some pretty classy mansions with Prohibition profits came to mind. They were too busy buying into the establishment to ever worry about anyone who fell by the wayside. I thought about guilt and where it really belonged. "Guilt. Was Gene preoccupied in any way with guilt?" I felt a bit foolish. Like I was a Viennese head-doctor with a patient on the couch. But the question did strike a nerve. I finished the beer and wished that I hadn't bypassed lunch.

"Gene's middle name was guilt," Moffat said. "And always over nothing. He'd get guilty if he forgot to leave money out for the milkman."

"That bad? Was he near-sighted?"

"No. The opposite. Gene had eyes like a friggin'cat. I swear he could practically see in the dark."

"What about when he was drinking?" I said, standing up to look outside. It was snowing so hard you couldn't see across the street.

"Mister, I'd be blind drunk and Gene would be sober as a judge. He *really* was an alcoholic. But unless he told you, you couldn't tell. That's how he kept his job."

"He sounds like he was a good fellow and a good friend," I said, pulling on my overcoat. "It's too bad he died so young."

Moffat controlled a sob. "I'm gonna miss him. And I can't believe that it was just your ordinary accident. But then I can't believe he won't be shooting pool with me at the Strand tonight, either. Funny, he was gray at the temples like you."

"Yeah, I know. It's a shame he's gone."

"You saw Gene, Detective Ireland?" Moffat said alertly. "You gotta tell me. Did he suffer?"

"Bill, listen to me," I said. "Gene died instantly. He never felt a thing." I had no way of knowing that but if it helped Moffat's bereavement then it was a lie for the good. If there is such a thing.

Moffat walked me to the door. "Thanks for coming, I appreciate it. Your visit made me feel better."

I nodded. We shook hands and said good-bye.

Down in the alley I stopped and tightened my scarf. It was getting damp – the snow on the verge of turning into rain.

As I crossed the street on my way to Hospital Hill a green Plymouth drove away from the curb. For a moment I could've sworn the mouthy seaman with the camera was eyeballing me from the back seat, but when I looked again there was no one visible in the car except the driver. And he was buried inside a hat and coat. I considered giving chase just for the hell of it but reminded myself that I'd seen the *Bergensfjord* cast off with my own eyes. Maybe the changeable weather had me seeing things. Or beer on an empty stomach.

I turned up my collar, put my gloves on and made for the General Hospital. A lab report on the blood sample from the wharf might prove revealing. Of what, I didn't know. There was something troubling about Robichaud's death, something unlikely. Somehow the circumstances just didn't add up. But so far I was shadow-boxing. Shadow-boxing in the dark.

TERRY CRAWFORD

CHAPTER TEN

THE HOSPITAL LOBBY was bustling. Somewhere down a side corridor a child wailed in agony. The scent of snow-dampened clothes mingled with an overriding trace of ether. I'd been told that besides knocking people out, ether was sometimes used as a supreme disinfectant. But the stuff was so volatile its smell escaped and wandered at large. It always made my nerves twitch a little at first. Probably the result of a forgotten memory.

I tapped the snow off my hat. While I unbuttoned my coat in the stifling heat a finger poked into my back and a familiar voice whispered, "Stick 'em up, Sarge."

I stomped the slush off my rubbers before turning around. "Hi, Penny. Just the gal I wanted to see."

"Oh, oh. Not another secret mission," Penny said in mock disgust. We had been friends since I first met her years ago when my wife was studying to become an R. N.

"Ssshhh, veddy hush hush," I said imitating her accent.

Penny had just come in off the street and was wearing a chic fitted coat and a blue hat in that Robin Hood style. She removed her gray velvet gloves finger by finger. Never one to rush, she smiled, "Right, then shall we discuss it in my den?"

Penny's "den" was a small laboratory used primarily as a classroom. When she wasn't teaching it served as a hideaway and study area. When we got there she hung a DO NOT DISTURB sign on the door knob.

I slouched onto a stool, offered Penny a cigarette, and passed over the blood sample I'd taken out of the snow on the pier. A line of red dots appeared in my mind like a postscript to murder. I think it was at that very moment I decided Eugene Robichaud was a homicide victim. And my decision was based on nothing more than a mental picture. An image somehow perversely beautiful.

Penny almost accepted a Philip Morris. "No, thanks, Jack. I'm experimenting with cork-tips for a while. These Black Cats aren't awfully bad, you know," she said, taking a pack out of her lab-coat.

"Miss Fairchild," I said. "Like all the other girls, you're in love with the package."

Penny laughed and turned away. She ignited a bunsen burner on a table beside the window. Then she filled a Florence flask with water and placed it on a ring above the burner. Bending over the flame she lit a smoke which she expertly French-inhaled. She had perfected the method after seeing Marlene Dietrich do it in a movie.

In no time at all the water came to a rolling boil.

"What do you hope to find out from this blood sample, Jack?" she asked, spooning tea leaves into an empty flask.

I filled her in on the day's events. I ended with, "So, what I'd like to determine is whether or not Robichaud's blood type is the same as the sample."

"And?" Penny said as she measured milk into a pair of graduated beakers.

"First things first. If it is, I'll go to the pathologist's for a sample of Robichaud's actual blood. If this sample belongs to Robichaud then I'll know which route he took to the ship. If it isn't then I'll try the impossible and find out who it does belong to. You can see that I'm clutching at straws. But you never know, I might get lucky."

Penny handed me a 250ml. beaker of tea.

"Scientific," I said. The tea was dandy but if I didn't eat soon I'd be too water-logged to move.

Penny shook her head ruefully. "Some fine day you're going to blunder into a hornet's nest on one of these private digressions of yours, Jack. And then where will you be?"

"At ease, Miss Fairchild," I muttered. "I'm in the dog-house with his lordship, Deputy Chief Hardfield, half the time as it is."

"Don't be flip. I'd hate to see you drummed off the force. There aren't enough compassionate policemen around these days," Penny said, squinting at a conglomeration of figures on a blackboard. Picking up a piece of chalk, she rubbed out a *cl*, replaced it with an *fl*, and muttered, "Silly students, think they're hilarious."

"What?"

"Students. Changing formulas. Likely thinking their old slave-driver will accidentally blow herself to bits."

"Could that happen?" I asked.

"Not with this. This is an innocent concoction. The reaction would be the wrong colour and give off a disagreeable odour. A prank in the category of a frog in teacher's desk. But, mind you, with some of the chemicals floating around loose it's a wonder more explosions don't occur," she said, as if lecturing a class.

"It's that easy?" I said.

"If one knows what one is doing it is surprisingly easy. Chemistry is no longer the deep, dark mystery it used to be for the layman."

"Don't say that, Penny, you'll give me nightmares. Molotov cocktails chucked at outhouses on Halloween are bad enough." I put on my overcoat and opened the office door. "Listen, for being a good sport, I'll take you to a movie some evening."

"No thanks," Penny protested. "The last one you took me to gave me a case of the blue devils for a week."

"What? *Boys Town*? That was schmaltzy."

"But it didn't prevent you from wiping away a few discreet tears, dear boy. I'll tell you what – if you'll lend me your motor – I'll keep it our secret. Do you still have the Studebaker?"

"Yeah. I just felt like walking today."

"I'd like to borrow it so I can visit a few college chums in Fredericton later this week, all right?"

"Sure, my pleasure. Telephone me at home about the blood sample, okay?"

"Right-O," she said, then touched my arm and whispered, "Do be careful, Jack. Sometimes I think you're walking on quicksand and don't even realize it."

Penny was so earnest I stopped. "What's the matter? You're usually upbeat."

"Oh, I don't know. Perhaps the rumours of war. It makes people seem all the more precious to me. The world's going to change so drastically. Things will never be the same."

I squeezed her hand. "I know what you mean, Penny, "I said. "But it doesn't do any good to fret about it. See you soon. And don't be such a stranger at the house. Come over for supper. I'll make Irish stew and biscuits."

She brightened. "You'll have to buy some records other than those jazz things in order to entice me."

"Not a chance. See you around."

As I left the hospital by way of Out-Patient's, Penny's forebodings got to me. The Movie-Tone News these days had some terrible footage of man-made death and destruction in Manchuria. And the European scene was like one of Penny's formulas – someone was going to tamper with a few things here and there and it would create one hell of an explosion. That someone wore a little black mustache and a mad glint in his eyes. And his name wasn't Charlie Chaplin.

CHAPTER ELEVEN

LINCOLN DRUMMOND'S HOUSE was at the top of the hill on Spar Cove Road. Its small picture window framed the cliffs of the limestone quarry rising straight up toward the spruce forest across the way. The unpaved street was a short stretch of rocky land unofficially reserved, or rather once assigned, to Negroes. A thousand feet away through an alder-choked gully in the other direction, the northern perimeter of Saint John ran a ragged crescent from horizon to horizon. Someday in the distant future the city would inevitably encroach upon the eight or nine houses on the road, perhaps forcing the residents even further into the hinterland of the white man's conscience. But for now it was a peaceful community of people left alone to themselves. Out of sight, out of mind.

It was twilight when I eased the Studebaker catlike through the potholes and turned into Lincoln's driveway. Stepping out, I took a deep breath of the frosty air. The snow had stopped, leaving behind a white carpet. Soon the night sky would be filled with brilliant stars. I stared at the frozen waterfalls in the quarries for a couple of minutes and then I tucked the new records I had ordered through the mail under my arm and went into the house.

Lincoln's place was more of a cottage than a full-sized house. He lived alone, employed a part-time housekeeper to do laundry and floors, and looked after the rest of the upkeep himself. The joint, as he called it, was always clean as a whistle. I pried off my rubbers at the back door, carried them inside and put them behind the stove along with my hat and overcoat.

"Hey, Drum, what's cookin'?" I yelled.

"Bang, bang, you're dead," Lincoln said, shooting me with his finger.

I nearly jumped out of my skin. He was standing in the pantry about four feet behind me.

"Been one of those days, Jack?" Lincoln chuckled, as he limped past me. He had taken a sniper's bullet in the right knee during the Great War. It was a day before the carnage at Vimy Ridge.

"You can say that again. Gimme a second to get my heart out of my mouth, will you?"

While Lincoln set the table I sauntered into the living room and listened to the Art Tatum record that was playing. When it finished I flipped it over and closed my eyes in the soft light. Intricate embellishments on the ivories. By the time the tune ended the cares of the day had disappeared. At least out of my head. For me, music, not laughter, was the best medicine.

"Supper's on," Lincoln said.

I joined him at the table. After the War, Lincoln had worked for a decade as a chef on the C.P.R. run from Saint John to Montreal. Since my wife died we usually had supper together twice a week, alternating between my apartment and his house. Lincoln was five years older than I was but we'd been best friends since 1912. Lincoln was more than a brother to me.

We ate a first-rate pot roast with extra vegetables on the side, followed by home-made apple pie washed down with fresh-perked coffee. While we supped we discussed the upcoming baseball season. Spring training was about to get under way.

"The Red Sox have a new kid they're bringing up this year. Name of Ted Williams," Lincoln said. "Supposed to be a holy terror at the plate."

"Yeah? It'll take some doing for him to live up to Jimmy Foxx. Did you read where Foxx is holding out for thirty-thousand bucks? A lot of fans are grumpy about that," I said, pouring both of us a second cup of coffee.

"Jack, Foxx is batting champ *and* M.V.P. The fans shouldn't be griping about Foxx. It's the owners who are really holding out. Foxx is their meal-ticket and they ought to share the wealth instead of being so damn stingy."

"Don't get steamed, Linc. I agree. One hundred per cent."

"Did I see you come in with some new records?" Lincoln asked.

"Indeed you did. Teddy Wilson, Coleman Hawkins, and Billie Holiday," I crowed. "Picked them up at the Post Office this afternoon."

"Oooee-E, baby. You sure good to me," Lincoln sang softly. "Let's take the java inside and catch a listen."

After we heard each record through twice without saying anything to one another, Lincoln said, "Great sounds, Jack. Notice how Hawkins seems on the brink of something new? Can't put my finger on it but that sax of his almost wants to go somewheres on its own."

"Outside?" I ventured. Musical thoughts were always hard for me to describe.

Lincoln nodded. "Right. Maybe it's because he's been overseas for the past few years. The Hawk's come a long ways since *Hello, Lola*. Remember that? With Red McKenzie's Mound City Blue Blowers?"

"How could I forget? We wore the grooves off it. Must be almost ten years old now."

"Damn, it is too," Lincoln said wistfully. "Just about the time I inherited this house and quit the railway. Still can't bring myself to scramble another egg. Must of cracked a million in those years."

I sipped the coffee and swung my feet up onto the chesterfield. Beside me on the wall Lincoln had hung some framed newspaper photos of Jesse Owens at the '36 summer Olympics in Berlin. One of them was of Owens taking a victory lap, arms stretched overhead, the crowd applauding wildly. Hitler had refused to shake hands with Owens even though Jesse had won four gold medals – more than any other athelete at the Games. "Do you think Owens will compete next year, Linc?"

Lincoln interwove his fingers, cracking his knuckles as he twisted them. "Ain't going to be any in '40. Maybe never again," he said glumly. His sadness worried me.

"What makes you say that, Drum?" I asked as he sat down at the piano and ran his fingers up and down the keyboard.

"Hell, Jack, the world's one big time-bomb. They thought the last was horrible – wait till the next one." He began playing a ragtime, taking it slow, syncopation swaying gently.

Linc's father had been a tremendous musician – the highlight of his life was meeting and talking with Scott Joplin at the St. Louis Exposition in 1904. When Linc and I were kids, we would sit spellbound while old man Drummond spun stories about life at the turn of the century. "1900 was sig-nif-i-cant," he would intone, and shivers would tingle up my spine; I was born on Dominion Day of that year. I'll never forget

Lincoln's dad telling us about seeing Geronimo on one of the first Ferris Wheels at "The Fair" and how ice cream cones were invented there by a clever biscuit vendor.

Lincoln picked up the tempo of the song he was improvising on. He played almost as if ragtime was classical music, something like the way my wife used to interpret Chopin nocturnes – reflective and dreamy.

"How about *Ghost of a Chance?*" I said, lying back and closing my tired eyes.

Without missing a beat Lincoln launched into the tune. He must have been feeling melancholy because he approached it a shade slower than usual. The effect was eerie, almost funereal. Maybe it was in the tune to begin with and I just never noticed it before. After Lincoln did a straight rendition he strolled around the block with it a couple of times. Insinuating, he called it. My eyelids were so heavy and belly so full I began to doze.

I woke about three hours later when I rolled off the chesterfield and hit the floor with a thump. A dream about Roxanne at Pepper's Diner had just gotten nicely started. We were alone in the restaurant and she was serving the meal Lincoln had prepared this evening. The red roses I'd sent were woven into her hair. Lincoln was out in the parking lot jazzing a snow-covered piano. Roxanne wore a long dress with a pattern identical to the wallpaper in the Moffat's flat – big yellow roses on a striped background.

The dream was so real that I entertained a notion of going back to sleep to try and catch it where it left off. Some dreams are like slow-moving trains. You can get off and get on again before they disappear out of sight.

I lay down again for a minute but the train must have gone around the bend. Tossing aside the blanket Lincoln must've draped over me, I went into the kitchen and poked the coals. The fire was just about gone so I added kindling and an armload of slabwood. After the flames burst into life I returned to the living room with the *Evening Times Globe*. Lincoln had retired to bed; no doubt worn out by my sparkling company.

I turned to the *News of the Port*, a regular feature in the paper. It would be interesting to see where the *Bergensfjord* was bound. I got an ugly shock when I saw that she essentially didn't go anywhere. She'd steamed out of the harbour, around the sugar refinery, and into

Courtenay Bay where she was tied up at the dry dock for minor refitting. A big U-turn. And that's just what I was thinking of doing. Just maybe Constable Waterman and I would pay a social call on our German photographer friend.

I borrowed four records from Lincoln's collection of over a thousand, wrote a note saying which ones, and turned off the lights.

Out in the yard I felt great in my stove-warmed clothes. It was snowing again, only big, wet flakes the size of quarters forecasting rain in the days ahead. As I stood beside the Studebaker I heard a car coasting slowly down the road. There were no streetlights and the nearest house was fifty feet away in the pitch black so I should have seen the car's headlights. But they weren't on. Maybe some goofball thinking that because the road's residents were coloured it was a red-light district. On second thought, it could be the teenagers Lincoln told me were harassing the neighbourhood lately. Kids driving through yelling "Niggerville" and "Coon Town" until a porch light came on.

I booted a chunk of frozen slush about the size of a milk bottle off my car and waited.

When the vehicle was in front of Drummond's house it slowed to a crawl. I lobbed the ice underhand high into the air. My aim was true. It came down with a resounding thud on the car's roof. The engine roared as the driver tramped on the accelerator and took off like a rocket.

I was still laughing to myself when I followed their tire tracks down the road. They would've been guaranteed a bone-jarring ride. It might be just the scare they needed to cure them of their nasty habits.

Strangely, the radio reception in the Studebaker was good even though the weather was unsettled. There was a live broadcast of a so-so swing band coming in loud and clear from a Valentine's Day Ball at the Royal Hotel. A woman's laughter in the background made me think of Roxanne in a romantic fashion. Even if I was going to turn forty in '40 it didn't mean I had to forego an interest in the ladies. Underneath her tough-girl exterior Roxy was probably the cat's meow. I'd seen her now and then out and about and around the town. Away from the diner she looked swell and acted ladylike so the wise-cracking waitress routine was likely a ruse. A protective shell. The mechanic at the Golden Ball Garage told me she was a widow but the way he said "widow" led me to believe there was more to Roxanne's situation than meets the eye.

I drove along by the river through Indian Town to where it connected with the end of Main Street, swung left for six blocks, then hung a right onto Douglas Avenue. My soft mattress beckoned from number sixty-five. I wondered if I even had a ghost of a chance with Roxanne. Roxanne of the roses.

TERRY CRAWFORD

CHAPTER TWELVE

I WAS ARM-WEARY and fagged out. Waterman had me in a corner and was doing his best to crack every rib in my body. I forced him into a clinch, spun him around, and pushed him against the ropes. Blood trickled out of his left nostril. We'd been sparring seriously for five rounds and Tom was losing his temper, getting wild and desperate, throwing vicious haymakers at my head that were missing by a mile. The blood ran onto his mouthpiece, turning it a gruesome pink. I bopped him on the forehead with a left jab that connected harder than I'd intended. He came off the ropes fast, faked a counterpunch, then hit me full force with a right cross over the heart. I staggered back winded and sat down in the middle of the ring. My mouthpiece popped out like a cork.

"Whoa, tiger, I submit," I said, laughing between gasps. "If we keep this up we'll be pronounced D.O.A."

Waterman glared but the fire in his eyes subsided as he helped me off the canvas. My experienced left jab and nimble footwork had frustrated him to no end. He was good, better than good, but relied too much on his knock-out punch. And he was a head-hunter. Which was too bad because his body-blows were a lot more effective than he realized. I eased my protective headgear off with my thumbs and held the ropes open for him to step through.

Kayo McClusky, the owner of the Monarch Boxing Club, watched us closely. It was a dull Wednesday night with hardly anyone around. Kayo's sidekick, a punch-drunk middleweight in his fifties, tossed us a couple of towels then shuffled off to stoke the furnace so there would be plenty of hot water in the shower stalls.

"You're dynamite, kid," Kayo said to Waterman. "Not too many guys around here can get past round three with Jack. But take some advice from an old puncher and remember one word – patience. With a capital P. Write that word on your bedroom ceiling so you can see it first thing every morning."

Waterman nodded.

"And loosen up. Relax. Boxing's a game. Have some fun. I figured for a while you was gonna punch holes in poor Jack there."

Kayo unlaced Waterman's gloves then turned to mine. "Ever since Joe Louis came along the young guys figure they gotta murderize the opposition in the first rounds," he said.

Kayo had sat ringside at Joe Louis's latest title defense a few weeks ago at the Gardens in New York. He worshipped the Brown Bomber. No wonder. Louis was twenty-five and after avenging his loss against Max Schmeling looked unbeatable. He had successfully defended his championship a record five times in the past year. In the most recent match Louis floored John Henry Lewis twice in the first round, pommeling his opponent so viciously the referee stopped the fight. It was the first time since 1913 that two Negroes fought one another for the Heavy-weight Crown. In Kayo's universe it was a landmark event.

"You can't blame them for wanting to emulate Louis's style," I said. "Joe is incredibly fast for a boxer weighing in at two-hundred plus. He's an athlete for the ages."

"What a specimen, what a specimen." Kayo said hoarsely.

Waterman laughed. Kayo had a habit of unintentionally imitating Jimmy Durante. Sometimes the boys in the gym would razz him, calling him Knobby Walsh after Durante's movie portrayal of Joe Palooka's manager. Of course everyone followed the adventures of Knobby and Joe in the funny papers. And it didn't help Kayo that he was bald as a billiard ball and actually resembled Knobby.

Kayo tugged off my gloves and helped me into a robe. "Listen, Jack," he said, "there's only one shower workin'. Damn pipes froze Sunday. Slugger's getting so punchy he forgets things. He closed up Saturday night then didn't remember to come in Sunday and shovel some coal into the boiler."

Waterman deposited his gloves in a basket and lay flat on his back on top of a bench.

Kayo screamed, "Slugger", so loudly it gave me a start.

"Slugger goes away and forgets where he is," he explained to Waterman. "Last week I went hunting for him and found him stoking the furnace like he was in the engine room of the Queen Mary. Poor bugger, I think he thought he was back in the Merchant Marine."

"Too many hard knocks," I said. "Do you want to flip for the shower, Tom?"

"No, you go ahead."

"I'll be a long time."

"It's okay, I'm going to read while I cool down," Waterman said.

I went to my locker for fresh underwear, clean socks, and a new bar of Lifebuoy. By the time I was in the shower and lathered from head to toe my skeleton began to creak a trifle from Waterman's pounding. The water felt soothing so I stood under the spray until the aching went away.

Tom Waterman was an interesting kid. I usually didn't choose to fraternize with the patrolmen, but he was different; deeper and more complex than the average run-of-the-mill recruit. It was a joke in some circles in Saint John that if you were a certified drugstore cowboy, looped King Square a hundred times by car every Sunday for two years in a row, and were male between eighteen and twenty-one you automatically qualified for the local constabulary. Like a lot of jokes it contained more than a grain of truth. I would have added dim-wittedness, laziness, and a violence-for-kicks mentality. It was a sorry situation. The force was divided between good cops, who conscientiously did their duty as servants of the people, and bad eggs who epitomized the public's view of the morally corrupt policeman. The ordinary Joe and Jane on the street had no inkling of how difficult it was for a young guy like Tom Waterman to thread his way through a department rife with back-stabbing, suspicion, and underhandedness. Maybe it was the depression we were just coming out of, or maybe it was the war I was positive we were going into – whatever the reason morale was low and tension was high. I sincerely hoped Waterman wouldn't become a casualty, wouldn't turn out jaded and cynical like so many other policemen.

The shower suddenly turned scalding hot. I jumped clear, grabbed a towel, and dried myself quickly in the chilly ante-chamber. A few minutes later I shut the water off, swiped the steam from the mirror and combed my hair. I was turning gray so fast my reflection sometimes took me by surprise. It didn't bother me though. My landlady said I was still a handsome rogue.

After I finished dressing and Waterman was in the shower, I sat down next to a stack of *New York Times*. Kayo's subscription went back to the

'20s. He saved every issue, always leaving the current month's copies in the gym.

Generalissimo Franco and his so-called rebels had taken Barcelona a couple of weeks ago. It was estimated that about one hundred thousand Spanish refugees were pouring into France every day. I sat back and considered the disquieting fact that without the aid of Hitler's National Socialists, Franco's victory might not have come for several years, if at all. The Nazis, in what surely was a dress rehearsal for something bigger, had supplied Franco's side with Heinkel bombers and Messerschmidt fighter planes. Some of the newsreels I'd seen when I went to *Gunga Din* at the Mayfair in January shocked the entire audience. Stark visions on the screen of women and children running in panic during an air-raid on Barcelona were harrowing enough, but to see – from the proximity of your neighbourhood theatre – their mangled bodies lying in a rubble-strewn street was too horrible for even the most avid warmonger.

Kayo brought me a cup of his good coffee and sat beside me while he lit a Cuban cigar. The java and the aroma of the cigar reminded me of climes where breezes blew warm and strong rum allowed you to briefly forget the troubles of the world. I mentioned this to Kayo who snorted knowingly and leafed through a January issue of the *Times*. He turned it back at a certain page then handed it to me folded book-size.

"Take a gander at this then," he said. "The Yanks are gonna be there until March."

It was an item dated January 22 – an account of the American Navy's wargames in the Caribbean. I'd almost forgotten about the operation and its enormous scale. One hundred and forty vessels, fifty-three thousand men, and five hundred planes were in the area for two months of naval exercises.

"Japan's got the hoodoo on them," Kayo said, clenching his cigar between his teeth. "F.D.R. himself's down there cruising the briny deeps."

"Probably the closest Roosevelt will get to a vacation in many a moon," I said, taking heart at reading an article about the inventor of a static-less radio system that one of the big networks was in the process of setting up. At least some of the news was from the sunny side of the street. And the world wasn't completely off its rocker – not as long as

Chick Webb and Ella Fitzgerald were making music at the Coconut Grove.

"Hey, your new sparring partner is quite the blade," Kayo said. "Look at the threads on that boy."

I smiled. Kayo wasn't known for his sartorial splendour but he had an eye for fashion. It was one of his numerous minor hobbies. Somewhere between fly-tying and bird-watching.

Waterman was adjusting a tie-bar on his shirt collar. He looked as stylish as Fred Astaire in his double-breasted suit and polished shoes.

"Sharp as a tack," I mumbled. My dress clothes were as gauche as civilization tolerated. I could never fathom what was so wrong about argyle socks with a blue-striped suit and brown shoes. A toff I am not.

Waterman donned his topcoat and overshoes. He studied the fight posters pasted over the walls while I got into my mackintosh and galoshes. The weather had turned mild. Along with the memory of Tom's punches I could feel rain in my bones.

We said our good-byes to Kayo and Slugger and waved to a couple of older pugs working out on the speed bags.

Outside on Sheriff Street the snow was melting so rapidly fog hung under the streetlamps like dirty curtains. My place was only a ten minute walk so I'd left the Studebaker home. Waterman lived five streets down toward the river from me in a spartan little flat on Kennedy Street.

When I called on him earlier he was dressed to the nines just to go out to *Jesse James*. Tyrone Power and Henry Fonda as the James brothers had people queueing around the block from the Paramount. It was a good enough duster – fantastic Technicolor – but I always got a bit miffed at the American tendency to glamourize bad guys. Even Cagney at his rottenest was somehow rendered heroic.

"Tom, how come your father changed his name?" I asked. "He wasn't ashamed of being German?"

"No. Dad was proud of his German heritage. But he hated the Kaiser and was anti-Prussian. Along with other pacifists from his village he was forced at gunpoint to be a stretcher-bearer during the War. He spent four years on the western front. Sometimes he woke up screaming at night. I've seen my father so shell-shocked he'd go to the basement and stay there for days on end. In the middle of the summer when the weather was beautiful. Anyway, he changed his name because he wanted to spare me the abuse he had to face almost every day on the job."

"What did your father do, Tom?"

"He was an electrician. Started from scratch with very little English and got his journeyman's papers in five years. If it wasn't for the War he would have been an electrical engineer. He had a scholarship at the University of Berlin." Tom said this with a mixture of pride and regret.

"Why the name Waterman? Is it a translation?"

"My father liked Waterman's pens the best. He signed the documents legalizing the name-change with one. His sense of humour always kept him going. I didn't mean to make him sound so grim. He was big-hearted and loved to laugh. Dad took me to all the Laurel and Hardy movies. It's a wonder he didn't die laughing."

Tom went quiet so we continued strolling in silence. Whenever a woman passed she would discreetly stare at him. Waterman's was a handsome face in a city of generally homely mugs. Since he had told me I could readily see the Teutonic qualities in his features: straight hair, pointed nose, thin lips, and square jaw. He could quit police work and model clothes in *Esquire*.

The boxing had invigorated me. Exercise usually affected me that way. As we were climbing the wooden staircase that led from the end of Sheriff up to Main, I said, "You're pensive. Cat got your tongue?"

"No, Mr. Ireland…"

"Jack. For the love of Mike, call me Jack."

"Fine. I was thinking about something I read in the *New York Times*."

"Oh? Such as?"

"Hitler's plan for the 'orderly emigration of Jews'. My grandmother is a quarter Jewish and still in Germany."

I raised my voice above the traffic noise. "I see. Why doesn't she emigrate to someplace desirable before she's forced to relocate somewhere she doesn't want to go?"

"She's more German than the Germans. She *is* German. Besides, Grandfather was a Lutheran lay preacher deeply involved with his church. He's gone now and Grandmother's never registered as a Jew and she never will. She converted to Christianity. She believes she's safe."

"Doesn't anyone know her?" I said.

"Not for long. Like so many retired people they settled in Dresden. They used to run a pharmacy in Munich."

"Well, Tom, maybe she will be safe."

"I don't know. In a letter smuggled out by a relative she said Jewish property is being confiscated outright or devalued then re-sold to pure Aryans," Tom said, emphasizing Aryans. "I'm afraid that it'll be just a matter of time before she's discovered."

"Pure Aryans, i.e. Nazis," I added.

Waterman went quiet again. While we were crossing an intersection I couldn't help thinking that Waterman's generation had inherited a world intent upon killing them off. The recurring dread of another Great War slipped over me like a funeral pall. Many of the best and the brightest from both sides had fallen during the war to end all war.

A car zipped behind us, spraying slush on my legs. It could've been that green Plymouth.

That green Plymouth? I mentally gave myself a kick in the pants. For some dumb reason I had green Plymouths on the brain.

"Here's my cut-off," I said, rounding the corner to Douglas Avenue. "Come on to my place, Tom. It's right there just before Saint Peter's Church."

Waterman hesitated.

"Come on," I urged. "I'll initiate you into the mysteries of jazz. Also, I've got an unopened fifth of Scotch. A four-dollar bottle of the grand stuff fit for the laird himself."

"Sure, that'd be swell. But I warn you in advance, my father introduced me to Mendelssohn when I was still in the cradle."

"Who? You mean Felix? That Mendelssohn?"

"Yes, the very one."

Before we reached the house the wind began blowing a gale and it started raining in buckets. I didn't mind. It'd be fine with me if the city's gray snow disappeared overnight.

CHAPTER THIRTEEN

THE STREET CAR rattled and shivered along Prince William Street in the freeze of early morning. Sometime before dawn the rain had turned into sleet, glazing everything with ice.

At the Duke Street corner a gang of port workers jumped off and went slipping and sliding down the hill to the piers. One fellow hit a bare patch and went flying like a trapeze artist with no one to catch him. His lunchbox struck the pavement and popped open, strewing sandwiches on the sidewalk. An orange rolled into the gutter and out of sight beneath a parked truck.

It wasn't quite eight o'clock when I stepped off at the end of the line and drank in the sights of the harbour. The day was so clear I could see Nova Scotia across the Bay of Fundy. On an impulse I'd decided to pay Shorty Long a visit. An impulse that was given a swift kick after I read in the paper that the coroner ruled an inquest into Eugene Robichaud's death was unnecessary.

Shorty Long was Saint John's nominal King of the Hobos. His father had bequeathed him the family business – a wood and coal yard, an enterprise complete with an office and some adjacent buildings, all of it enclosed behind a tall wooden fence that made it seem like a stockade stuck in the city's South End. Shorty paid the taxes by running a bottle exchange and a ten-cent a night flophouse for those, like himself, who rode the rails west during the dirtiest days of the Depression.

Shorty and I went a long way back. From the time we were old enough to pronounce the word we had played baseball together on the South End diamond. But as we approached early manhood I became a rookie cop whereas Shorty became an apprentice derelict. His was one of those shining minds tarnished by the bloodshed of the Great War and the breadlines of the 30's. Instead of the college professor he should have become, he was a boozing Bolshevik with a library of socialist literature that filled two or three coal bins. Half his pals called him Freud and the others nicknamed him the Professor. I was probably the only person living who still introduced him as Shorty.

I held tightly onto the railing while I traversed the boardwalk on the train trestle leading to the landward side of the sugar refinery. The tide was out and the gulls bobbed on the water a long way down.

Nervous after my feat of derring-do, I stopped on Vulcan Street and peered through the windows of the Ironworks. The shop rang with a ceaseless clanging and banging. Welders were raining blue sparks onto the floor. In heavy masks and leather aprons they looked like half-human creatures out of H.G. Wells.

I lurked in the protection of the window. A City Works employee walked by paddling sand out of a galvanized bucket. I followed him up the icy sidewalk and past the Armoury. Scattered squads of infantrymen were out huffing and puffing on the barrack green. Drills of any kind bored me to death. It was one of the reasons why I disliked Deputy Chief Hardfield. He was crazy for the drill – the absolute blind obedience of it. And his inspections smacked of an obsession for spit and polish, as if the men were nothing more than well-oiled automatons.

When I looped back to Vulcan Street and opened the door through the high wooden gates to Long's Coal & Wood, a pair of the resident winos were already up and about. An old bearded geezer everyone knew only as Gabby was busy splitting kindling which a workmate then gathered into bundles and secured with wire. Many of the neighbourhood corner stores were good enough to buy their wood from Gabby and his motley crew of drifters. Gabby was also the South End's premier window-washer. His industriousness kept him solvent and usually pickled in gin.

"Gabby, where's Shorty?" I asked, offering him a cigarette which he accepted and tucked into a tobacco pouch.

"Freud? Up in his orifice," Gabby said, displaying a row of perfectly rotten teeth.

"Thanks. How's business?" I asked, already climbing the stairs to Shorty's H.Q.

"Fourteen new stores this winter," Gabby shouted. "The woodyard down on Celebration Street complained to the Better Business Boobs. Seems they're scared I'm gonna get as big as K.C. Irving."

"Dandy. Keep punching," I yelled, giving Shorty's door a hard thump-thump with the flat of my hand.

"Enter at your own risk," someone warned from inside.

I opened the door. "Shorty?" When my eyes adjusted to the murky light I could see him standing on a chair ready to fling a snowboot at any intruder's unsuspecting head. "Well, if it isn't the man of a thousand voices," I said.

"Ireland, John Errol, protector of the common herd and keeper of the faithless. Welcome," Shorty said jauntily.

He dismounted the chair and dumped the boot into a barrel of discarded footwear. Walking over to me he held out a hand. "Good to see you, Jack."

"You too, Shorty." At six-two there weren't many men I met who were taller than I was but Shorty had me by a couple of inches. From a middle distance his blue eyes were so pale they faded into nothing. Combined with his lanky frame and a fondness for black suits, Shorty's eyes lent him the appearance of a demented mystic. Or a saint gone strange from too many weeks alone in the wilderness.

"What brings you into my humble abode?" he asked, dragging a chair out of a corner. "Take a load off."

"Social call, mostly," I said, reading a couple of quotes Shorty had chalked in big letters on a cracked blackboard scrounged from a demolished school-house. The first went: the abnormal is the normal carried to its logical extremes. Beneath it, the by now familiar: Religion is the opiate of the masses.

"Mostly?" Shorty said, digging into a filing cabinet.

"I've a small favour to ask."

"Say but the word and thy will be done," Shorty said. "But first, how about breakfast?"

"No, thanks," I said, inwardly cringing at the sherry he was attentively pouring into a beer mug.

"Coffee?"

"Swell."

Shorty grabbed a rope dangling over his desk, pulled it three times, and hesitated. "Two more will get you toast."

"Grand. Fire away."

Shorty took a swig of sherry, shuddered from the shock to his stomach, then put his endless legs up on the desk. "Now, what are the misguided denizens of the criminal underworld up to?"

"The usual: B and Es, burglary, auto-theft, fraud, get-rich quick schemes... you know the score."

"Whoa, partner, I thought we single-handedly wiped out car rustling."

"We did, on a big scale. For the time being."

Three years ago, when I was unsuccessfully attempting to bust an auto-theft ring, Shorty and his comrades had done a considerable amount of undercover spying for me. I owed them my promotion to Sergeant. It had been an ugly affair. Along with an assortment of smalltime hoods rounded-up at the end of the investigation there were two cops who drove stolen vehicles to Montreal. That hurt. I liked them both but they turned out to be crooked bastards. If it hadn't been for Shorty's Irregulars, as he called them, I'd have batted zero. No one pays particular attention to bums and panhandlers: pariahs who rank with the angels in terms of near invisibility.

The door burst open. A bald guy in his early twenties marched in with a tray of coffee and toasted raisin bread smothered with peanut butter. He set the order down, saluted, did an about-face, and departed.

A few lumps of coal dislodged and dropped from the self-feeder into the belly of the stove. Through the isinglass windows hard embers twinkled and glowed sleepily.

"This is substantial stuff," I said, munching the toast.

"These lads recognize sustenance when they see it," Shorty said, nabbing a slice. "It comes of not knowing when or if you'll eat again."

The coffee tasted as if brewed in a hobo jungle - a handful of grounds boiled in a can of water. It brought back memories of bivouacs with my wife on salmon fishing trips to the Miramichi.

"Shorty, I need your eyes and ears again," I said. "About ten pairs. I want to know if anyone spots anything unusual on the waterfront. Forget the standard disappearing stalk of bananas. I mean *unusual*."

"Some members of our fraternity managed to finagle longshoreman's tickets," Shorty said. "Their numbers don't get called too often. Hardly ever. But they hang around the sheds anyway."

"Good. I'm particularly interested in the *Bergensfjord*."

Shorty finished off his sherry and plunked the mug down like a pirate. "Avast! Now there be a vessel on our craplist."

"Oh?" Now that Shorty was warmed-up I decided to take my hat off.

"Hostiles on board. Suspected Nazi infiltrators. Stay away," he read from a note on his clipboard.

Shorty saw Nazis everywhere. When he was tight he'd claim that the Holy Name Society was a Fascist front supported by the Knights of Columbus.

"Nazis?" I ventured.

"German nationals, at least."

"That I already know, Shorty."

"But what you don't know, my dear Inspector Heat, is that a pair of these louts beat the living tar out of Randy Murphy last week," Shorty said triumphantly.

"How come?"

"Murph sometimes offers his services as a tour guide to the more adventurous seamen and officers."

"Tour guide?"

"To the bootleggers and cathouses. The establishments with the slogan 'We Never Close'."

"Sweet Jesus. So why did they put the boots to Murphy?"

"Unadulterated meanness. All Murphy expects is free liquor and the odd damsel of the night by way of a finder's fee. Mind you, he gets it coming and going. The houses give him a percentage of whatever business he steers their way. Murph's a rather well-to-do bum."

"Lovely. And?"

"Well, it seems Molly's on Station Street have a couple of new girls from Montreal of the Hebrew persuasion – St. Urbain Street graduates. A pair of *Bergensfjord* Germans took umbrage to their lineage."

It might have been the oily peanut butter sticking to my ribs, or the hobo coffee in my gut, but I had a queasy feeling – something like the alarm I always get before impending danger.

"Those goons waited to nail Murph until after they satisfied their carnal desires," Shorty added. "They're pure slime."

"I agree," I said quietly. "How's Murphy?"

"All right. He'll survive. He's taking his food through a straw but he can afford to lose his spare tire."

"Would it do me any good to talk to him?"

"I don't think so, Jack. Murph's badge-shy."

I got up to leave. "This is unofficial, Shorty. And, as you've already seen, possibly hazardous to your health."

"As always, you may rely on my discretion," Shorty said, accompanying me to the door. The sherry had him unsteady on his feet.

"The National Harbours Board doesn't appreciate us meddling with foreign nationals," I said, stepping out onto the stoop. "Some of these sailors practically get away with murder."

"Leave us hope it never comes to that," Shorty said, spitting over the railing.

"Amen. See you, pal."

"Okay, Jack. I'll contact you in the usual way."

I retraced my route back to the streetcar line, hoping as I went that I wasn't tilting at windmills. If Deputy Chief Hardfield were to get an earful of what I was up to I'd be in more hot water than a boiled dinner.

CHAPTER FOURTEEN

D OCTOR CROMARTY PUSHED his way through a gaggle of student nurses at the entrance to the Pathology Lab, spent a moment admiring a well-turned ankle, winked when the owner glared, and then ambled like a tweed camel toward his office.

Cromarty was a lumbering, angular man about my age who could be blustery and jovial in the same breath. A changeable character, but I liked and trusted him. Trust was a rare commodity on the force, not to mention on its outer reaches. Cromarty did all the department's autopsies – mostly motor- vehicle accidents and the inevitable drownings in summer – and was our forensic medicine-man. He bristled whenever I called him that so I reminded myself to shelve the moniker for today. I required a good deed regarding a delicate matter on this particular morning.

I was sitting on a bench in the corridor, my face hidden behind a T.B. pamphlet and the water-cooler, when Cromarty unlocked his door. Giving him ten seconds, I rapped on the glass and turned the knob.

"Go away," he growled into his doctor's bag.

"You're too late."

"Ireland, do you ever sleep? It's seven-thirty in the goddamn A.M."

Cromarty took a Thermos bottle from the bag and poured two cups of coffee.

"You're in, you might as well stay," he said, settling his two-hundred and ten pounds into a swivel chair. "Don't say another word until I get a mouthful of coffee."

I honoured the Doc's request, and then some, allowing him to finish the cup and start consuming what looked like a lettuce sandwich on rye bread. A plaster model of the human heart sat partly disassembled beside a now ringing telephone.

He picked up the receiver and said soothingly, "This is Doctor Angus Cromarty. I am not in until eight o'clock. Thank you," and hung up.

He crunched three fat red radishes slowly and deliberately between his molars before he looked at me with what seemed to be a disturbingly pathological interest. I could almost feel him dissecting my thoughts.

His freckled face crinkled into a smile. "Go ahead, Jack, I dare you to say this is just a friendly visit."

I tipped my hat back with a finger. "This is just a friendly visit," I said solemnly.

"Son-of-a-bitch," Cromarty hissed.

"Doctor, you know I can't resist a dare."

Cromarty put his battleship-sized oxfords up on the desk.

"Or sticking your nose into something you've been warned away from, Jack," he said. "Deputy-Chief Hardfield is already a step ahead of you."

"Meaning? Enlighten me, Doc."

"Hardfield's wise to your extra-curricular activities, Jack. He told me, in the nature of a threat, not to show you anything on the Eugene Robichaud accident," Cromarty said, retrieving a banana big enough for King Kong out of his bag. He made it disappear faster than Mandrake the Magician.

"Why? Where's the harm?" I poured myself more coffee. It'd been sweetened with maple syrup. Doctor Cromarty called refined sugar white poison. Ditto for white bread and white rice. I've seen him eat a bowl of boiled seaweed. Which is bad enough, but the worst part is he enjoyed the purple sludge.

Cromarty folded his hands; a sign that he was serious. "No harm, Jack. Deep down, I think Hardfield has a grudging respect for you. But his kick is obedience. He resented you double-checking the Robichaud thing after he had handled it personally. Can't say I blame him. I would hit the roof if another pathologist went over ground I'd already covered. It's a personal insult, Jack. Jesus, you step on people's toes with the greatest aplomb."

"It's a gift," I said, lighting my third Philip Morris of the day. The T.B. pamphlet's caution was still fresh in my mind: Stop Smoking – Save Lungs. What about my sanity?

Cromarty sighed. Swivelling about in his chair, he extracted a file-folder from a roll-top desk.

He stood over me in his three-piece suit like a glowering Scottish giant. "If you weren't such a sawed-off runt, Ireland, I'd toss you end over end like a caber. Maybe then you'd gain some sense. In the meantime, I'm going to brush my teeth and visit the boy's room. If you choose to amuse yourself with a little light reading while I'm gone, that's up to you."

I smiled meekly. Angus *could* toss me like a caber. There wasn't an ounce of flab on his towering frame and he was fit as a fiddle. He still anchored the scrum of one of New Brunswick's toughest rugby squads. Nobody messed with Doc Cromarty.

As soon as he shut the door I slipped into his chair and opened the folder. It contained the requisite photographs and documents in proper sequence. A closed case if ever I saw one. Hardfield had conducted the investigation with military precision, noting the exact time of his arrival, when the photographs were taken, the phone call placed for the hearse (his word), and his departure from the scene. All very efficient. Curious for its lack of curiosity. I'd delved into other reports in which Hardfield decided to play the part of active investigator. They were invariably riddled with procedural oversights. Inept would be too kind a word. So why the new-found professionalism? My instincts told me to find my patrolman's whistle and blow it on the Deputy-Chief. But why? Something. Somewhere.

"Jack, your nose is twitching like a bloodhound's. Now, be a good lad and close the folder before you start barking up the wrong tree," Cromarty said in a jocular mood. He took off his suit jacket and put on a lab coat spattered with ink along the left sleeve. The Doc had the world's finest collection of leaky pens. It was a kind of sacrificial rite with him. Whenever I teased him about it he'd mumble something about Druidic ancestors. After a last long look at the file I gave him his seat back. He shook a pen over a blotter to make sure it leaked then clipped it into his breast pocket.

"A couple of questions, Doc?" I asked timidly.

"What? Did you forget how to read? Everything is there in the report, Jack."

I shrugged. "Yeah, but…"

"You've got until eight o'clock and then make yourself scarce. I shouldn't even be discussing this with you. If Hardfield finds out we'll both be hauled over the coals."

"Thanks. I appreciate you sticking your neck out, Doc." I kept quiet for a minute while Cromarty idly reassembled the plaster heart.

"Blood," I said. "I expected to find Robichaud awash in blood. Broken open like a ripe tomato."

"Very picturesque description, Jack. Remind me to relay that to the *Canadian Medical Journal*," Cromarty said. "He wasn't split open anywhere and none of his internal organs were damaged. Don't forget that Robichaud died, probably instantly, of a broken neck."

"What about the bruise on the chin?"

"Consistent with the break. His neck was snapped backwards. My educated guess is that Robichaud missed a rung on the ladder, panicked, and hooked his chin two or three rungs lower down. And he didn't slip until he was almost at the bottom."

I was stumped. All along I'd been taking it for granted that Robichaud died of the fall. Now Doc Cromarty was saying he was dead before he hit the floor of the hold. A lot of vague theories were going up in smoke.

"Robichaud's blood-alcohol level wasn't very high, Doc. That puzzles me. I've got information from a reliable source that he telephoned his sister in a drunken state maybe two to four hours before he died."

"He wasn't drunk, Jack. However, he was a small, weak-muscled man with hardly enough fat to fry an egg. A few drinks on an empty stomach could have got him rolling. His liver was in the most deplorable condition I've ever seen for a man his age."

"So he didn't drink the Chivas Regal?"

"You just lost me, Jack. Go back up the path a wee bit and run that by me again," Cromarty said, producing a russet apple from his doctor's bag.

"Is that the latest thing in lunchboxes?" I asked. He was getting me hungry even if he habitually ate like a mammoth squirrel. Any second now Cromarty would start in on his can of mixed nuts.

"Don't get impertinent, Ireland, or I'll work up an autopsy on those sausages you prize so much."

"There was a broken forty-ounce bottle of Chivas Regal underneath Robichaud," I said, wondering at the same time if the horror stories I heard about sausages were true.

"There you go. Maybe I should be the detective. Robichaud's climbing down the ladder, fumbles the bottle, is inebriated enough to reach for it, and wham! Literally loses his grip and the rest is history. Elementary, my dear Ireland."

"Not too shabby, Doc. But it begs the question: What was Eugene Robichaud doing in the middle of the night entering the hold of a ship he surely knew was empty?" I said, lighting another cigarette to stave off hunger. Oh, for a fried-egg sandwich.

"You might have the answer in your hand," Cromarty said, pointing at the match I just blew out. "Robichaud's shirt had about a dozen burnt matches in the right pocket and another dozen live ones in the left. He may have been behaving in a surreptitious manner, I'll grant you that. Perhaps searching for something."

"I repeat – there was nothing to find in the hold. Unless whatever was there had been moved or hidden. Also, you said he was feeble – weak muscled. I'm positive the hatch cover above the ladder outweighed him. I don't think he could've moved it all by himself. In other words – he needed help."

Cromarty laughed. "Damn your hide, Jack. If I listen to you for another minute you'll have me believing that with an accomplice this little man murdered himself."

"Or curiosity killed the cat?"

Cromarty leaned over the desk with his boarding-house reach and snatched my cigarette. "One or two puffs and I'll give it back."

He turned in his chair and took a couple of contemplative drags on the smoke. While he did, I studied an Easter Seals poster of two rosy-cheeked kids zooming along on a toboggan. My wife and I used to toboggan twice a week on the run at Lily Lake. Since she died I hadn't done anything by way of recreation. I didn't count boxing at the Monarch Club – that was therapy. Every punch was good for the soul.

Cromarty derailed my train of thought. "Eugene Robichaud was simply in the wrong place at the wrong time."

"No kiddin'," I said. "And Einstein is a dumb cluck. Gimme that cigarette before your brainwaves drown you."

Cromarty was serious. "Look," he said patiently, "there's no evidence whatsoever to indicate that Robichaud didn't die in the manner I described. It's up to you to discover the why. I've given what I think is the how. Fair enough?"

"Fair enough," I echoed. "You've been a big help, Doctor. As always. And I'm thankful." I stood and went to the door. "That's a swell poster. Could I have it when you're done with it?"

Cromarty rose, came to the door, and clamped a big hand on my shoulder. "Sure. Take it easy, Jack. Go slow. You sometimes can smell a rat where there isn't one."

I did a double-take. "Are you questioning my zeal? Take another look at that report. A hearse is a vehicle for carrying the dead to the grave. Hardfield's awfully anxious to see Robichaud buried."

Cromarty seemed genuinely surprised. "You're going to pursue this because of a Freudian slip?"

"Come again?" I knew what a Freudian slip was, but I pretended ignorance. "What's lingerie got to do with it?"

Cromarty suppressed a laugh. "Never mind. You told me you can't stand psychological theories." He checked his wristwatch. "It's nearly eight. Go forth and detect. Catch a crook."

"Yes, Sir." I saluted. "See you around."

"Not if I see you first," Cromarty shot back over his shoulder as he bounded down the hall toward the lab.

I watched him climb a staircase, then I slowly wended my way to the rear exit.

A sub-zero February gale whipped around the streets on Hospital Hill. Nurses wrapped in navy-blue capes scurried between the residence and the General, white caps securely bobby-pinned to their hair, white shoes and hose flashing in the gray morning. They were enough to make a soon-to-be-forty detective's heart ache for his lost youth.

CHAPTER FIFTEEN

I STAGGERED BACKWARDS from the brink of the dry dock and scrambled onto a hillock infested with weeds and burdocks. All I'd wanted was a look at the *Bergensfjord* from above, not the scare of my life.

Saint John has one of the five largest dry docks on earth but I'd never been any closer than the view from across Courtenay Bay. Many's the time I'd stood on the high embankment and leaned against the black-and-white checkered dead-end sign at the foot of King Street East and gazed over at the shipyards. From a distance the dry dock looked benign and industrious. And human scale, not so deep and awe-inspiring.

I felt a little ashamed at not knowing this part of the city better. But there wasn't much out here besides the dry dock, the poorhouse, the T.B. hospital, the fertilizer plant (which stank of dead fish), and the Boys' Industrial Home where I delivered juvenile offenders from time to time. Except for the parish of Simonds, the city's population was concentrated across the bay and around the harbour.

"Ireland, you're white as a ghost," Jock McMillan said. "Into the liquor last night, were you?"

I muttered, "If only," then I picked the burdocks off my clothes while I explained my fear of heights to McMillan, the Saint John Shipbuilding Company's head nautical engineer. A transplanted Glaswegian, he was supervisor for the *Bergensfjord's* refitting.

A steam whistle shrieked, signalling the noon hour. Within seconds the various commotions in the shipyard ceased as the men knocked off for lunch. It was strange the way the silence took over. It came from below, sweeping up and past us like an invisible wave.

McMillan guided me to an elevator cage. From on high the *Bergensfjord* looked small and insignificant, hardly big enough to cross the North Atlantic.

We descended smoothly to sea-level where the platform gently smacked the floor of the dry dock. It was an interesting ride. I didn't mind the height so much as long as I was enclosed. Maybe there was hope for me yet.

The *Bergensfjord* cast its shadow over us as we walked beneath it through a maze of pilings. The barnacled underside of the ship smelled of the ocean.

We climbed a scaffolding that swung to and fro a little too much for my liking. "See these plates we're replacing here?" Jock said, facing a gaping hole amidships at the waterline.

I hooked an arm around the scaffold and nodded. "Mind if I smoke, Jock?"

"No, give me one. I gave up buying them."

We lit our cigarettes and stood silently examining the work underway. It wasn't far from where Eugene Robichaud had met his doom. I finally said, "Pardon my ignorance, but so what about the plates?"

Jock inhaled deeply then exhaled twin streams of smoke through his nostrils. "The ship's log says they incurred this damage – popped rivets, a number of stress fractures – when they struck submerged ice off Newfoundland," he said, "but I've ne'er seen results quite like this from ice. There'd be no possible way I can prove it but I'd say this ship ran aground." Jock's *r*'s rolled liked rocks in a keg. "Aground, man."

I took a hard puff on my cigarette. Jock McMillan was a serious Scotsman not given to idle speculation.

"Ran aground?" I said, stepping out and away from the shadow of the ship and into the sun. The sides of the dry dock loomed like a canyon wall. Our voices reverberated incoherently.

"More probably 'drifted' aground. They may have cut the engines and allowed the vessel to lie dead in the water," Jock said, taking off his plaid cap and passing a hand over his bald pate. Iron-red hair feathered out like wings over his fleshy ears.

We transferred to a staircase secured alongside and went aboard. I didn't say anything else until we were solidly on deck. "Why cut the engines? And why concoct a fable about ice? I don't get it, Jock," I said then.

Jock said hello to a couple of welders eating lunch in a sunny spot beside the funnel, then led me to the first mate's quarters.

"I don't know why, Ireland," Jock muttered angrily. "But it's a grave matter to wander off the prescribed shipping lanes without a crackin' good reason,"

With keys he had brought with him Jock unlocked the cabin door. He barred my way with an arm. "I don't want what I've said to go any further. You must promise me tha', Ireland."

"My word of honour, Jock."

"I stand by wha' I say. I wouldn't have revealed my thoughts to you if you hadn't been so candid with me about your own suspicions. That and the fact that your mother's parents were related to relatives of mine in Aberfoyle."

"Thanks. I appreciate it more than you know." I was sincere but I didn't buy the kinship angle. There were enough black sheep in my mother's family to cover King Square knee-deep in worsted.

The inside of the cabin was clean and bright. I had expected to find some sort of mad scientist's photographic laboratory. The man standing watch on Valentine's Day said there were photos hanging everywhere. Photos of everything.

McMillan unscrewed the porthole. "Place reeks of photographic chemicals. Phew!"

I searched the locker and the desk but found nothing out of the ordinary. The fellow sure liked *LIFE* magazine. He seemed to have every copy since it started in December '36 stowed in chronological order under his bunk. However, other than the telltale odour of chemicals, there was nothing to suggest the cabin had ever been used as a darkroom.

Jock sat beside me on the bunk. "A blind alley, Ireland?"

"Naw. I'll just have to snoop elsewhere. Why would this guy dismantle his workshop? The dry dock crew would never disturb it, would they?"

McMillan was shocked at the suggestion. "Definitely not. It would cost them their jobs."

"Where's the ship's crew holed-up, Jock?" I asked as I knelt to find the October '38 copies of *LIFE*. They had some terrific photos of the World Series. The Yankees had won the championship title for the third year in a row, wiping out the hapless Chicago Cubs four games to zero.

"Far as I know, the captain and officers are at the Royal Hotel. The crew members are at the Seamen's Mission and billeted here and there at boarding houses."

I pulled a handful of magazines out of the pile. "The Royal? Talk about high class. Meanwhile, the crew's likely fighting over beans and brown bread at the Mission."

"On board the *Bergensfjord* the officers and crew do not mingle. It's one of the more strictly disciplined ships I've come across in recent years," Jock said.

"Is that so?" I flipped open a copy of *LIFE*. Dizzy Dean was warming up his sore arm in a valiant but ultimately losing effort. "Why do you say that, Jock?"

"Since the Great War the distinctions between classes have been less sharply defined. It's been my experience to witness a general relaxation of formalities aboard merchant vessels. But the *Bergensfjord* is a throwback to the old days of iron-fisted command."

"Hello? What's this?" I said, discovering a photograph pressed between two sheets of onionskin in one of the magazines.

Jock sat up straight. "That's the approach to Halifax harbour. I know from taking ships there on sea trials."

I systematically went through the rest of the magazines. When I finished I counted two dozen photographs. They'd been interspersed throughout the first week of the month's issues for 1937 and 1938. He had faithfully collected every issue up until last week. The man's fastidious organization would make it easy for me to leave everything as I'd found it.

"Good Lord, Ireland, these are photographs of every major harbour from St. John's to New York. And there's Portsmouth, New Hampshire, an American naval base. I've a dirty feeling about all of this," Jock said, wiping his bifocals with a plaid handkerchief. He put his glasses back on and studied the photographs for a good ten minutes without speaking.

I had seen enough to fuel my worst nightmares. Jock helped me replace the photos in their respective hiding places and stow the magazines. Before we left the cabin we smoothed the blankets on the bunk, screwed the porthole tight, and pocketed our cigarette butts.

We made a slow and thoughtful journey back to McMillan's office. Jock swept his desk clear of blueprints and produced a bottle of Dewar's Scotch. He measured a double shot into each of two tumblers decorated with a painted-on tartan ribbon surmounted by the McLeod coat-of-arms; his wife's clan. "Here's to Robert Burns," he said.

"And the 'twa corbies' – Jock and Jack."

McMillan allowed a rare smile to lighten his otherwise dour face. "That's why I never call you Jack, Ireland. It would sound infantile if two grown men went around going Jock and Jack, Jack and Jock."

"Like twa corbies cawin'," I said, sipping the Scotch. It seeped down the walls of my empty stomach like slow fire.

"What are you going to do about this man, Ireland?" McMillan asked, downing his drink.

"Nothing for the time being. He's done nothing illegal, Jock. All he's done is take pictures of various ports of call. We may think it's with dastardly motives at heart but where's the proof? Many a sailor collects pictures of the places he's been without being accused of espionage. Besides, we're not at war."

"Yet," McMillan said, grimly pouring another drink. He wiped the desktop with a plaid washcloth.

"My God, Jock, it wouldn't surprise me if you wear tartan boxer shorts," I said.

He looked at me with mild alarm, as if he did wear tartan boxer shorts.

I decided to leave before I stumbled on to any more family secrets. "Thanks a million for your co-operation, Jock. Say hello to Murdena and the little tykes for me. I'll let you know if there are any more developments."

I took a last look down into the depths of the dry dock from behind the security of a chain-link fence and then I drove out of the shipyard. In the rearview mirror my face was flushed with the glow of the whiskey but Jock's "yet" hung in my brain like a warning light. War seemed as inevitable as the damn Yankees winning the Worlds Series again this year.

CHAPTER SIXTEEN

BEYOND A SHADOW of a doubt, I was in Deputy Chief Hardfield's dog house. Proof positive was in my vest pocket in the form of a name and address – Mrs. Prudence Reilly, 28 Garden Street. Mrs. Reilly's name struck fear and trepidation into many a Catholic under the auspices of the Cathedral of the Immaculate Conception. It was rumoured that the Bishop himself cringed and rapidly concurred whenever Perfection Prudence barked her wishes within earshot of His Excellency. I thought I'd seen the last of her prissy snout – elevated at an angle into the sanctified air of her good works – after my wife and I moved to St. Peter's parish. But the gods were not kind. Neither was the Deputy Chief. He knew I'd had run-ins with Prudence since we were kids at Holy Trinity elementary. And had practically started wholesale warfare when we were teenagers. It was the classic confrontation of the dirt-poor spudhead versus the monied Catholic gentry. Prudence was born with enough silver spoons in her mouth to feed the Dionne Quintuplets with a different utensil every day of the month. That was enough on its own to make an enemy of me but it was her avowed aspiration to become some sort of lay pope that really stuck in my craw. If you could buy your way into heaven, Prudence had a fifty-room mansion already reserved on high.

I parked the Studebaker around the corner from the Reilly property. Prudence and her husband lived alone in a turreted Victorian house midway up the steep hill that was Garden Street. A stone wall shielded the elevated lawn from the inquiring eyes of the common folk. In summer a hedge of blooming hydrangea bushes insured even greater privacy. It was a classy joint. If the house could talk it wouldn't condescend to speak to me.

I tarried on the curved wraparound porch, enjoying the afternoon view before I pushed the doorbell. A deep-voiced dong, bong resonated within, like the ringing of the angelus in a secret church. All the shutters in the big windows on the main floor were closed, blocking out the sun.

A single louver opened, then fell shut. Seconds later a stout maid entered the vestibule, peeked at me through the door's purple stained glass, and said, "Police?"

I flashed my I.D. She pulled back the deadbolt as if my badge possessed the authority of a sacred relic. I stepped inside before she started kissing the hem of my topcoat. Prudence's servants were nothing if not subservient. Superstitious and devoutly religious, all four were Irish landed immigrants. Prudence Reilly had put the fear of something into them but it sure as Hades wasn't God.

"Sir, could I take your hat and coat?" the woman said, trembling on her thick ankles.

"Why? What are you gonna do with 'em?"

Flustered, the poor dear almost burst into tears. "Nuttin', sar," she said, reverting to her country accent.

"It's okay, dear. I'll take care of them," I said quietly.

"M'Lady is in the parlour by the fire." The maid pointed unceremoniously then beat a retreat into the nether regions of the house.

I hung my coat over the arm of a bronze statue of a musketeer with a case of the jollies. He looked dashing in my fedora.

In the dim light of the oak-paneled front room I could see Prudence Reilly's slender hands primly folded on her lap. The wing chair she was sitting in completely hid her face and shoulders. The shuttered room with its cheerless fire was the picture of loneliness. Prudence didn't so much as twitch while I strode the length of the room, footfalls resounding off the hardwood floor.

I stood between Prudence and the fireplace. She was sound asleep, regal head tilted to one side. I'd be able to tell her girlfriends that Prudence snored. Not loudly, but gently like a cat with a head cold. I directed a bellows at the fire until the flames danced. Then I knelt and gently shook Prudence by the knee. Gradually she came out of what I presumed to be a drug-induced rest.

Prudence and I were contemporaries but she looked seven or eight years younger. Some of the C.W.L. ladies said it was pure spite that kept Prudence wrinkle-free. My theory was probably closer to the truth. I figured she was a vampire who never went out in the sun. But enemies and allies alike agreed that Prudence was a beautiful specimen. Tall, statuesque, auburn-haired, and green-eyed, she was photogenic enough to grace the pages of *VOGUE*. When she smiled – a rarity since Prudence was a teen – she could light a dozen Edison lamps. For all the skin-deep glamour though, Prudence was the closest thing you could get to a secular nun. Her nastier rivals claimed she only married for social reasons, that Prudence and James Reilly were a childless couple because immaculate conceptions had gone out with the birth of the Saviour. I wasn't quite as mean as all that. Even an ice queen like Prudence needed to thaw out once in a while.

Prudence slowly blinked the cobwebs away. I have to admit she looked like a movie star sitting there in her black velvet dress and frilly blouse. She started to drift off again. Damn it, what were those doctor friends of her late father's giving her to slow down? I tapped her knee until she opened her eyes wide.

"Jack? They sent *you*?" Prudence said, applying a lace handkerchief to the corners of her mouth. She raised herself up but fell down clumsily. Not at all like a lady. But it would've looked enticing to a stranger with no good on his mind.

She rearranged her bodice and covered her legs. A cologne that would've cost me a week's wages wafted toward me. I guess I was supposed to swoon at a glimpse of those perfect thighs but I managed to remain conscious.

"Jack Ireland?"

I stepped away from the fire before my behind roasted like an Easter ham, and said dryly, "In person."

Prudence turned away from the firelight. She'd been crying. Prudence Reilly crying was bigger news than Garbo talks. I couldn't quite believe my eyes.

"You're staring," Prudence said, cold enough to freeze my overheated derriere.

"It's not a capital crime," I said. "Or a mortal sin."

"Oh, clam up and sit down, Jack."

I moved a hassock to the side of the fireplace, opened my suit jacket, and obediently sat. Prudence gazed into the fire. Before she could nod off to dreamland again I cleared my throat rudely, "I'm gonna have a smoke, Mrs. Reilly."

"If you must, you must. And drop the Mrs. Reilly, Jack. Manners never did suit you."

I found Prudence's drowsiness downright alluring. What was the matter with me? Opposites attracting? "It's been eight or nine years since I've seen you, Prudence. You haven't aged a day. And I'm not being sarcastic."

Prudence regarded me for a moment as if she were judging a dog show and disapproved of the mutt's bloodlines. She rang one of those dinky little handbells snobs jingle in limey movies. She sighed, "Oh, I've aged, Jack. A hundred years."

I believed her. There was a century of suppressed heartache in her voice and the slouch of her shoulders. But before I blubbered in sympathy for this woman who could spread misery with a wave of her diamond-encrusted fingers, I thought I'd ask why she had summoned the police to her mansion on the hill and determine why Deputy Chief Hardfield instructed me not to take a statement or file a report. I was still stinging from his assertion that I "was more secretive than a cat-burglar" and that "as a result discretion should be as natural to you as wearing those heinous neckties."

The maid pushed a trolley into the room and nervously poured coffee for us as we watched. After she left all atremble and short of breath, I handed Prudence a cup and saucer. The china had a pattern of delicate shamrocks and was light as a feather. The coffee was just about the best I ever tasted. "This is grand stuff," I said, referring to the java.

"Belleek. Made in Ireland," Prudence said. She was adrift somewhere in her own world.

I let the fire hypnotize me, had more coffee, and took the plunge. "What's up, Prudence?"

She took half a minute to respond. "Blackmail," she said so softly, I almost didn't hear her.

"Who's being blackmailed?"

"Me."

"Who's doing the blackmailing?"

"Molly Higgins and her brother Conner," Prudence said, holding her cup for a refill.

I obliged and repeated the names, "Molly and Conner?" They were a brother and sister duo who worked, if you could call it that, for Barry Stratton, whoremaster and bootlegger to most of southern New Brunswick. Stratton owned a couple of houses on Station Street and a string of expensive painted ladies who made house calls. And they weren't selling Fuller brushes. The son-of-a-bitch had clients too big to even think of touching. It wasn't the whoring I objected to so much, or the bootlegging, but the despicable hypocrisy of the high and mighty. Before my blood started to boil, I said, "Tell me more."

Prudence suddenly came out of the fog and into the glaring light of her predicament. "You will not tell a soul. A single soul about this, Jack Ireland."

"Your secret will go to the grave with me, Prudence."

"Don't mock me, Jack. I'm in dire straits," she said, taking the cigarette I'd just lit. Which was damn curious because I never knew her to smoke.

"Since when did you take up the habit?"

"I've smoked since I was fifteen."

"Where? In the outhouse at your summer cottage?"

"Oh, hush," she said, dragging deeply. "You're not here to criticize my personal habits. You did enough of that when we were children to last a dozen lifetimes."

Now, there's an admission I liked. If I'd been a rooster I would've hopped onto the mantelpiece and crowed until midnight. Instead, I buttoned my lip and assumed the posture of an avid listener.

"It seems that my husband has been making rather regular visits to a certain house of ill-repute on Station Street. The damned fool went there yesterday and in a drunken stupor left his tweed jacket draped over a chair and didn't miss it until Molly Higgins telephoned me this morning. The inside pocket contained his wallet and one-hundred and fifty numbered invitations to a benefit dance at the Admiral Beatty Hotel that must be delivered no later than four this afternoon." Prudence was fuming like a she-devil. The Prudence of old.

I nodded. "When Molly phoned why didn't you simply tell her you'd reprint the invitations?"

"I told her exactly that but then she threatened to have Conner and his cronies hand-deliver each and every ticket. You see, Jack, a volunteer wrote the names of the recipients on the invitations. Some of them are very influential people in the community."

"What does Conner want for playing Mr. Postman?"

"Ten dollars per invitation. I would, without hesitation, pay him fifteen-hundred dollars but I don't trust him to leave it at that."

"No. And you shouldn't. Molly and Conner will do anything for a buck. I didn't think they'd stoop this low. Business must be hurting," I said, staring into Prudence's dilated pupils. Her gaze did not waver.

"You don't consider prostitution low?" she said wearily.

"As they say, 'The oldest profession'. You might as well try to eliminate inclement weather. Sometimes it's a necessary evil." I was tempted to ask her what medication she was on but thought I'd better not tread on thin ice. Her father had been a well known M.D. with a reputation as a pill-pusher. One of his faithful cohorts probably had Prudence full of candy of some sort. "How do you want me to handle this, Prudence?"

"I want the tickets, my husband's wallet, and I want Molly and Conner to develop complete amnesia regarding the entire incident," Prudence said, slurring a word here and there. She was struggling to stay awake.

"Is that all? How about we get Father Creary to absolve them of all their sins while we're at it, Prudence. For the love of Mike, I'm about as popular as a skunk at a garden party on Barry Stratton's turf. If I try to make a deal with him he'll hook me for the rest of my life." I was seriously contemplating throwing Prudence to the wolves and myself off the Reversing Falls bridge.

Prudence arose, held her forehead with both hands, then resolutely walked in slippered feet to a cabinet beside the phonograph. I watched in disbelieving fascination as she opened a fifth of Jameson's and drank straight from the bottle. It had the immediate effect of reviving her senses. A smoker and a secret tippler too? No wonder she did so much penance. For the first time I realized how desperately lonely Prudence had been all these years. It was almost enough to make me feel sorry for her. But not quite. I hadn't lost my mind yet. She took another long swallow and grew two inches taller.

"You'll manage a solution, Jack. You always do," Prudence said, holding onto the liquor cabinet.

"And If I don't?"

"Deputy-Chief Hardfield assured me that if you don't follow my instructions to the letter that I can have your head in a handbasket."

"You have such a nice way with words, Prudence. How come you don't teach school?" I said. "Come and sit down before you fall flat on your face."

She walked the few feet in a dream, sat down, and allowed me to prop her feet up on the hassock.

"Don't order me around, Jack," she said, head lolling against the side of the wing chair.

I smirked. "In the bishop's absence, I thought someone should."

Prudence didn't care what I said. She was gone again, floating on a pharmaceutical cloud. I studied her for a minute. How could someone so lovely to look at, be so nasty?

Before I left I threw a couple of logs on the fire. Getting Prudence out of this jam with the Higginses wasn't going to be simple. I could imagine their gloating faces and piggy eyes when I strolled into their place of business.

I got my hat and coat back from the gay cavalier and let myself out after I informed the frightened maid that madam was asleep and didn't wish to be disturbed.

On the way down the hill to Station Street my brain did its best to formulate a plan but it wouldn't shift into gear. Prudence had given it too many things to think about. I'd told the maid that she didn't want to be disturbed. But Prudence was already disturbed. Deeply. I'd known her almost all my life and didn't really know her at all. She probably had skeletons in her closet that would scare the daylights out of a common Mick like me.

CHAPTER SEVENTEEN

MOLLY AND CONNER'S house was a flat-roofed, two-storey affair painted forest green with black trim. Since I last looked at the place closely the Higginses had attached heavy gauge screens to the window casings facing the street and side alley. Schoolboys more or less regularly stoned the building despite, or maybe because of, the unleashing of a pair of aggressive mongrels Conner kept to make the unwanted stay away from his yard. The dogs were muzzled but they scared the bejesus out of me anyway. Molly, in her cursed arrogance and obstinacy, had the red light on in the back porch. I'd warned her to employ a less universal symbol but she told me it was either that or her red bloomers flying on a flagpole on the roof. So the red light beamed 364 days a year. Molly Higgins was sentimental about Saint Patrick and on his day didn't allow customers to darken her doorway no matter whose sexual or alcoholic urgency she had to deny. Sometimes the Irish can be a peculiar lot, given as they are to strange gestures of faith.

Wary of the dogs, I kept going past the house. A seated figure in a knit shawl stirred behind a downstairs window. That would be Mom Higgins, the seventy-two-year- old matriarch of the family and official sentinel. She knew me from when I went to school with her children. I let her have a good look while I lit a cigarette in the lee of a telephone pole. She recognized me but was sly enough to stay put behind her row of prize geraniums. One thing that old bat did have was a green thumb.

Satisfied that the house would be all agog with false alarms, I sauntered half a block down the street to the Atlantic Dairy. Milk bottles clinked together in wooden cases as they rolled along a conveyor and into a delivery truck. I went into the clatter of the shipping bay where a phone sat on a milk can. I dialled Doc Cromarty's office during a break in the din of rattling bottles. Angus didn't like the Higgins bunch so when I explained my predicament he agreed to Plan B – a ruse we'd used before under similar circumstances. After I hung up I felt a hundred pounds lighter. Maybe the Deputy Chief was right; I should have been a confidence man. When the game was on, my fingertips tingled like a safecracker's.

"Hey Sarge, how's tricks?"

I turned and looked straight over the top of Tiny Miller's head. Even standing on a milk crate he was scarcely five-eight. "Not bad, Tiny. What are you drinking that's good?"

"I got some Jersey milk. Want a glass?"

"Sounds like the cat's meow," I said, trailing him into his office. He opened a spanking new refrigerator and handed me a pint labeled JERSEY in blue letters. My insides purred in appreciation.

"What's the verdict?" Tiny asked, lighting the butt of a foul-smelling stogie. Clenched between his teeth, it made him look like the littlest of Little Caesars.

"Grand. Sure is creamy."

"It's got about four per-cent more butter-fat than Guernsey milk. We're gonna try it out for a couple cents more a quart. Rich man's milk. We're getting it from a farmer up near Hampton. You should see Jersey cows. Talk about beauties. Got eyelashes like Joan Blondell."

"You better stop, Tiny, before I have to arrest you," I said. Nobody could wax poetic about cows the way Tiny did. "You should be down on the farm instead of pencil pushing."

"Too small. I couldn't lift a bale of hay to save my soul."

I got up to leave before Tiny's cigar asphyxiated me. "I used to like dropping in here for a pint on my beat. Those were simpler days, my friend."

"You're right, Sarge. Me, I got two boys who outweigh me by fifty pounds apiece and tell me to take a hike if I yell at them to finish their homework. If I ever backtalked my old man he'd immobilize me," Tiny said, adjusting a lopsided picture of a herd of Ayrshires that hung behind his desk. "Want a calendar, Sarge? I got lots left. Got a dandy painting of the world's record-breaking Holstein on it."

"Mail it to me, Tiny. I have to go into Higgins's and handle a complaint."

"Must be that Randy Murphy beating, eh?"

"No. But I'm glad you reminded me. I'll have to ask Conner about it."

Tiny marched around the desk like an impatient steeplechase jockey waiting for his mount. "If you was to ask me, I'd tell you Randy had it comin'. He's a good-for-nothin' layabout. I offered him a job here as a driver's helper but he'd rather assist the likes of that Higgins crowd."

"No great loss, Tiny. Murphy'd probably break out in hives at the sight of plain milk. Closest he ever gets to it is in rum egg-nog," I said, offering Tiny a cigarette before he lit a fresh cigar. Mercifully, he took one. "What do you know about the guys who put the boots to Randy?"

"Nothin' much. I was working the midnight shift and heard a hullabaloo behind the railway sheds across the street. I went over with a driver and had a look. These two guys were givin' Murphy a good goin' over. They spoke some kinda gobbledygook but lemme tell you they were cool customers. That's what scared me. It was like they'd taken a course in beatin' up people. All business, you know. I've seen plenty of scraps but these guys were handin' out punishment like they was licensed for it."

"And then?"

"They walked off in one direction and Murphy staggered away in another. I asked him if he wanted some help but he told me to F-off and mind my own business. His jaw hung real slack. Randy's usually sort of friendly but I think – I *know* he was scared shitless. They could've killed him if they wanted to and it wouldn't of bothered them a bit."

I feared Tiny was right. I sighed and shook my head.

"What's it all about, Sarge?" Tiny asked, walking me to the door.

"Ideology."

"Wha? You lost me, Sarge."

"I'm lost too, Tiny. Thanks for the drink," I said, pulling up my collar as I stepped outside and ducked under the conveyor. "If you have any more trouble with your young fellows, tell me and I'll pick them up and give them the guided tour of the Boys' Industrial Home. Believe me, they won't give you any grief after that."

I took the back route to Higginses', cutting through the woodyard and the bottle exchange's excuse for a scrap heap. They hadn't sold a piece of junk in ten years. And they didn't exactly burn down the house buying and selling bottles either. But then certain residents of the street had no visible means of support so any front would do. A front was a front. Except in the upper crust where it became a façade. Or a veneer of respectability.

I kept an eye peeled for Conner's guard dogs but it must've been too cold even for their mangy hides.

The rear stairs were well used. The snow on the steps was packed hard and scrunched under my feet. When I was a young buck assigned to the Morality Squad I dislocated my shoulder bashing the second-storey door in but today it was ajar. They were expecting me and no doubt waiting with open arms. And upturned palms.

The door swung fully open before I reached the knob. I walked into an overheated room crammed with overstuffed furniture. Conner Higgins poked the door closed behind me with one of his feet. He was wearing moccasins, flannel pyjamas, and a loud checked bathrobe. His porcine eyes looked rheumy and flu-bitten. My sympathies were with the unfortunate virus.

Molly, nestled in an armchair that could have swallowed five of her, coughed a little cough. It was not a healthy household. Conner blew his nose with a blat worthy of Bix Beiderbecke. All of which made me smile my most aggravating smile. A grin to grate the skin off a rhinoceros.

I took a chair because I knew they'd never ask me to sit down. Molly proceeded to have a real coughing fit. I reached over and handed her a box of Kleenex. She tugged out four or five tissues and pressed them to her quickly reddening face. Conner slapped her scrawny back hard enough to dislodge her lungs. Catching her breath, she leaned back and retrieved a pint of rum from between the cushions of the sofa. After a long pull on the bottle her colour returned to its normal ashen hue. "We don't know nothin' about Randy Murphy," she said, "Nothin'."

"That's right, nothin'," Conner piped in. "Two-bit chiseller always trying to put the bite on us for 'services rendered'."

I lit a smoke and counted the blue ribbons old lady Higgins had won over the years for her houseplants at the Exhibition. She could grow grass on a bald man's head. I stopped counting at forty. "Randy who?" I got a boost out of lying to liars.

Molly and Conner exchanged sly glances. They weren't fooled for a second. "Murphy," he said, "M-U-R-F-Y."

Brother and sister had a right jolly laugh over that. When they finished wheezing and wiping the tears from their eyes, I said, "Prudence, T-R-O-U-B-L-E period. J-A-I-L period."

Conner suddenly lost his sense of humour.

"Listen, you two," I said. "I'm not gonna beat around the bush. I came here for James Reilly's wallet and the dance tickets, or invitations, whatever you want to call them."

"We don't know what you're talkin' about," Molly whined. "Mister Prudence Reilly wouldn't be caught dead here."

"My lips are moving but you're not hearing me, Molly."

A car horn sounded on the street. One long-one short-one long.

I watched as Conner went into the upstairs hall and peered out the front window. He drew back the curtains and yelled something unrepeatable. A heavy-breasted girl wearing only a bra and panties came out of a side room. No more than nineteen or twenty, she was an ivory-skinned beauty with wavy black hair and million-dollar legs. What a waste. Conner barked, "Hannah, get back in your room."

At that moment Doc Cromarty threw open the back door, letting in a swirl of Arctic air. Molly shivered convulsively. Angus removed his homburg, bowed at the waist, and presented Conner with a handful of QUARANTINED – BY ORDER OF THE BOARD OF HEALTH signs. "Doctor Angus Cromarty, at your service."

Conner sat down. He glumly eyeballed the notices. Doc had marked the dates Feb 20th to June 20th in the appropriate spaces.

"Diphtheria is an acutely contagious disease," Cromarty announced officiously.

"You're bluffing. Barry Stratton will get you for this," Molly said as if we'd incurred the wrath of the devil.

"Angus took a stapler out of his overcoat pocket. "Stratton? That self-important pantywaist?" He snatched the signs from Conner and made for the door.

"Wait. Wait a minute." It was old lady Higgins. "Give him Reilly's goddamned wallet."

"Mom," Conner protested.

"Do it, you stupid lug," the old lady screeched. "Before I box your ears."

"Oh, Mom," Conner said, pulling the wallet from behind an embroidered souvenir pillow of Niagara Falls. Mom Higgins went there every summer to see the gardens and the honeymooners.

I made sure all the tickets were accounted for and pocketed the wallet. "Thanks for making him see the light, Mrs. Higgins."

The old lady snarled, "Don't 'Mrs.' me, Jack, you son of a whore. I never thought I'd live to see the day you'd be running errands for Prudence Reilly. Since when did you get so cozy with her?"

Her accusation hit the target. And hurt. "I'm protecting my own interests, Mom. Aren't we all?"

"I'd throw you ass over teakettle down them back stairs if I wasn't so sick," Conner snuffled, brave now that Mom was in the room.

"On your best day you couldn't beat your way out of a wet paper bag," I said, still smarting from the old lady's remarks.

Doc Cromarty looked coldly from face to face. "I don't want to come back here. Understand?" The Higginses nodded. "I'll meet you back in the vehicle, Detective Ireland. Try not to be too long with these riff-raff."

"Fine. Thank you, Doctor," I said formally. "Conner, get Hannah. I've got a couple of questions for her."

"If you're wondering if James Reilly poked her, forget it," Molly said. "He doesn't do anything but sit and drink and hobnob with the boozers."

"And play crib with Mom," Conner added.

They obviously liked Reilly. Probably gave the dump a touch of class. I liked James myself. He was a decent man but a dipsomaniac since the Dark Ages. "Very interesting. I'll submit it to the society page. Get Hannah, Conner."

Conner glanced at his mother. She nodded and eased into a chair.

"What's with you and Prudence, Jack? You used to hate her in school," Molly said, taking a sip of rum.

"Orders are orders, Molly. If you're so hot to trot to humiliate Prudence then wise up and do it legit."

Molly's tiny frame shifted inside her housecoat. She could've been at death's door. "Hah. And how exactly would I manage that?"

"Take your mother's example. She wins top prizes for her plants at every exhibition and fair from here to Kent County. Those snooty dames in the garden clubs can't stand it but there's not a damn thing they can do about it."

The old lady grinned from ear to ear with malicious glee. She took a Philip Morris from me and lit us up with a gold cigarette lighter. When I admired the lighter, she said, "Customers leave some nice things behind.

This was a high school principal's. He liked to screw with worksocks and mittens on."

Hannah appeared in the doorway. She was dressed for the outdoors in a ski outfit that made her look more like a college co-ed than a prostitute who'd been around the block a few hundred times. "Whadya want? I don't have all day to jaw with coppers," she said in a voice hard as nails.

"You had a pair of clients…" Everybody must've been breathing laughing gas but me because they all laughed. When the mirth died down, I continued, "Two German sailors. Just before Valentine's Day. What were their names?"

Hannah hesitated then said, "Don't know. They were German jerks, that's all."

I stared at Molly. "Well?"

"Rolf and Fritz is all," Molly said, blowing her nose. "Now what's this about gettin' Prudence legit?"

"Go up to the Cathedral and sit next to her at eleven o'clock Mass every Sunday for the rest of her natural life. That should do it."

"Yeah, but I can't stand church."

"Take a book. What can I tell you? I have to go. Can we drop you anywhere, Hannah?"

I couldn't have shocked the girl more if I'd punched her in the face.

Mom Higgins nodded. "Go ahead but be back by six."

I glared hard at Molly and Conner. "So long. If you can't be good, be careful."

Conner mumbled, "Shove off," and went downstairs to answer the doorbell.

"Mom Higgins," I said, "I want to get a cutting off one of your shamrocks. Mine was knocked over by the landlady's cat one too many times."

"Take one of the ones on the radiator. I got dozens," the old lady said. "My ribbon winners are in the kitchen."

"Okay. I'll leave a quarter for it. That way it won't constitute a bribe," I said, putting the plant under the protection of my overcoat.

"Jack, you always could be a snide prick," Mom Higgins said with all the venom she could spit out.

Hannah went outside ahead of me. Before I closed the door, I said, "Thanks, Mom. After all these years I'm glad you still hold me in such high esteem."

I held on to the stoop railing while my eyes got used to the sunshine reflecting off the snow. Inside, Molly and her mother cackled like a couple of witches.

CHAPTER EIGHTEEN

I T TOOK MY nose a minute after I got into the Department of Health's midnight-black Chevrolet to identify Hannah's talcum powder. Lily of the valley. It'd been my wife's favourite. At Grace's funeral Aunt Hilda had placed a bouquet of the tiny white flowers in the casket. I could almost see Grace now, as if time had cruelly reversed.

"Where to, young lady?" Doc Cromarty asked. He was having a terrible time shifting the gears. Hannah was apt to guess he hardly ever drove and probably didn't represent the branch of medicine he claimed. Old lady Higgins wasn't stupid; we had a spy in our midst. Sitting between us to be exact. Angus jerked the car to a stop at the bottom of Garden Street. It was a long steep hill that ended at the top of the highest ridge in Saint John.

"The General Hospital," Hannah said. She had a French accent. Shades of Montreal. "I'm going to visit my friend Abby."

"Oh?" Cromarty said. "She's not very ill I hope."

"She doesn't have diphtheria," Hannah said. "Not unless you want her to. Naw, she's got mumps. A stupid kid's disease."

"That can be very serious at her age. How old is she?"

"Legal age," Hannah said, cutting Cromarty short before he could turn on the charm. She was too hard-boiled for Angus to crack but I knew he'd take on the challenge.

"Got a smoke?" she asked me. "They don't let me. Says it'll give me wrinkles."

I gave her a cigarette. "Rolf and Fritz will give you permanent wrinkles. How come you didn't tell me they beat up Randy Murphy after he brought them to you and Abby? You must've known about it. Word gets around."

Partway up the hill she absent-mindedly helped Angus shift into gear. We were almost to the Reillys' place but I nodded to Cromarty to keep going.

"Mom Higgins don't want me talking," she said.

"Try again, dear. Old lady Higgins thinks more of Randy than she does her own son, Conner," I chided, pretending to be annoyed.

Hannah puffed hard on the cigarette, her eyes glistening with fear. Angus steered the Chevrolet around the corner and pulled over to the curb on Coburg Street near St. Joseph's Nurses' Residence. Old habits die hard.

"I'm on your side, Hannah. So give," I said.

"Believe him, young lady," Angus said. "Jack is a straight shooter."

She kept her eyes, which were filling with tears, fixed dead ahead. "Those bastards told me and Abby if we talked…"

Angus touched her on the arm.

"If we talked they'd cut off our nipples and shove them up our twats."

Angus whispered, "Jesus Christ."

Hannah sobbed for a minute like someone's little sister then regained control. "They said Jews should be ex ex what's the…?"

"Exterminated," I said.

"Yes. And me and Abby never seen the insides of a synagogue. If they let us, the roof'd cave in," Hannah said, tough again in the time it took to snap your fingers. "Ain't that rich?"

"Rich as Rockefeller," I said, getting out of the car before I did get annoyed. "I'll speak with you later, Doctor. Hannah, if those cruds threaten you again, telephone me. I'll be there like gangbusters."

Hannah nodded, wiping her tears on the sleeves of her ski-jacket. I felt sorry for her. Before she knew it, she'd be a worn-out whore in some backwater. And Barry Stratton's bank balance would be none the worse for wear.

I walked briskly in the biting wind. It started to snow again by the time I got to the Reillys' front porch. Like a beacon, a light was on in the top of the turret.

The nervous maid came to the door. I waltzed right past her before she could say a word. "I want to talk to Mr. Reilly."

"He's working," the maid said, fluttering like a worried hen.

I swept the snow off my fedora onto the polished hardwood floors. "Well, unwork him. Tell him Jack Ireland's here."

She plodded up the curved staircase, every ten steps or so casting doleful glances over her heavy shoulders. I could've been Attila the Hun invading the private chambers of the Vatican.

Prudence was still asleep in front of the fireplace, one arm cramped at an awkward angle. The fire was blazing and looked dangerously close to her dress. Putting a finger to my lips, I muttered, "Don't say a word," to the laughing cavalier standing guard in the hall and went on tip-toes across to Prudence's liquor cabinet. She'd taken quite a bite out of the bottle, not bothering to wipe the lipstick off the neck. I poured a stiff belt into a monogrammed glass then sat down beside the fire to warm my ice-cold feet. Ah, the life of the idle rich.

Prudence stirred, gave a wobbly smile to someone I couldn't see, and conked out again.

"Mr. Reilly would like you to go up to his study," the maid said from the parlour door.

I rose slowly, whiskey and warmth too comfortable to break away from abruptly. Emboldened by drink, I spilled a large one into my glass. James Reilly would just have to put up with me imbibing his liquor.

"At the top of the stairs to your right in the tower," the maid said, obviously not in the mood to escort me.

"Thanks, dearie. You better stick a fork in Mrs. Reilly. I think she's done. Then you better turn her chair around before she overcooks."

Much to my surprise, the woman laughed. "Yes, saar, is dere anyting else?" she said with an Irish lilt.

"In five minutes bring the Jameson's up with two clean glasses. The master and I will be getting smashed."

I draped my topcoat over the cavalier's head. "Leave that there so I won't forget it."

The woman moved away and turned Prudence, chair and all, in one powerful lift. She'd probably been lugging water pails since she was two years old.

I climbed a stairwell hung with oil portraits of James Reilly's relatives. A seascape on the highest landing must have been a case of saving the best for last. I sat on a bench in front of it and stared at the ocean. Isolation and serenity. What I probably needed this coming summer was a long voyage on calm seas.

"Like it, Jack?" James Reilly asked. Apparently he'd been watching me watching the water.

"It's a Duesie, Jim. If it was mine I'd have it in the front hall instead of the bronze."

"Then I couldn't do what you've been doing just now. No, it stays. Sometimes I think that painting preserves my sanity. It's an early John Singer Sargent. With his prices these days I'm fortunate to have it. Grandfather purchased it for a song when he attended university in New England."

"I'd like to know the song. Hum me a few bars and I'll see if I remember the tune," I said, standing. My landlegs weren't the best. One of these years I'd have to give up drinking on an empty stomach. I was about ready to glow in the dark.

"Let's go into my study, shall we," James said, extending an arm. His shirt sleeves were rolled up and his vest was unbuttoned.

It'd been nearly a decade since I'd seen him. Ever the snappy dresser, it wasn't like him to be seen in less than impeccable form. He had gone gray at the temples. We had that and a love of whiskey in common. He studied the leaping gazelles on my necktie and momentarily frowned with disapproval. James was one of those guys who wore ties when he didn't have to; a class distinction of some sort that always irked me.

I flopped into a leather chair so soft I thought it was going to swallow me. James Reilly sat opposite beside a book-binding contraption strung with counterweights. In the small circular room the scent of glue and aromatic pipe smoke rubbed elbows with the odour of leather.

"Cozy spot, Jim," I said, toasting him. "I didn't know you bound books. I'm impressed."

"Thank you," he said humbly. "I hand-sew and leather-bind certain valuable books for the Provincial Archives and the Public Library, on a volunteer basis. A worthwhile hobby."

I drained my glass and placed his wallet on the work bench. He grabbed it like a starving man attacking a roast chicken.

A sheet of gold leaf feathered to the floor. Clamped in a vise, a book bound in green leather had the names *ULYSSES* and JAMES JOYCE embossed on the spine in gold. On a shelf nearby there were five additional copies. I mumbled, "Banned in Boston." The U.S. authorities lifted the ban on *Ulysses* in '33, the same year Prohibition ended. They must've been in a charitable frame of mind. I wondered why.

Reilly glanced up from counting the invitations to the ball. "Pardon?"

"Nothin', Jim. I took the liberty of instructing Nervous Nellie to bring a tray of drinks."

"Fine. Whew, I guess I've caused you no end of trouble over this, this oversight of mine," Reilly said. "I apologize, sincerely."

"I accept, sincerely." I smiled back at James as the maid clomped into the room, deposited the tray on a settee, and disappeared without a word.

"Miss Congeniality," James commented. "Ice?"

"Why not?"

We drank in silence, one glass, two glasses. Somewhere in the house the hired help were listening to a soap opera. A jingle for Oxydol interrupted the heroine's current dilemma.

"Aren't you going to ask me?" James said, his eyes bright from the liquor.

"Ask what?" I said. My tongue was sprouting fur faster than a werewolf. "Got a smoke? I'm out."

He opened the lid of a copper box on his desk and offered me a Pall-Mall. "What I was doing on Station Street?"

"No." I exhaled a perfect zero toward the books.

"Why, Jack, why?" he said fervently. Then he did a funny thing. He rolled down his sleeves, tightened the knot on his tie, buttoned his vest, and put his cuff-links back on. All with meticulous concentration.

"Because I know."

"I don't cheat on Prudence. I swear. Prudence is a profoundly troubled woman, Jack."

"Prudence was a troubled girl. There's a streak of I-don't-know-what inside her that used to make my hair stand on end." My mind was beginning to dredge up memories that were better left submerged.

James Reilly turned in his chair and gazed out the window, hypnotized by the snow flurries. I could sense that he was a haunted man, bedeviled by dreams that didn't turn out the way he had hoped. He blinked and shook his head. "Tell me what I was doing on Station Street. You said you knew."

"No one judges you there. No one looks down on you. No one looks up to you. No one envies you. What I call uncritical company. It's a far cry from the Knights of Columbus bashes where the bootlickers would just as soon sink a knife in your back."

Reilly almost sobbed. "Yes, yes, yes."

I had said more than enough to this tortured man. And to his tortured wife for that matter. "I have to leave while I can still walk," I said, finishing my whiskey. "No need to show me out."

Reilly put his face into his hands and started to weep.

I went down the carpeted stairs, gathered my hat and coat, looked in on Prudence, and left. So much for the lives of the idle rich.

CHAPTER NINETEEN

 OR THE LIFE of me I didn't know why there was scattered laughter in the audience. You'd think people had seen enough goose-stepping fascists in the newsreels by now to render the spectacle worrisome instead of humorous. Hitler's and Mussolini's crapulous behaviour was no longer the daily fun and games of a pair of comic-opera generals. Generals with the unbridled authority of ancient kings. Mad kings with mad dreams.

I finished my popcorn and washed it down with a small Coke. Hitler was ranting and raving to an unbroken sea of bodies at an outdoor rally. The devout and deranged alike stared with intense fervour at their Fuehrer. Before I jumped up and yelled, "Fanatical idiots," at the screen, I took off to the canteen for another Coke.

"Are you staying for the other movie, Jack?" the manager of the *EMPIRE* asked while I lit a cigarette and sat in one of the armchairs in the lobby.

"Don't think so, Pete. I fell asleep in the first one. Good picture, though. Always did like Gary Cooper. God, can you imagine joining the Foreign Legion? It'd be like jumping into a bathtub full of rattlesnakes."

Pete chuckled. We'd been schoolmates and went to Saturday matinees together long before the advent of sound. I sometimes missed the piano players and the old flicks but nowadays movies were better than ever.

"Don't miss *Gone with the Wind* when it comes out later this year, Jack. It'll be one of the best. I guarantee it," Pete said, handing me a couple of free passes. "Those are for being my most loyal customer. A lot of the regulars deserted me for the Paramount. It's a great house but they don't show double bills like we do."

"Thanks, Pete. I shouldn't take these, but I will."

"Sure. Why not? You pay to get in and most times all you watch is the *News of the Day*."

"That's when I'm working, Pete. Instead of a coffee break, I take a news break. A bugger for punishment."

"Yeah, I catch the sports and that's it. After what the I-ties did in Abyssinia I had enough. Probably not good to turn a blind eye but what can you do?"

I got up and looked at the posters and the stills for the coming attractions. "Nothing, Pete. We're all going to get our eyes opened pretty soon, anyway." I stopped dead in front of a black-and-white of Lana Turner.

"There oughta be a law the way she fills a sweater. You'd get a charge out of the way kids howl at her. You'd think they knew something," Pete said, tidying the chocolate bars at the concession stand. Then he combed his twenty or thirty strands of hair in one of the circular mirrors lining the lobby.

"More than we ever did, Pete. We might as well have grown up during the Middle Ages."

A loud clamour arose from inside the theatre followed by the rhythmic tramping of feet. It sounded like a Nazi rally right here in Saint John.

"New projectionist gets balled up when he's changing reels. Gotta run, Jack," Pete said, running for the booth before the crowd shook the building apart.

I buried my cigarette butt in a sandtrap that passed for an ashtray and pushed open the glass doors to the street. The fresh air reminded my sorry head that it was nursing a hangover, the kind that begged to be put to bed with an icebag and a bottle of Aspirin. It was nobody's fault but mine. When I'd left the Reillys' place I went straight home and raided my own liquor cabinet like some dipso seeking wisdom in a bottle. All I found was one complicated question after another. It didn't take me long to give up trying to fathom the nature of the human creature and get on with listening to music into the wee small hours. I must've had a blinding glow on because I didn't hit the sack until I dropped one of my favourite Art Tatum records, shattering it into a dozen pieces. After a dreamless sleep I woke up around noon with a tongue like coarse sandpaper and a brain soggy as a wet mattress. If I keep at it long enough, I might learn how to drink someday.

I stood under the shelter of the *EMPIRE'S* marquee for a minute and watched the traffic making slush on Coburg Street.

It was one of those mild days in late February when a balmy breeze sweeps up from the south and gets us a little bit goofy after a long winter. I was wearing a leather jacket and my Red Sox cap. Jumping the gun on spring but chipper despite yesterday's alcohol abuse.

There was a restaurant called The Silver Rail at the bottom of the hill on the corner of Union. I let my feet take me there to a phone booth where I could ring Doc Cromarty about our Station Street adventure. The ding-ding-a-ling of the nickel tumbling in the machine was enough to make me cry, "Uncle."

Doc Cromarty, short of breath, caught the phone on the fifth ring.

"Chasing the nurses through the infirmary again," I said. "You ought to be ashamed."

"I am. I am," he said. "Seriously, Ireland. I'm expecting a call from a colleague, so make it short."

"Just wanted to thank you for the able-bodied assistance yesterday. Did Hannah say anything after you dropped me?"

"Very little. The Higginses have got her well trained. She's frightened out of her wits by Rolf and Fritz. And I can't say as I blame her."

"She's a hard ticket, Doc. When push comes to shove she'll be able to take care of herself," I folded the phonebooth door to turn the overhead light off. If I didn't soon get something on my stomach besides popcorn and Coke I'd collapse in a blithering heap.

A familiar-looking woman walked into the restaurant with a handsome boy of about twelve. She was wearing a beret and a stylish short coat. They slid into one of the red leather booths.

"What are you going to do about Rolf and Fritz?" Doc asked. "Or have they sailed for parts unknown?"

I could hear him munching a celery stalk, his only addiction besides nurses. Then again, he was making so much noise it could've been a leg off his chair. I told him about the *Bergensfjord* and made him privy to some of my suspicions. It actually stopped his ungodly chomping.

"And I had someone nose around for me at the Port Authority," I said. "Rolf and Fritz are false monikers. Try Werner and Herman on for size."

"Very strange, Ireland."

TERRY CRAWFORD

"Not so, Doc. It isn't the first time someone's used an alias in a whorehouse."

"Come to think of it, something peculiar did happen when I was parked outside waiting for the moment to honk," Doc said. "I didn't want to say anything in front of Hannah."

"Oh? What's that?"

I had just remembered who the woman with the boy was – it was Roxanne from Pepper's Diner. With her face on and dressed up for the world she didn't much resemble the wise-cracking waitress. I liked the improvement.

"A car cruised by twice, stopping for a minute each time," Doc Cromarty said. "The occupants seemed inordinately interested in the Department of Health vehicle. Perhaps it was nothing of consequence. Customers scared off by officialdom."

"Lemme guess, Doc. A green Plymouth. Am I right?"

"You *are* a detective, Jack. How did you know? One of your hobo spies?"

"No, Doc. Merely the hard work and diligence of one individual with an uncommon intellect."

The green Plymouth was a shot-in-the dark fired off by the slack condition of my brain in its hungover state. Someone was shadowing me and I'd just gotten the verification.

"Modesty is a virtue with which you are apparently unacquainted, Ireland," Doc said. "Say good-bye before I vomit."

"Bye, Doc. Thanks a bunch."

I huddled in the phone-box and waited for my slight dizziness to pass. There was so much Scotch still in my system it was a wonder I didn't hear bagpipes screeling a plaintive air everytime I inhaled. I burped Highland gas, the smoky scent of peat and malt, and vowed to switch to ale. For a week or so, anyway.

I sat on a stool at the fountain and convinced the owner to let me have a double order of scrambled eggs, bacon, and toast even though it was mid-afternoon. He poured me a cup of coffee and went into the kitchen, grumbling under his breath. He'd tried to talk me into a hot pork sandwich, one of the worst abominations yet invented. But it did cost twice as much as breakfast. The old geezer had a cash register for a heart but he also had the best jukebox in town. I should know, I pumped enough nickels into the thing to send an entire orchestra to Juilliard.

Roxanne walked behind me to the jukebox. I sneaked a peek as she pushed B-4, D-7, and K-3. Not bad. Two Billie Holiday tunes and a Benny Goodman rouser. If she'd played Louis Prima's *The Lady in Red*, or some such silliness, I might've asked for the return of the Valentine roses.

She looked good out of uniform. A sight for sore eyes in a beret and blue angora sweater. I must've been staring in the mirror behind the counter because she caught my eye and said hello.

I spun on the stool and touched my cap.

"The flowers were lovely, Mr. Ireland," she said. "It was the first time I ever had roses sent to me. First time ever for flowers. Thank you."

"My pleasure. How'd you know my name?"

"That should be easy for a detective – I phoned the florist's."

"Elementary, my dear Roxanne."

"Roxy will do."

The boy with her seemed both shy and protective. He looked at me with a flash of suspicion when Roxanne said detective. I hoped he wasn't another kid who didn't like cops. It was a prevalent disease of unknown origin that afflicted the high and the low.

"Jack, then," I said.

"This is my son. Leonard. He's off school today for a check-up with the doctor. Leonard has asthma."

"Oh, Mom," Leonard said. "I wish you wouldn't tell everybody." It was more of a plea than a bratty remark. The kid didn't appear to be shallow-chested or particularly frail. In fact, he was a hale and hearty sort.

"Lots of guys have asthma, Leonard," I said. "Even professional athletes."

He sipped orangeade through a straw and muttered, "Lenny."

"Lenny, don't be rude," his mother said evenly.

"It's okay, Roxy. I hate being called John so I know the feeling."

The owner refilled my coffee cup. "Yer order," he spat, "will be a while. The cook gimme a hard time. He don't like fixing breakfast after ten o'clock."

"It's a rough life," I said. With my head pounding the way it was, I wasn't much interested in kitchen politics.

"Why don't you join us?" Roxanne said. "We're having a late lunch."

"Glad to."

I sat next to Lenny so I could eyeball the street. A few young sports were wearing windbreakers and no gloves or hats. A blond head stepped out of the Federal Five & Dime on the corner opposite. It was Werner Strasser, the first mate of the *Bergensfjord*. He was carrying a shopping bag in each hand. Maybe it was me but he looked like an arrogant cavalry officer too proud to come down off his high horse.

The waitress placed hot pork sandwiches drowned in caramel-coloured gravy in front of Roxanne and Leonard. The boy promptly decorated the fries with a spiral of catsup and dug into the boiled-for-forty-eight-hours peas. He ate with a dreamy expression. It was probably a treat even though his mother worked in a diner.

A minute later my breakfast arrived. The eggs weren't scrambled and the bacon was limp as a pansy's wrist. I devised a double-decker sandwich that my innards didn't exactly appreciate but at least it was sustenance. Somewhere down below, the popcorn was deciding whether or not to revolt. I squelched the uprising with coffee, sat back and enjoyed Billie Holiday's *Say it with a Kiss*, and felt not too bad for a young/old fella.

I asked Roxanne, "Do you like Billie a lot?"

She daintily daubed the corners of her mouth with a napkin, a different woman away from work. "She sends me. And Teddy Wilson's piano really. But I like Teddy's whole band. When I get home from the job it's the only way I can get relaxed."

"Same here," I said.

Leonard sopped up the last of the gravy with a French fry that he dropped in his mouth like a worm into a hungry bird.

"Want to play pinball, Lenny?" I said, giving him three nickels.

"Could I, Mom, could I?" he said, excited.

"I don't usually let him but I suppose," she said, cornered by the circumstances.

I let the boy out of the booth just as Werner Strasser came in off the street. He sat on the first stool at the fountain. Because of the booth's high back, I could watch him without his knowledge.

Roxanne and I sat in silence, looking into one another's eyes like bashful teenagers. I glanced at Roxanne's hands then at Werner who was trading small talk with the owner. Strasser's English was perfect except for the *k's* which clinked like loose chains on a smoothly running tire. He was somewhat of a charmer and had a handsome, sinister face. I thought about the ugly threats against Hannah and Abby. It made my blood run cold.

Roxanne said, "I notice you don't wear a ring, Jack, aren't…"

"I'm a widower," I interrupted. "I noticed you don't, either."

"My husband deserted me nine years ago when Leonard was two and a half. No one's seen or heard of him since. He was declared legally dead last fall. I don't know why I bothered with the courts. He's been dead to me since the day he walked out. I guess I did it for Leonard's sake. Or my own peace of mind. Who knows why we do things?"

"What about your family?" I asked.

"They disowned me when I married Rupert. Turned out they were right about him. He never wanted children," Roxanne stated flatly. As the sun broke through the clouds she looked out at the traffic-snarled street but didn't see it. She was a thousand miles away.

I waited for her to come back. "You don't seem bitter. Are you?"

Roxanne considered the question for a minute. "No. For years I hated the insinuations that I was to blame, but I'm not bitter. It does make me mad, though, that the sympathy usually goes to the man even when he's in the wrong. That's not fair but life isn't always played by the rules, is it?"

I didn't respond. If she was looking for an argument she'd have to pick another subject.

"Enough about my trials and tribulations. When did your wife die?" Roxanne asked, signalling the waitress for more coffee.

"Four years, last December," I said. It seemed like a distant nightmare. Maybe time was finally healing the wounds.

"Was her health bad or do you mind me asking?"

"No. Grace was killed by a hit-and-run driver who was never caught." I peeked at Leonard, who'd just tallied up two free games and was grinning at us with a 100- watt smile. "She was three months' pregnant."

"Oh, God, I'm sorry, Jack. I shouldn't…"

A great weight lifted off my shoulders. I'd never told anyone Grace was expecting our first child. I thought when I did it'd be to Lincoln

Drummond, my best friend, after we'd downed a bottle of Scotch and were having a head-to-head tell-all. Now I'd have to tell him or take it to the grave with me.

The waitress smacked her chewing gum and poured the coffee. "Give us three slices of butterscotch cream pie and another orangeade for the boy, will you," I asked quietly, not wanting Werner to notice me. I shouldn't have worried. He was transfixed by *LIFE* magazine.

"On me," I winked to Roxanne.

She smiled, the serious talk behind us. I felt at ease with her for some reason. Maybe it was shared anguish or just relief from our respective burdens. Then again I didn't meet too many women who went for Teddy Wilson. They were mostly gone on Artie Shaw. Which was okay but I liked my jazz closer to the alley than the dance floor.

"Leonard's having fun," Roxanne said. "Those pinball machines are a scourge, though. Some of the kids on our block pump every cent they get their hands on into those machines. Some of them even swipe money out of their mothers' purses."

"Yeah, they can get hooked on pinball, Roxanne. Become regular little wizards. Hell, we've got cops on the force who can't stay away from those contraptions. Some example. Mind you, I shoot a mean game of snooker. Even the police gotta enjoy life once in a while. What do you do to get away from it all?"

"When I can afford a babysitter I love going to the movies. And call me Roxy. My mother's name is Anne," she said. "It kind of grates on my nerves."

"Sure. Movies? What do you like?" I said, sliding along the booth to let Leonard sit on the outside. When the pie came his eyes popped. "Grab your weapon and dig in, Lenny."

He didn't need prompting, eating the meringue first then the butterscotch filling.

"Detective stories," Roxy said, blushing. "Honest. But I can't stand Westerns. Cowboys chasing one another around the same boulders for an hour."

I took the passes for the *EMPIRE* out of my shirt pocket. "Here, Roxy, use these, you can take Lenny with you. There's a Thin Man double-bill next week and some new cartoons."

"I couldn't, Jack. Really."

"I insist. You can splurge on the popcorn and buy Lenny an extra orangeade."

Werner Strasser walked past the window and glanced over his shoulder. The way he flinched I knew that he recognized me. I tipped my cap at him to let him think I was a bloodhound on his trail. It worked. He gave a hurried look around and disappeared into a crowd of high school boys from St. Vincent's on their way to a hockey game.

"You know him?" Roxy asked.

"Not personally. Why?"

"He came into Pepper's and got into an argument with some sailors from away."

"An argument? About what?"

"We don't know. It was in a foreign language. Mr. Pepper says German because he knows the words *schweinehund* and *dummkopf.*"

I nodded. The day Eugene Robichaud died Werner Strasser refused to speak English. Or didn't want his command of the language known. Stupid like a fox. Or a Nazi brown-shirt. When that thought occurred to me I could almost hear glass breaking. It was like a warning from the ghosts of my ancestors. A Celtic tremor.

The waitress added up our checks. Against Roxanne's protests, I paid hers as well as mine.

"That was awful good of you, Jack," she said, when we were on Charlotte Street strolling toward the bus-stop at King Square.

"My pleasure, Roxy. I didn't feel like eating alone today."

"Mom, there's our bus," Lenny said, breaking into a run.

"I've got to rush, Jack. I'm on at four. Drop by for coffee sometime," Roxanne said. "I work days next week."

"Will do," I said. Lenny was already aboard the bus, watching us guardedly. He turned away when Roxanne gave me a quick peck on the cheek. Damned if my ticker didn't beat a little faster.

I waved as the bus pulled around the corner and then I went across the street and into the City Market.

There wasn't much activity along the centre aisle. Only a few stalls were rented, most of them displaying home-made baked goods, knitted mittens, stocking hats, and sweaters. On both sides of the building various butchers, fish mongers, and grocers operated permanent businesses. An occasional housewife browsed with basket in hand, looking over the produce, stopping to haggle over a piece of meat, or complaining about fish prices. The Depression had made many of us moneywise to the point of Scrooginess.

I bought a pound of cheddar at Fenwick's and walked down the paved slope to McCavour's fish stall beside the Germain Street entrance. The haddock was fresh that morning so I picked out one big enough for Lincoln and me to have for supper. He was probably already at my place preparing the vegetable stew we both liked so much in the wintertime. The fish, baked with lemon slices and ground pepper, would make a nice side-dish and could be combined with leftovers into a dandy chowder. My insides grumbled in not-so-silent approval. If I didn't know better I'd say my hangover was over.

I went outside and stood in the alcove of the arched portal. For a second, I thought the six-pounder under my arm was going to swim away. I lit a cigarette to quell the dizzies. I then entertained the notion of going on the wagon before John Barleycorn counted me as one of his slaves. After I argued the point and won, I decided to loop around the block and visit the Federal Stores.

The going was rough but the walk did me the world of good. I described Werner Strasser to a salesgirl and was referred to Men's Clothing. A spiffy, bespectacled man with a pencil-thin mustache managed the section. He wasn't about to tell me anything until I showed him I.D. I didn't mind. Too many people opened up without hesitation, as if they couldn't wait to implicate an associate or neighbour in something illegal.

"I'll keep it simple," I said to the clerk, who was standing at rigid attention. "What did Strasser purchase?"

"I'll be happy to show you exactly what he bought," the little man said, polishing his glasses with a linen handkerchief. "Right this way, if you please."

We stopped in an adjoining aisle beside an arrangement of men's work-clothes. The clerk put his spectacles back on and peered over the rims. "Four of each of the following items." He built a stack of clothing. "Workpants – black; wool turtleneck sweater black; stocking hats…"

"Black," I said. "Thank you. I get the picture." Crystal clear. Werner and his cronies masquerading as cat-burglars. And it not even close to Halloween.

"Fine, Sir. Will that be all?"

"No. I want to buy one of those ties you were putting into a box when I came in."

"Are you sure, Sir? We're returning those to the manufacturer. We haven't been able to sell a single one. Not even to the Zoot-suiters."

"In that case, I'll buy two."

He draped a selection of the beauties over his arm as if they smelled bad. I chose an aquamarine with copper and bronze triangles and then deliberated over my second choice. The man had that patient quality a good salesclerk should have in the face of a sure purchase. But maybe he just pitied me. After all, I was wearing a baseball hat and a leather jacket. He probably expected a detective to dress like William Powell. I drank like the Thin Man but the resemblance ended there. I selected chartreuse with flying V's and small vortexes spinning before the eye. You'd have to go to Timbuktu to find an outfit to match it.

I took the Union Street exit and began the long trek homeward. Walking kept me trim, and my stomach and feet flat.

TERRY CRAWFORD

CHAPTER TWENTY

L INCOLN OPENED THE baked haddock, inserted a fork below the head, and extracted the backbone in one piece. He held it suspended for my inspection as if I were an expert on fish skeletons. I applauded softly. I swallowed a fish bone when I was nine and nearly choked to death. I'd been leery of them ever since.

While Lincoln loaded our plates with fish I added the baby carrots I stored in boxes of sawdust in the basement especially for the dreary days of winter. They were perfectly cooked, with a bit of snap in the core, not boiled down to orange mush.

Lincoln sprinkled pepper over his fish, made a quick sign of the cross, and went to work on the carrots, crunching them in the silence. We ordinarily saved the chit-chat till after we ate but tonight he pointed his knife and said, "I've been thinking about that Werner what's-his-face and what you told me, Jack."

"Yeah?" I prompted. I often laid out cases for Lincoln but he seldom commented on them, knowing that I did it mainly to get the facts straight in my own head.

"Couldn't he just be buying extra clothes for work on the ship? It could be innocent enough."

I savoured a few bites of haddock before answering. "That's possible, Linc. Maybe I'm too suspicious. But four identically clothed men conjures a vision of a co-ordinated stake-out or manoeuvre of some kind. I did some reading up on what the Brits are calling 'commandos' – specially trained marines for operations behind enemy lines. Part of their strategy is to create confusion by being identically dressed. In a night operation it'd be impossible to count heads accurately."

"Commandos? That's a new one on me."

"Military jargon. Anyway, Werner Strasser is a first mate, not just an ordinary seaman. The steamship company would supply his gear."

Lincoln poured two cups of strong tea and shoved one in my direction. "Not to get you going, but what do you think Werner's up to?"

After last night, tea was the only thing that could slake my thirst. I drained the cup. "Shipyards. Harbours. Possible sabotage."

Lincoln objected, "Jack, give your head a shake. If there is another war it'll be like the last one, it'll never reach our shores."

"I hope you're right, but I have my doubts. There *is* going to be war and the next one will be a real world war. Hitler put the Sudetenland into his back pocket last October and the Czechs were left hanging out to dry by their so-called allies. Hitler knows now that he'll be appeased. The maniac won't stop until somebody kills him."

Lincoln gazed at me for a minute. "The Great White World – I'll never understand it. It staggers onto its feet, back toward prosperity, and for what? So it can murder more efficiently?"

He said it with such weariness I almost kidded him about us being the Black Man's Burden. But I didn't. I'd save it until we were in a mood to laugh.

I wolfed down the rest of my supper and drank a whole pot of tea. I was beginning to feel half-human. Good enough to have a shot of rum with Lincoln before we went bowling at the St. Peter's Lanes. Behind our backs the alley rats called us Salt and Pepper, which of course made us never miss our four strings every Wednesday through the season. For a man with a limp, Lincoln was one of the best bowlers in the city but he'd never had a single team invite him to join. He didn't care. It was satisfaction enough to see his name posted regularly for high string and pocket the five dollar prize.

The doorbell buzzed while we were clearing the table. There was plenty of haddock left over for a chowder on Friday so I wrapped it for Lincoln to take home. He went down to answer the door and came back bewildered. "No one there, Jack. That happened about an hour before you got in, too. Kids goofin' around?"

"Probably," I said. "Did you see anything?"

"No. A car rolled by kind of slow is all."

"Green Plymouth?"

"No. Black Ford. It might've been my imagination but I thought I heard a two-way radio squelched when I unlocked the vestibule."

My head was still a bit light from my highland fling with the Scotch but it suddenly got lighter than air. I sat down beside the icebox and had a feeling of terrible dread come over me. What I was thinking wasn't fit to utter aloud. But, damn it, if I didn't chase the thought I'd never have another moment's peace.

"What's the matter, Jack? You okay?" Lincoln said

"Nothing. Get me a glass of milk, will you?"

"Sure. You look like you were hit by lightning. You're not in trouble, are you?"

"Trouble? What kind of trouble?"

"How would I know? You tell me."

Lincoln offered me a bag of sugared doughnuts. Who said lightning didn't strike twice? I almost gagged.

"Maybe we should skip the bowling, Jack. You don't look so good."

I guzzled the milk. It hit my stomach like an overweight Holstein. "I'll be fine once I get my bearings. Let me brush my teeth and then we'll take off."

In the bathroom my feelings of dread turned to anger. Tomorrow would be an eventful day or my name wasn't John Errol Ireland.

Lincoln and I went out the backdoor and hopped the fence into St. Peter's churchyard.

We had an alley reserved for seven o'clock and didn't want to miss it.

The night was balmy but not half as balmy as the idea that kept nagging me. Nagging me through the background noise of bowling balls rumbling down the lanes and the knock-knocking of the candlepins.

CHAPTER TWENTY-ONE

T HE DETECTIVES' BASEMENT locker-room was empty. A dusky bar of sunlight shone on the bulletin board through the window. It was barely 7:30. The way I felt, too early for me to be up and about but I had business. Business.

Something in Doctor Cromarty's autopsy report on Eugene Robichaud had bothered me: the deceased had eaten his last food approximately twelve hours before his death.

I took my coffee and stretched out on the leather chesterfield we bought last autumn at a fire-sale. Its stiffness creaked. I clicked off the lamp. Up above a door opened and closed, men exchanged "mornings", the janitor's scrub-bucket rattled on worn wheels. An inmate in the jail shrieked "Up the I.R.A," his voice almost lost in the intervening corridors.

I scratched a match along the stone wall, momentarily lighting up the dark corner. My first smoke of the day. It was times like this when the building felt really old. Older than its nearly one-hundred years. If the Count of Monte Cristo tunneled out of the wall beside me I wouldn't have been taken by surprise. There were persistent rumours of a new police headquarters but I liked the station we were in – the heavy mass of quarried stone, the wide exterior steps, the carved balustrade overlooking the Loyalist Burial Grounds. I preferred the time-after-time of old places.

Sluggish footsteps came down the backstairs. The locker-room door swung open and Sullivan dragged his feet across the threshold. The goof was eating a doughnut. When he walked towards me I could see that he had two doughnuts in his hand and was actually eating the top one first. Then he did something only a bona-fide slob would do – he polished off number one and rammed all of number two into his fat trap. This he washed down with the last of a chocolate milkshake. He tossed the paper cup into a wastebasket and belched. His gluttonous eyes glinted in the dim light. Glinted with the look of religious ecstasy. Food was the Blessed Eucharist of Sullivan's existence.

He didn't even see me.

Sullivan was the only detective on the squad who used a padlock on his locker. Probably kept emergency peanut butter sandwiches in it. I know he had some Swedish *Health* magazines he kept in there under wraps. After a minute of watching him fruitlessly search for something, I turned the lamp back on. He just about jumped out of his tight skin. It gave me a major kick.

"For Chrissakes, Ireland," he bellowed. "Why don't ya just shoot me? My heart'd stop faster that way."

I couldn't stop laughing. Maybe I was giddy from tossing and turning most of the night. Or maybe it was just hilarious seeing a hog levitate.

"What're you doin'? Sleepin' here nights now?"

Sullivan sat down and stuck his chin out. "Geeze, I just don't know about you anymore, Jack."

My mirth was enveloped by a fogbank of dark thoughts. I decided to get down to brass tacks. "I don't know about *you* anymore, Sully."

"Wha? I oughta clobber you. Sayin' a thing like that."

I rose and walked toward him. For all his extra blubber Sullivan was one hell of a scrapper. But he knew better than to tangle with me even on his best days.

He stood up to me. Defiant, arrogant, and pugnacious. I offered him a cigarette which he accepted with apparent relief. He muttered nervously, "What's with you?"

"You," I said. "Francis X. Sullivan is doing a lot of added duty that you haven't logged in."

"What are you yammering about, Ireland?" Sullivan dead-panned. He stared into my eyes then nonchalantly went to the chesterfield.

I thought, Go ahead, play hard to get. I said, "Quit the runaround, Sully. Why are you dogging me?"

"For the last time, Jack, I don't know what you're talking about," Sullivan yelled, edgy before I really started to probe. He took off his hat and combed the hair around his bald spot, a sure sign that he was distressed. I knew him that well so I just let him squirm on the hook. After a few minutes in the loud silence he said, "What? What?"

I decided to reel him in slow. "Doughnuts. And a weakness for sugar, Sully. Maybe a *fatal* weakness."

The colour drained out of his apple-red cheeks. He was confused and I could sense that his mind was racing. Flicking his lighter in agitation, he finally produced a tiny flame which made him seem vulnerable and pathetic.

"Sometimes clues, even answers, hide in plain sight. Maybe enemies, too," I said, sitting astride the bench in front of the lockers. "Doughnuts. I would've never connected Shed 7 with those blubber manufacturers if you hadn't driven past my apartment last night. You'll have to learn to use the two-way someday, Sully. You're like a mobile radio station. Every two-bit hood in town knows when you're in the vicinity. But I'm straying from the subject. When I checked Eugene Robichaud's cubbyhole there were sugar crystals in most of the drawers. I figured him stealing a bite on the job but it was you, Sully. Wasn't it?"

Sullivan didn't answer. He didn't have to. I took his silence for an affirmative. "Why root through his office when he was found in the hold of the *Bergensfjord* unless there was more to it than a drunk falling down a hole? What was there to find?"

"I don't know, Ireland. You tell me," Sullivan smirked.

I didn't like it. He was far too smug. Why? The answer dawned on me like the sun rising in the east. He was *relieved* when I mentioned Robichaud. There was something else. But what?

"Nix on Dicks, eh Sully? You made sure I was home after you and Deputy Chief Hardfield finished on the waterfront. But being your average nitwit you couldn't resist writing Nix on Dicks in the snow on my windshield. And later on that day it was you who tailed me back to the pier."

"So? If you got a point, make it, Jack. Elsewise stop pestering me. I was just doing my job."

"Job? You're sweeping something under the rug, Sullivan, and I'm going to find out what it is. As for your job, it doesn't include pulling jokes on a fellow officer. Or keeping him under surveillance as if he did something wrong."

Sullivan blew smoke at me. "Preventative measures." The smirk. That damned smirk.

"Against what?" I exploded.

"Your secret missions, Jack. Your private crusades."

TERRY CRAWFORD

He had turned the tables on me and I was getting nowhere. All I'd done was come out with my suspicions. But he knew I was sniffing around so it wasn't a total waste. I had a brainstorm. "Who are you working for, Sully?"

Sullivan gawked at me as if he'd just had bamboo slivers slipped under his toenails. "Aw… get away from me, you bastard," he said without an ounce of conviction.

"Got a secret mission of your own?" I said.

He wouldn't look at me. A pair of senior detectives, Breen and Shea, came breezing in, chattering about last night's hockey game at the Forum. The old guys nodded hello and went into the adjoining room, a kitchenette where the janitor always made sure there was coffee ready in the mornings. They were used to me and Sullivan crossing swords so they ignored us.

I persisted, "Moonlighting with a mission?"

"I got nothing to say, Ireland. It ain't your business what I do. Christ, we used to be friends."

The colour was returning to Sullivan's cheeks. He clenched his fists and gave me his best bulldog imitation.

"What's your connection with Eugene Robichaud, Sully?"

Sullivan stood up, cinched his belt under his pot belly, and went into the kitchenette without a look or a word. I was skating on thin ice but after careful consideration I followed him.

"Answer me, Sully, never mind the silent treatment."

Breen and Shea were reading a notice on the wall. They glanced at me then deliberately started staring holes in an announcement about a St. Paddy's Day variety show at Saint Vincent's High School.

Sullivan blew up. "I didn't have nothin' to do with that nosy little frog gettin' killed."

"Nosy. So he was nosy. What else?"

Sullivan slammed down the coffee pot, splattering the burner. There was a hiss in the room like a snake about to strike.

Breen said, "Knock it off, you two." He was a couple of years away from retirement and used to conciliation. I shut up because I respected him.

"Watch your step, Ireland. You might wind up down a hole one of these days yourself," Sullivan said.

"Don't threaten me, you crooked piece of crap."

"Drop dead, Ireland. You and that spear-chucking nigger. What's his name? Drummond the drum-beater? Where's he from anyway? Out of *darkest* Africa? Boogie-boogie…" Sullivan taunted.

He was a racist bigot but Sullivan wasn't alone in that category. I took a deep breath and counted to ten.

Shea said, "Don't pay any attention to him, Jack."

"Somebody might run over Drummond's black carcass, Ireland. You know you can't see them coons at night till you see the whites of their eyes."

Breen ordered Sullivan to shut up but it was already too much for me to endure. Before I really knew what happened I hit Sullivan with a crunching right cross that, because his big mouth was open, broke his jaw with a snap like the breaking of balsa-wood. His lights went out in a second.

"Get up, you slob," I said, prodding him with a foot in the ribs.

Shea restrained me with a half-nelson. "That's enough, Ireland. You really did it this time. Better run and get Doctor Jennings, Breen."

I wrestled free and knelt down to unfasten Sullivan's shirt collar. He was breathing with difficulty; spitting blood in fits and starts. "Let's roll him onto his side, Shea."

We no sooner had Sullivan situated so he wouldn't drown in his own blood than he regained consciousness and slugged Shea on the forehead.

Shea sneered, "Nice one, Sullivan, you big ape," and pinned him to the floor.

Sullivan went out cold again but not before mumbling, "I'm warning you. Robichaud was a dumb frog."

"Did you hear that, Shea?" I asked.

"Yes. And for the record – for the umpteenth time – I wish you'd confide in me and Breen. Hardfield would like to crucify you and you just went and handed him the hammer and nails. Will you tell us what's going on?"

"It's too soon, Shea. Until a few minutes ago it was more of a sense of something wrong. Something I didn't want to think, let alone say out loud."

"Christ, Jack. You don't think Sullivan killed Robichaud?"

"No. But I can't say that he didn't."

Shea rubbed his bruised forehead. He had a shock of unruly white hair that made him look older than fifty. "That's a grave matter, Jack. Very."

Breen rushed into the room with Doctor Jennings. The doctor's house was only a hop, skip, and jump away from the station. Rumpled and tired, Jennings yawned. He was still wearing pyjamas and slippers underneath his top coat.

"You could have held off until I finished my scrambled eggs, Ireland," the doctor said, briskly going to work on Sullivan. He set the broken jaw with a practised hand. "Better do this before he comes to or it'll be worse than it already is. What did you hit him with, Jack? An iron pipe?"

Breen and Shea relaxed, chuckling to one another. Shea said, "An iron fist."

"Speaking of which," Breen interjected. "Jack, Deputy Chief Hardfield wants you in his office, pronto."

I waited until Sullivan's eyelids flickered open.

Doctor Jennings had fastened a sling under Sullivan's chin to hold the slack jaw in place. "Get up, slowly, Sullivan," he said, "and don't say a word. We have to get you to the O.R. fast."

Sullivan glared hatefully at me. He started to talk but the pain almost made him faint. His knees wobbled.

"Do you want another one," I said. "This time it won't be a love-tap. You ever say anything to me about Lincoln Drummond or anybody of race again and I'll kick the stuffing out of you."

"I think he already got the message, Ireland," Breen said, escorting him by the elbow. "C'mon, Sully, let's go bye-byes."

I was left alone to weigh the consequences of what I'd done. Regret was not an issue. Doc Jennings was put out but he would pad the bill and come away smiling. An "inconvenience charge" he called it. I was tired, even a bit exhausted. I had an image of the doctor's scrambled eggs slowly losing their steam, little cartoon dollar signs evaporating into the air above the breakfast table.

The phone jangled in the detectives' room. That would be Hardfield eager to roast my lower extremities. I drank a cup of coffee then went in and dug around in my locker for a tie. I came up with a burgundy number with dice on it. Roll them bones. Life is a gamble we all lose.

I grinned into the cracked mirror over the sink. Time to face the music.

I walked upstairs with the plodding footsteps of the condemned ascending a scaffold.

CHAPTER TWENTY-TWO

I'D BEEN ENSCONCED in a sound-booth in Benny Goldstein's Music Store for over an hour without hearing anything I really liked. Which was strange because the Duke and the Count always did something for me. If music has sounds to soothe the savage beast then I must've been really wild. And if the truth be known, I had the urge to kill. Deputy Chief Hardfield had suspended me for a month without pay. All of my protests were to no avail. I'd reminded the little dictator that an independent panel had to be convened to investigate my "transgression". That it wasn't up to him to punish me out of hand as if I were an errant schoolboy. I almost hit *him*. There was something sorely amiss. It wasn't like Hardfield to stray off the prescribed path. He was a militaristic boob who had the virtue of predictability. The Deputy Chief was letting his emotions run away with him and I wanted to find out why. Sullivan was the key. A big fat key. And in a moment of blind rage I'd stupidly clamped his filthy mouth shut.

Someone rat-a-tatted with their fingernails on the sound-booth window. I lifted the record I'd been listening to but not hearing off the felt-covered turntable and slipped it back into its jacket. Because I was a big customer Benny Goldstein didn't mind if I hid all day in one of the six booths but every once in a while the bobby-soxers would put the run to me. There was another rat-a-tat. I twisted around on the stool to plead for a moment's patience. Penny Fairchild smooched the glass and batted her eyelashes at me like Betty Boop.

She opened the door and climbed onto the other stool. "I should have guessed where you would be," she said. "Been telephoning your place all morning. If I'd put my thinking cap on sooner I could have walked around the block from my flat and fetched you." The cold came off her serge coat and gray slacks, a reminder that Old Man Winter hadn't yet returned to the north. She patted her mittens together in muffled applause. "So now that I've found you, Jack, come and have lunch with me like a good boy."

Penny must have sensed I was going to decline because her eyes showed disappointment. She touched me on the knee. "I know about your trouble. Don't be angry, but I looked in on Sullivan. He's doing fine even if you 'cleaned his clock' as Detective Shea so quaintly put it."

I stacked the records and vacated the booth with Penny. She was studying my silence as if it was one of her chemistry formulas. I suppose, looking for a reaction that wasn't taking place.

I didn't say anything until we were out on the sidewalk. "Sullivan had it coming," I said then. "He was overdue. He threatened Lincoln." The cold light of day made everything clear. I'd give Sullivan more of the same if he made the same mistake twice. If I was sorry, it was probably for my own miserable hide. It was the first morning of my suspension and already time weighed heavily on my hands. I said as much to Penny with a shrug.

Penny tugged my sleeve. "Dear boy, you haven't said yes to lunch."

"Sorry. Too busy stewing in my own juices. Yes. Providing you're not fixing cucumber and watercress sandwiches."

"Only for lady friends. Rest assured, I've prepared something manly for you."

She interlocked elbows with me and clutched my upper arm with her free hand. I stiffened. She felt it and eyed me apologetically. "Streets are bloody slippery."

There was enough sand shovelled onto the sidewalks to build beaches from Saint John to Boston. I walked around the block with her clinging to my arm like a star-crossed lover. It was an uncomfortable feeling. I'd always thought Penny Fairchild was a stunning beauty but because she was my late wife's best friend I'd never allowed myself to go beyond a certain boundary. In thought, word, and deed. But in an instant, something had changed. Maybe I was all at sea but she was sending me strong signals and I was afraid of receiving them. Afraid of what I might want. Or need.

Penny had a rambling but cozy set of rooms on the top floor of an old, well-kept house on Peter Street not far from the hurly-burly of Waterloo Street's commercial section. Compared to me she was uptown and close to the thick of things. And a ten- minute walk to the hospitals.

I sat down in a rocking chair beside the fireplace in the parlour. Coal glowed warmly in the grate. On the mantel paperwhites forced into bloom perfumed the room with a strong whiff of spring. The scent made me yearn for warm days in King Square where I often ate my lunch in nice weather.

Penny called from the kitchen, "Coffee or tea, Jack?"

I'd smelled coffee when we came in so I said, "Coffee."

A minute later she appeared with a tray of home-made scones and preserves then went back for the coffee. The scones were from an old family recipe of Grace's. She'd taught me how to make them and I passed the technique on to Penny. I felt a terrible pang of loss for Grace. Some of the photos of her and Penny during their student days were arranged on the bookcase beside me. They didn't help my confusion or heartsickness.

Penny handed me a cup about half the size of a chamberpot. I ate a couple of scones with blackberries. It was the first solid food since before I'd hit Sullivan.

Penny sprawled on a divan opposite me, almost lost among the knick-knacks and bric-a-brac cramming the room. She hadn't said much but Penny wasn't by nature a chirpy bird.

I devoured another scone and broke the silence. "Delicious."

Penny stirred a little, trying not to study my face too microscopically. Past her shoulder the sun fingered through the clouds, casting a net of lacy shadows onto the hardwood floor. She responded to a dinging timer in the kitchen. I watched her leave the room. God, she was a lovely woman. Svelte and lithe. Penny exercised regularly at the Y.W.C.A., conscientiously adhering to her belief in the Greek ideal.

"Dinner is served," she announced amid a clatter of pots and pans. I tipped the coal scuttle into the fireplace then went to my chair by the kitchen window. The Angelus rang deep and sonorously from the spire of the cathedral. When I glanced out over the housetops toward the church a flock of pigeons burst from the copper roof. Penny set a heaping plate of macaroni and cheese with ham slices in front of me. I gave it a good dose of H.P. Sauce and dug in for the duration.

"Lord, you were ravenous," Penny said when I'd finished wiping my plate clean with a slice of whole wheat bread.

"Outstanding grub."

"My pleasure, Jack. If only I could cook for you more often," Penny said coyly.

I got up and poured coffee for us both. "Mind if I smoke?" Penny smoked at work but not at home.

"No. Be my guest," she said, stretching her long legs underneath the table.

I found an ashtray behind the African violets on the windowsill and sat back down. The meal had made me drowsy.

"You look worn-out, Jack," Penny said. "What are your plans for the next while?"

"I'm getting away from it all. Going to visit my cousin Marvin in Nova Scotia. He lives on the Fundy shore over the mountain from Annapolis Royal. No electricity. Or phones to bother me. I'll be *incommunicado*."

"Oh," Penny said, disappointed. "I wanted to borrow the Studebaker."

"For the trip to Fredericton? I didn't forget."

"Yes. It's Winter Carnival time at the University of New Brunswick. I'd hoped to surprise some of my chums from college days."

My overcoat was hanging on the kitchen door. I reached into the inside pocket and retrieved the car keys. "Here you go. I filled the gas tank this morning. The heater goes on the blink sometimes so I left a coat and stocking hat along with an Indian blanket in the back seat. The car's parked on Union across the street from Bardsley's Hats."

Penny fairly sparkled. "Oh, super! It'll be so much easier getting about Fredericton with a motor."

I laughed. "Car.Auto.Wheels. Get with it, Penny. You still call the trunk, boot and the hood, bonnet."

Penny nudged my shins with a foot. "There will always be an England, Jack. But how will you get to Nova Scotia?"

"I'm going to take the *Princess Helene* to Digby. I always liked the ferry trip. It's long enough to qualify as a sea voyage but short enough not to get boring."

Penny suddenly grew serious. "I almost forgot this," she said, handing me a slip of paper. "This is the analysis of the blood sample you gave me."

"Group B?"

"Yes. Only about eight to ten per cent of North Americans of Caucasian descent are Group B. Is it any help?"

"It eliminates Eugene Robichaud. He was AB." I set fire to the note and dropped it into the ashtray. It burned brightly and disappeared into a wisp of smoke. For all anyone in authority cared, Eugene Robichaud had vanished as suddenly and completely.

Penny placed a hand over mine and kept it there. "Don't take any more risks. If Deputy Chief Hardfield discovers you're sleuthing around for clues about Robichaud against his orders he'll destroy your career."

I stared at Penny goggle-eyed. "Sleuthing around for clues? Buy me a magnifying glass and a pipe and point me in the right direction. For instance, Hollywood."

"Oh, Jack. Don't make light of it," Penny said, squeezing my hand tighter.

Her touch felt good but I was getting embarrassed. "I have to go. Sleuthing to do."

"Not so fast. I've something very serious to take up with you."

Why did I have a bad case of the butterflies? Was it the way Penny's face glowed? Or was I panicking like an animal in a trap? The tender trap?

Penny released my hand. "Breathe easy, Jack. Your worry lines are showing."

"Is it any wonder?" I muttered. "With you looking into my eyes like Svengali?"

"If only I could hypnotize you," Penny said with unmistakable longing.

It was time for me to beat a hasty retreat. "I think I'll hit the road. The meal was grand. Thanks."

Penny watched as I fastened the buckles on my overshoes and put on my overcoat and hat. She stood up, even in stocking feet almost as tall as I, and began adjusting my plaid scarf. She'd never before gotten so close to me. I could smell her cologne, hear her quickened breathing.

"Who was the woman I saw you with the day before yesterday?" She blurted.

I stepped backwards, dumbfounded, then let out a nervous laugh.

Penny still had a grip on my scarf. She idly tucked it into place. "My apologies. I've gone and made a proper mess of this."

"That was Roxanne. She's a waitress at Pepper's Diner. I wanted to know if she could give me any information about a German seaman."

"I see. And do most women you question kiss you?"

"Only the pretty ones," I said, feeling behind my back for the doorknob.

Penny snapped to attention, a sharp but bemused expression on her face. "Detective Sergeant Jack Ireland," she said. "I'm serving you fair warning of my intentions. If you're going to allow pretty waitresses to make passes at you then I'm coming on like Marlene Dietrich."

I laughed again. Nervously. "The Blue Angel strikes again?"

"Don't be flip. I'm serious," Penny said. "Damn it. I need a cigarette."

She went into the living room and got a deck of Black Cat cork-tips out of her purse. She came back to me for a light. "That's better," she said, taking a drag. "Do I stand a chance with you, Jack? Because I'm telling you that I've been waiting for what seems a lot longer than four years. And for the record – when you married Grace it was the only time I was jealous of her. Do you get my meaning?"

"Loud and clear."

"Well? What *are* my chances?"

I cleared my throat. "Um...good to excellent."

"All right then," Penny said, smiling. "I shan't require any preliminaries, no boxes of sweets, pretty posies, or candlelight dinners. I'll save you the trouble and expense of courtship."

"But I like the preliminaries. Moon and June, and all that."

"Smashing. But you know where I hide my key. You can come up the backstairs any time of day or night. I'm always alone. I've been waiting for you..." she said, holding back tears.

I kissed her gently on the forehead, the eyes, then passionately on the mouth. She stood there trembling in the hallway as I stepped out onto the back landing. "Catch you later," I said, closing the door.

She pulled the curtains open. "Any time, day or night."

I went down the three flights of stairs so aroused my knees were a bit weak. I wasn't used to such declarations of intention. Especially from someone I cared for so deeply. It had happened with breathtaking suddenness. Was I so blind?

I walked around town in a daze. It started snowing. Big soggy flakes. When they weighed down my hat brim I ducked into M.R.A's Department Store where I brushed them off with a whisk in the men's room. In the mirror a middle-aged man with graying temples stared at me. He didn't want to admit how terrible the loneliness had been. How lovely he thought Penny Fairchild. He swept the snow off his coat.

In the Dock Street Liquor Commission he bought a bottle of Harvey's Bristol Creme. An hour later after much soul-searching he unlocked Penny Fairchild's door. Without a word, he poured two glasses of sherry and went into her bedroom. She'd dozed off while reading a collection of Dorothy Parker's short stories. He took the book out of her hand, inserted a bookmark, and set it aside. She felt him sit down on the bed and took her time awakening.

They had two glasses of sherry, talked about the strange weather of late, then she turned out the lamp attached to the headboard.

CHAPTER TWENTY-THREE

A DOUBLE BLAST from the smokestack jettisoned my slumber into the deeps. I took a minute to let my brain defog then went out on deck to breathe the sea air. The Digby Gut lay dead ahead, an opening in a wall of stone. To starboard and portside, the rockbound coast of Nova Scotia stretched as far as the eye could see. The *Princess Helene* steamed through the narrow Gut and into the calm waters of the Annapolis Basin, gulls calling plaintively in its wake.

The forty-five mile crossing took almost three hours but I didn't mind. I wasn't in a hurry to get anywhere fast. The suspension from work still rankled but had taken a back seat to yesterday and the night I'd spent with Penny. I was lovestruck as surely as if Cupid had pierced my heart with a quiverful of arrows. Something had been reawakened in me – not the desire for a woman's body, that never leaves – but the need for female companionship. The bond that is like no other. In one day the world had become a better and brighter place for me. Despite my troubles, I was the luckiest man alive.

Deckhands appeared fore and aft, scurrying in the bitter cold. When we embarked from Saint John it was snowing hard but here in Nova Scotia the sun shone brilliantly in an unblemished blue sky. Scallop draggers, some of the crew members waving their hats overhead, chugged astern of the ferry on their way toward the Gut and out into the rough waters of the Bay of Fundy.

A couple of men slid open the doors of the shed on the Dominion Atlantic Railway wharf and stood by to await the mooring lines. I went aft to watch the docking as the engines were thrown into reverse and the ship drifted toward the pier. A young seaman was twirling a weighted leader around his head like a lariat. When we were close in he let it zing with deadly accuracy. On the wharf men ran for the leaders and pulled in the hawsers, looping them over the bollards.

While the ship was secured I dodged inside and returned to my seat for a cigarette. There weren't many other passengers on board. A few travelling salesmen and a handful of sailors stationed at Stadacona Naval Base in Halifax. I put my feet up on my duffel bag and snuggled into the warm upholstery. Sailors. They were getting younger and I was getting older. Day by tick-tocking day.

The public address system announced in a nasal whine that disembarkation would be in five minutes. A purser in greatcoat and mittens passed by ensuring that no one was asleep and apt to miss his connection. I folded the copy of *The Saturday Evening Post* I'd purchased in the *Princess*'s gift shop under my arm and made for the gangplank.

The gangplank had a canvas roof and partially enclosed sides so that I wasn't forced to experience any sensation of height. Nevertheless, I hurried down the thirty feet like a rat deserting the ship. Safely on the pier, I stretched my legs and let my heartbeat return to normal before I continued into the shed where the train waited out of the weather.

The puffing of the engine echoing off the blackened rafters sounded like two pillows pounding together in slow motion. A brakeman whistled *Lady of Spain* while he checked the air hoses and undercarriage of the coaches, now and then stealing a glance at the women on the platform. A third seasick, I stood back until everyone else boarded the train. I'd soon be trading the rolling of the waves for the rocking of the rails. The conductor eyed me to see if I was okay or perhaps drunk, then yelled, "All aboard!"

The coach was dimly lighted and smelled of pine air-freshener. I stowed my duffel bag in the luggage rack and chose a seat to the left so I could view the Annapolis Basin instead of staring inland at the forest. As I was about to sit down the train lurched, hurling me with a thud into my seat. I didn't mind. It shook up my insides and I was the better for it.

The engine pulled out of the shed and into the dazzling sunlight. We lumbered jerkily off the pier and threaded through Digby toward the main line. At times we were so close to the houses we could've reached out and plucked milk bottles off the windowsills. A pair of wide-eyed toddlers with chubby faces returned my salute, waving frantically from their back stoop. At the end of the spur a beagle hitched to a post howled balefully in response to the train whistle.

We switched to the main line, picked up speed, and hurtled toward the next stop. The conductor and his assistant zig-zagged down the aisle, collecting tickets and recording destinations. I sat back, grateful at last to be away from home. Surely, Saint John could survive without the great Jack Ireland for three or four days.

The train snaked along the shoreline, seldom losing sight of the water. At Bear River Station the engine throttled out of a dense stand of evergreens and onto a trestle so narrow it seemed to suspend us in mid-air high above the river until we reached the woods on the other side. Before long the screech of metal on metal heralded a stop at Clementsport.

A trio of young ladies, pert and trim in short coats and slacks boarded the train with the help of a bearded sailor. He sat across from me and grinned like an old sea-dog after the women found seats at the other end of the car. Before he could roll a cigarette I offered him one of my tailor-mades.

"Thank you, sir. Goin' far?" he said, striking a match.

"Annapolis Royal."

"Nice town," he said, inhaling the cigarette as if it were the elixir of life. The fingers of his right hand were stained orange with nicotine. He coughed huskily. "That's where I grew up. Right near the old fort. Used to play soldiers there. Fighting the Frenchman and Indians, eh?"

I laughed. "Yeah. We used to do that up on Fort Howe in Saint John. I always had to be an Indian, though."

"Fort Howe? I know the place. Overlooks the harbour," he said, scratching his coarse beard.

I nodded.

"Geeze. You'd best watch your step up there. Fall off and you'd kill yourself or worse. Saint John must be the hilliest city I ever been to."

"Hills and more hills," I said. His hatband identified him as a crew member of the *Saguenay.* "Are you going out to sea?"

"Nope. Been reassigned to Stadacona to teach them boys how to operate gunnery emplacements."

"What for? Coastal defenses?"

"What kinda question is that?" he said. "I hope you ain't plainclothes S.P. testin' me."

The train rattled down a slope and into a salt marsh. A flock of ducks took to the air, their flight silhouetted against the remains of the day.

"Sorry. Force of habit," I said, breaking the seal on a mickey of rum I'd secreted in my jacket pocket. I took a pull and handed it to him. "I'm a detective with the Saint John Police."

"Ah," he said, making sure the conductor didn't see the bottle. He showed the same enthusiasm for drink as he had for tobacco. "I'm a friendly sort but you gotta be careful."

I waved the bottle away, urging him to take another swig. "Is security all that rigid?"

"Not so's you'd notice but lately we're gettin' a few lectures. Basic stuff. A 'better safe than sorry' routine." He took off his flat-topped hat and revealed a closely cropped head of jet black hair.

I accepted one of his makings and a light. Vogue tobacco. Sweet and a bit sickening. I shared the last of the mickey with him and decided to tell him about Werner Strasser and his fellow "wunderkinders".

He listened with the intensity of a scientist discovering a new element. By the time I'd finished the story he appeared ready to exclaim, "Eureka!"

"I seen the guy," he said. "Right out there in the basin."

I glanced toward the water and back. It was getting dark enough for me to see my face, flushed with alcohol, reflected in the window. "Couldn't be," I said.

"Look, pal. You said this fella was right handsome. Well, I got a skiff I sail when I'm on leave and I'm tellin' you I seen him. There's lotsa different vessels hereabouts but I remember him because he was on a small yacht – pretty thing – and he had a camera rigged up on deck on one of them tripods."

I was skeptical. "Too much of a coincidence. He wouldn't have had time to get over here last week."

"No. No. No. Last summer. You don't think I'd be out in a skiff in February. You must be a landlubber," he said, rubbing his beard so hard I thought it'd burst into flames.

"You should suds your beard with lanolin shampoo," I said. "It'll take the itch out."

The sailor laughed as if he had pirate blood in his veins. "Don't alter the course, mate. It was the same fella. As sure as there's salt in the ocean, I'm right. I'd stake a keg of dark rum on it."

The conductor passed down the aisle. "Annapolis Royal, next stop."

I put on my hat and scarf. "How can you be so sure?"

The sailor rubbed his hairy chin for a minute. "Blonde as Jean Harlow? Baby blue eyes?"

"Yeah."

"Whenever he looks into the sun he squints. Makes him look angry as a rat in a trap. Say it ain't so."

I couldn't help smiling. "You're very observant. Anything else?"

"Come to think of it," he said, excited. "He's got one of them Nazi thing-a-ma-jigs tattooed over his heart."

"A swastika? How'd you see that?"

"Put the binoculars on him and his buddies. The three of them were in nothing but skimpy bathing trunks. They had women on board. Your Werner fellow planked one of them in broad daylight up against the wheelhouse. That was an eyeful. I should have been the one with the camera."

"His buddies?"

"Two others with swastikas. And another older guy, maybe your age. Not that you're old."

I was beginning to feel ancient. "Did he have a tattoo, this other fellow?"

"Yes. But it was a mermaid or pin-up doll on his arm. And there was a real old guy. Retirement age but he had his paws all over the women. Fat slob. He kinda made me sick."

Across the tidal flats the chimneys of Fort Anne came into view. The rest of the garrison was hidden behind the seaward earthworks. Aimed at the basin, the muzzle of a huge old cannon protruded through an embrasure.

"The women," I said, shouldering my duffel bag. "Hired for the occasion?"

"They looked like high class fluff to me. Drop dead legs and ba-zongs gunny sacks couldn't harness," the sailor said, drawing the contours of an Amazon with his hands.

"Do you remember what the yacht was called?"

"Nope. Foreign word. It slips my mind. I have trouble with words outside of English."

The train slowed as it veered away from the stucco courthouse looming in the twilight ahead and approached the station. My cousin Marvin was leaning against a freight wagon on the platform.

I shook hands with the sailor and thanked him.

"Name's Hudson, George Hudson. It's been nice talkin' to you."

"Same here." I gave him one of my cards. "Here's my address. If you remember the name of the yacht, would you drop me a line? Or telephone me collect? It might be important."

"Sure thing. I'll be seeing the brother sometime this month. He might remember." He read the card. "Jack Ireland? Well, I'll be damned. You're Marvin Halliday's cousin."

"That's right."

"We played hockey together. Hooky too, if you want to know the truth. The way Marvin minded nets was a caution. He was better than Turk Broda. Say hi for me."

"Marv is on the platform, George. You'll have to give him a wave."

The train eased to a stop and I got off with George Hudson hot on my heels. He talked up a storm with my cousin then bolted for the train before it left without him. He stood on the steps waving to us until he disappeared around a bend and into the gathering darkness.

I grinned at Marvin, happy to be on solid ground for a couple of minutes before we'd have to jump into his truck for the bumpy ride over the mountain.

CHAPTER TWENTY-FOUR

IN THE DARKNESS and silence of my room in Marvin's house my wristwatch ticked louder than a grandfather clock. And no matter how hard my eyes strained I couldn't see the time. Even though there was a window somewhere by my bunk the room was as dark as a crooked lawyer's soul. I turned my warm ear outward, pressed my cold ear to the pillow, and tried to get back to sleep. My poor nose felt like a frozen tomato.

During waking spells throughout the night I'd thought about the journey from the valley to the fishing village where Marvin and his wife Peg lived. Shifting his pipe with his teeth, he would give me an impish grin before smacking the holes in the road with bone-jarring precision. He must have thought it was good for the wheel-alignment. Or he just plain didn't like machines. If there had been more snow and it wasn't so bitterly cold he would've brought the horse and sleigh, transportation more suited to my idea of woods travel.

I'd been robbed of a sound sleep by a hair-raising dream that kept chasing me. Marvin and I were in the deep woods at the top of the mountain, making our way at a breakneck clip along the narrow road, when suddenly everything slowed to a snail's pace. I elbowed Marvin but he didn't respond, just kept on driving, steering as if he were hell-bent. Hollow, drunken laughter came from the back of the truck. My skin crawled. In the rearview mirror Werner Strasser and a squad of Brownshirts, truncheons in hand, barked and bayed like hunting dogs. I feverishly opened the truck door and jumped, waking each time with a start in the pitch black room.

Sometime before dawn I managed to shake the dreams and shiver back to sleep. When I opened my eyes it seemed like a few minutes later but there was a pearl-gray sunrise showing behind the fir trees crowding the window.

Downstairs, someone lifted the lid on the stove. One thought entered my mind – heat. I grabbed my socks and went into the hall.

The intoxicating aroma of coffee and bacon wafted up from below. I didn't waste any time getting to the kitchen.

Peg turned to me with a smile, coffee percolator in hand. "Morning, sleepyhead," she said. "Marv's out feeding the animals."

She was wearing the new housecoat I'd bought for her in Saint John. Over her dungarees and bulky wool sweater. I grinned. She didn't give a damn what people thought. Not that there were many people around to think much of anything. Marv and Peg lived apart from the village in a house built by my reclusive Uncle Philip after he'd come back lame from the Boer War. Uncle Philip was a kind, gentle man who had lost faith in the human race. It was probably why Marvin was cynical about authority. What he called, "Big Powers".

I sat on the cot beside the stove and pulled on my socks. Then I wrapped my fingers around a mug of coffee. My teeth were chattering.

Marvin stamped the snow off his boots at the back door after letting in a blast of frigid air. He didn't say anything until he filled the pitcher on the table with fresh milk. "Here you go, Jack, my boy."

I put milk in my coffee. It was still warm from the cow. I didn't want to let go of the pitcher but Peg needed it for pancakes.

Marvin smiled. "Quite the togs you got on there, Jack."

I modeled my purple and white striped pyjamas, doing a tour around the table. "If you want, I'll give them to you. They're all the rage with the swells."

"And I thought you liked me," Marvin said, as he fired a couple of sticks of hardwood into the stove.

Peg laughed.

"There's work clothes and overalls on the trunk at the foot of your bed, Jack. Why don't you run up and get dressed. There's something I want to show you down on the shore," Marvin said. "We can take bacon and egg sandwiches with us."

"Why don't you boys sit down and eat a proper breakfast?" Peg said. "In this cold you'll need fuel to keep you warm."

"Have to beat the tide, Peg," Marvin said. "We won't be long."

It felt good to wear a woodsman's garb again. If Marvin was true to form, he'd have me felling trees with him before noon. He knew I liked hard labour, especially if I had a problem bothering my mind.

Outdoors, tramping in rubber boots through the snow, I was as awkward as a toddler stuffed into a snowsuit. It didn't take me long to break into a sweat even with the cold whipping through the trees.

We stopped and ate our sandwiches on a bench made of logs on a cliff overlooking the village. I say village but it was closer to what the backwoods people of New Brunswick call a settlement, a cluster of buildings huddled in the leeside of a cove as if tossed in like a pile of driftwood. Even the rickety wharf looked as if it could float away on the next tide. There wasn't a soul out and about. Unless you counted a shaggy dog gnawing on a bone.

Marvin nudged me with his knee. "Let's make tracks."

He led me along a path that was too close to the cliff for comfort. Whenever I caught a glimpse of the rocks below I'd grab a branch until we turned back into the woods. This amused Marvin to no end. I wondered what he had in store for me.

About a quarter mile further on I found out. We were halted by a narrow fissure which cut like an axe into the cliff face. Wind-stunted trees clung to the sides of the opening. I could see daylight at the bottom of a steep trail strewn with boulders and loose rock. The pungent smell of seaweed and salt water hung in the chasm. Before I had a chance to stop him, Marvin was twenty feet down the split and out of sight behind an outcropping covered with faded moss and rusty ferns. I reluctantly followed.

We scrabbled our way down the incline until we reached the high watermark. The walls of the fissure rose up on both sides almost like a sea cave. Between them there was a miniature beach of small stones rubbed smooth by the action of the waves. I made for the sunlight, rocks rattling under my feet, the sound ricocheting off the cliffs.

The water was a long way out but I knew only too well that the incoming tide could trap us against the cliffs if we wandered too far from the rift in the wall.

Marvin walked on ahead, setting a brisk pace. The coast here was wild and spectacular. The isolated villages hidden in the protected inlets were without electricity or telephone service, cut off from the world yet so close to it. Most of the fishing boats were without anything but running lights and a compass. Marvin's vessel, the *Barbara Ellen*, did have radio. Through a fisherman friend in Saint John I relayed messages to Marvin via a system the men had worked out for weather warnings. I was code name Pluto, nicknamed after the planet discovered in '30 when Grace and I exchanged marriage vows.

Marvin waved then disappeared past an icy headland. I rushed to catch up but the going was treacherous on the slippery rocks. When I rounded the headland I caught sight of him standing in the centre of a weir. From a distance he looked like a man corralled behind a fence made without pickets. He had his hands on his hips and was staring at a row of poles, the tops of which had been broken clean off. Tattered netting streamed in the wind.

By the time I reached him, Marvin had shinnied up a pole and was busy examining the break. He tore off a kindling-sized piece of wood, dropped it to me, and slid down.

I turned it over in my hand. It had been struck by something painted with an aluminum-based paint. Silvery gray. Marvin nodded, a knowing smile on his lips.

"You're the detective, Jack. Add it all up."

"Busman's holiday, eh?" I said, pacing off the distance from the first to last broken pole. Twenty feet or so. I then calculated by eyeball how much had been busted off the tops. About eight feet. Most of the poles were approximately fifteen feet high with a few crossmembers to hold them in place.

I glanced out at Fundy's jade green water. The white caps were now close enough for me to hear the crashing of the waves. "How high's the tide here?"

"Thirty-five, thirty-seven feet. Thereabouts. Depending on the moon," Marvin said.

I looked at the foot of the cliffs. We were standing on a kind of shelf. "So at high tide the water would be near the top of the weir?"

"Just about, Jack. How'd you expect us to catch any fish?"

"Only making sure. Speaking of the tide… let's head back. I don't like how fast it's coming in." Beyond the headland, spray was flying into the air as the waves crashed into the shallows.

"All right. Sometimes you're an awful 'fraidy cat," Marvin said.

"I don't want to trade in any of my nine lives, Marv. I need all of 'em."

We took a final look at the rent in the weir and started back. Marvin didn't say anything until after we had clambered up the fissure and were catching a breather on the log bench. The mouth of the harbour was rapidly flooding with seawater. The weir was probably neck deep in the ocean waves. I didn't like the thought.

"Well?" Marvin puffed, pipe smoke mingling with the scent of the surrounding evergreens.

"The weir was struck by a fast-moving heavy vessel. That's why the clean break on the poles. The paint? I'm not sure. I'd guess it's the type used on steel hulls. I've ruled out fishing boats. What about the navy?"

Marvin bristled. "Contacted them. They deny knowing anything."

"What do you think, Marv?"

"I'm inclined to believe them this time. The buggers tear up our nets once in a while and wreck a few lobster traps but they always own up to it. Even compensate us. This is different. Something strange."

"I agree. Try this on for size. Whatever it was, hit the poles and *stopped*. It didn't rip out the other side of the weir. That vessel was at least twenty feet wide. It would have a draft of say, ten feet. At high tide it could have sailed right into the weir without seeing it in time. Or maybe it happened at night?"

Marvin turned to me. "It did. But the vessel should've kept on goin' straight for the shoreline and been wrecked on the leeward shoal."

I scratched my head. "Have you ruled out the possibility of a U-Boat?"

Marvin's jaw went slack. "A submarine?"

"Why not? A submarine could have got in there and hooked up on the weir, thrown its engines into reverse and backed off."

"That's a wild notion, Jack," Marvin said. "But you might be right. Some of the boys in the village were scared lately by a craft out in the bay running without lights. And running quiet like. When they yelled ahoy they didn't get an answer. It spooked them bad. Yessir, Jack, submarines. Go to the head of the class, son."

I laughed. "Not just yet. Are there any submarines tied up in Halifax?"

"Beats me. Maybe the Brits. The yanks have submarines. It'd be like them."

"Or somebody else. Somebody acting in secret."

"Who would that be? And what were they doing there, Jack?"

"I noticed a waterfall near the headland. It rushes so fast it doesn't even freeze. Fresh water?"

Marvin poked me in the ribs. "You've been watching them serials at the movies too much. Next thing you'll have the evil Fu Manchu sneaking into the village. Let's go eat. I could handle a pile of pancakes about now."

"Sounds good," I said, following him into the bush where a well-beaten path meandered back to the house.

Peg was leaning out of the porch feeding sunflower seeds to the chickadees from the palm of her hand. One by one they'd flit in from the lilac bush by the clothesline, alight long enough for a seed then retreat back to their perch. She sprinkled a few seeds onto my hand and went inside with Marvin.

The only birds I'd ever fed by hand were the pigeons in King Square. But they didn't count – city slickers with pot bellies and bad manners. Oh, I'd fed whiskeyjacks before, on tenting trips, but always with bread crusts balanced on the brim of my hat. Besides, they were camp robbers and hardly seemed wild. This was the first time I'd had chickadees land on my hand. I liked the way they trusted me.

"Okay, Snow White, let's eat," Marvin said, opening the kitchen door.

I peeled the overalls off and went in. Peg had the cast-iron stove in the parlour burning full blast. We sat at a card table near the heat and ate a breakfast of pancakes, sausages, scrambled eggs, and toast with Marvin's maple syrup and Peg's blueberry jam. The syrup and the jam put me in seventh heaven.

Peg poured me another cup of coffee. She'd put on a lot of weight since last fall. "Margaret," I said, looking askance at Marvin, "if I were to hazard a guess, I'd say you're expecting."

Marvin nodded. "Chickadees and now the stork," he said with a laugh.

CHAPTER TWENTY-FIVE

BACK IN SAINT John, the snowdrifts on the Dominion Atlantic Railway wharf were waist-deep. I dragged my galoshes along a recently shovelled path and on into the empty waiting room. While I was aboard the ferry the third snowstorm in as many days had passed through Southern New Brunswick, dumping another four inches on top of us. I was starting to get winter-weary. It was nearly March. Enough already.

I propped my duffel bag in a corner and stretched out on a bench. The crossing had been rough, giving my stomach a sloshy, loose feel that would take a few minutes to go away. A cabby stuck his head through the swinging doors at the end of the room and asked if I wanted a taxi. I shook my head. "No, thanks. What are the roads like?"

"Somethin' fierce," he said over his shoulder as he went out into the biting wind.

I glanced through the narrow window beside me and out at the ferry. Her prow towered above the pier, out of range of the meagre wharf lights. There was a blackness, then stars by the millions beyond the outline of the ship.

I dug into my innermost pocket for a cigarette. The seas on the Bay of Fundy were too rough for me to even think of having a puff on board. I was wearing enough layers of clothing to stuff a mattress. Finally, I got through to my old pal Philip Morris and greeted him with a light. Aahh. My head spun. Three days working in the woods with Cousin Marvin had increased my lung capacity. Half the cigarette disappeared with the first deep haul. I exhaled slowly. The smoke craved the company of a double Scotch on the rocks.

"Hey, mister, don't mean to disturb you, but I'm gonna close up early," the ticket-master said in a voice scratchy with age. "If you want to, you can wait in the freight shed by the stove until the boys there are done."

"Thanks. I'm just sitting. My car's parked a couple of blocks from here."

"Probably buried in snow," the old gent said, pulling on his overcoat. He took a battered homburg off a peg and tugged it down as far as his eyebrows. The brim touched the tips of his ears, folding them like bat wings. The wind wasn't about to claim this guy's topper.

"That's all I need," I said. "Let me stow my duffel bag before you go. I'll pick it up in the morning."

I butted my cigarette before it gave me a case of the permanent dizzies, then I secured my gear in a locker.

The ticket-master and I left together, walked a ways with heads down to protect our faces from the windblown snow, then nodded good-bye. I watched him until he disappeared around the corner of one of the tea warehouses on Market Slip. The night was quiet enough to hear the dynamos humming in the generating plant a hundred feet away at the foot of Union Street.

Shortly before the ferry docked the snow had stopped falling. So, all in all, it wasn't such a bad evening. A silent wind swirled snow off the roofs of buildings and parked cars.

I made my way toward Water Street where Penny was supposed to have left the Studebaker. But when I got there all I could find were a few old heaps sleeping in the snow. Maybe the weather was so treacherous Penny didn't dare venture out. Can't say as I could blame her. The steep hills of Saint John are a living nightmare when the pavements are slippery.

I plodded through a snowbank and crossed the street to the power plant where I found a sheltered spot out of the wind. Up the slope on Dock Street, a North End bus slid to a halt for a pick-up but I stayed put. Behind me, the dynamos hummed harder, vibrating the air with a kind of musical whir. If I worked there I'd probably wind up walking into walls. Or climbing them.

It occurred to me that I was about the same distance from home as I was from Penny's. I wanted to see her but, then again, maybe she wasn't back from Fredericton. That would be a better explanation for the Studebaker not being on Water Street. If she had been afraid of driving she would have gotten someone from the hospital to drop the car off. I could phone her but if she was in, the sound of her voice would only get my dynamo humming. After the strenuous work of the past few days it would be practical if I got my rest instead of romance. I was just too worn out. Besides, there was always another day.

A string of boxcars rumbled through the railyard intersection, the ding-ding of the crossing signals alerting motor vehicles of the hazard.

I waited for the quiet to return then headed for the tracks where I could shortcut to High Street and loop over to Main.

Men in scattered gangs of three or four were digging out the switches in the train yard. They had lanterns suspended on portable tripods to light their work. If you didn't know better, they could've been labourers from a bygone era searching for something lost. The way they were stamping their feet it might have been warmth. I watched them from a loading dock by the freight sheds until I got cold, then I continued walking in the dark.

LeBlanc's bootleggers at the bottom of High Street was doing a brisk business. I saw a couple of the younger guys from the Monarch Boxing Club stagger down the steps and into a waiting panel truck. They were hardly old enough to shave let alone destroy their virgin livers. I'd have to stop by some night for a quart of beer and remind Hector LeBlanc not to be so eager to contribute to the delinquincy of minors.

The city was peaceful, almost hushed, like it often was after a heavy snowfall. And now, it was starting to snow again. Softly and hypnotically.

There wasn't much activity on Main Street. The pharmacies were open, with a few drugstore cowboys riding stools at the fountains, but otherwise everything seemed drowsy and ready for a night's rest.

I almost went into Welsford's Drugs, which faced Douglas Avenue and was a stone's throw away from my apartment, for a bottle of ginger ale. But I decided to slip away unseen when I noticed one of the neighbourhood busybodies yammering old man Welsford's ear off. I had an unopened fifth of Canadian Club left over from Christmas locked inside my rolltop desk in the front room. It would have to get along without mix.

Public Works was fighting a losing battle against the snow piled high along the sidewalks and in the gutters. Many of the sidestreets hadn't even been plowed yet. Luckily for me, I lived on one of the main arteries or I would have had to dig my way into the house. As it was, Mrs.

Cronin, the landlady must have hired a street kid to shovel and sweep the front steps, saving me the trouble.

I kicked the snow off my boots and stepped into the vestibule. I was glad to be home and looked forward to my own bed in a room that didn't feel like a meat freezer. I noticed that I'd forgotten to turn the upstairs hall light off. No wonder the bills were getting higher all the time.

I hung my hat and coat on a hook in the hall. It was warm by the radiator so they'd be good and dry by morning. When I got into the apartment and turned on a light, I froze. Someone had ransacked the place, going through my belongings in a methodical way. They'd found the Canadian Club and helped themselves to a healthy drink. I picked up the bottle by the neck and had a stiff belt that cried out for a cigarette accompaniment. After going to the liquor cabinet and filling a glass, I answered the call and lit a smoke. Time to think. What the hell was going on?

No sooner had the cogs and wheels in my head started spinning than I heard cautious footsteps creaking up the back stairs. I took my grandfather's oak shillelagh out of the umbrella stand, turned out the light, and waited, heart pounding like a jack-hammer.

Mrs. Cronin's cat streaked into the room, hunted around for me, then leapt onto the back of the chesterfield and began rubbing its head on my elbow. So much for hiding in the dark. I tried to shoo the animal away but only got it purring louder and louder. Whoever had come into the house had stopped in the kitchen and was no doubt listening.

I crept on tiptoes down the hall toward the kitchen. If I could sneak into the bedroom for my revolver then I could play a waiting game. Because, for all I knew, the intruder might be packing a gun. At least we'd be on even terms.

Hugging the wall, I slid around the corner. The cat might have been able to see but I sure couldn't. The hall was dark as a coffin. I'd almost reached the bedroom when the light came on and a figure came at me from out of the darkened kitchen. I sidestepped into the bedroom and raised the shillelagh over my head. I was about to strike when I saw the blade of one of my hockey sticks. Lincoln Drummond was attached to the other end.

I yelled in relief, "Lincoln."

Before I knew it he nearly speared me in the ribs.

"Hey, pal, watch it, that's a five minute penalty," I said, fending off the stick.

Lincoln stared in astonishment. "Jack, glory be to God, you're safe."

"And sound," I said. Soberly. Very soberly. Lincoln looked exhausted and at wit's end. Dread flooded into my guts. "Lincoln, what do you mean, 'safe'?" I put my grandfather's skullcracker back in the umbrella stand.

Lincoln didn't answer me but went straight for the whiskey, draining the glass in a single gulp. He shuddered when the liquor invaded his stomach. "I went out and bought some ginger ale. It's at the foot of the back steps."

Rather than persist with my questions, I did as I was told. I returned with a couple of highball glasses half filled with ice and ginger ale.

Lincoln topped up the glasses with rye. I was anxious to hear what he had to say. He reached over to the pack of Philip Morris on the mantel, passed me one, and lit a cigarette for himself. Something was up. Lincoln hadn't touched tobacco in over five years. He sat on the chesterfield and took a drag like an old pro.

I sat down in the armchair and waited until I couldn't take it any longer. "Lincoln, the suspense is killing me. Would you mind telling me what's going on?"

He leaned forward, surprised at the question. "I don't know, Jack. You tell me."

"Whoa. Let's back up. What did you mean by safe?"

Lincoln took a thoughtful pull on the cigarette. "They towed your car out of the St. John River late this afternoon."

I felt a terrible fear. It made me as wide awake as I'd ever been. "What?"

"I thought you were dead, Jack. Drowned under the ice. Or lost in the woods. Frozen to death."

I sat next to Lincoln on the chesterfield. My best friend looked woebegone. And aged. "I was in Nova Scotia at my cousin Marvin's. I phoned you before I left but there was no answer."

Lincoln smiled and let out a big sigh. "I was worried half to death. And then when I came back into the house you scared me half to death. I didn't think I'd ever see you alive again."

We drank and smoked in silence. My mind was beginning to see things. There was an awful clarity. I could hear the blood rushing in my ears.

Lincoln mashed out his cigarette in the ashtray. "What do you figure? Somebody swiped the Studebaker for a joyride then ditched it? A couple of boys out rabbit hunting came across it below Fish-Hawk Bluff about twenty miles upriver from Grand Bay."

I went to the telephone and dialled Penny's number. No answer. Knowing it wasn't any use, I called the hospital and was informed that Miss Fairchild was on vacation. I turned to Lincoln. "I let Penny borrow the car to go to Winter Carnival in Fredericton."

Lincoln groaned. "Not Penny. Not her."

"No, Linc, I don't believe it. *I can't*. Not now. The way things are."

Lincoln stood up, wavered a little, then went to the kitchen and prepared tea. A minute or two later he telephoned my father and the R.C.M.P. to let them know that I was all right. That I was safe and sound. All I could think of was Penny.

Lincoln handed me a cup of tea. "What about Penny? Should we report her missing?"

"Did the Mounties search for me, Lincoln? They must have."

"Yes. But it's been snowing off and on for the last three days. Harder up there than down here. The Mounties no sooner got started than they had to call off the search. Besides, they couldn't find a trace of you. I mean Penny."

I thought for a minute at the rate of a thousand thoughts a second. "Where's the car?"

"At the police pound. The tow truck operator said they had one bastard of a time getting the thing pulled back up the hill to the road. Used extra winches and cables. And four-letter words."

"I'll bet. How'd you find out?"

"About?"

"Where the Studebaker was, Lincoln," I said impatiently, then added, "Sorry, pal."

"It's okay, Jack. Get this. Your favourite partner, Sully Sullivan, came and told me what happened then drove me to see the car. I looked it over but didn't find anything. The mechanic has a hunch the brakeline might have been tampered with but the undercarriage of the car was so badly damaged he can't say for sure."

"So it may not have been an accident?" I was beginning to feel sick to my stomach.

"There's a hairpin turn where the car went down and it's known as an icy spot because the wind sifts through there at a good clip. The R.C.M.P. are treating it as a single-car accident. Shouldn't we tell them about Penny?"

"Lincoln, we'll set out before dawn and hunt for Penny on our own. Your uncle Louis will let us borrow his hound, won't he?"

"Sure."

"I'm curious about Sullivan," I said. "How is he?"

"He looks terrible. Sounds terrible with his jaws wired. He apologized to me. Said he had a big mouth and said awful things about me just to bug you. Jack, he burst into tears when he told me you were missing."

"He did? Jesus."

"I'm going to head home. I'll pick you up at six o'clock. We'll use Uncle Louis' truck," Lincoln said, motioning for me to remain seated. "I'll let myself out. You try and get some sleep."

"Thanks, Lincoln."

"It's okay, Jack, welcome home."

I watched Lincoln leave then went to the window, opened the drapes, and gazed after him until he was out of sight. It was snowing but not so peacefully now.

Before I went to bed I emptied my insides into the bathroom sink. It helped me sleep, a troubled sleep that scared me because I kept dreaming of a snow-covered, empty world. A frozen world where the wind whispered answers to unknown questions.

CHAPTER TWENTY-SIX

WITH SWOLLEN EYELIDS at half-mast and a face that felt as slack as Uncle Louis' bloodhound's pile of wrinkles and folds, I wasn't sure who looked more sorrowful – the dog or me. As if reading what little was left of my mind, the old fella turned his big brown head toward me and fixed his bleary eyes on mine. Oh, the wisdom there in that canine face. The answer was evident. He was the life of the party and I was the real dog.

I glanced at Lincoln as he shifted the truck into gear to make the steep grade ahead. One last, long hill and we'd reach the bluff where the Studebaker took a plunge off the road and down to the river. Across the snow-covered ice the sun appeared over the rim of a slope dense with evergreens.

The dog let out a slobbery sigh full of bloodhound woe, then flopped his head onto my lap, one big ear draping over my knees. I rubbed his neck and he slumped into a deep slumber.

Lincoln elbowed the hound's haunches. "Jupiter, sit up." The dog obeyed, yawning drearily.

"Pour me some tea out of the thermos, Jack," Lincoln went on, "I'm going to nod off here any minute now."

"I'll drive if you want, Linc," I said.

"No need. We're almost there," Lincoln said.

Anticipation gnawed at me as we drew nearer our destination. I'd reported Penny missing to the R.C.M.P. about an hour ago and received considerable grief for not saying anything last night even though it wouldn't have made one iota of difference. One thing about the Mounties is that they're sticklers for details, something of which you couldn't accuse our poorly trained city force.

I ate a hard-boiled egg and a cold sausage, washing them down with Lincoln's sugary tea. The food had mitigated my pounding headache by the time we reached Fish-Hawk Bluff and I stepped out onto the shoulder of the road and breathed in the frosty air of the dawn. On another day, under different circumstances, it would have felt great to be alive. But I felt awful, even though in my heart of hearts I refused to believe that Penny had come to grievous harm.

An hour before Lincoln and I had dropped by the police holding pen to have a look at the Studebaker. The night watchman was surprised to see me but only because it was so early in the morning. He wouldn't even glance at Lincoln, his loathing hidden under a cool veneer of yessirs. We were used to that kind of treatment. Unfortunately, almost hardened to it. You had to have skin as tough as a crocodile to get past that brand of silent racism, the type of hatred that renders people of colour invisible in their own country.

The Studebaker was well and truly smashed up. Judging by the condition of the roof, I'd say the old girl had pitch-poled at least once, maybe twice. The door pillars had bent at the knees but not collapsed. I opened the trunk with my extra set of keys. The lock gave me a fair bit of trouble. Nothing but the spare tire and the jack. No luggage. The back seat was empty as well. My greatcoat, stocking hat, and Indian blanket were gone.

The door on the driver's side had popped and refused to close. No wonder the boys who had found the car, then later the police, presumed I was driving. There was nothing to indicate otherwise. This worried me. It was as if Penny had vanished into thin air. Lincoln and I left the garage in silence, the grim realization that this might not have been an accident nagging like a bad tooth.

Lincoln poked my shoulder with a mittened hand. "There's the spot up ahead, Jack, about fifty feet. You can see where the alders on the side of the road were sheared off."

I climbed back into the truck and finished the thermos of tea. Lincoln walked slowly toward the breach in the wall of bushes tracing the sharp curve in the road. When he reached the bluff a strong wind swept off the river, pushing against him.

Jupiter raised his head above the dashboard, watched Lincoln disappear into the alders, then curled into a ball behind the steering wheel and went back to sleep, snoring as softly and contentedly as a baby. I didn't bother rousting him out of the truck. With all the snow, his nose wouldn't be of much use to us. Besides, it was too damn cold for a thin-skinned old bloodhound. Or for me, but I went and got the snowshoes and knapsack out of the box anyway.

Lincoln was part way down the bluff, skidding on his heels, then on his behind, on a rockslide. I yelled, "Be careful." He stopped a yard or so from the edge of a lower cliff where the ground was bare because of the prevailing winds. I followed, more surefooted in my hiking boots.

We gazed down at the river. The hole in the ice where the Studebaker had broken through was already partially frozen over. I glanced backwards to determine the path the car had taken in its downward flight. It must have sailed into the alders, become airborne, smashed its nose into the rocks at our feet, then pitch-poled over the cliff and down the thirty or forty feet to the river. It was hard to see how anyone could have survived such a crash.

To our left the snow had piled up against the westward wall of the small promontory we were standing on, providing us with an easy way down. I foolishly stepped into the snow and immediately sank up to my armpits.

Lincoln pulled me out. "That wasn't too swift, Jack," he said. "Most of that's new snow and I'll bet it's at least fifteen feet deep, the way it blows in there."

We slipped the snowshoes on, fastened the harnesses tight for one another, then side-stepped like penguins down to the riverbank. The northwest wind was raw and bone-chilling. Lincoln took off his stocking hat, replacing it with an army green balaclava. A minute later he put the stocking hat back on too for good measure. The breath from his mouth and nostrils was ghostly in the early light.

I took my hunting knife out of its sheath and cut a stout branch off a nearby maple. After I'd fashioned it into a staff, I used it to shatter the skin of ice where the Studebaker had come to rest. The water was clear and crisp as gin.

Lincoln handed me a Jersey Milk bar. I peeled off the wrapper and tossed it into the river. It bobbed like a cork for a few seconds then disappeared under the ice, sucked down by a deep-running current. I let the chocolate melt in my mouth.

There was an outcropping of rock three or four feet below the surface. I'd been told by the Mounties that the rear axle had hooked over it, preventing the car from sinking to a depth of five fathoms. It was easy to see why they'd thought the driver was lost and presumed drowned. If someone went under here they wouldn't wash up for miles, if ever. The river itself was a quarter-mile wide at this point and kept many secrets.

Lincoln snowshoed along the shoreline around the foot of the bluff. In places there was absolutely no snow while a short distance away high drifts, sculpted by the wind, made the going difficult. He stopped and bent over to tighten the straps on his boots.

I made a rough estimate of how far the trunk of the Studebaker would have been from where I was standing. It was possible that the trunk had been emptied after the car was in the river. But who or why eluded me. For the time being I was betting that Penny herself had salvaged the luggage. Then again, it wouldn't be the first time that a car wreck was looted. It was grisly business, akin to grave-robbing.

Lincoln yelled, disrupting my morbid thoughts. "Come here, Jack. What do you make of this?"

I tottered on the rough terrain, unused to snowshoes on bare ground. Lincoln was standing at the river's edge, actually on the ice. He turned his back to the wind and pointed to something on the shoreline.

There was the impression of a small semi-circle with spokes frozen into the mossy lichen. It was almost like a petroglyph, a deliberate sign of some sort. I pushed aside the blueberry bushes surrounding the spot and searched for other marks. A couple of feet away, I found a complete circle with spokes.

"Take a look." I couldn't stand it anymore. I reached into my coat and lit a cigarette to calm my nerves.

"What is it?" Lincoln asked, reaching for a drag on my smoke. I gave him a cigarette of his own which he lit off mine. It was odd to see him smoking again.

"It's the indentation made by a ski pole."

Lincoln shrugged, his expression hidden beneath the mask. He started to cough violently and threw his cigarette away. "So?" he said hoarsely, unable to find his voice.

"Penny took up skiing almost the first day she moved to Canada."

Clearing his throat, Lincoln said, "Jack, you're clutching at straws."

"Maybe so, but it puzzled me not finding skis in the car."

"Or suitcases."

"Right. You said it snowed to beat the band up this way yesterday. It'd cover any footprints. Look around. You can hardly see a sign that a towing crew was here. Broken branches, skinned bark from the pulleys and chains. Right? Now, let's suppose that Penny was thrown clear of the car, then, afraid that it was going to disappear into the river she somehow managed to open the trunk and retrieve her belongings."

"And?"

"And set out on skis. If she wasn't injured Penny could cover a lot of miles in no time at all," I said, trying to convince myself even more than Lincoln.

"Where would she go? There isn't a house for miles in either direction. Make sense, Jack," Lincoln said calmly.

He placed a hand on my shoulder and spun me around. I could hear but not feel him unbuckling the straps on my knapsack. After he rebuckled the straps, I faced him. He reached into his pocket for an opener and snapped the caps off a couple of bottles of Coca-Cola he had taken from the sack.

I took a long swallow, dry from last night's booze. On the other side of the river smoke rose like a signal. "There." I pointed. "On the peninsula. Maybe that farmhouse or one of the cabins along the river."

"Cabins? What cabins? I don't see any cabins," Lincoln said, tossing his empty bottle back toward the truck.

"To the left of the smoke plume. You can't see them because they're in an inlet called Church Cove. It was a Bible camp at one time until it went private. Grace and I used to go there to get away from it all. Nice place. Rustic."

I finished my Coca-Cola. Across the ice where the river swung in a wide curve south, the sun had risen above the tree-smothered point.

"Penny's smart. She knows she'd have to find cover," I said with renewed hope. "She went to Church Cove with Grace on nurses' retreats years ago." It was a slim chance but a chance.

We headed directly for the farmhouse. Now and then we slid over bare patches of ice smooth as glass. In mid-river we waved as an R.C.M.P. search plane tipped its wings in recognition as it flew low through the morning sky. The aircraft would be able to cover a lot more territory than we could on foot. And the pilot had the advantage when it came to spotting distress signals.

By the time we crossed the river I was soaked in sweat. "What did you pack in this knapsack, anyway?" I asked. "Half a dozen anvils?"

Lincoln grinned. "No. Eight or nine Cokes. A pile of corned beef sandwiches. Few cans of kippers. Four tins of sardines. Maybe ten or twelve chocolate bars."

"Yeah, and a partridge in a pear tree."

"Just the tree, Jack," Lincoln said, staring up the riverbank. "We're going to have to scrap the snowshoes. It's too steep here."

We leaned against the bank and took one another's snowshoes off. I had a cigarette and a Coca-Cola while Lincoln ate a sandwich. The wintry air was so fresh that the pungent aroma of mustard and pepper wafted temptingly after every bite.

Lincoln brushed the bread crumbs off his coat, then he folded and pocketed the wax paper. Tucking both pairs of snowshoes under one arm, he grabbed a strong branch, pulled himself off the ice, and began traversing the slope.

There was a clock within me that was beginning to panic. A road ran parallel to the river. I doubted if it was plowed but at least we wouldn't have to battle through the underbrush and trees. It would make the going faster.

Lincoln's black and green buffalo checks disappeared behind a tall spruce. A second later he shouted in alarm, "Jack, get up here quick."

Grasping brambles hand over hand, I followed him as fast as I could go. In my rush I burst through a row of trees and wound up somersaulting head over heels down a gravel embankment. Later, I couldn't remember hitting the road face-first.

Both nostrils were plugged with snow. Lincoln thumped me on the back to get my wind started then hauled me upright by the armpits. I shook my head to get rid of the ringing in my ears. For a moment I was blinded by the sunlight glaring off the snow. Everything pulsated red.

Lincoln steadied me by the elbow. "Brace yourself," he said, guiding me toward the side of the road.

There was a shape covered with snow in the ditch. My breathing came hard and fast. I recognized my stocking hat and greatcoat.

Wordlessly, Lincoln went up the windswept embankment and sat down.

TERRY CRAWFORD

I ran to the shape and stood for a moment before I knelt. I took the huddled form by the shoulders and almost screamed. The greatcoat was empty and had been draped over a boulder with the stocking hat placed on top. That clock inside me rang its alarm.

I realized that somewhere I'd let myself despair of ever seeing Penny alive again. And that finding her this way, curled up and frozen, was what I'd really expected.

Lincoln turned the stocking hat inside out. It was blood-stained. He rubbed the wool between his thumbs. A reddish-black powder fell to the snow and lay there until it was dispersed by the wind.

Lincoln said, "She's hurt, Jack. But she made it this far."

"You're wrong, Lincoln. She made it farther. Let's go."

CHAPTER TWENTY-SEVEN

"**I** DON'T SEE any signs of activity, Jack," Lincoln said, unconsciously rubbing his bad leg. He hadn't done anything until now to show that it might be bothering him. Even at the worst of times, Lincoln was never one to complain.

We were standing atop a low ridge overlooking the site of the cabins strung out along Church Cove. Yesterday's new snow reflected a faint blue in the shaded inlet. All the cabins had little porches that protected the doors from the weather. Long icicles hung over the eaves of every one of them except the nearest one to us. There the icicles had been broken off, stubs left suspended like blunt instruments.

"Let's check number eight," I muttered. "Come on."

We snowshoed across the inlet and up the beach. I was getting a flood of memories of when my wife and I came here years ago. When we were young. Something about buoys. White buoys roped together with white rope. So you wouldn't go in over your head. But Grace swam under the rope and out into the wide river. In her red bathing cap. A red bathing cap in the distance. Bobbing like a child's balloon lost on the water. I was calling frantically to her, afraid she was out too far.

Lincoln turned around and sat on the icy cabin steps. He unstrapped his snowshoes, stood them up in the snow, and waited for me on the stoop. I did as he did and followed.

The door was slightly ajar. I guessed that it had been forced open with a ski pole. Hoped, really. The doorjamb near the knob had been stabbed repeatedly with a sharp object, splintering the wood enough to release the lock.

We went inside. Lincoln was breathing hard. Apprehension. I was nervous myself. The interior of the cabin was dark with the curtains drawn on the small windows. I knew there were kerosene lamps to the right of the doors in all the cabins. Striking a match, I lit the lamp and turned up the wick.

Releasing a sigh, Lincoln walked into the room with me close behind.

"Well, whoever was here is gone," he said.

His breath was visible in the cold, still air of the cabin. He sat at the table and looked at me through the mask. It shouldn't have, but the sight spooked me.

"Why don't you take off the balaclava, Lincoln?" I asked, moving toward the open-shelved cupboard.

"Too cold," he said, rubbing his thighs. "Wouldn't want my face getting frostbite and turning white, would we?"

"Definitely not," I said, picking up a tobacco tin and giving it a shake. Wooden matches. Beside them, a Mason jar full of teabags and another of sugar. I checked behind the Franklin stove. There was left-over kindling, old newspapers, and plenty of logs in the woodbox. I had a brainstorm. No, I take that back. It was more like a mild squall. "Let's build a fire."

Lincoln found another lantern. Lighting it, he placed it in the center of the table. I tended to the stove and in minutes had a roaring fire on the go. We stood with our backsides to the heat, grateful for the penetrating warmth after the trek across the ice. I was feeling pretty rocky. What I really needed was about twelve hours sleep.

While Lincoln stayed by the stove, I wandered aimlessly around the cabin. If Penny had broken in I had to figure out where she had gone. The farmhouse further down the road would be the logical place to try next. From Fish-Hawk Bluff the cabins and farmhouse looked close together but when you got over here they were quite a distance apart. My guess was that Penny had rested in the cabin, then moved on.

I looked underneath the dry-sink for a pot to boil water. There were mugs hanging on nails by the window beside the cupboard. I unhooked two. One of them had a lipstick smear on the rim. It proved to be so fresh that it wiped off easily. We were close. Very close.

But instead of giving me a boost, it sapped me. I lay down on the cot in the corner and closed my eyes. A white rosary floated on the water. Children clung to it, laughing and squealing with delight. A woman in a red bathing cap swam past, beckoning them into the deep river. The rosary beads bobbed up and down as the children disappeared one by one. Someone who looked like me watched from the shore. Powerless.

"Jack. Wake up. Jack." Lincoln shook me. "You've been conked out for over an hour."

My eyes opened and I came to from a long way off. "Wha? An hour?"

"Yes."

It was so warm Lincoln had taken off the balaclava and his coat. I stared groggily into the room. There were empty Coca-Cola bottles and candy wrappers on the table. A veil of cigarette smoke drifted at eye-level. Sun streamed obliquely through the south-facing windows. Lincoln had discovered a stack of old *Star Weeklys* and apparently had been toiling over the crossword puzzles while I slept.

I staggered to my feet, knocking a saucepan on to the floor with a clang. It was enough to wake the dead. Namely me. I picked up the pan and made for the door.

"What are you up to? Sleepwalking?" Lincoln said, pencilling in a long word.

"Practically," I said. "The old dog needs something hot to drink. I left the thermos in the truck."

Stepping out onto the stoop, I broke off several icicles. The thermometer read 10 degrees above zero. No wonder the cold slapped me in the face. I took a couple of deep breaths and felt like a true northerner; strong and free.

Lincoln watched inquisitively as I put the pan on the stove. "Quite the Boy Scout, aren't we, Jack?"

I smiled. "Hidden talents." Turning serious, I told him about the lipstick traces on the mug. It led me to believe that Penny wasn't badly hurt. That she was coping well with her situation. There were also scratch marks on the floor that I guessed were made by the cot which Penny must have dragged in front of the stove. I was at a loss about her missing luggage. I couldn't imagine her on skis trying to handle a suitcase. And why did she abandon my greatcoat? Was it just too heavy? Or a deliberate trail?

The ice hissed in the pot. I sat beside Lincoln until he finished the crossword puzzle. Then I tossed a couple of teabags into the boiling water. While the tea brewed I put a tablespoon of powdered milk into a mug. I ate one of the corned beef sandwiches and a nutbar. Before drinking the tea, I enjoyed a cigarette. I wasn't feeling too bad. The sleep, strange dreams notwithstanding, had revived me.

I threw the stocking hat into the fire and decided to wear the greatcoat. Lincoln had spread it out by the stove so it was nice and warm. I was overdressed but I didn't care. The substantial weight was nothing compared to the weight on my mind. For some reason I thought about the little man in the hold of the *Bergensfjord*. The little dead man. He was the beginning of all this. The link in a chain of events that led nowhere. And everywhere.

We tidied the cabin and dampened the fire. I left an unsigned note of explanation along with two dollars to pay the costs of repairing the damage caused by the forced entry. Lincoln shouldered the knapsack, smirking when I kidded him about it being safe now that it was five pounds lighter.

Outside, the wind had ceased swirling the snow. All was calm. We snowshoed into the unbearable peacefulness of the woods.

CHAPTER TWENTY-EIGHT

I ASKED LINCOLN to stay undercover in a clump of spruce trees at the edge of a plowed field above the farm. From there he could see the house, a rambling Victorian gingerbread with a rickety verandah.

I snowshoed down the hill toward the outbuildings, which included a chicken coop connected by an open-walled woodshed to a cattle barn. A dapple-gray Percheron tramped back and forth in a paddock near the river. The horse's ears pricked up when I came down the hill. She looked at me, then went on pacing the fence, big hooves flattening a path in the snow. A crow alighted in a dead maple and cawed three times.

I stopped in the shadow of the barn and listened. Inside, a voice echoed off the rafters. A boy acting out scenes from Flash Gordon with himself cast as the flamboyant hero. He had Merciless Ming the Magnificent ready for annihilation. Z-z-zap! Z-z-zap! His sound effects were practiced and pitched to perfection. I peered through a cobwebbed window. The young fellow, tall, gangly, maybe thirteen or fourteen, was using a funnel for a megaphone. Aiming his zings and zaps toward the high roof, he'd listen to the reverberations, think for a moment, then let loose another blast from his ray-gun.

I let the boy drift undisturbed in a distant galaxy where there weren't any cows to milk or eggs to gather and quietly crossed the barnyard to the side door of the house.

A cross-eyed black and white cat squinted suspiciously from the kitchen windowsill. Somewhere in a faraway room a dog started yapping the instant I touched the horseshoe doorknocker. The drapes parted on a second floor bay window. Four kids arranged themselves in a row behind the panes and stared in mute wonder. I waved. They took off like frightened partridges.

A raw-boned, homely woman almost my height opened the door. She was wearing an out-of-date housedress beneath a home-made wool cardigan that reached to her knees. It made her look oddly modish.

I took off my hat. "Good morning, Ma'am. I'm Detective Sergeant Ireland, Saint John Police."

She regarded me with steely indifference.

I tried one of my better make-them-feel-at-ease smiles. It usually worked, but not today.

"What do you want?" she said. The four kids appeared in the kitchen behind her, each sliding to a stop on sock feet. With the exception of a cute, redheaded girl they were as unbecoming as the mother. The house released a smell of fresh-baked bread and percolated coffee.

A sturdy boy in suspenders approached and brazenly inspected my snowshoes. I hastily took them off. "Want to try them out, Sonny?"

"Yes, yes," he said. "Mom, can I? Please."

"Liam, go inside, be quiet, and don't move till I say so," his mother commanded. The boy obeyed but studied me with interest. So did the other children. They seemed alert and bright, not the least bit shy or backward. A huge map of the world, tacked to the wall, dominated the kitchen. There were books, magazines, and scribblers strewn everywhere. By all appearances this was one of those country families where education enlivened the long winter evenings. It gave me hope. In too many other places I'd found a self-defeating, carefully maintained ignorance. A fear of learning and a stubborn unwillingness to learn.

My protracted silence unnerved the woman. When she spoke, her voice quavered. "Mister, I've got my hands full, as you can plainly see. So, what is it?"

I didn't answer but instead turned around, watching as the boy from the barn cautiously went to the woodpile and sat on the chopping block. He too, seemed alert and intense. I wondered about the father of the family.

"Is your husband home?" I asked.

"No."

"When will he be back?"

"Any time now."

One of the children gasped. Mom had told a big fib.

"I'm looking for a lady who came this way. Maybe early yesterday or the day before. She might have been lost in the storm."

"I don't know anything," the woman said, regaining her composure.

The children sidled together into a little knot of conspiracy. An enjoyable game that visibly excited them. I stared, making each one in turn squirm under my gaze. I felt like the Big Bad Wolf.

"I see," I said. "Could I buy a couple of cups of coffee from you, Ma'am?"

The request completely flabbergasted the woman. She started to stammer something but I cut her short. "Thanks. I'll signal my friend," I said, taking my patrolman's whistle out of my pocket. I gave it a shrill burst that almost sent the children and their mother into a dither.

Lincoln came down the hill on the trot, probably happy just to move into the sunshine. The spindling boy, cool as a cucumber, sauntered over from the chopping block and stood on the steps. I don't know what he thought he'd be able to do if there was trouble. I didn't see any ray-guns. He smiled uncertainly but without a hint of fear. There was a quality of strength about him which I immediately liked. "Hello, Space Ranger," I said.

He blushed, unable to contain a smile. His mother pulled him abruptly by the arm into the house, an act which made him burn with humiliation. "Stay right there, Joseph," she said.

An aeroplane flew low over the house, the drone of the engine agitating the Percheron. I glanced up. It was the R.C.M.P. ski plane, flying systematic grids in its search pattern.

"What's up?" Lincoln said.

"We'll soon see," I answered. "For starters, we're going to have some fresh coffee."

"Sounds good. *Smells* good," Lincoln said.

The children couldn't take their eyes off him. Perhaps they'd never seen anyone wearing a balaclava. I suppose he did look frightening. When he bent over to unstrap his snowshoes I whisked off the balaclava in a single tug. It was obvious by their amazed expressions that the children had never seen a black man before, except in the numerous copies of *The National Geographic* crammed into the bookshelves beside the stove.

Lincoln cupped a hand over my ear and whispered, "Did I go and forget to take the bone out of my nose?"

Even though the joke was worn out, we laughed anyway.

The woman of the house seemed torn between curiosity and protectiveness. She folded her arms and leaned against the door-frame, blocking the entry. Alarmed, I stared at her left wrist. The hour hand on her watch was red and the minute hand black. Somewhere deep inside, I trembled. I decided to unload rather than pussyfoot around anymore. "Penny Fairchild was here and I know you've seen her. Why don't you tell me all about it?" I said, but not in a threatening way. "I know Miss Fairchild personally. You're wearing her wristwatch. When she broke it in a skiing accident Penny had the hour hand replaced with a red one because she liked the look of it. The English. You know. Eccentric."

"We haven't done anything wrong," the woman said, putting an arm around her son. "She..."

I blurted, "Is Penny all right?"

"Yes."

"Thank God. Where is she? Inside?"

"No. She went to Saint John with my husband," the woman said listlessly. "I wasn't supposed to tell anyone. *Anyone.*" She stepped aside. "You and your friend better come in. She insisted I keep her timepiece. I said no but she left it on my dresser."

We took off our boots and followed her into the kitchen. I hung the greatcoat behind the stove. When I sat down the cross-eyed cat jumped onto my lap. The little ones giggled. I rubbed it behind the ears for a few seconds before the woman made it scat. She placed two of the biggest teacups I'd ever seen on the table.

Lincoln drank in silence, the object of close scrutiny by the motionless children. He reached into the knapsack on the floor and produced the last of the nutbars. Six in all. The children stirred like roused honeybees. "Do you mind if the kids eat candy, Mrs.?" he asked.

Lost in thought, she shook her head. The lanky boy accepted the nutbars from Lincoln and dispensed them to his brothers and sisters, then set one in front of his mother. She slipped it into the pocket of her cardigan.

"This coffee is grand," I said.

Lincoln nodded. "A-1."

The woman looked into my eyes. "What's your first name?"

"Jack."

She relaxed and leaned towards me across the table. "Does your friend, Penny, go by any other name?"

"Why?"

"Does she use any other name?"

"Sometimes. Her middle name's Charlotte. What's going on?" I wasn't used to being questioned. And I didn't like it now that the shoe was on the other foot.

"I had to be sure," the woman said. "Charlotte... *Penny* was here. She left yesterday morning with Fred. He had a hundred chickens we had to get to the City Market."

"But there was a snowstorm," I said.

"It's been storming on-again, off-again, for the last while. There was a break in the weather, so Fred decided to chance it. We just finished killing and cleaning the chickens. Unless Fred got them to market we'd lose money. As you can see, we're not well off."

The house was humble enough, but comfortable. And though rough-hewn, the children were the most well-behaved I'd seen in a long time. I noticed a piano in the big room off the kitchen. "Are there any Coca-Colas left in the knapsack, Linc?"

"Three."

"If it's okay with the Mrs., why don't you give them to the kids and treat them to a concert," I said, then addressed the woman. "I don't think they have to be privy to what we're talking about, Mrs."

She agreed. "That'd be best."

"And Joseph," I said. "How would you like to earn a dollar?"

The boy leapt to attention. "A whole dollar?"

"Yes. Here's what I want you to do: There's an emergency flare in the knapsack. Take it down to the river, go about fifty yards off shore, and when you see the R.C.M.P. ski plane, fire the flare. All you have to do is pull the tab and stick it into the snow. The chemicals will do the rest. You'll hear a bang when the rocket goes off – it'll shoot a light into the sky – then the bottom of the flare will emit a cloud of red smoke for three or four minutes. Got it?"

"Yes, sir."

"Use a pair of the snowshoes if you like. Here's your dollar. When the ski plane lands, tell the pilot Sergeant Ireland says Miss Fairchild is safe and has returned to Saint John. Okay?"

TERRY CRAWFORD

"Yes, sir."

I watched until the boy was out of the yard. The way he was manoeuvering, it wouldn't take him long to get the hang of the snowshoes.

"That was good of you," his mother said. "Joseph has an overactive imagination. He can use a real adventure for a change. When Penny was here Joseph was seeing mobsters behind every tree."

"Mobsters?"

"Joseph's word. The men Penny was afraid of. The ones who forced her off the road. They thought she drowned under the ice in the river."

I poured myself more coffee. No wonder this woman was on guard when I showed up at the door. I was lucky she didn't pepper my hide with buckshot. She eyed my cigarette pack for a moment. "Have one, please," I said.

"Thanks. I haven't had a tailor-made since Christmas." She struck a match off the stovetop and took a long first drag. "If it wasn't for the dog, Charlotte... Penny might have got lost on the river. Penny followed him to the cabins. Later, we heard him barking and sent Joseph down to fetch him home. Joseph found Miss Fairchild asleep in front of the stove. Unconscious. Sort of. Kept saying, 'Must tell Jack,' over and over."

"When was this?" I asked. Lincoln launched into *The Maple Leaf Rag* and had the kids enraptured.

"The day before yesterday. In the morning. About ten."

"Was she badly hurt?"

"She was quite forgetful. Told us it was because of the concussion she suffered when she was thrown out of the car and over a cliff."

That would be the cliff I stepped off and into the snow, I thought, but... there were all those buts. "Anything else?"

"Just that she was knocked unconscious and when she came to she saw some men dragging her luggage up the hill."

"Some men?"

"Three men. She didn't see their faces. I guess she feared for her life."

"What did the men do after they stole the luggage?" Last night's lack of sleep caught up with me in a sudden avalanche of weariness.

"Drove away as fast as they could go."

Stifling a yawn, I asked, "What else did Penny say?"

"Hardly anything. She mentioned a coat that got too heavy to wear. She wanted to get it but couldn't remember where it was. She would have forgot her skis if we hadn't put them on the truck."

"I see. Don't worry about the coat. We found it by the road. That's it hanging there. Can you recall anything else?"

"No. Penny was in a daze. Hardly talked at all. She mostly sat close to the stove to stay warm. Because of the concussion she got me to keep her awake until the evening. When she did go to bed she slept through till morning. Then it was time to go."

I rose and stretched my back, sore from too much snowshoeing at one go. "Help yourself to the smokes. I've got plenty."

The woman looked in on the children. Aglow with the entertainment, they beamed at her as if she were a fairy godmother and had granted them their most precious wish.

"Does he work in a band?" the woman asked, lighting a cigarette after admiring its perfectly cylindrical shape. "Or in nightclubs?" she added in a secretive tone as if the question were risqué.

"No. But he's easily good enough. He usually only plays for me and his relatives. Lincoln's probably more dedicated than a lot of piano players who do it for a living." As I spoke, he sailed into a medley of waltzes that soon had the kids merrily skating around the room in sock feet.

The woman smiled, content to smoke and bask in the sounds of her laughing children.

Joseph burst through the door, the cold clinging to his clothes. "I did the job," he announced proudly. "The pilot even let me talk on the radio myself. Oh, Mom, it was swell." The spent flare protruded from his pants pocket, a souvenir of the adult world of intrigue. He threw himself down so clumsily onto a chair, the coffee pot danced on the stove. He fidgeted, then shot out of the room and joined the others.

I hated to break up the party but I was dead tired and itching to get back to Saint John. "You said your husband and Penny left yesterday. Wouldn't he get to town by suppertime?"

"If the roads were good. Fred has a cousin in Hampton. If the snow was bad he would've stopped there for a while. Maybe only an hour or two. Or maybe overnight, but I don't think so."

"And then?" I put my boots on to let her know I was preparing to leave.

TERRY CRAWFORD

"He'd make the delivery to the City Market and visit his brother in Saint John," she said, accepting half a bottle of Coca-Cola from Joseph.

"Could you give me his name and address?"

"James Quinlan, forty-eight Exmouth Street."

One of the kids collided with a long low table, strewing crayons and watercolour brushes onto the linoleum. "That's enough, sit," the woman said, without looking. Obedience was immediate. Joseph and the redheaded girl hastily cleaned up the mess.

I arched my eyebrows at Lincoln and nodded. He left the piano to wild applause, bowed to one and all, and joined me.

Dressed for the great outdoors, I placed my extra pack of cigarettes on the windowsill and asked the woman her name.

"Mrs. will do fine," she said. "Mother gave me a name that's as homely as I am."

I started to protest.

"No need to flatter me, Sergeant. I saw the look on your face when I answered the door. If they had ugly pageants, I'd be Miss World." She suddenly laughed, a throaty warble that had real beauty. "Thank you for the treats. And thank you," she said to Lincoln, "for the wonderful music. Our children will never forget today."

"My pleasure, Mrs.," Lincoln said. "Never had a better audience."

We followed Joseph's easy trail to the river. It wasn't ten o'clock yet but I could've laid down in the snow and slept until spring. At least when we got back to the truck we'd only have a drive of a few hours to Saint John. On the other side of the river, Penny and the farmer would've had to go the long way around the peninsula, all the way to Hampton, then down to the city from the other direction.

I tried to picture Penny hidden inside my greatcoat, wandering alone on the ice. Out here, a sudden snow-squall could turn a person around. Make them see things.

CHAPTER TWENTY-NINE

THE OVERHEAD LIGHT blinked off when I opened the folding door of the phone booth in Pepper's Diner and stepped out onto the tiled floor. Lincoln raised a hand from behind a newspaper to let me know where he was sitting. It was noontime and the place was hopping, alive with restaurant noises and the chatter of people. I glanced toward the soda fountain to see if Roxanne was working but she wasn't there. Then, right on cue, the swinging doors of the kitchen parted and Roxanne, carrying a tray of sandwiches and pie, backed neatly into the room. Under the bright lights she looked harried, ten years older than thirty-two. She saw me as I was about to sit down, and smiled, at once fresh-faced and young. On another day it would've made me feel good but I was too tired and worried to smile back. She didn't seem to mind, which was one of the things I liked about her – a lack of unnecessary fuss.

"I think she likes you, Jack," Lincoln said, folding the newspaper at the sports-page.

Coffee was already on the table. I rubbed my eyes, sore from squinting at too much sunlight reflected off too much snow. I was a city boy accustomed to soot and ashes, slush-covered sidewalks, the dull grays of railyards and industry.

I slipped my boots off and put my feet up beside Lincoln. He had let me and the dog sleep for most of the drive into the city, awaking us on the outskirts where all three of us got out to relieve ourselves in the woods. I drove the rest of the way to Pepper's, the window rolled down in a worthless attempt to enliven my senses. Weariness and worry weighed me down.

"What's up?" Lincoln said, clearly glad to be back in known territory and off snowshoes.

My thighs ached from the weird walking. We had compared notes about just the way it hurt and laid bets concerning the duration. I was finding it harder to bounce back these days. Whenever I sparred at the Monarch Boxing Club it took me days to stop hurting.

"There's no answer at Penny's flat. I tried the hospital but they said she's still on holidays."

"Maybe she's out shopping," Lincoln said. "Or so beat she's sleeping and can't hear the phone."

"I hope you're right but I won't be satisfied until I see her live and in Technicolour. Quinlan's brother doesn't have a telephone so I'll have to go to Exmouth Street for a talk with him."

"What's going on, Jack?" Lincoln said, putting the menu aside.

"Your guess is as good as mine," I answered, sick at heart at the dead truth of it. I'd stumbled onto something but it was in the dark and I didn't know what it was. I would have to go about eliminating the possibilities I knew of. A mere handful.

"What'll it be, gents?" the waitress asked, smacking her bubblegum between ruby-red lips. She had a spare pencil tucked over one ear and a cork-tip cigarette over the other.

"What's the special?" I asked.

"Hot pork sandwich," she said, writing it down.

I shrugged. "I guess I'll have it then." She'd jumped to a conclusion and my hunch was that somebody else had done the same. But what about? Question marks floated around in my head like fish-hooks. Sooner or later I'd get a bite. Or get bitten.

Lincoln ordered not one, but two club sandwiches, and a strawberry milkshake. He could eat like a horse and never gain an ounce. I figured it had something to do with pounding the piano for five hours every day.

I butted my cigarette and read a section of the newspaper while we waited for the food. The New York World's Fair was coming up later this year and was promising an astounding glimpse into the world of tomorrow. I'm not sure I wanted to know what the big brains predicted cities and towns would resemble in faraway 1960. Like the century, I'd be sixty then and probably yearning for the days of my grandfather.

I consulted the want ads for a good deal on a car but came up empty. New Pontiacs were $758.00 and up, which was a fair bit of change, but the style was sharp. Maybe I'd pay that if they tossed in a radio for free. One thing was sure, my Studebaker wouldn't fetch enough on a trade-in for a set of windshield wipers. Fortunately, my insurance was paid up.

The food arrived and we ate diligently. Lincoln solved the crossword puzzle between mouthfuls, staring off into the distance as if the answers were written on the wall. After I finished eating, I could've curled up in the booth and gone to sleep for a week but I had to hit the streets.

The cash register clinged and clanged like a three-alarm fire. I *was* tired. Worn to a frazzle. Our ruby-lipped waitress approached and said, "Roxy wants to see you in the kitchen. Says it's important."

Lincoln sat at the fountain and ordered another milkshake. He always did have the patience of Job. I went through the swinging doors and into the kitchen.

One of Lincoln's cousins, Rodney, was scrubbing pots and pans. A handsome devil, he looked even more Satanic as steam rose in clouds under his armpits and formed a halo around his head before it was drawn out through the exhaust fan. He was a mulatto with white features but dark skin. Catching sight of me, Rodney beckoned me further into the kitchen.

"Man, what brings you into these precincts? Some fool report me for scoffin' leftovers?"

"At ease, Rod, I'm looking for Roxanne," I said, lighting a cigarette. "Have one?"

He quickly dried his hands and accepted a smoke. Inhaling extravagantly, he performed a little soft-shoe, knowing I was a large fan. Hobbled, Rodney could dance the feet off Nijinsky.

"Roxy's in the supply room," he said. "Her and the girls got a mirror and a little dressing table in there so they can rouge and lipstick in peace."

Sidestepping the short-order cook, I went past the deep-fryer and grill to a metal door marked SUPPLIES. Beneath the sign someone had written 'Girls Only' with fingernail polish. I entered without knocking. The room was cool, almost cold, after the heat of the kitchen. Off in a corner Roxanne stood with her back to a full-length mirror. She was busy straightening the seams on her stockings and didn't notice me. I let her finish fastening her garter belt before I coughed into my fist. She glanced up with mild surprise, smoothed her uniform, and said, "Hello, Jack."

A Kewpie doll hung from the pull-chain of the light. Under the bare bulb, I realized for the first time that Roxanne's eyes were more gray than pale blue. She directed me toward a collection of butter boxes that served as furniture. It was like sitting down in a cozy little kid's club.

"Long time, no see," Roxanne said, lighting a cigarette off mine. "I've been trying to reach you on the telephone."

I nodded. I didn't want to be, but I was strongly attracted to Roxanne.

"I've been out of the city," I explained. "Beyond reach."

Roxanne froze, as if expecting me to elaborate further, then spoke softly. "I've got a problem and I didn't know who to turn to. Can I talk to you?"

"Go ahead, shoot."

She lifted the window a bit to let the smoke out. The glass was painted dark green. The sun shone over the sill, bouncing its light off a rouge compact and onto the dark ceiling. Roxanne gazed at the shimmering circle for a long while then said, "Someone's following Leonard."

"Leonard? Your boy?"

"Yes."

"Who?"

There was withheld desperation in Roxanne's voice. "A man. Skinny. About forty. Leonard thinks he's that old. But how could he know? He's just a kid. Besides, the guy's got a long beard."

"This is important, Roxy. You said, 'following'. Why?"

She thought the question over for a minute and said, "Because Leonard's seen the man wandering near the schoolyard, at hockey games at the Forum, twice on the bus, in the Tobacco Store where the kids buy penny candy, and hanging around the Ludlow Street playground."

"H'mm. Why does Leonard think this guy's trailing him?"

"I don't follow you, Jack," Roxanne said, nervously punching her cigarette into the ashtray.

"Let me put it this way – do any of the other kids in Lenny's circle feel threatened?"

"That's just it, Jack, some of them have seen this man but he doesn't seem to upset them."

"Upset them?"

"Make them nervous. Some of them even think he's nifty because of his beard. Oh, Jack, Leonard's had two asthma attacks since last Wednesday. It's drivin' me around the bend."

I put out a hand, which she took and clung tightly onto. "There now, Roxy. Easy does it. Where is Lenny now?"

"It's a Holy Day, so he's off school. After he attended Mass he went to a friend's house. A whole gang of them are going to the movies up the street this afternoon."

"Okay. Safety in numbers. What school? Assumption?"

"Yes."

"I'll enlist Tom Waterman. His beat includes that parish. He can keep an eye out for Leonard *and* this creep who's haunting the neighbourhood."

"Oh, Jack. Would you?"

"It's *done*, Roxy. Now, before I leave – have you seen this character?"

"No. None of the parents have. Some of them are accusing Leonard of trying to scare his classmates in order to get attention."

"Lamebrains. If it was their kid they'd be screaming for blood," I said, getting up. "I gotta go. Constable Waterman will get to the bottom of this business. Have you got a photograph of Leonard?"

"Yes. In my purse. It was taken at New Year's."

"Good. Lend it to Waterman. I'll tell him to pick it up here at the diner. In the meantime, if you remember anything you forgot to tell me, tell him."

Roxanne had risen with me, still clutching my hand. I gave her a light kiss on the cheek and said, "Could I have my hand back?"

She laughed and let go. "Sorry."

"Anytime, Roxy. You can trust Waterman. He's a good man. I'd handle this myself but I'm on suspension and up to my eyeballs in something smelly. If Waterman needs it he's got a squad car at his disposal and, of course, the resources of the department."

"Thanks, Jack. I feel better now, knowing you're in my corner," Roxy said, smiling. It was a smile that had "come hither" in it. But it also had a big chunk of regret.

When I opened the supply room door I glanced back and saw her sit down forlornly on one of the butter boxes, light a cigarette, and exhale a smoky sigh. A lost angel if ever there was one.

Lincoln was still sitting at the fountain, an empty stool on either side even though the restaurant was jammed to the rafters. I sat beside him while he finished reading an article in *LIFE* on the Japanese/Chinese question. Odd, how reporters could call mass murder a question. What the hell would an answer be?

Lincoln returned the magazine to the rack at the end of the counter. There were hateful eyes upon him and he knew it. Buttoning his coat, he said, "All set?"

I handed him a paper napkin. "I'm not going anywhere with you until you wipe off that pink mustache. Wouldn't want people to stare, would we?"

"At a magnificent specimen like me? Can't have that."

Feeling like the good sports we, of course, were, we waved good-bye to Debra and Bill Pepper. Then we went arm in arm out through the revolving doors.

Jupiter yowled at us from inside the truck as we mounted the running boards. It was a somber reminder that we had to stay on track until we found Penny.

CHAPTER THIRTY

4 8 EXMOUTH STREET was a ramshackle tenement house stuck to the side of a hill like a wrecked ship about to founder in the next strong wind. It was painted sky-blue with yellow trim in an attempt at beautification. It didn't work. The dump looked cheaper than a week-old birthday cake.

I hauled the demonstrator I picked up at the Pontiac dealer's over to the curb and pulled on the parking brake. I didn't want the thing sailing down the hill and into traffic on Prince Edward Street before I'd even made a payment on it. As it was, in the fifteen minutes I'd been behind the wheel I almost cracked it up twice. She was peppy and more streamlined than my Studebaker. A thoroughbred instead of a draft horse. The salesman begged me to try it for a day or two, so I didn't object. Why should I? It was the dealership's gas and they were willing to trust me with a new car. Trust? It might have had more to do with the peculiar regard a policeman is sometimes afforded when he shows a mere mortal his I.D. Something I'm not altogether comfortable about, but I needed my own transportation so I accepted the offer.

I got out of the Pontiac and crossed the slushy street. A well-greased chain-driven Ford truck was parked in front of a fire hydrant. Empty chicken crates covered a flatbed ringed with spruce posts connected together with page-wire. The truck had to belong to Fred Quinlan or my name wasn't Jack Ireland. And it was.

I found Quinlan's registration papers in an oilskin envelope under the dashboard. They confirmed ownership and also indicated that the man was at least ten years younger than his wife. I leaned over and put the envelope back and caught a glint of something shiny beneath the driver's seat.

It was an antique Colt .45, oiled and polished like new. There were five bullets in the cylinder. For someone who left his truck unlocked a small concession to safety, but it did lead me to think that Fred knew how to use the monster. And that he was ready and willing if pressed. Penny had travelled through the snowy woods with an able bodyguard.

I tucked the pistol under my belt. It felt heavy and deadly. A threat to life. I don't care for firearms. Never did. Whatever dangerous glamour radiates from them is lost on me. And the bottom line is that guns are just too damn easy to use.

Wood ashes were scattered over the steps of 48 Exmouth. The firm imprint of gumrubber boots, as distinct as freshly inked fingerprints, led upwards to the hallways. I checked the names beneath the seven doorbells. A crudely scrawled Q designated flat six as Quinlan's brother's place. There was a stencilled sign beside the bells which said: FARM BUTTER & EGGS but didn't state where.

The halls and narrow staircases listed worse than a drunken sailor. I followed the fading outline of the ashes to the third floor. The gumboots stood sentinel outside the door of number six. I stopped on the landing to blow my nose. Could it have been possible that every tomcat in the known universe had left its irresistible aroma in these stinking corridors? As if to answer yes, a pair of mangy calico cats jumped from behind a battered settee and onto the hall windowsill. A flyweight rat could've licked either one of them.

Another stencilled sign was pinned to the crumbling plaster wall with red thumbtacks: FARM GOODS – HERE.

I rapped on Quinlan's door. Inside, Jimmie Rodgers was Blue Mountain yodelling at the top of his tubercular lungs. I knocked louder. The music abruptly stopped. A man with an up-country accent said, "What is it and what do you want?" from a couple of rooms away.

"Customer. Two pounds of butter and a dozen eggs."

The door swung open and a small, trim man in a vest and dress shirt with sleeves rolled up confronted me. "And who might you be?" he asked, giving me the once over.

I reached for my wallet and extracted a five-spot. It was enough of an answer. The little man stepped aside and led the way to the kitchen.

After the dingy blight of the halls, the room was as sanitary and bright as a surgery. An icebox, painted white to match the surroundings, stood by the window. Another man, who could've been a twin to the fellow who opened the door, sat in a chair and gazed out at the view without so much as a glance in my direction. His coveralls smelled of hay and half-decomposed straw. The not unpleasant odour of the barn.

"Nice day," I said.

The farmer's brother pulled a strip of brown paper off a roller bolted to a chopping block, then grabbed the end of a string dangling from a holder overhead and wrapped the butter as if he could do it blindfolded.

Fred Quinlan looked at me for the first time. He was as handsome as his wife was homely. One of the children had luckily taken after his side of the family.

His brother James went to the icebox and removed a dozen eggs two by two, placing them into a used carton. He announced, "That'll be two-bits for the butter and two-bits for the eggs. I ain't got change for a five."

I laid the bill on the table. "That's all I have," I said. "That, and this." I put the Colt .45 on top of the money. The air in the room seemed to galvanize.

"I knew you were trouble the second I saw you," James said. "You're too tall and strapping to be anything but some kind of cop. Listen, I ain't got no vendor's license. All my brother and I do is sell a little produce on the side. Cut out the middleman, see? Where's the harm?"

I shrugged.

He rolled down his sleeves and fastened his cuff links with a snap and a click. I suppose he thought he now presented a picture of legitimacy.

"Where's the harm?" he repeated. "The little guy's gotta make a dime too."

"If you're looking for an argument, pick another subject," I said.

My lack of concern bewildered him. He ran a hand through his brilliantined hair, then wiped the oil off on a tea towel. "I don't get it," he said. "You ain't from the authorities?"

Fred Quinlan, without taking his gaze off the pistol, calmly rolled a cigarette. I admired his nerve. He struck a match underneath the table, the sudden flare scaring a drowsing cat off the chair beside him. I bent over and got a light for my Philip Morris. He nodded when I said thanks.

I pulled out the deserted chair. Brushing away the cat hairs, I sat down and waited for the talk to begin.

"Tea, Jimmy," the farmer said. His brother hopped to it, setting a pair of chipped Blue Willow cups and saucers in front of us. He then poured a dark brew that had been simmering on the stove.

TERRY CRAWFORD

A pitcher of milk appeared on the table. I added some to the tea, which tasted a bit burnt. "Your milk, Fred?"

"Yes, Jack." He glanced at his brother. "That's Uncle Desmond's old revolver restored good as new, Jimmy."

"Ah," James said, taking a seat in the corner. "Ah." He folded his arms and watched, perfectly still.

"How did you know me, Fred?" I asked.

"Miss Fairchild – Penny – said you'd find me before the others. Besides you're like she described you. Tall. Gray at the temples with a scar on your left eyebrow."

I felt the scar with a fingertip. I'd forgotten it even though the hair never did grow back. "The others?"

"Those that ran her off the road. The ones the revolver's for."

Scratching the stubble on my chin, I murmured, "I see."

I tossed a tailor-made to James, which he lit with a grin, and then I gave one to Fred. After a minute's thought, I explained to them what had happened and why I believed that neither they or any member of their family was in danger. I felt satisfied that Fred wasn't entertaining any doubts before I asked him about Penny.

"She was quiet as a mouse on the trip down. I didn't stop over in Hampton like I sometimes do but kept on going. I had extra gasoline on the truck for the trip so we wheeled into town yesterday afternoon."

"Can you be more specific about the time, Fred?"

"First thing I did was deliver the chickens to the City Market. Lemme see, I remember, that big neon clock said ten after three."

"Did Penny walk home from the Market?" I said, disturbed that she had arrived in Saint John even before I boarded the ferry in Digby. Disturbed, because I'd tried to reach her at all the obvious places and couldn't. Damn it all, she was in the city as least five hours before the ferry docked. Where the hell did she get to?

"No. I drove her."

"Drove?" She could've walked home in three or four minutes. "Was she feeling that bad?"

"I should say not," Fred chuckled. "She helped me unload the truck. That woman's as good as any man."

"Was she afraid? Did you see her to the door?"

"Nope. I dropped her off then turned around and came back down Main Street and through town to Jimmy's with butter and eggs and a few chickens for him to sell."

"Wait a minute. Main Street is nowhere near Penny's."

"I don't know anything about that, Jack. I left her at a drugstore on Main Street," Fred said, concerned.

"Which drugstore?"

"Welsford's."

I sat back, not knowing what to think. "I must be exhausted from all the snowshoeing I did around your neck of the woods, Fred. My head is in a muddle. Penny must have gone to my house looking for me. Meanwhile, I was still in Nova Scotia on my way to catch the ferry."

"My neck of the woods?" Fred traded worried looks with his brother. "What were you doing there?"

"Searching for Penny. I wasn't after your hard cider operation, if that's what you're worried about," I said, going to the icebox and pulling out a sample. They'd not too cleverly put it in Sussex Ginger Ale bottles. "Your house smells like fermented apples, Fred. It drifts right up through the floorboards. Kinda nice."

Fred slumped against the wall, discouraged at being exposed. I pointed to the cider, indicating that we try a round. James uncapped the bottle and poured three tall glasses. It was divine; dry tasting and light golden in colour. These lads were masters of an old and venerable tradition. To allay their fears, I told them just that, and how, through an educated guess, I trailed Penny to the cabins in Church Cove. From there it didn't take Sherlock Holmes to deduce that she would be found at the only inhabited house on the peninsula.

The Quinlan brothers listened breathlessly like two schoolboys hearing *Treasure Island* read aloud for the first time.

"So that's how you knew Jimmy's address, you got it from Hortense. I figured Miss Fairchild must've told you where to find me," Fred said. He grew silent and fell into pondering something.

I downed the cider and helped myself to another. Hortense. A truly homely name. I didn't blame Fred's wife for not revealing it, although I might've been able to convince her that it didn't matter. What's in a name? Who am I kidding? Everything. My own father threatened to divorce my mother while she was still in the maternity ward if she wrote Orville Edison Ireland on my birth certificate.

The tin clock on the windowsill pinged as it passed the hour. Four o'clock. James was an early riser. At least he was this morning. Cider deliveries? He seemed to know what I was thinking when I checked the alarm setting. He shook his head and smiled.

Someone downstairs started beating a child. The kid shrieked and pleaded and pleaded, "Stop, stop." James banged with his heel on the floor and all went quiet except for the muffled sobbing of what sounded like a young boy.

"Cursed woman's too handy with the belt," James said, blood rushing to his face. "Some oughtn't to have kids. For Christ's sake, that goes on day and night."

I nodded. "It ought to be a crime. Maybe someday it will be."

Fred came out of his deliberations, rubbing his eyes as if he'd been slumbering. "Penny said she had a concussion. That's why she asked Hortense to make sure she didn't sleep too long at a stretch. You don't suppose that had her balled-up? Made her forgetful-like?"

"Could be," I said. "You said she was quiet in the truck. It isn't like Penny not to make conversation." I tucked the butter and eggs under my arm and made ready to leave.

James slipped the five-dollar bill from beneath the Colt .45. "You might as well take this, I haven't got change. Drop fifty-cents into my mailbox next time you're in the neighbourhood."

"Give me a bottle of cider and we'll call it even," I said.

"It's still way too much."

"Give the rest to Fred for gas money and the trouble he took with Penny."

"She wasn't any trouble. Not a stitch," Fred said.

"Take the money anyway," I said, picking up the Colt. "And put this someplace safe." Taking the bullets out of my pocket, I dropped them on the table. They were brutish things that could shatter bones, crippling a person for life.

James took the instrument and hid it in the cupboard behind a box of Rice Krispies. He shook my hand when he gave me the cider and thanked me for being a straight arrow.

Fred got up on his feet. "I hope everything's fine with Miss Fairchild. Now, you two take care of yourselves, hear?"

"We will," I said, going to the door and letting myself out.

The two scruffy cats were still in the hall on the sill. They were watching the snow coming down in big wet flakes that occasionally hit the window and slid down the glass like white spiders.

I descended the slanting staircase not feeling much better than when I entered the tenement house. Penny's whereabouts and behaviour were a mystery to me.

A child yelped behind the wall to my right as a belt swished through the air and landed on bare flesh. I pounded on the door with my fist. A haggard woman, overweight to the point of obesity, filled the doorframe. Behind her, a frail boy of seven or eight wiped away tears.

"Stop beating this boy," I said evenly, wanting to scream.

"Ain't none of your business," the woman bellowed. "It's my kid."

I shoved my badge in front of her bloodshot eyes. "He won't be for long. You smarten to hell up. We've had complaints about you and if we get one more, *one more*, I'll have you standing in front of a judge so quick it'll make your thick skull spin."

The woman dropped the belt, kicking it with a slippered foot into a corner.

"Understand?" I said.

"Yeah, yeah."

"Good. I'll be back to make certain you don't backslide. In the meantime, you seek advice from your minister or priest."

"Ain't got none," the woman said defiantly.

"Then go see Chaplain Harris at the Prince Edward Street Sally Ann store. And I don't mean next week. Understood?"

"Yes," the woman said, slamming the door in my face.

I listened but could hear nothing but the frightened sobbing of the boy. His mother muttered, "Aw, shut up," then shuffled away to another room.

In the vestibule I wrote down the woman's name. In a couple of days I'd telephone Chaplain Harris and get him to make a house call if she didn't show. I had a feeling I was fighting a lost cause. But there were certain things you had to fight. You just had to.

TERRY CRAWFORD

I locked the cider in the trunk of the Pontiac, so vexed that for a minute or two I'd actually searched for my trusty Studebaker. My battered and broken Studebaker. As beat up as God knows how many kids in this city. In this world.

I put the car in gear and tramped on the accelerator. The snow slid off the windshield in a soggy sheet.

CHAPTER THIRTY-ONE

A WOMAN I remembered from the days of my First Communion walked slowly down the centre aisle of the Cathedral, genuflected with apparent effort, and turned toward a bank of votive candles at the side altar. She was an elderly spinster, so devout a Catholic she practically lived in the church. She lit a candle and bowed her head in prayer, a solitary figure in the flickering light, a light that didn't seem to give off any illumination but spread darkness instead into the dim corners of the transept.

We were alone with the exception of a few other worshippers. At least, based on the evidence of rosaries and moving lips, I took them for worshippers. I certainly wasn't. It had been years since I last visited the Cathedral of the Immaculate Conception. Or attended Mass or took any of the sacraments. But from time to time I found the quiet of an empty church helpful when I was troubled. Usually, that meant slipping over to St. Peter's via my backyard. But the Cathedral was only a block away from Exmouth Street so I parked out front and came in and sat near one of the big stained glass windows.

Weary, almost to the point of sleep, I was staring at one of the Stations of the Cross – Christ falls for the third time – when someone shook me roughly by the shoulders. It was Doctor Cromarty, dressed in a natty dark suit instead of his usual baggy tweeds. He grinned, exhaling unadulterated garlic. It woke me up faster than a dose of smelling salts.

"Aren't you afraid the pillars are going to shake apart and the roof collapse?" he asked archly.

"I could put the same question to you, Doc. Maybe now that you're here we're in double jeopardy."

Cromarty smiled and nodded. "Why do you find that particular bas-relief so interesting?"

I looked at Christ on His hands and knees with the cross on His back. Ever since I was a kid it was an image of torture and suffering that bothered me. Used to give me nightmares. "Why don't they just leave him alone?" I mumbled without thinking.

The Doc sighed garlic. "You are under a cloud, but take heart I've got good news."

"What? Penny's turned up?" I said eagerly. Too eagerly.

"Penelope Fairchild? What about her?" Cromarty said. Locked away in his lab, he obviously didn't know about her disappearance, appearance, and disappearance.

I gave him a quick synopsis of what had happened up until now, holding back that Penny had been forced off the road, referring to the wreck of the Studebaker as an accident.

"Strange," he said, probably suspecting that I wasn't telling him the whole truth and nothing but. "How very strange."

"What brings your Presbyterian hide into this palace of idolatry?" I said. "Expecting a brigade of nurses from Saint Joe's?"

"Jack, did anybody ever tell you, 'Blasphemy becomes you'?"

"Not lately."

"Enough of your withering wit, Ireland. I'm on a serious errand."

His stern tone told me that Cromarty was suddenly all business. "Deputy Chief Hardfield contacted me less than an hour ago and ordered me to find you."

"How *did* you find me?" I asked, taking a cigarette out of my pocket. Cromarty immediately seized it.

"When I didn't get an answer at your place, I telephoned Lincoln Drummond. I was on my way to Exmouth on foot when I saw you climbing the Cathedral steps. At first I didn't think it was you because you were walking like a zombie in a trance."

"Nice to see you too, Doc."

"Don't interrupt. The good news is that Hardfield's lifted your suspension. As of today you're on active duty again. Besides, Hardfield told me that he's been aware all along that you never did hand in your badge and identification. Maybe that stuffed shirt knows you better than you think, Jack."

"Hah, he should, he has me surveiled enough," I fumed. "Why the turnaround? He would've skinned me alive if it wasn't against Canadian law."

"I don't know. He sounded distracted and, if I'm not mistaken, scared."

The sun came streaming through the stained glass window, bathing the pew in purple, burgundy, and gold light. It startled and hushed us.

"Scared?" I whispered.

Doc Cromarty stood up. He brushed the front of his new suit with the palms of his hands as if it had been contaminated by the refracted light of the stained glass window. I followed as he marched to the front entrance and pushed open the heavy door.

Outside, on the wide steps leading down to Waterloo Street, he gave me back the cigarette. I stopped to light it, inhaling the first drag like a true slave to Mother Tobacco.

"Hardfield wants us to go to Sullivan's home," Cromarty said.

"Sullivan's home? Sully separated from Dorothy four years ago. He lives in a heated flat not far from me down on Victoria Street," I said, steering Cromarty toward the Pontiac. "This is mine."

The Doc looked at me as if I was the Prince of Car Thieves. When we were seated in the car, I added, "For a day or two. It's a demonstrator. But I'm gonna keep it."

"It's swanky, Jack, but somehow I can't picture you in anything new."

"Yeah, the Studebaker was a '35 Dictator– God rest its trusty soul," I said, wheeling into traffic. I tried the radio and got a dial full of stations, finally zeroing in on a swing tune.

I turned right onto Union Street and headed for the North End. Sullivan's home had to mean Victoria. The slob had a nice wife and three bright kids in a house he bought on Elliot Row but he hadn't darkened the threshold there in three years. Not since the time he showed up with a moving van and took some of "his" furniture to the doghouse he inhabited.

I applied the brakes at the railway crossing by Union Station. Good new brakes as tight as a miser. A string of freight trains and flatcars seemed to take an hour to roll past. Cromarty was unusually quiet. Finally, the caboose went through the intersection, a brakeman swinging up and onto the stairs.

It wasn't like Cromarty not to comment on the women walking along the sidewalk, let alone ignore them.

I said, "What's the matter, Doc? Cat got your tongue?"

"I was thinking about Hardfield, how nervous he sounded on the telephone. Ever since, I've felt a foreboding. And why has he got me consorting with you?"

"Doc, I don't know. Christ, I'm sorry I said anything. You got me nervous now."

And he had. Hardfield and I were direct opposites. He hated me and I hated him. That was about the only thing we agreed on. Now here he was reinstating me three weeks early and getting me to go to Sullivan's before Sully's jaw was even mended. A forced reconciliation for the sake of department morale? Maybe. But foreboding wasn't something I was susceptible to and neither was Cromarty. That worried me. The Doc was often gruff but always in command of his emotions. Except with the opposite sex and there he was a fool for love.

We parked in front of Sullivan's. A pair of veteran patrolmen were jawing in a black-and-white that blocked the driveway. They saw me and tried to hide their bottles of Seven-Up and bologna sandwiches. I waved, motioning for them to roll down the window.

"At ease, you birds," I said. "I know it's past your teatime."

They laughed with their mouths full, a couple of right jolly old elves. I snatched a cookie out of a package on the dash. Cromarty just stood there on the sidewalk with that look.

That look.

The officer behind the wheel handed me a set of keys. "Sergeant Sullivan's. The Deputy Chief wants you to let yourself in."

"Oh, yeah?" I said, stealing another ginger snap. "Where is Hardfield?"

"He flew the coop maybe an hour ago. White as a ghost, he was. What the frig's goin' on, Sarge?"

I glanced at Doc Cromarty. That look, again. "Don't know, Butch. What did Hardfield say to you?"

"Told us to stay put till you and some other guy showed, then we was to take orders from you. Is that the fella?"

I nodded. Foreboding turned into dread.

"Who's he?" the other cop asked.

"The coroner," I said.

The two officers looked at one another, then straight ahead.

I wondered if Cromarty's arrival on the scene usually had this grim effect on people, a sense that something was terribly wrong.

"Stay here," I said, "until I say different."

They said, "Right, Jack," quietly and at the same time.

We squeezed by the squad car and went into Sullivan's yard. A boy of twelve or so was shovelling the snow in carefully carved-out blocks, which he nonchalantly pitched over the neighbour's fence. He'd progressed almost to the back steps, the path an architectural model of precise right angles. There were no tracks in the snow on the wooden stairs attached to the rear of the house. I watched as the boy set the shovel aside and swept the snow off the sheltered stairs with a broom. He'd seen us waiting but made no attempt to hurry.

Cromarty said, "A capable boy," in a sarcastic voice.

The kid came down the steps three at a time, adept as an escape artist. "Do you know where Mr. Sullivan is?" he asked.

"Home," I said.

"No, he ain't. Or he's soused and ain't answering the door," the boy said, wiping sweat off his brow. "He's supposed to pay me."

Cromarty climbed the stairs and surveyed the yard next door from the vantage point of the second-storey landing. I could hear a couple of housewives gossiping while they were hanging out clothes, the pulleys squawking like alarmed blue-jays. The ladies must've been pretty because for a few minutes Cromarty seemed alive to the outer world again.

I flipped the kid a fifty-cent piece.

He looked at the coin as if it was the Kohinoor diamond, then slowly closed his fingers around it.

"Do you live around here?" I asked.

"Acrossed the street," he said warily.

"See anyone calling on Sullivan lately?"

"When?" The boy buried the 50¢ piece inside a Roy Rogers wallet that zippered on three sides.

"Today. Yesterday. Whenever." I lit a smoke which the kid followed with his eyes. The small fist around the money had been nicotine-stained. A sorry sight.

"Those mugs out front and the other cop."

"The other cop?"

"The guy who comes here all the time but in clothes. I seen him today in a uniform. The others saluted him like he was a bigwig."

I took an extra deep drag on my cigarette. A capable boy. A most capable boy. "Does he come at night or in the morning?"

"In the morning 'bout the time I'm delivering papers. Six, six-thirty."

"Are you sure it's him?" I said. The boy was frail and sickly for all his apparent toughness. Dark rings circled his eyes, eyes that didn't get enough sleep. He probably had three or four odd jobs like a lot of other boys around his age in the neighbourhood.

"I got good peepers," he said indignantly, tired of questions. Fed-up with yet another authority figure.

"Okay, I believe you. Now, make yourself scarce."

The boy shouldered the shovel and broom. "I'm supposed to do out front too," he said. "It's bad enough I had to wait till after school to get here but I'll lose the job for sure if I don't do it all."

"I'll fix it," I said. "Go on, scram. And don't come back today."

I lingered on the shovelled path between the straight walls of the snowbanks until I finished my cigarette. The only footprints leading into the house were on the front walk. Hardfield's army issues. It had stopped snowing in earnest just before sun-up so he would've been the only person to come and go since at least late last evening. I don't know why it mattered but it seemed to be important.

"Can we get on with it?" Cromarty said from above, his breath visible under the shadow of the porch roof. Even without an overcoat he never felt the cold. Diet, he said. Garlic and onions. Carrot juice and plenty of tropical fruit.

I took my time going up the stairs. The two women next door fell silent, watching us as if we were well-dressed burglars with stolen keys.

"You got a weakness for housewives who tie their hair up in bandanas, Doc?" I said.

"The mysterious domestic arts," Cromarty said. "Tell me, why would they wear lipstick to hang out the clothes?"

I glanced over at them. He was right. And those ruby red lips were freshly painted. "Dunno. Must've seen us coming."

The back door opened into a woodshed and had a Yale lock. I inserted the key and gave it a turn. There was resistance of some kind on the other side. I tried again, this time shoving hard. The door jogged open far enough for us to step inside.

Doc Cromarty waved a hand overhead in the dark until he found a string dangling from the ceiling. The instant the light bulb came on we stepped toward one another in fright.

Sullivan owned a purebred boxer named Duke. The dog was hanging off the knob of the Yale lock, held fast by the throat with naked wire. The animal's tongue and eyes protruded hideously. Scratch marks where he had struggled in vain to save his life scarred the back of the door, bare wood vivid against the brown paint.

I pushed aside the sawhorse that had prevented the door from opening all the way. Cromarty severed the wire with a pair of pliers he picked up off the workbench. He laid the dog on the floor and placed a burlap sack over its body.

It didn't take much figuring to guess that the sawhorse had been used as a makeshift scaffold with the door as a kind of vertical trap. The wire had been twisted like a noose and attached to the lock and in similar fashion around the dog's neck. Then the door would've been slammed shut. Duke was always a big friendly sap who loved to be handled. I almost sobbed when I thought about how trusting he would've been.

"This isn't your average garden variety cruelty – it's sadism," Cromarty said. "That poor dog died a slow, agonizing death."

I inspected the wire. It occurred to me that the very pliers the Doc used to release the dog had been employed to make the hangman's noose. Whoever had done the task was sadistic. Yes. And patient. Enjoying the work at hand. It made me shudder. And it made me not want to enter Sullivan's flat for fear of what awaited us there.

I sat beside Cromarty on the sawhorse, both of us shaken by our discovery. I lit a cigarette while he tamped tobacco into his briar pipe. It had already been too long a day for me. I was near exhaustion and now it seemed the worst was yet to come. A match glowed and the Doc's fragrant mixture filled the shed, the aroma reminding me more of fusty men's clubs than a place of death.

CHAPTER THIRTY-TWO

T HE NEXT THING I knew, Doc Cromarty took the skeleton key from my hand and opened Sullivan's kitchen door. I was angry but calm. Angry at every sicko on earth, every twisted creep who could torture a person or a dumb animal.

Cromarty knocked his pipe against a heel of his big brogues then clenched the empty briar between his teeth. He put an arm in front of me, barring the way before I could enter. "Age before beauty," he said. All things considered, I guess we were both pretty calm.

Sun shone through the windows over the sink, a sink full of last year's dirty dishes. A green and gray substance was growing on what might have been left-over macaroni and cheese. It was that strange fungi that gives off an antiseptic smell; the cleansing side of corruption.

There was another odour though, coming from somewhere inside. I couldn't quite put a finger on it. But it was vaguely familiar. And nauseating. Cromarty caught a whiff about the same time I did and stopped dead in his tracks. We were standing in what seemed the brightest sunlight of a long winter. Some other time the heat on my face would've suggested a late afternoon nap.

Sullivan's cuckoo clock went off like some loony bird in a Warner Brother's cartoon. I reached over and grabbed the counter-weights, stifling the cockamaimie thing in mid-cuckoo. There was silence but for the hiss and static of a radio tuned to a weak signal. That would be the ultra-deluxe number in which Sully had practically invested his life savings. It was a floor-model cathedral that could haul in stations from around the globe. When we were on friendlier terms we used to listen to Irish music from Dublin every St. Patrick's Day.

Cromarty, sweating at the temples, undid his necktie. I'd never seen him so self-contained. He stepped into the living room. The curtains were drawn across the big window, leaving the room dim, dozing in a hazy half-light. Furniture was tossed left, right, and centre. A table lamp had been smashed on the floor, shards of pottery and tangled wire marking the spot. The bulb hadn't broken and was still alight inside the crumpled lampshade.

I unplugged the lamp cord and clicked off the radio. The band was tuned to an overseas station. Consulting the map on the console cover, I determined exactly where. Cromarty cleared his throat, impatient at my stalling tactics. I went to his side and together we slid open the paneled doors to the dining room.

What greeted our eyes was an unholy nightmare. The scent turned out to be dried blood, the odour of the killing floor. It was splattered everywhere as if it had been shot out of a squirt gun.

I sincerely felt like uttering "Saints preserve us" and blessing myself but I'd already committed enough sacrilege for one day.

Cromarty let out a world-weary sigh as sorrowful and resigned as Methuselah. He touched my arm. "Stay still for a minute."

I didn't move a muscle. Sullivan lay on his back on top of the dining table, trussed to it with baling wire. Again, that noose connecting the loose ends. There was a tea towel over his face, a silly thing with shamrocks and leprechauns and a stupid pot of gold. Sully was dressed in dungarees and a red flannel shirt – his deer hunting outfit. His feet were bare, soles facing me. When my eyes adjusted better to the light I realized they'd been burned – X's seared into both heels. A poker from the coal fireplace he kept lit seven months of the year was obscenely propped between his legs.

I held onto the doorframe with one hand and dug out a cigarette with the other. Sully wouldn't have minded. Cromarty snapped his fingers for one so I tossed him the pack. He struck a match and inhaled, letting out the smoke in a steady stream, then threw the pack to me in a perfect arc. After a few minutes spent staring at the tea towel he lifted it by the corners. The expression on Doc's face hadn't changed until now. He winced very slightly, almost as an afterthought, and replaced the tea towel.

I turned on the light fixture above the table, startling Cromarty quite a bit. He was examining Sullivan's arms, cigarette held between his teeth. Taking another deep drag, he crushed out the butt in an ashstand. It occurred to me, not for the first time, that he was disturbing potential evidence at a crime scene but I wasn't about to say anything. If I had, I'm sure my voice would've faltered.

Ever since we entered the room my heart had been beating like a bird trapped in a cage. With an effort, I got hold of myself and returned to that strange calm I'd felt in the woodshed. Once a thing was done, it was done. What remained was to do something about it. I vowed then and there that I'd get the inhuman bastards who killed Sullivan come hell or high water.

I went to the table and removed the poker from between Sullivan's legs. There were bits of blackened skin and hair stuck to the business end. I almost gagged.

"Shouldn't you wait for the photographer before you move anything?" Cromarty asked. His voice sounded disembodied, as if it came out of an old-time wax cylinder.

I was trying to control my emotions, blood pounding in my ears like a kettle drum. Thrusting the poker into the dead coals to wipe it clean, I dislodged something that fell through the grate onto the hearth.

"Shouldn't you…" Cromarty said, bending nearer.

"I don't want anybody else to see Sully this way," I said, kneeling and raking the object closer with the poker.

Doc Cromarty knelt beside me. Perhaps we should've done that in the Cathedral earlier. It might've dispelled the awful feeling I had that we'd walked into a room where devils had done their damnedest. But deep down I wasn't all that superstitious. We were after men, demonic maybe, but men after all.

Cromarty took a pair of tweezers out of his pocket and picked up the object. It was made of metal and glass, melted into a shapeless glob. "God Almighty, Jack. I've never seen anything to surpass this," he said. "Do you know what this is?"

"No, but I've got a feeling you're going to tell me."

"It's a hypodermic syringe."

"Is that why you were looking at Sullivan's arms?" I said, wanting to sit but I couldn't find a chair that wasn't splattered with blood.

"Yes. Let's go into the other room. For now, I've seen all I need to see here. I'll find out more when I do the autopsy."

Cromarty took me by the elbow and urged me toward the sliding doors.

I stepped backwards and stood over Sullivan.

"Don't," Cromarty said as I moved to lift the tea towel. "Don't."

"I want to see his face," I said. "He might've turned shifty the last few years but he used to be my partner."

"Then brace yourself, Jack."

For once I wish I had listened. Sullivan's face was bluish-white, his mouth stuffed with a handkerchief to muffle his screams. There were needle marks on his neck. But his eyes were the worst. They were charred holes, black with coagulated blood. I gasped and dropped the tea towel back in place.

We slid the doors closed. I set a pair of chairs upright and sat down amidst the wreckage of the living room. Before Cromarty could notice I used my hand to erase a footprint in the cigarette ashes spilled on the floor. It was the imprint of a woman's ski-boot, size 7. I didn't know what to make of it and, for the time being, I didn't want anybody else wondering.

"What do you think, Doc?" I wanted to scream bloody murder on every street corner in town but I already knew we'd have to hush this up. It was too deliberate. Too much a ritual killing.

Brushing dust off his new suit, Cromarty thought for a minute. "Torture is the first thing that comes to mind."

"Torture? What for?"

"The usual," Doc looked straight at me. "Information."

"But who?"

"I don't know. Whoever it was had a rudimentary knowledge of the arterial system and an exemplary knowledge of terror. Pure terror. Jack, I think they used the hypodermic to drain blood out of Sullivan 100cc's at a time, squirting it around the room in full sight of the man. Combined with a red hot poker applied to the genitalia and feet, any normal person would give up their own mother under the circumstances."

My privates shrank. For a moment the room seemed pervaded by an evil I could feel in my guts.

Cromarty massaged his forehead. "You don't suppose there would be any tea or coffee here?"

I went into the kitchen and found a packet of Red Rose tea, then I put the kettle on the hot plate. The appliance was brand new. Just like the top-of-the-line refrigerator. And the electric coffee percolator. I shut off the hotplate. The percolator had never been used so I decided to give it a try. The Doc didn't care if I puttered for a while. I knew he asked me to fix hot drinks to give me something to do. To get my mind off Sullivan. But it didn't work.

Sullivan's alimony was stiff to the extent of impoverishment, yet all around me were signs of affluence. Newly acquired. A light bulb came on over my head. I knew Sully kept his spare cash in a sugar bowl because that's where he went whenever he lost bets we made on ball games. When it came to wagering Sully was funny/peculiar, a supporter of hopeless underdogs. Sentimental to a fault.

The coffee was perking softly, the most soothing thing I'd heard all day. Attracted by the aroma, Cromarty came into the room just as I removed the lid of the sugar bowl.

"What is it?" he said, extracting a couple of mugs from the sink and rinsing them under the tap. Like an overgrown kid he dried them on the curtains.

I pushed the sugar bowl along the countertop. "Have a gander."

Cromarty took a roll of twenties out of the sugar bowl and didn't stop counting for a long time. "Seven hundred and sixty dollars. That's a lot of money for a rainy day."

"Yeah, some rainy day."

"How's your bank balance? Are police detectives hauling down this kind of money?" Cromarty said, twisting an elastic band back around the wad. He stuffed it into the sugar bowl and handed it to me.

"Are you joking? You know better," I said. "Half the force moonlights. Guys come to work baggy-eyed and half asleep. If you're a flatfoot you're not exactly on the road to riches."

"Well, how did Sullivan amass such a sum? The bingo jackpots aren't that good even at St. Peter's," Cromarty said. Being a Protestant, he considered gambling the foundation of the Catholic Church. The one true faith.

"Maybe under the G for Greed." I was surprised at how surprised Cromarty was.

"Let me put it this way – I don't think Sullivan saw into the future and collected his life insurance policy early."

Doc poured the coffee then went to the refrigerator. It was so recently acquired there was only a quart of milk and a pound of butter in the gleaming interior. In the slovenly kitchen the new appliances stood out like diamonds in a dustbin.

"Somebody must have heard or seen something, Jack. Who lives downstairs?"

I tried a mouthful of coffee. It was as good as regular perked. "No one. It used to be the landlord's mother's place but since she died he hasn't rented it. The blinds have been drawn for three years."

"And upstairs?"

"Landlord's aunt. She spends the winters in Florida."

"A ghost and a snowbird. That's not much help."

The telephone rang and we both just about jumped. I spilled coffee on the floor but when I wiped the area with a dish-rag all it did was leave a clean streak on the linoleum.

Laughing nervously, Cromarty picked up the receiver. His expression changed from chagrin to professional seriousness as he repeated a solemn yes several times. The colour drained from his face. It made his rusty hair redder and his freckles multiply before my eyes. He hung up the phone then stood with a faraway look at the window. After a few minutes of loud silence he resumed drinking his coffee. "Not bad," he said quietly. "How about a cigarette?"

I lit two and handed him one. "You and Lincoln. I don't get it."

"Get what?"

"Huffing the butts. It has to be more than nerves."

"I suppose," Cromarty said, returning to the living room.

I refilled my cup and followed. He was leaning against the bookcase, having cleared away enough debris to set down his coffee and an ashtray. A hand covered his mouth and the glow from the cigarette turned it orange. "That was Hardfield on the line. He wants this mess cleaned up."

"Cleaned up?"

Cromarty kicked a wastebasket against the wall, sending the contents flying. "Yes. We...you and I are to handle it personally. No one else is to be involved. When I make the appropriate phone call a hearse will arrive from the funeral parlour for Sullivan's remains."

"What? No autopsy?" I mumbled, head crowded with thoughts. That awful feeling of dread returned – walked right into the room like an uninvited guest.

"No autopsy. Hardfield has a report prepared and I'm to sign it. We are to do as he says 'without fail or suffer dire consequences'," Cromarty said, pulling a sofa chair onto its feet. I didn't like the resignation in his voice. It wasn't like him to be bullied into anything. Especially regarding his duties as coroner.

"What about the funeral people?" I said, helping him flip the overturned chesterfield. It was new and made of leather and had hardly ever been sat in. I fixed that. Sitting down, I repeated the question.

"They're in Hardfield's pocket," Cromarty said. "As silent as the graves they plant coffins in."

"This has been done before?" I said, maybe too angrily.

Cromarty shrugged. He went to the bookcase and took a haul off the cigarette. "In gory suicide cases."

"Such as?" I persisted.

"Men who blow their heads off with shotguns. It's done to protect the next of kin. I had a case last year of a man who attached wires to his wrists and ankles and electrocuted himself. The result was ghastly."

"Okay. Enough already. Doc, before you start to wax poetic remember that Sullivan's in the next room and *he* didn't take his own life."

"I know that, Jack," Cromarty yelled. He seemed frustrated and hurt.

I felt like an idiot. "I'm sorry, Doc. I apologize. But what's this humbug about cleaning up? It's more like covering up."

Cromarty sat beside me. The new leather creaked whenever he spoke. "Hardfield is the party responsible. Put the question to him. Until then, well…" He inspected his cigarette as if it were full of answers. "You said it wasn't like me to smoke these. Well, you're right, it is more than nerves. I can't explain it but I feel that we're being inexorably drawn into something beyond our control. Something far-reaching and complicated, that won't unravel easily."

"That's reassuring. You're a real barrel of laughs." While we'd been sitting the sun had gone down, leaving us in near darkness. I switched on the overhead lights and looked around. "All right, Angus. I'll do what I can in here but don't ask me to help you with Sullivan."

Cromarty stared. I didn't often call him by his first name. "Fair enough. I'll need rags, a bucket of hot water, and a pair of clean sheets."

I nodded and did as he asked. After that I put the room back in order and swept up the broken glass. I was in a mental fog. Nothing seemed real. Nothing but the ache in my heart.

I talked to Cromarty through the closed sliding doors, informing him that I was leaving. He croaked, "Yes, see you tomorrow," and that was that.

In the kitchen I placed the electric percolator and the sugar bowl in a shopping bag. The money would go to Sullivan's wife and kids. It was probably dirty but they were clean. The coffee percolator was mine. A kind of trophy as a reward for all the ignorant digs I'd endured from Sullivan. Any one of which I'd be glad to hear from him now. If only.

Outside, in the cold evening I gazed above the rooftops. Stars shone in an inky firmament.

I dismissed the squad car and carried my booty to the Pontiac. While I waited for the engine to warm up I listened to music on the radio. It was one of those smoldering love songs so popular with the younger set. The last station tuned in on Sullivan's radio probably didn't broadcast such degenerate trash.

CHAPTER THIRTY-THREE

I PARKED THE Pontiac in front of St. Peter's steps and walked the stone's throw from there to my place. Snow was piled high on both sides of the path. The churchyard was about the only area in the neighbourhood plowed free of deep drifts. It was a beautiful winter evening but all I could think of was Sullivan.

Earlier, I'd been too shaken-up to think straight. Now, as I put the key into the front door, questions haunted me like ghosts. Who? And why? If I figured out why, I'd have the who. But I'd never seen anything like the torture chamber at Sullivan's. Never in my life imagined such a hell on earth.

Dragging my feet on the carpet, I went upstairs step by weary step. Too tired to hang them up, I dumped my outer clothes in a heap in the hall.

In the parlour, there was a lamp on beside the gramophone and wisps of cigarette smoke hung in layers in the room. Someone had tidied up the disorder Lincoln created while searching for my funeral arrangements. Probably Lincoln himself or my father. Anyway, I must have just missed whoever was here. Thankfully, they left the thermostat turned up so that the radiators were warm to the touch. I stood with my rear glued to the rad by the front window and lit a cigarette. The heat worked its way into my sore muscles, but I was still wound up tighter than a watchman's clock. It was only nine-fifteen on what seemed an eternal day.

I toted the shopping bag into the kitchen and stored the money in an empty shortbread tin, carefully hiding it in plain sight among some others in the pantry. If I was a bad actor I could take the money and pay cash for my new Pontiac but the percolator was my limit. And I felt guilty enough about that to go to Confession. Well… not quite.

Silence ruled the roost except for the plip-plop of the kitchen faucet. I felt a sudden chill. I needed a fire in the range. Maybe if I got a good blaze going and lay down on the cot near the stove I'd be able to get some shut-eye.

The comforting sound of kindling crackling in the stove must have set me off because I took to weeping once the fire got started. Sullivan and I had known one another since we were mouthy little punks running around the East End. We'd had our quarrels but we always shared a loyalty to the past that kept us from drifting too far apart. That is, until the last couple of years when for no reason I could figure Sully had grown antagonistic. And took to spying on me with no apparent motive other than driving me into the nuthouse.

I put an extra quilt on the cot, crawled under the covers, and cried into the pillow like an orphan. I slept until dawn, awakening with thoughts of Penny. Where was she? My wife used to call her Fairchild the Intrepid. I hoped Grace was right.

Sunlight penetrated the front window and beamed through the hall, bouncing off the linoleum beside the cot. Sleepily, I reached out as if I could catch the rays in my fist.

Tossing the blankets aside, I got up and built another fire then prepared a pot of coffee. I wasn't someone who quite trusted new-fangled gadgets, but even in my jaundiced view the electric percolator was a dandy rig. As for the noise it made, I didn't mind because with each chug-chug it released a steamy puff of coffee aroma. It gave the apartment a cozy and welcoming smell.

When the stove started kicking out so much heat I thought it'd set my bathrobe on fire, I put in a couple of chunks of hardwood and turned the damper down. The news would be on in a few minutes. I wondered if they'd say anything about Sullivan. I clicked on the mantel radio in the kitchen and hunted for a cigarette. An obnoxious song later, I raised the volume to Loud. It didn't take long to get to Sullivan. "Yesterday, a North End man, Detective Sergeant Francis Xavier Sullivan, a twenty-year veteran of the Saint John Police force, passed away suddenly at home. Mr. Sullivan lived alone. He is survived by his wife, the former Dorothy Cummings, and three children. In other local news…"

I killed the broadcast. So that was it – "Passed away suddenly". They might as well have spelled out s-u-i-c-i-d-e. It amounted to the same thing. It angered and made me more determined than ever to seek justice for Sullivan's murder.

I had just finished rotating the stove-grate when I heard someone behind me. Brandishing the crank, I spun around.

"The coffee smells frightfully good, Jack."

My mouth hung open a mile. Standing barefoot in the kitchen doorway, dressed in nothing but my flannel pyjama top, Penny smiled a smile of relief. Her hair was tousled, falling onto her shoulders, partially hiding a garish bruise that ran the width of her forehead. There was an ugly blue shiner under her right eye. Despite her injuries I couldn't help thinking she looked beautiful.

Choked-up, I said, "It's grand to see you. Where have you been?"

She padded across the floor and kissed me on the lips. "It's a long story. Most of it a bad dream."

Penny was still warm from the bedclothes. I placed a couple of chairs in front of the stove, sat her in one, stripped a blanket from the cot to cover her legs, and filled two mugs with coffee. "Were you here all night?" I asked.

"Yes. I don't think I've ever slept as soundly."

"So you did the housekeeping in the front room?"

"And Lincoln. He didn't know where you'd gotten to. I was knackered. And too frightened to go home. Maybe I should have left a note. I was sure you'd find me asleep in your bed."

"I was exhausted and half-crazed when I came home. I slept on the cot. After seeing Sully my bedroom would have been too dark."

"So it's true," Penny said.

"What?"

"The radio. Sullivan's dead?"

"Yes. He ended it all. Himself."

"My God, Jack. What is going on?"

"I wish I knew. Somebody's shadowing me. They must think I'm onto something. I don't know what. I can't tell you any more than that, Penny."

I felt like a first-rate slob for prevaricating, but Penny had been through enough of an ordeal and didn't need to be any more frightened. If anything, she could probably tell me a few things I needed to know. "Fred Quinlan told me your story," I said, "but I'd like to hear it in your own words. Would you mind?"

"No. But after the Studebaker went off the road and I was thrown clear, everything fades in and out. I may not be of much help."

"That's all right, Penny," I said, getting up to fix bacon and eggs. It'd be best if I didn't watch her too closely. "I'll make breakfast and you relax. Start before the accident, okay?"

"Fine," Penny said, reaching over to the table for a cigarette. She lit it and exhaled thoughtfully.

"It had snowed like the dickens for two days," she said," but on the day I planned on leaving for Fredericton the skies were crystal clear and the weather report promised no more snow. Famous last words. I was on the road for perhaps an hour when the first flakes started falling. And to make matters worse the car heater went on the blink. It was damned cold. I nearly turned back then. Would that I had."

"How come you didn't?" I said, breaking three eggs into a bowl.

"I pulled over to the side of the road, fully intending to, but then I remembered your greatcoat and stocking hat in the back seat. The sky wasn't terribly overcast so I decided to carry on."

"Where were you then?"

"Perhaps ten miles past Westfield."

"Wearing my hat and coat?"

"Yes. Virtually wrapped up in them. And I had the Indian blanket over my legs."

"What was the traffic situation?" I asked.

"I saw a snowplow and several lumber trucks. That was all until I was on the River Road motoring toward Fish-Hawk Bluff."

"Where you went off?"

"Yes. A car came out of nowhere, overtook me, and disappeared in a whirl of snow. But the next thing I knew it was coming back toward me on my side of the road. And there was a big log obstructing the other lane. I applied the brakes but they were mushy."

"Mushy?"

"Well, you know, soft. They were hardly grabbing."

"And then?"

"I swerved to avoid a head-on collision, slewed, and lost control of the car. It went crashing down through the bushes, struck something solid, at which point I went flying out of the door, cartwheeling through the air and over a cliff into the deep snow."

"Jumpin' Jesus. It's a miracle you weren't killed. If you'd stayed in the car it would've been curtains for sure. You would've drowned."

Penny shivered as if she had been dipped in ice-water. She huddled deeper into the blanket. "How did you know where I was?"

"An educated guess. Tell me about the three men the Quinlans told me you saw," I said.

"They were wearing parkas so I couldn't see their faces and they weren't saying anything. Very businesslike. I tried to cry out to them for help but I fainted and fell back into the snow."

"Cry out?"

"Well, I didn't suspect them of any wrongdoing, Jack. It wasn't until after I came to and discovered my luggage missing that I knew something was seriously awry."

"What about them blocking the road?"

Penny eyed me with what could be taken for contempt. "I thought they might have been warning me about trouble ahead."

"Trouble ahead, all right," I said, wondering aloud.

"Jack, I don't appreciate this cross-examination. You must know all this if you've spoken with Mr. and Mrs. Quinlan."

"Now, now," I said, somewhat irritated myself. "I'm just searching for some detail that might…"

"Detail!"

"Was the car new? Old? Were the men big? Small?"

"The car was three feet long and the men were a foot high and hailed from Mars. Satisfied?"

I didn't dare laugh. "Are you always like this before breakfast?" I asked. "Come on, let's eat."

I toasted two slices of raisin bread and put a jar of shredded marmalade on the table. When everything was ready, Penny was sulking. "Look, let's bury the hatchet," I pleaded. "And not in one another, okay? I act like a heavy-handed lug sometimes but it's only because I want to solve something. To get to the bottom…"

"I know, Jack. I'm sorry. My nerves are frayed. When you weren't here I didn't know what to do. I wandered around the North End for hours imagining all manner of terrible things. I wasn't even sure if you were safe. If perhaps something hadn't happened to *you*. After I saw Sullivan come out of here and spoke with him, I went into a sort of numb panic. Perhaps the after-effects of the concussion made me easily confused."

"Sully was here at my place?"

"Just leaving. I asked him if you were home and he merely glanced at me and kept walking past in a daze. I held him by the elbow and repeated the question. All he said was, 'We went too far. Got in too deep.' He looked absolutely dreadful."

"Did you go to Sully's place with him?"

"Goodness, no. Why would I do that?"

"I don't know. Someplace to go. Get in out of the weather." While I was cooking I'd spied Penny's ski-boots behind the stove. Without her noticing, I moved them closer to the heat. They were size 7. I was getting to the point where I didn't know whether to trust myself. I'd already smudged out evidence and otherwise withheld information. I watched Penny eating. She was ravenous but her table manners were as delicate as ever. Put her in an evening gown and she could've been an angel dining at the Ritz.

I banished my darkest thoughts and decided to believe her. After all, she was battered and bruised, prone to staring vacantly into a corner of the room as if she'd misplaced something she couldn't remember. Maybe she was having blackouts.

I reached across the table and touched her on the hand. For a moment it seemed she didn't know me. When her eyes focused, I said, "I'm going to take you to the doctor's for a check-up. You're not quite right."

"I was thinking about Sullivan. It's unbelievable."

I thought, You don't know the half of it. Or do you?, then regretted it. "Get dressed. I'll drop you off before I go to work."

"Work? Aren't you on suspension?" Penny said, stacking the dishes and carrying them to the sink.

"Leave those," I said. "The elves will do them while we're gone."

Penny laughed. "What happened to your suspension?"

"I was unsuspended. Now, hurry up and get ready. I'll take you for a ride in my new car."

"Really? What is it?"

"A Pontiac with a swell radio."

Penny went down the hall and into my bedroom. I had to follow her for a change of underwear and clothes. At the door, I said, "Are you decent?"

She turned toward me and dropped my pyjama top to the floor.

I stared without embarrassment. It was a new feeling for me to be at ease at the sight of a beautiful woman. Particularly a naked woman.

"Can you be late for work?" Penny asked.

I undid the belt on my robe. "I can be late."

CHAPTER THIRTY-FOUR

I WAS LATE for work. But, frankly, I didn't give a damn. At least one thing was right with the world and that was whatever Penny and I had going for us. I couldn't put a label on it but it just felt so right.

She climbed the granite steps to Dr. Jenning's first-floor office, pushed open the cut-glass door, and a second later passed the bay window to the receptionist's desk. The smell of bath salts and shampooed hair lingered in the car like a sweet promise.

I lit a cigarette and blew an O toward the dashboard. From where I was sitting the station was in clear view. Three constables were chatting behind the balustrade in front of the jail. The weather had turned mild, snow melting everywhere under the strong sun of late winter. I could, and should, report to Deputy Chief Hardfield right away but he would have to wait. Sullivan's money was in my overcoat pocket and I wanted to give it to his wife before too many relatives arrived at her house.

Penny gave me the high sign from Dr. Jenning's waiting room. It meant the doctor would see her and that I should go ahead instead of waiting to take her to Outpatients. Jennings was the department physician and an experienced specialist when it came to head injuries.

Rather than drive, it was just as convenient to leave the car and walk around the block to Dorothy Sullivan's. Penny watched as I got out of the Pontiac and promptly stepped into a pile of slush. Giggling, she discreetly blew me a kiss. I shrugged, shook my pantlegs, and winked. That's what comes of wearing my best suit.

Penny was dressed in some of Grace's casual clothes borrowed from a closet I hadn't opened since the hit-and-run accident. I suppose it was about time I leapt that hurdle. It turned out not to be so bad. Besides, Penny looked terrific in slacks, short coat, and plaid tam. A little out-of-date but that appealed to me, if for no other reason than it forced me to confront physical traces of my deceased wife. Deceased? My dead wife. There, I'd said it, *dead*. If to no one else at least to myself.

It was a cloudless morning, seagulls soaring in the high sky. The sun was warm, almost hot, so I unbuttoned my overcoat for ventilation while I walked. Water from the melting snow gleamed and sparkled as it coursed down the hill toward Union. I stopped on the corner of Carmarthen Street and Elliot Row and gazed over at the Loyalist Burial Grounds. It was too nice a day for the mournful business at hand.

I turned on my heels and headed for the Sullivans' place, five numbers from the corner. Their house was above the street, two flights of concrete stairs up from the sidewalk. Someone had sprinkled cinders on the steps.

Standing at the front door I could smell hops from the Red Ball Brewery on Union Street. Taking a deep breath, I pressed the bell. Gone was the polished brass Mr. & Mrs. F.X. Sullivan plaque, replaced by a green bakelite sign with white lettering that simply said Dorothy Sullivan.

Her mother answered the door. A dour grouch of a woman on her best days, she greeted me with unadulterated hatred. "What do you want?"

"Is Dot here? It's Jack Ireland."

"I know you," Dot's mother said, taking my hat and coat and flinging them onto a wicker rocker surrounded by Boston ferns the size of small shrubs. "She's in the parlour."

I followed the old crone. She slouched past the parlour and on toward the kitchen. Listening for voices before entering, I parted the heavy brocade curtains drawn across the opening. Dot was alone and didn't see me at first.

Without thinking, I lit a cigarette. The hiss of the match seemed to rouse her from a dream. She was still in housecoat and slippers. She'd put on lipstick and rouge and with her hair down looked younger than thirty-nine.

"Oh, hi. Jack, it's you," Dot said. "Got a spare fag? Mom doesn't know I indulge but that's just too friggin' bad, isn't it?"

I nodded, handed her my cigarette, and lit another. "How are you?"

"Awful," she said, puffing hard on the Philip Morris. "Still go for these Yankee smokes, eh?"

I sat down beside her on the divan. We didn't say anything for a long time. Two votive candles set in front of a picture of St. Bernadette flickered red on the side table. A dime-store crucifix was propped against the wall along with a bouquet of artificial roses. The arrangement was a heathenish blot. Dot's mother's doing. She was more pagan than Catholic. For the sake of the children, Dot paid a begrudging kind of lip-service to the Church, keeping her anti-clerical opinions submerged.

"Where are the kids?" I asked.

"I sent them to school," Dot said. "That might seem hard-hearted but they hardly knew their father. Anyways, it'll keep them out of the clutches of Mom's people when they start arriving."

I loosened my necktie, the only solid-coloured one I owned.

"Geeze, Jack, you look nice when you dress up," Dot said.

"Instead of dressing down?"

"You said it, not me."

Dot rose and went to the china cabinet. "I got a pint of Boodles Gin that's been in here for five years." She placed two whiskey glasses on the table in front of me and filled them to the rim. "Waiting for a special occasion." Her voice broke when she said special.

I made her sit down. "Take it easy, Dot."

"Easy? It hasn't been easy these last years."

"I know." And I did know. An attractive woman separated from her husband had to bear the brunt of too much idle gossip. Malicious speculation, and the unwanted advances of men who in their male vanity assumed she wanted only one thing.

Dot clinked her glass against mine. "Here's to Sully. A great guy. Once upon a time."

I didn't care for the bitterness. In Dot or in the gin. The pungent scent of juniper caught in my nostrils. "When did you find out about Sully?"

"Last night. I was listening to *The Jack Benny Show*. Having a good laugh, too," Dot said, taking a large mouthful of gin that made her shudder and a little breathless. "A real good laugh."

"Last night? Who came to see you?"

"Nobody. Hardfield telephoned."

"Christ. That was big of him. What did he say?"

Dot gave me a hard look, then she sat back and sighed. "I'd really like to know what's going on, Jack. Can you help me understand?"

"Understand what?"

Dot got up and started pacing the room. Before she wore out the carpet, I repeated, "Understand what?" Her eyes flashed. "Why is it that Sully – sonofabitch Sully – passes away suddenly at home of a heart attack and yet, and yet, oh Jesus, he's going to have a closed casket. *I'm* not even allowed to see him."

I lit a cigarette and stalled. Dot swooped and snatched it out of my hand. I lit another. I had foreseen the problem of a closed casket but for once I was at a loss for words. Maybe I hadn't expected Dot to be so aggressive. Or angry.

She spilled gin into the glasses and said, "Bottoms up."

I didn't say anything. In my mind's eye all I could see was the last, horrible glimpse I'd had of Sully's mutilated face.

"You know what that means, Jack. They might as well have chanted suicide over the f'ing radio. And just wait until the evening paper."

Trapped, I got to my feet and stretched. "I know the reporter who handles that stuff. He owes me one. I'll tell him it was in Sully's will that the casket be closed. He'll print whatever I dictate."

"Thanks. That'd be a great help."

"Well…"

"I'm sorry, Jack, honest. That sounded sarcastic. I didn't mean it to come out that way, but that sorry excuse for a priest, Father Mitchel, was here at the crack of dawn insinuating that Sully couldn't be buried in hallowed ground."

"Mitchel! Forget him, he's a twist. I'll phone him and if I have to I'll march up to the Cathedral and knock his stupid block off."

Dot laughed. "I wish you would anyway, just for the fun of it."

"It would be fun, wouldn't it?" I laughed. Mitchel was a fire and brimstone woman-hater who loved to terrify children with tales of the devil. I got a knot in my stomach just thinking about him.

Dot grew serious again. "Were you at Sully's yesterday?"

"Yes."

"Did you see him?"

"No. I got there after they took him away."

"You'd tell me, wouldn't you, Jack? If he killed himself? I need to know."

I placed my hands on her shoulders. "Sully didn't take his own life and he didn't die of any heart attack. That's between just you and me,

Dot. I'm only telling you this because we go back a long way and because I care about you."

"What did happen?"

I put a finger to my lips and stepped through the curtains and into the hall. The last thing I wanted was to have her mother eavesdrop on us. I needn't have worried. The old woman was still in the kitchen. She was listening to a game show, her ear pressed against the radio. The set was loud enough for the whole house to hear it. I returned to the parlour.

I went to Dot and said, "Sully was murdered. Killed instantly."

Dot gasped. "Who?"

"I don't know and I don't know why it's being hushed up. Someone's clamped a tight lid on the case. That's all I can tell you for now, Dot. Trust me, someday I'll let you know the rest. Okay?"

"Okay. You were always a good influence on Sully, Jack. But he took a wrong turn somewhere. These last years he was ashamed about something. And, of course, he wouldn't talk to me."

"I know, Dot. It must've been hell-on-earth for you."

"Truer words were never spoken. It's a relief to hear someone say it. You can't imagine how much of a relief."

Our eyes met and we fell silent. The room smelled of gin and smoke and dusty old furniture. Dot and I were chums as kids, running around the Albion Street playground till all hours. She always had great spirit and more energy than a locomotive. The spirit was still there but I wasn't sure about the energy anymore.

After a time I broke the silence. "I've got something for you, Dot. And I don't want you to spend a nickel of it on funeral expenses. Let the department cover those."

I handed Dot the money. She counted it in disbelief. "Jack, you keep this. I haven't got enough for a decent housedress, much less widow's weeds, but I can't take this."

"It's not mine, Dot. I wish it was. I found it at Sully's."

"In one lump sum?" Dot said. To my dismay she topped up the glasses, handed me one, and waited for an answer.

"That's an odd question."

"Not so, Jack. Sully said he'd have something extra for me around the end of the month. He phoned drunk as a lord one night last week. I couldn't make head or tails of what he was mumbling about but I do remember that. Cripes, Easter's not that far off. The kids need spring clothes."

I didn't say anything. Instead, I sipped the gin. It was starting to taste good. Dot was watching me the way she used to when we were teenagers and I was about to tell her something only boys were supposed to know. My mind had slipped into its police uniform. The end of the month suggested a reckoning: a balancing of accounts for services rendered. But for what? Sully always accepted minor favours. Hockey tickets, lunches, new socks. That kind of petty thing. But cash? That was something else again. Maybe that was the "too far, too deep," he'd babbled to Penny Fairchild.

If Dot tried any harder she'd stare a hole through me. I gently coughed smoke rings toward her mother's tawdry little shrine.

Dot smiled. "Secrets, Jack?"

"Puzzles."

She swallowed the gin and lit a cigarette off mine. Then she hid the money under some old snapshots in a chocolate box buried beneath the quilts in a trunk beside the fireplace. Replacing the throw, she sat down heavily on the trunk. "Whew. I guess I'm under the influence."

"Get something to eat," I suggested. "You're probably in for a long day."

I tightened the knot on my necktie. "By the way, Sully had a new refrigerator. I mean *new*. That and some other appliances. Do you want them?"

"I couldn't set foot in that place, Jack."

"No need to, Dot. I'll contact your brothers after the funeral's over. I'll wait a few days to let things settle down. Okay? Leave the timing up to me."

An old-fashioned car horn a-hoo-gawed twice down on the street.

"Grand. That'd be grand, Jack. Thanks for everything. Now you better scoot. That sounds like Harold's Model A. The whole gang will be here soon. Don't you just adore Irish wakes?"

"I don't like wakes, period. Lemme out, will you?"

Dot helped me with my overcoat. "Nice fedora," she remarked. "Green always suited you."

I put it on and snapped the brim smartly. "Thanks."

"Don't ever dye your hair, Jack. It looks good with that touch of gray." She brushed my cheek with her hand, eyes brimmed with tears.

I hugged her while she wept softly into my shoulder. My throat was raw with trying to be manly. Then we both cried. A small flood. When it was over I wiped my eyes with a handkerchief and gave it to Dot. It was monogrammed with my initials. I'd found a package of them in Grace's closet. They must've been a gift she never had a chance to give to me.

I declined the handkerchief when Dot offered it back. "Keep it. A memento," I said, opening the door. "Phone me if you need me for anything, Dot. Anything."

She watched me descend the steps to the lawn and cross over to the steep stairs that led down to the street. After the gin, a street that seemed very far below. There were four cars at the curb, each one packed with Sully's red-headed relatives. They started pouring onto the sidewalk, not one of them empty-handed. There'd be food enough for an army at Dot's before the noon whistle.

When I reached street-level, I nodded to the men and tipped my hat to the ladies. I turned and waved up to Dot. She fluttered the handkerchief like a flag of truce and yelled, "Don't walk under any ladders."

CHAPTER THIRTY-FIVE

I MEANDERED UP and down the walks of the Loyalist Burial Grounds for a good twenty minutes before I went to the station. I spotted Hardfield glaring out of his office window but I didn't care if he was waiting for me or not. He could get hotter than Hades under his starched collar and it wouldn't bother me today. Filled with gin and grief, I'd reached a place beyond anger where nothing could touch me.

The desk sergeant gave me an amiable handshake and a slap on the back. "Welcome back, Ireland. Somehow the old dump isn't the same without you around to stir up the proverbial."

"Thanks. I appreciate it. Any messages while I was away?"

The sergeant leaned into me and smelled my breath. "Whew. That's quite the aftershave. What is that? I'll have to get a jug."

I burped on cue. "Excuse. Boodles juniper juice. I called on Dot Sullivan."

A couple of older constables came out from behind the desk where they'd been checking the log book. "How is she?" one asked.

I removed my fedora and wiped the sweatband with my sleeve. "Dot's holding up pretty well. She's going to have a whack of Sully's relatives on her hands so it'd be good if a few of the men from the force were there to help out. Spread condolences and keep the drunks in line."

The desk sergeant said, "Consider it done. Can you tell us about Sully? What the bejesus happened?"

"Something godawful. The official word is heart attack. But no one's swallowing that hogwash. I've gotta phone Father Mitchel. That moron already made noises to Dot about not burying Sully in hallowed ground."

"Official? So what was it really?" one of the constables asked.

"Officially, it's heart attack. I already let out too much. So forget everything I said. Someday it'll all come out in the wash. Right now, Holy Mother Church is the problem. So, we make sure Sully's buried in the family plot by saying zero about his death. Once he's in his grave not even Father Mitchel would dare disturb his final resting place."

The three men regarded me in silence but with inquiring eyes. I knew I could trust them or I wouldn't have uttered a word. But I realized right then and there that I'd have to clam up from now on. It wasn't wise to involve anyone else, perhaps to place them in danger. Especially when I didn't know what was going on myself. It had been less than twenty-four hours since I'd seen the unholy horrors at Sullivan's and it was likely that the perpetrators were keeping tabs on me. A thought that sent icy fingers up and down my spine.

"See you gents later," I said to the men, then I went downstairs to the locker room.

The room was empty but someone had purposely left the hot-water tap dribbling so the sink would overflow. It was almost full. I ran over and unplugged it, drained half the water, then soaked my face and hands in an attempt to sober up. I had toothpaste and Old Spice in my locker that would help mask the gin.

I swung the door open and found my tube of Ipana had been squeezed in squiggles all over my spare jacket.

The padlock was gone from Sully's locker. I opened it. Someone had taken his belongings, including his Swedish nudist colony magazines. Maybe they could read Swedish. The locker was clean except for a bag of jam-filled doughnuts. Sully and his sweet-tooth. Damn. Damn it all.

I took the bag into the lunch room and put the doughnuts on a plate near the coffee pot. It was a crying shame, but I had a picture in my head of Sully grinning, mouth full, lips dusted with icing sugar. I smiled and felt a little better.

I drank a cup of coffee and ate two doughnuts. Someone had made a proper mess of my locker. Strangely, it was the type of practical joke that Sully used to pull. It could be an inside joke. Or an inside job. Anyhow, it spooked me. Maybe that was the point – a warning from someone with a sick sense of humour. And a sick mind.

I brushed the powdered sugar off my sleeve. It made me think of the ashes on Sully's living room floor and the footprint I rubbed out before anyone could see it. It matched Penny's ski-boots. I knew that in advance without having to double-check at my house. In my bedroom where Penny and I had...

"Here you be, Jack," the desk sergeant said. "I've been ringing down but the line's busy. Wait a second, the phone's off the hook."

TERRY CRAWFORD

"Don't look at me," I said. "I didn't touch the thing."

"Well, I'll be jiggered. Ain't that odd," the sergeant said, picking up a doughnut. "Never knew you to be one for sweets, Jack."

"Hungry all of a sudden," I said, hiccupping gin and jam filling.

"Deputy Chief wants you in his office, double-quick. It's nothing new, but he sounded steamed. Wondered what you were doing 'lolly-gagging around'."

I poured more coffee. "Lolly-gagging is my true calling in life. That's why I became a cop. So I could loiter and get paid for it."

The desk sergeant grinned. "You're too young to be a cynic, Jack."

"Yeah, and too old to be an optimist." I pushed my chair away from the table. "I better see what his royal-pain-in-the-ass wants."

The sergeant snickered, spitting bits of doughnut onto the floor. "Jack, you slay me."

I shut the lunchroom door behind me and stood in the corridor for a minute at the foot of the stairs. For a public building the station was poorly lighted and cheerless. There were times when I could almost hear the ghosts of jailbirds from the 1800s scrubbing the walls and floors in the murky half-light. I went up the stairs and into a slightly dimmer hallway, feeling somewhat like a prisoner myself. A prisoner of deep shadows and dark secrets.

I rapped a rhythmic rappity-rap-rap on Hardfields's gold-lettered door.

The old guard dog barked, "Enter."

The Deputy Chief was seated bolt-upright at his desk, mustaches quivering, the veins on his temples bulging like blue rivers. He tried to stare me down with those coal-black eyes as if he were a python hypnotizing a chicken. "What have you been doing, Ireland?"

I almost clucked. Gin and giggles. Clicking my heels together I saluted. "Lolly-gagging around, Sir." The words came out with true solemnity, if not sobriety.

"You were to report for duty this morning at eight o'clock sharp," Hardfield said. "I am not amused."

"I reported for duty yesterday, Sir."

Hardfield rolled his eyes but when he looked back at me they were glistening with fear. Sullivan's murder had terrified him to the depths.

"As you requested," I added. Then I boldly asked, "May I smoke?"

"If you must."

I reached inside my suit jacket.

"Try one of mine," a voice out of nowhere said.

I turned and saw a pair of brilliantly polished wingtips protruding from behind Hardfield's titanic filing cabinet. They belonged to a slinky fellow dressed in a light-brown summer suit. Beneath his ginger coloured hair, his face was sunburnt and peeling across the bridge of his very straight nose.

I stepped toward him and he produced a silver cigarette case with the initials W.H.

"That's if you can abide American," he said.

I took a cigarette and accepted a light from a small flame-thrower. It almost singed my eyelashes. "Thanks. I don't mind. As it is, I smoke Philip Morris."

We stood there and smoked as if we were tobacco connoisseurs at a cougher's convention. It was a custom blend, smooth-burning with a sweet aftertaste. But when I stepped back, a cloying aroma hung in the air. The scent of exclusivity, of private clubs and boardrooms. The executive privilege of the wealthy.

"Allow me to introduce myself. Name's Wilder Hunter. Friends call me Wylie."

His spidery fingers gripped mine so tightly that I knew it would be hard to shake him off if he didn't want to let go.

"Jack Ireland," I said. "Friends call me whatever they can get away with."

"Very good. I can tell we'll get along fine."

Hunter spoke with an accent that wasn't an accent. It was American all right, but it wasn't north or south, east or west. It was as flat and plain as the prairies. My guess was that he came from the heartland.

"Where are you from?" I asked. Hardfield joined us, nose twitching like a subordinate rat. He was obviously in awe of the easy-going American.

"Nebraska, but I went to college in Chicago. Little Catholic school name of Notre Dame. Ever hear of it?"

"Rings a bell," I said. Although my parents wanted me to become a teacher, college was never my idea of something to do. Too much rah-rah and shish-boom-bah. "What brings you to our fair city, Mr. Hunter?"

"Wylie, please. Or Wilder. I wasn't baptized Mister. It doesn't suit me."

"Wilder, then," I said.

Hardfield was about to speak but remained silent when Hunter raised a hand. It was as if the American had bestowed a blessing upon him. Such reverence was hard for me to tolerate.

"I'm with the C.I.C. – Army Branch. Your government has kindly allowed me to enter the country incognito in order that I might observe certain foreign nationals believed to be operational in this region."

Hardfield nodded. A man in the know. One of the anointed. I could've kicked him in the shins. Instead, I played the ignoramus. "C.I.C.?"

"Hang it all, man. Counter Intelligence Corp," Hardfield snapped.

Hunter adjusted the knot on his silk tie and this time raised both hands in benediction. "Please, Deputy Chief Hardfield, such acrimony is uncalled for. We're all gentlemen here, aren't we?"

Chastised, Hardfield quick-stepped around his desk and sat down hard enough to make himself grimace. He impatiently motioned us into chairs.

I faced Hunter. He was a relaxed customer but didn't seem arrogant or cocky for all his sureness. "Foreign nationals? What's the connection with us? Shouldn't you be talking to our Secret Service?"

"The Official Secrets Act forbids me to comment on that. However, we needn't be concerned with such matters. You are acquainted with a Norwegian freighter, the *Bergensfjord?*"

I glanced at Hardfield, who nodded. "I have been," I said cautiously.

"In what regard?" Hunter asked.

"There was a longshoreman, actually a shipping clerk, found dead in the hold a while ago. St. Valentine's Day."

Hardfield, never subtle, flinched as if I'd given the wrong answer.

Hunter noticed and seemed annoyed. At what it was hard to guess. "Dead? The circumstances?"

Hardfield bellowed, "What are you talking about, Ireland?"

"Eugene Robichaud, late of St. Patrick Street. Remember him?" I said bitterly. "Death by misadventure?"

"Yes. Yes. That matter is over and done with. An open-and-shut case, Ireland."

"Allow me to intervene," Wilder Hunter said, "before we get off on a tangent. You are aware of the National Socialists?"

My mouth must've fallen open a bit. I tried to recover by putting a cigarette into the gap. Hunter watched me light up and inhale.

"The Nazi Party?" he said.

I exhaled. "I'm alive and living on the planet Earth."

Hunter laughed. It was a laugh as flat and dry as his voice. "Touché. I deserved that. Anyhow, in a nutshell, we believe there are Nazis aboard the *Bergensfjord*. Members of a fifth column, if you like, intent on espionage and, not to be alarmist, possible sabotage in the event of war."

I could hardly contain my excitement at having my suspicions confirmed. "That's quite a nutshell."

"You appear taken aback," Hunter said. "It was our understanding that you already had prior knowledge of some of these individuals."

"*Our* understanding?"

Hardfield squirmed out of his chair and went to the window, eyes downcast. It was snowing again, big flakes whirling around in a white sky. I wanted another drink of gin. Chilled and with ice cubes.

Hunter's eyes narrowed. "The department's."

"Oh," I muttered. "You'll have to spell it out. The understanding, I mean."

"This travels no further than this room. It does not go beyond the three of us," Hunter said, calmly lighting a cigarette. He unfolded his long legs and dangled his arms between them like a rower at rest. He let everything drift for a minute, comfortable with the long silence.

"When you went aboard the *Bergensfjord* you came in contact with some of the men in question – no need to name names – and since then you've been in close proximity more than once."

I interrupted Hunter's careful monologue. "How do you know that? Or are you guessing?"

"We've had you under surveillance."

"Since when?"

"Valentine's Day."

"Why?"

"We've been monitoring the activities of these Nazis. Mind you, they're not doing anything illegal. That is, nothing that most seafaring men don't do while in port. Boozing, whoring around, that sort of thing..."

"Including beating derelicts half to death?"

Hunter didn't look up or move. "I can't and will not comment on that incident."

I wanted to add, "Ritual murder," but despite my anger knew better.

Hunter continued. "We're following their moves closely. They mustn't suspect that they are being observed. You, Ireland, have upset them for some reason. We want you to lay off."

"Why should I?"

Hardfield was still standing by the window, his meticulously brushed hair silhouetted against the snow squall. He seemed empty of emotion, not all there.

Wilder Hunter stood up and stretched his lanky frame, arms extended overhead in an odd stance of exaltation. "Because we have a man inside. All our painstaking work will have gone for nought if his true identity is somehow revealed as a result of your interference."

I was in a state somewhere between shock and bewilderment. Hardfield had a decanter in the bottom drawer of his filing cabinet. It was the worst kept secret in the station. Without ceremony, I went and splashed three stiff belts into the prissy glass tumblers he had and then passed them around. The liquor turned out to be an excellent Scotch.

CHAPTER THIRTY-SIX

I STEERED THE Pontiac around the corner and down Wentworth toward Union Street. The sudden snow squall had passed, leaving the city blanketed white beneath a blinding sun. I put the visor down and squinted through the windshield. The car upholstery smelled too new and untainted to suit me so I lit a cigarette. I was as unsettled as the weather.

Wilder Hunter crossed his legs and then his arms. He was staring at my hat as if trying to read the turbulent thoughts flying around beneath it. I glanced at him and he averted his eyes. He'd bummed a ride to his hotel because his car was in the garage for repairs. I was in the mood for driving somewhere, anywhere, alone but I couldn't say no.

"Mind if I ask you something?" he said.

"No, fire away."

"What's with Father Mitchel? Why get the Deputy Chief involved?"

"Why not?"

"You seem eminently capable of handling such a matter on your own," Hunter said without a hint of flattery. "Holy Mother Church or no."

"The Church and I reached a fork in the road years ago," I said. The Cathedral, on the high ground, loomed over the neighbourhood ahead. I nodded toward the spire, a towering spike in the underbelly of the sky. "Father Mitchel's a born tyrant but he's also the kind of man who joined the priesthood so he could wield the absolute power the Roman collar gives him over certain people. Mitchel would swallow his tongue before he'd give in to my requests."

"So I take it you're a lapsed Catholic?"

"More like collapsed."

Hunter laughed dryly. "Very good. Anyway, Hardfield played hardball when he threatened to withdraw any and all future police escorts for funeral processions emanating from the Cathedral."

"Yes." For a change, I was proud of Hardfield. "I didn't know he had it in him."

"Had what in him?"

"Guts. Intestinal fortitude. He usually lets someone else do his dirty work for him. Maybe he cared more about Sullivan than I thought."

I thought back to the kid shovelling snow at Sullivan's place and what he said about seeing Hardfield there more than once. Sully and the Deputy Chief had some kind of working relationship that superseded ordinary police work and I wanted to find out more. I'd have to return to the scene of the crime. A thing I dreaded.

"Why don't we stop somewhere and catch a bite," Hunter suggested. "I'm famished."

"That's an idea," I said, and pulled the car over in front of The Silver Rail. "This place isn't fancy but it'll do the trick."

The noon crowd, mostly shop clerks and office workers, was dispersing. We slid into a booth by the window. I liked to watch people coming and going. Union and Charlotte was a bustling corner in a busy uptown.

I ordered vegetable soup, a fish dinner, and raisin pie. Hunter decided on steak and potatoes. While waiting for the food, I vowed to ease off the booze. There was a rough road ahead. I'd need an alert mind and a body ready for any emergency. The smokes too would have to go, I thought, lighting one up. Well, maybe next year.

Hunter was sipping black tea and listening to the juke box. He was certainly an easy guy to be around.

"Hey, I know that tune," he said quietly, as if talking to himself. "That's Charlie Barnet on *Overheard in a Cocktail Lounge*. I wonder if *Surrealism* is on the flip-side."

He slipped out of the booth and sauntered over to the juke box. A couple of young ladies seated at the fountain exchanged arched eyebrows. Hunter noticed and said, "How y'all doin', girls?" They turned their backs and shyly tittered into their Cokes. He studied the selections one by one then pumped a handful of nickels into the machine.

I finished my soup by the time he returned and plonked himself down in front of his steak. He ate like a young wolf, barely pausing to catch a breath. Jazz plainly excited him. He seemed to know every note, every riff. And he had savvy. None of the tunes were the obvious swing things that were all the rage, but real jazz with brains *and* beauty.

Impressed, I complimented him on his good taste.

"You're a fan?" he said.

I nodded. Then I told him about the collection Lincoln Drummond and I had put together over the years. And how we had to order most of the records we wanted through the mail.

"That's too bad. You should visit New York. It's a paradise for someone hip to the music, like yourself."

I was surprised to hear Hunter use jive but that passed when he went on to tell me about all the bands he had seen – Jimmie Lunceford, Bennie Moten, Duke Ellington, Count Basie, Charlie Barnet, and scores of others, most of which I knew from records or had heard on the radio. He had travelled the U.S. and had taken the time to dig deep into the music world. I would've given my eye-teeth to have seen a tenth of the bands he mentioned.

"How do you manage it?" I asked. "With work and all?"

"I get around on field assignments. Otherwise, I take side trips on my own initiative."

"Nice work if you can get it," I said, a bit skeptically. I wondered how many C.I.C. agents wandered far and wide like Hunter. And what they were really doing on civvie street.

Over coffee, we chatted a while longer about music, avoiding any political or departmental talk. I found myself liking Hunter even though I was averse to foreigners observing foreigners on our soil. That seemed to be a job for our people – whoever the hell *they* were. Besides, there was too much risk of innocent bystanders getting caught in the crossfire. Meaning me and mine. I didn't need to be convinced that Penny's "accident" was intended for me. I'd thought that all along but I couldn't figure who or why. When Hunter let the cat out of the bag about me being under surveillance I knew who but I still didn't know why. And now I had been officially told to lay off. Fat chance. I always was a disobedient S.O.B. and couldn't see myself changing old habits. But it would take cunning. There were eyes and ears everywhere.

I smoked another one of Hunter's custom-made cigarettes and then we left for his hotel. He was staying, more like hiding out, at the Ten Eych Hotel just two blocks down Union Street from The Silver Rail.

Hatless, and with his topcoat draped over his shoulders like a cloak, he stepped regally out of the car.

"Thanks, Ireland," he said. "I think I'll breakfast at The Silver Rail for the duration. That's a hip juke box. How come? You'd never expect to find it in a burg like this."

"Dunno. Surprising what you'll find in Saint John."

"You can say that again." Hunter tipped an imaginary hat. "See you around."

I watched him disappear into the recessed entrance of the Ten Eych. He had an aristocratic bearing that made him seem aloof, set apart from commoners such as myself. There are certain things you can't hide no matter how clever you are, and one of those things is background. Hunter's blue-blooded pedigree didn't add up but then neither did much of anything else about him. Maybe I was wrong. Maybe I was right. I did know that I was entertaining a lot of bad thoughts about too many people. Not just the Germans aboard the *Bergensfjord*. Hardfield. Sullivan. Penny. Penny – everytime I thought about her I felt a warm stirring. I didn't want anything to be wrong about Penny.

A cabbie leaned on his horn and hurled a few choice obscenities at me before I broadsided him between the T and the X. I jammed on the brakes. It was a close call. I'd rolled right through a red light and almost sent him into eternity. I shrugged, mouthed "Sorry," then I pulled into the nearest parking space. It was only a block to the Dominion Atlantic Railway wharf. The best thing now would be to go over on foot and get my duffel bag out of the locker in the waiting room.

I stopped at Market Slip. It was coming on high tide and the air was brisk and salty. It helped clear my foggy brain. A tugboat chugged alongside, a pair of ruddy-faced crewmen with hawsers at the ready. I watched them tie up and secure the mooring. The rest of the crew came on deck. They started gesturing and talking all at once. I overheard the word drowned and asked permission to come aboard, although I had already leapt from the dock and landed amidships. A stout, bearded man the others addressed as Cap stepped forward and checked my I.D. "That was quick. Were you waiting for us?"

"Yeah." I didn't like to horn in on the Harbour Police's jurisdiction but anything out of the ordinary that happened around the waterfront these days was of concern to me.

The captain said, "I want you men to keep your traps shut about all this. Now, take the rest of the day off. I'll see you at sun-up."

Glad to oblige, the men grabbed their gear and scrambled ashore. The stout man motioned toward the wheelhouse. "Cook left me a pot o' tea. Let's get in out of the sea breeze and have a sit-down."

I sat on a padded bench beside the charts. An X was pencilled in red a short distance off Partridge Island outside the mouth of the harbour. A log book lay open on top of the map. An entry noted: *Remains of man presumed drowned brought aboard 13:20 hrs. Harbour Police removed same 13:50. Instructed to say nothing about above.*

The captain tamped tobacco into a meerschaum, struck a match, then said in a low voice, "Are you supposed to be in on this, Ireland?"

I admitted that I wasn't but that I had an interest which I couldn't reveal. Shades of Wilder Hunter and his convenient veil of secrecy.

"I would've had your tail tossed back onto the pier if it weren't for knowing your dad, Jack."

I laughed at the man's frankness. He looked at me steadily while he poured two mugs of tea.

"I knew you when you were in kneepants, long before I grew this fur coat for my face. Warren Armstrong's the name."

I shook his hand. "Of course. You used to play cribbage with Dad. How are you?"

"No complaints, Jack. How is the old fella?"

"Grand. He's been ice-fishing almost every day since New Year's."

"Wha? You don't say? Out freezin' his arse off in a fishing shack in Drury Cove, I suppose?"

"You got him nailed down tight. Dad's hooked enough fish to fill a warehouse."

Captain Armstrong grinned. "Don't that beat all? What can I do for you, Jack? Off the record, to be sure. I can't have the harbour master revoking my ticket. Regulations, you know. Them things that keep civil servants serving."

"Tell me about this." I tapped the log book with a cigarette then lit up. "What makes it so different that it should be hushed?"

"Beats me. Coroner came aboard, examined the remains of the poor bastard, wrapped him in a tarpaulin, spoke to the Harbour Police, then they told us not to say a word. Nothing. They were real emphatic about that issue." Armstrong talked in a rush as if speaking rapidly made him less guilty of disobeying an order.

"The coroner? Doc Cromarty?"

"Hulking brute of a fella with reddish hair?"

"Yeah. He usually lets the bodies come to him. Unless…"

"Unless what?"

"Nothing, Cap. Did you find the man?"

"Wished to Christ I didn't. Strange things happen on the water. 'Specially the Fundy. We were gaffin' lines from a freighter, gettin' set to pilot her into harbour, when this body, more like a thing, came out of the deep sort of tangled on the ship's anchor. It were a chillin' sight, make no mistake."

Warren Armstrong didn't relish the memory. "Chances are one in a thousand of recovering a body that way. If it wasn't for the wind and the heavy swell the anchor chain wouldn't of dragged the way it did on the shoal. It was as if it weren't intended that the man be eaten by the fishes. I may be a superstitious old bugger but that's what I believe."

"It sounds grisly," I said.

"Saints alive, yes. He was tethered with a cable to a pair of car tires that had ballast bricks in 'em."

"Jesus."

"I never uttered a word to you, Jack."

"No. 'Course not, Cap," I said, looking over my shoulder. The Harbour Police had hauled up in a paddy wagon on the other side of the slip and were eyeballing us. "If they ask, tell them I was delivering a message from Dad about ice-fishing. I'll make sure the story is covered."

A couple of uniformed officers got out of the truck and started around the wharf. I scribbled a note to Cap about smelt runs in Drury Cove and signed my father's name.

I said, "Safe seas," then I hurried ashore and ducked into the Brookes Bond warehouse. A minute later I'd wound through a labyrinth of teaboxes, whisked past an astonished shipper and was out the receiving door. The D.A.R. wharf lay dead ahead.

The waiting room was deserted. I entered a phone booth, dialled my father, and explained about Warren Armstrong.

"It sounds like you're in it up to your gills," Dad said. "Watch out. You don't want to be stepping on the wrong toes."

"I'll be caution itself," I said, ringing off. Yeah, sure. Why did I feel like I was being lowered into a snake pit?

The ticket-master's wicket had a *Back in Ten Minutes* sign hanging from the bars. I was about to head for the lockers when I noticed my empty duffel bag sitting on his desk. Also my belongings, which were arranged as if ready for inspection. Someone had folded my shirts, pants, and longjohns, matched the socks, and sorted out the toiletries. My spare stocking hat, a scarlet number with a long tassel, was stretched over a lamp and stood guard over all.

I went to locker 16 and found it jimmied open. Alarms went off in my skull. Loud and clear.

I shut myself in the phone booth. What was it I had that somebody else wanted? Besides brains and good looks? "Shut up, Jack," I said aloud. Whenever I was rattled, I cracked wise. And I was rattled.

The day had too many surprises. I phoned the desk sergeant and asked him if anyone strange had been in the station that morning.

"Naw. Only a couple of guys here early to fix the circulator on the boiler."

"Early? What time?"

"Eight. I was on the desk. They were in overalls and waved a fistful of slips at me."

"Overalls?"

"Yeah. Nelson's Coal."

"You sure they were legit?"

"They were grimy enough to be boiler men. Black faces and hands. Covered in soot from head to toe. I didn't want them near me."

The ticket-master, in homburg and greatcoat, passed by with a bundle of posters under each arm.

"Anybody go with them to the boiler room?" I asked.

"Jack, there's fourteen men out with the flu. We couldn't cope with a minor traffic jam much less escorting boiler men on guided tours."

"All right, Sarge. Do me a favour? Ring Nelson's and check up on these birds, will you?"

"What's cookin', Jack?"

"Maybe my goose. Just do it okay? I'm at a pay phone. Number is 3-8006."

I mashed out my cigarette in the ashtray on the ticket-master's desk. He glanced up from beneath his homburg, emptied the butt in a wastebasket, then wiped the tray clean with a rag.

TERRY CRAWFORD

"Sorry," I said. "Didn't mean to invade your territory."

He looked at me like Grumpy then broke into a smile like Happy. I watched as he fetched an ashstand from the waiting room and placed it next to a chair in front of his desk. "Take a load off," he said. "These articles yours?"

"I'm afraid so."

The old fellow reached down and pulled a couple of Lime Rickys from a case. He snapped the caps off and handed me one. It was warm and fizzy.

"Anything missing?" he asked, guzzling half the bottle of soda pop.

"Doesn't appear to be," I said. "What's the scoop?"

"About five this morning one of the stevedores was loading the stove in the freight shed and thought he heard a noise. That time of day this place is locked up tighter than a drum. When he came in to investigate, two fellows took off out of here like bats out of hell. The stevedore chased them but they jumped into a car and were gone lickity-split. Your stuff was spread all over the floor."

I gathered it together and shoved it into the duffel bag. Handing over the key to locker 16, I said, "Thanks for everything. Don't know if this key's any good to you."

"Souvenir. This is a first for us. Now, is there anything else I can do for you?"

"No. I'm expecting a call on your pay phone. Tell me something though, did the stevedore mention what these guys were wearing?"

"Coveralls."

I put my duffel bag on a bench and went outside on the wharf. The harbour was alive, ships moored at every pier. The sun came out from behind the clouds but it didn't lift my spirits. New wood surrounded the door handle where it had been splintered.

A minute or two after I went back inside, the phone rang.

"Jack?"

"Yes, Sarge."

"Nelson's Coalyard didn't send anybody out this morning. But get this. Those buggers repaired the circulator. It's workin' better than it ever did. I'm actually gettin' heat in the radiator behind my desk."

"Hurrah," I said quietly. "See you tomorrow."

"Don't hang up, Jack. What's going on?"

"Crazy mischief. I don't know. Send the janitor downstairs to clean up my locker, will you, Sarge? And mum's the word."

"Right. You know best."

"I hope so, Sarge, but don't bet on it."

I slung the duffel bag over my shoulder and walked the long way back to the Pontiac. I didn't know best, but I did know better. I was keeping too much to myself. Sooner or later I'd have to confide in someone outside my immediate circle. But who could I trust?

CHAPTER THIRTY-SEVEN

I STEPPED INTO the alley beside the ironworks on Vulcan Street, pulled up my collar, and hunched deeper inside my coat. It was damp and freezing, the sun barely over the South End rooftops. I could smell woodfires on the wind and hear boys whooping in the Saint John the Baptist schoolyard, early birds playing street hockey. They stopped running and leaned on their sticks while they watched me cut behind the school and disappear between the church and the rectory. Tough kids with knee patches and the elbows out of their sweaters. Rough boys not much different than I was at their age. Sometimes when I saw them I wondered if I should've become a school teacher instead of a cop. An ounce of prevention and all that.

Shorty Long had contacted me in the usual way – a note under the milk bottle. COME SEE ME in green crayon. I'd phoned Tom Waterman and told him to come in plainclothes to the ironworks. It was time Tom was introduced to Shorty and the gang at Long's Woodyard.

The Pontiac was at my place where I parked it for all to see. Under cover of darkness I'd slipped out to a rendezvous with a cabbie on Adelaide Street and got him to drive me around the North End until I was convinced we weren't being followed. Then he put the accelerator to the floor and took me to the streetcar line where I rode as far as the Three Sisters lamp at the end of Prince William Street. From there I wandered up and down and in and around St. James and Britain until it was light enough to see faces from across the pavement.

Dressed as sharp as a blade, Waterman came around the corner and into view. He loitered for a while across the street then joined me. "Is that your idea of plainclothes?" I said, offering him a cigarette.

Tom held up a kid glove. "No thanks. Gave 'em up for Lent. What's the matter? Was I supposed to come in disguise? The latest in rugged longshoreman?"

I laughed. "Forget it. It's good to see you, Tom. Punchin' a bag at all?"

"I went to the Monarch Club three or four times after you were suspended but no one knew where you were. You dropped out of sight. Turned out you were in Nova Scotia but how was I to know that? I didn't know whether you were dead or alive until you phoned me about Roxanne's son and that guy lurking around their neighbourhood."

"Sorry, didn't mean to be secretive."

"We've got some catching up to do, Jack. I want to be let in on things, not left out. If you want my help I'll go to the wall but you have to keep me informed. Deal?"

"Deal. Let's get in out of the cold."

We walked up the street and crossed the road to Long's Woodyard. The big folding gates were closed but behind them there were sounds of activity. I tried the latch on the door in the gate, opened it, and ushered Waterman through to the inside. Gabby and a couple of helpers were splitting slabwood into kindling, faces red with the effort. Another man, a light-skinned Negro, was loading coal into paper bags for the cornerstore trade. No one paid any particular attention as we climbed the stairs to the second-storey porch that overlooked the yard.

Shorty's office was empty but the coffee pot was percolating on the stove. He couldn't be too far away. I waved Waterman into a chair and searched the two adjoining rooms. They were filled with cartons marked with issue numbers of foreign newspapers and socialist magazines but no Shorty.

I rejoined Waterman. He was reading the latest quote written large on Shorty's blackboard: Life consists of what a man is thinking all day. Ralph Waldo Emerson.

The room had been newly painted and the furniture polished and rearranged. There were even pictures in fancy frames on the wall: a group of photographs of Saint John harbour in the days when sailing ships crammed the quays.

Cups and spoons surrounded a sugar bowl and a pitcher of milk on a tray on the desk. While I was pouring coffee the phone rang. I let it jangle four times, then I picked up the receiver. It was Shorty, out of breath and excited for one usually so deadpan. "Jack, I'm at my sister's on Germain Street. Minnie's in bed with the flu, sick as a dog. I'm going to make porridge for the kids and shove them off to school. Coffee should be ready. Help yourself. I have to go. Someone's burning the toast."

TERRY CRAWFORD

"What was that all about?" Tom Waterman said, accepting a cup of coffee. He'd removed his topcoat and hat and looked even more dapper in suit and tie.

"Shorty's held up for a while. Just as well. I want to talk to you in private."

Tom moved onto a chair closer to the pot-bellied stove. He seemed mesmerized by the twinkle and glow of the coal behind the isinglass windows.

"Careful. Fire is hypnotic," I said. "Now, tell me about this character that's been seen watching young Leonard."

Tom carefully measured his words. "*Alleged* to be watching him. When I knocked off duty the day before yesterday I dropped by Pepper's Diner and had a talk with Roxanne. She's never laid eyes on the guy. She traded shifts one day with the intention of confronting him but he was nowhere to be found. What we're left with is two or three jittery boys who think the guy might be after them, although he does seem to zero in on Leonard."

"Zero in? How so?"

"Well, he just watches him. Or *seems* to. From a healthy distance at that, I might add. I don't have to tell you that area is very hilly with quite a few look-outs. He doesn't appear to want to attract attention."

"H'mm. Leonard strikes me as a sensible kid. I don't think he'd make up stories."

"The fellow might be a harmless dawdler. I did talk to him."

"You what!"

Tom got up and poured more coffee. "Easy does it. I was in Darrah's Lunch on Ludlow Street. He was at the magazine stand, leafing through the latest *LIFE*. I sat at the fountain and ordered tea and doughnuts. After a minute or so I turned and asked him if the March *Argosy* was in. He said it wasn't and came and sat on the stool next to me and ordered coffee. I started talking about the weather and he said he hadn't seen snow in nine years. Said how much he hated the cold. I asked him what brought him back north, presuming he'd been south, and he said a banana boat."

I interrupted. "Banana? That'd mean Willett Fruit. I'll phone the warehouse on Paradise Row and find out the name of the ship."

"Do you want me to still keep an eye on him, Jack?" Tom said, standing to get a better look at one of the photographs. "He wasn't menacing or anything like that. In fact, kind of sad and lost. Lonely. Really lonely."

"You sound sorry for him, Tom."

"Maybe I am. His face is tanned like leather and that beard, geeze, that beard makes him look fifteen years older than he is. But he wouldn't be more than thirty-five, I'd say. People in the neighbourhood treat him like dirt and yet he was polite enough."

"Yeah. Well, keep an eye peeled for the next while anyway. Okay, Tom? Maybe the guy's waiting for another ship out and he'll be gone and that's all there is to it. But, better safe than sorry. I got a lot on my slate. If something doesn't happen with this buzzard in the next week I'll visit Roxanne and we'll resolve the situation one way or the other."

Bashfully, Tom said, "Roxanne is nice. Although she can be two different people."

"I agree. The hard-ticket waitress and the pretty young mother. You're not soft on her, are you?"

"Roxanne must be seven or eight years older than me."

"That's not what I asked you."

"She's a real dish." Tom blushed. "Let's talk about something else."

"What? The price of meat and potatoes?"

Tom smiled. "As important as that is, no. Fill me in on what happened to the Studebaker. Then tell me about Sullivan."

The phone rang. It was Shorty Long. He was going to be another half hour. "If you want breakfast, pull the cord back of the desk. You know the routine."

I did just that. In no time at all, the young bald fellow who was manservant and chief cook and bottlewasher for Shorty served us a breakfast of eggs, sausages, brown bread, and strawberry preserves.

I confided in Tom while we ate. I didn't spare any of the lurid details, surprised that I could keep my food down. Tom appeared to have no problems either. Maybe it was morbid fascination that made us so voracious. Or the unspoken recognition that in the midst of life...

I yanked the cord. "You guys was hungry," the bald man said, grinning. A gold filling glinted. "I brought youse some tea."

TERRY CRAWFORD

"Good grub, thanks," I said, helping him stack the dishes on a tray. I opened the door for him and tucked a deuce into his apron pocket.

"Strange bedfellows you have, Detective Ireland," Tom said.

"Trust. Stick with the people you trust."

To further show Waterman that I fully trusted him I mentioned the American C.I.C. man, Wilder Hunter. I underscored the pertinent fact that Hunter had had me under surveillance since Eugene Robichaud's death on Valentine's Day.

"Speaking of Gene, my brother-in-law says Gene seems to have been forgotten," Tom said.

"Tell Billy for me that nothing could be further from the truth."

"You remember Billy's name?"

"Billy Moffat. I never forget the little guy, Tom. That's who keeps this country going – ordinary men and women."

Tom nodded. "I believe that myself."

"Besides, Eugene Robichaud is the key. When we find out how he fits into this whole sorry mess it'll unlock the question box."

"In the meantime..." Tom said.

I cut him off. "Keep one eye on the rearview mirror."

"Something like that was on the tip of my tongue," Tom said, getting up with a start, ready to fight, as Shorty Long crashed into the room.

CHAPTER THIRTY-EIGHT

"WHOA," SHORTY SAID, in three strides bounding behind the protection of his desk. "Who is this warrior, Jack?"

"Constable Tom Waterman, Shorty Long."

They shook hands.

Shorty was panting from running. Many's the time I'd seen him loping through the neighbourhood like a giraffe in a navy-blue Burburry, coat-tails flying in the slipstream. The temporary colour in his cheeks flattered him, otherwise he was a pale drink of water. A broom-handle in a tight suit.

"Pleased to meet you, Tom. You're too handsome to be a policeman. Have you ever dreamed of a life on the stage?" Shorty said, pouring sherry into a cup, then filling it with tea.

Tom frowned, tired of people commenting on his looks. "All the world's a stage," he said, declining the sherry.

I took a small shot as a digestive aid. It was Harvey's Bristol Cream, not Shorty's usual paint-stripper.

"And all the men and women merely players," Shorty said. "They have their exits and their entrances, and one man in his time plays many parts…"

"All right, Barrymore. Cease and desist," I said. "You got my vote for the Oscar. Now, can we come down to earth?"

Tom Waterman was having a good laugh. "You guys crack me up. Talk about the stage. You ought to be in vaudeville."

I stood with my hindquarters to the stove. Tramping through the snow, combined with too much drink of late, had me feeling rundown and rheumy. The heat only a coal stove can provide insinuated its way into my stiffening joints.

"So, why the summons?" I said to Shorty.

Shorty glanced at Tom Waterman then back at me.

"Tom's trustworthy. Go ahead, gimme the goods."

"That matter we discussed the last time you were here?" Shorty said, consulting a notebook. "We have news. Not much, but some. The *Bergensfjord* is in the dry dock. You know that because you went there and were aboard for, let's see, forty-two minutes. The crew is spread out over Saint John and Lancaster. However, the German gentlemen are, to a man, boarding in Wellington Hall next to the Y.M.C.A. where two of them toil long hours building the perfect Aryan body for the fatherland and the Führer."

Waterman didn't seem to know what to think.

"Shorty is what the American G-men label a P.A.F.," I said.

"Which is?"

"A Premature Anti-Fascist."

Shorty huffed into his teacup. "Isolationist morons."

Tom said heatedly, "How could you be a P.A.F. when the fascists are a clear and present danger to democracy? If you ask me, there's too damn much sympathy in the form of silence for Hitler and Mussolini. Hasn't anyone learned anything from the Spanish example? Franco's a dictator, for God's sake!"

"Well said, hear, hear," Shorty said, thumping his desk. "Bright lad you've got here, Jack."

"Beyond a doubt. But he's not Bolshevik material, so hands off. We're getting sidetracked. What else have you got?"

Shorty flipped through his notebook. "These guys are avid sightseers. Reversing Falls, Martello Tower, shipyards, cat houses, et cetera… and, get this, excursions along the coast to fishing villages. Beaver Harbour. Black's Harbour on a tour of the fish plant."

"Jack, what are they up to?" Tom asked.

"Seems like straightforward espionage in the guise of tourism. This fellow Werner Strasser is an ace shutterbug."

"So what are we going to do?" Tom said.

"Remember, we're not supposed to be doing anything. Wilder Hunter and his C.I.C. people are keeping them under surveillance and us in the bargain. That's why I'm relying on Shorty's men. No one pays much attention to supposed winos and derelicts. They can be *our* secret agents. Look what they've come up with so far."

"I'm impressed," Tom said. "Shorty, you've got quite the underground network at your command."

Shorty shrugged. "We get along. These thugs made a big mistake when they beat up Randy Murphy – one of ours."

Tom turned to me. "What did you make of Wilder Hunter?"

"I did think it peculiar that he was staying at the Ten Eych Hotel. Didn't fit his style. But it's just across the street and down the block from Wellington Hall. He won't talk about the Germans. Claims the C.I.C. has a man inside and me nosing around might expose him."

Feeling a chill, I moved closer to the stove and turned the damper up. Influenza was creeping into my bones like fog ruining a sunny day.

"What about Sullivan?" Tom said. "Do you think he stumbled onto something and was murdered for his troubles?"

"That possibility looms large. Torture. Whoever killed him wanted information. The padlock was gone from Sully's locker at the station. Sully kept the key in his pants pocket. I think his killers and the phony boilermen were one and the same. They also jimmied the locker at the D.A.R. wharf then ransacked my duffel bag. And don't forget, two days before that, probably stole Penny's luggage out of the Studebaker. They're after some *thing*. But what?"

Shorty put his feet up on the desk and clasped his hands behind his head. "Sullivan? Murder? Torture? Lockers? Penny? This is all news to me."

Shorty never listened to the radio or read the local dailies. He kept abreast of the European and Russian "theatres," as he called them, through dozens of subscriptions to foreign journals. I told him about Sullivan, again not sparing any of the gruesome details. An image of that damn footprint in the ashes came into my head and wouldn't go away. Oh, Penny. Penny. I was sick at heart at the thought…

Shorty stared knowingly. "There's something else, Jack. You look like somebody just walked over your grave."

I mustered myself together and evaded with, "Sully had a fantastic floor model radio. You could pull in Zanzibar at night. The radio was tuned to an odd spot on the dial. I memorized the numbers and telephoned a ham operator I know to find out what broadcast might have been on that evening."

Stepping away from the stove before my backside scorched, I sat down and drank some more tea. I was feverish and my joints were beginning to ache.

TERRY CRAWFORD

"And?" Shorty said.

Tom Waterman leaned toward me and placed a hand over my forehead. "You're burning up."

"I'll survive." I hadn't told anybody about my initial hunch regarding the radio. It was a hunch that struck paydirt.

"And?" Shorty repeated.

"Berlin."

Shorty sat back. "Why doesn't that surprise me? And the broadcast?"

"A Nazi rally with major speeches by Goebbels and Hitler."

A chill not only went through me but I'm sure Shorty and Tom as well. We sat in silence for a time, the only sounds the whining of the big circular saw and the steady whack of an axe outside in the woodyard.

Shorty searched the recesses of his desk and tossed me a tin of Aspirin. "Better take four or five. If you're coming down with what my sister's got you'll hardly be able to move by this afternoon."

I did as I was told. Damn, I didn't have time to get sick. But germs were germs and kept their own schedules so I'd just have to ride it out.

There was a knock on the door. The young bald fellow who brought us breakfast stepped in and spoke to Shorty. "He's here."

"Whereabouts?" Shorty asked.

"In the kitchen. I made an eggnog for him."

"Does he suspect anything?"

"Naw. He's reading my friggin' *Screen Romance* and won't give it back."

"Okay. We'll be down in a couple of minutes. Take some coffee and sandwiches out to the men and tell them not to interrupt us."

"Gotcha. Next time I'm gonna put a laxative in his f'ing eggnog."

"What's that rigamorole about?" I asked.

"Randy Murphy's here. I knew you wanted to talk to him about Werner Strasser and accomplice whaling the crap out of him."

"Aces. How'd you get him here?"

"Against my nature, I lied. That'll cost you a pint of rye."

"Done," I said. "Tom, Murphy is the guy who was beat up down on Station Street. I told you about him the first time we sparred at the boxing club."

"Sure, I remember. You said he was a cop-hater and wouldn't talk to us."

"That's right, but thanks to Shorty we've got him on neutral ground. Actually, more like home turf."

"Let me get this straight," Tom said. "Randy Murphy's the guy who picks up money directing sailors and soldiers to the whorehouses and bootleggers. A kind of procurer or third-rate pimp."

Shorty arose and went to the door. "Randy prefers 'facilitator'," he said, vexed at Waterman's harsh judgement.

"Facilitator? That's rich," I said. "Randy always was a card."

We stepped outside onto the porch. There was a streak of blue sky surrounded by gun-metal gray out over the bay. I hoped the skies would clear and along with it my cloudy brain. Shorty escorted us to a door three away from his office. We went inside and tiptoed single-file down a narrow staircase.

Randy Murphy was seated at the kitchen table with his back to us. He didn't bother to look around to see who entered the room. He had plowed a path in the clutter of milk bottles and cereal boxes so he could prop up the *Screen Romance* for maximum ogling. A top-heavy, leggy Hollywood starlet with bedroom eyes had Murphy hypnotized.

"Don't set the page on fire," I said.

He recognized my voice and started to get up. I put both hands on his bony shoulders and rammed him back into the chair. "Sit still and be nice," I instructed.

Waterman was embarrassed at the way I manhandled Murphy. Little did he know what a tough nut we were up against. We sat on opposite sides of Randy while Shorty cleared the table and swabbed the oilcloth with a dishrag.

I gave Randy a cigarette, which he coolly lit, blowing out the match as I leaned into the flame. I took his smoke and handed him mine. He found all this mildly amusing.

"Enjoy your little shenanigans while you can, Murphy," I said, "because before you leave you'll answer some questions. Understand?"

He closed his eyes and nodded. Murphy had lost about twenty pounds. It suited him. His vanished midriff made his suit and vest fit properly for the first time in a decade. When he tipped his head to sip eggnog through a straw I noticed a congregation of pink scars along the part in his hair.

"How'd you get those?" I said. They looked itchy, as if the stitches had been recently removed.

From between clenched teeth, he muttered, "Knuckles. The brass variety. It was like the *Anvil Chorus* ringing off my dome." His voice sounded normal enough with the exception of a slight slur. He'd had a few weeks' practice mastering the knack of speaking from his diaphragm.

"I want to get these guys, Randy," I said. "But I can't go the usual route. The higher-ups won't let me."

"So fuckin' what?" he said with such vehemence it startled Waterman and Shorty.

I calmly replied, "So I need your help."

He took a noisy drag off his cigarette and exhaled through his nostrils. "Deep six that. I'll get 'em myself."

"What you'll get is a pauper's grave. These bastards are killers. They took pleasure doing what they did to you."

"How do you know?"

"An eyewitness. If he hadn't shone a flashlight in their direction, that blockhead of yours would be nothing more than jelly with ears."

"Eyewitness? Who?"

"Tiny Miller."

"The dairy guy?"

"Yeah."

"Well, I guess I owe him one. Gutsy little shrimp."

"At the time, you told him to mind his own fucking business."

Randy pouted then glanced at Waterman with something approaching total disgust. Or jealousy. "What is it you want I should do?"

"That's more like it," I said. "You're on the cathouse/bootlegger grapevine. Keep your ear to the ground and let me know what these characters are up to. Their basic itinerary. Don't shadow them. I don't want you to get hurt again."

"Stop. You'll make me cry."

"Shut your festering gob. I'm in no mood for wisecracks." I wasn't, either. My head was pounding like a pile driver. I wrote down a telephone number on a piece of paper. "This is a safe number. Call it every day at ten in the evening and leave a message. If the person on the other end doesn't say Scott Joplin, hang up."

"Why all the cloak and dagger?" Murphy said.

I stood up. Murphy's eyes widened in fear. "Life and death," I said. "Take your pick."

The remark caught his attention. He grew solemn and shook my hand. A pact now existed between us.

"And respect this man," I said, pointing to Waterman. "He's solid as a rock."

Murphy nodded, his gaze returning to the Hollywood starlet. I think Randy was a watcher. Women were safe as long as they were isolated on the page or with someone else in real life.

We went back up the narrow staircase. I was feeling worse than something the cat dragged in. Shorty bade farewell and left us standing on the outside landing from where Tom and I could observe the men working in the woodyard below.

Tom asked, "Who's Scott Joplin?"

"Lincoln Drummond. He takes messages for me under that name. I want to protect his identity."

Gabby yanked a canvas tarp over the stack of freshly split kindling to protect it from the rain that had suddenly started to pelt down. Everyone else ran for cover, abandoning their work in mid-stroke. In the space of an hour it had turned mild, almost balmy, the wind driving hard from the south. Maybe winter's back had finally broken.

"Industrious place," Tom said.

"Yeah. It's like a monastery for bums. Let's get out of here."

We stepped out through the door in the high gate and secured the latch. I watched as Tom went up the street toward the red stone wall of the Armouries, then I turned away and walked down to the harbour.

Stevedores were unloading a sugar boat at the first wharf I came to. It made me think about the fellow off the banana boat. Roxanne probably needed reassurance. I put my head into the wind and made for the sugar refinery's gatehouse. Once there, I phoned the station and told the desk sergeant that I was down with influenza and wouldn't be in to work. Then I phoned a taxi to take me to Pepper's Diner.

TERRY CRAWFORD

CHAPTER THIRTY-NINE

T HE RIDE TO Lancaster wasn't any picnic. When the jalopy of a taxi turned onto Douglas Avenue I almost got out at my place but told the cigar-smoking cabbie to keep going up the Avenue and across the bridge. Fearing I was going to throw up, I had him drop me in front of Simms Brush Factory. It was still spitting rain but the fresh air and lack of jostling were lifesavers.

I leaned with both elbows on the railing that bordered the sidewalk and spied on the factory workers through the wall of windows. In about ten minutes the nausea subsided. My confab with Roxanne was going to have to be short and not very sweet.

The brief stroll from Simms Corner to Pepper's Diner seemed to take forever. When I shouldered through the revolving door I was perspiring and short of breath, ready to fall flat on my face.

There were only four patrons in the restaurant, all of them seated in the same booth at the back. Roxanne was sitting at the fountain, her back and arms tense as she concentrated on rolling a cigarette. "Be right with you," she said, twisting the tobacco together in a mangled mess.

I slid my cigarette pack down the counter. It came to rest against her elbow. Flinching, she ripped apart the makings. "Wha! Oh. Hello, Jack." She swept the spilled tobacco into an ashtray with the edge of her hands. "Thanks. I will have one."

Saying no to coffee, I mounted a stool beside her. Roxanne looked fine and I told her so.

"I've been taking Leonard skating. It's doing me more good than it is him. His feet get cramps. Most of the time he hangs onto the boards and watches me. The fresh air helps his asthma, though."

"That's great, Roxy. I came to see you about the fellow who's worrying you. Tom Waterman came up with a few details. It seems the guy's a seaman and hasn't been in northern climes for almost ten years. I'll ask around and see if I can find out more about him. Name, rank, and serial number. Then, if you really think there's a problem we'll work something out. So far he's law-abiding, and on the surface appears for all intents and purposes, harmless. I know how you feel but that's the legal point of view."

Roxanne picked a shred of tobacco off her tongue.

"Fair enough?" I said.

Roxanne didn't budge.

"Misgivings, my dear?" I said, gently prodding her arm.

"Fair enough. Better than fair. But something is bugging me. Something that won't quit."

"Out with it. Don't be shy."

"I'm not the shy type. What's bothering me is that Leonard had a dream about this man."

"Dream? A nightmare?" I reached over the counter for a glass and pumped myself enough Coca-Cola to wash down five Aspirins.

"No. In the dream Leonard's in a rowboat with the man out at Lily Lake. It wasn't a nightmare but Leonard is uneasy about it. I can tell."

"It was the bearded man and not someone else?"

"The bearded man."

"Whew. It's got me flummoxed. Sounds like a case for Sigmund Freud."

"Who?" Roxanne said, a bit fearfully.

"Never mind." I smiled and covered her hand. "Everything will be all right."

"My Gawd, Jack. Are your hands ever clammy."

"I know. I'm not well. Flu bug bit me." While I spoke I realized that I could've curled up in a booth and gone straight to sleep.

"You should be home in bed. We're not busy. Why don't you give me your car keys and I'll drive you home."

At the mention of bed my insides slumped. The lights in the diner were giving me a fierce headache, particularly the blue and pink neon circles around the clock in back of the fountain. I couldn't take my eyes off the illuminated numbers on the clock face. It was as if they were trying to change into letters of the alphabet. A man in my head moaned, "Spell it out," in a voice as disembodied as a ventriloquist's dummy. I gripped the counter as everything pulsed in one lumbering heartbeat.

"Jack, you don't look so hot," Roxanne said.

TERRY CRAWFORD

I wobbled into the men's room, took a deep breath, and vomited into the toilet bowl. Sweating profusely, I got up off my knees and flushed the toilet. Then I filled the sink with cold water and drenched my face and neck. Roxanne appeared behind me in the mirror. She had her hat and coat on and was wearing a vermilion muffler that made her pretty face radiant.

"I didn't bring the car, Roxy."

"Oh. Then, I'll walk you across the tracks to Star Taxi."

On the slushy sidewalk Roxanne hooked an arm around mine. She was steady and strong so with the rotten way I felt I didn't mind the extra support.

"I'll get the cook to make a pot of chicken soup for you," she said. "Me and Leonard can bring it over tomorrow. He likes walking over the bridge and looking at all the big houses on Douglas Avenue."

"H'mm. Maybe he's going to be an architect."

"I don't know. He doesn't like new buildings but he's real interested in anything old. He loves the museum."

"Good for him. Too many kids have their heads buried in funny books all day."

I waited in front of the taxi stand while Roxanne went in and ordered a cab. Call it a sixth sense but I had the feeling we were being watched. Scanning the bus stops on Simms Corner, I didn't notice anyone out of the ordinary. Neither could I detect anybody suspicious on the Asylum property on the elevated ground overlooking the intersection, unless you wanted to count the poor woman pulling at the bars on the third floor.

"Five minutes, Jack. I better get back to Pepper's. Go right to bed when you get home. One of our waitresses caught this flu and she was miserable for three days."

I nodded, too weak to respond. Roxanne turned and ran with surprising speed down the sidewalk, across the railway tracks, and into the diner. A minute or two later I saw the silhouette of her head looking out of a window and thought she waved as I got into a taxi.

I fell asleep on the Reversing Falls Bridge and had to be nudged awake by the cabbie in front of St. Peter's Church. I gave him a tip even though he muttered something about drunkards.

It was everything I could do to get up the stairs and into the apartment. After what seemed a millennium, I managed to strip down to my underwear, find an old stewpot in case I threw up again, and lower my aching bones into bed.

The sleep I fell into was heavy and awful, beset by worries and moving shadows. Over and over, I dreamt about men without hats who surrounded the bed, their heads bowed like pallbearers at a gravesite.

TERRY CRAWFORD

CHAPTER FORTY

WOMEN'S VOICES. SOMETHING about spring dresses and the new pumps. More coffee? Help yourself to the sandwiches. Away off in the blue an orchestra played a Gershwin tune. "S'wonderful, s'marvellous…"

Waking up, or more like coming to, I didn't know where I was. The sheets were soaked with perspiration and smelled of the sickbed. My tongue was thick, dry, and prickly as a cactus. Clicking on the headboard light, I found myself in my own bed but couldn't remember how I came to be there. From head to toe every joint ached and their attached muscles throbbed in sympathy. I put my feet on the floor and stood up. The room revolved. *Fascinatin' rhythm got me all aquiver.* A medley was all I needed. Where was *Someone to Watch Over Me?* After I got into my bathrobe and moccasins and opened the door and shuffled into the hall it started as if by request.

The sun was all the way to the back of the house. I'd slept round the clock and then some.

Roxanne's son Leonard was in the front room sitting Indian-style on the floor with his back turned. He appeared to be going systematically through the back issues of the *Saturday Evening Post,* large stack to his left, small to the right. He was a serious kid given to long silences, probably the brainy sort.

The music was coming from the mantel radio in the kitchen. It sounded like a Broadway orchestra with a flair for Gershwin, not one of the ricky-ticky dance bands that committed murder day and night. Judging by the conversation, Roxanne and Penny were getting along like a house on fire. That pleased me to no end. I peeked in on them, then pulled my head back. They were seated comfortably at the table with their sock feet up on chairs, soles facing the stove. The aroma of simmering chicken soup almost made me puke.

I walked into the room. When Roxanne and Penny saw me they burst into gales of laughter.

I had to laugh. "What gives?"

Penny held on to her sides. "Oh, Jack. Look in the mirror. Your hair is a fright. It's standing up every which way."

I dragged onward to the sink I agreed. My hair was comical but the face beneath it was a mask of tragedy. I inspected my coated tongue and bloodshot eyes. More signs of misery. Before despair set in, I washed my face and ran a comb through my locks. All of which caused pain. Was it possible for each and every hair on your head to ache?

At the table, the women gave me the once over. I still wasn't quite awake and could've gone back to sleep there and then.

Penny placed a cool hand on mine. "Good afternoon, Rip Van Winkle," she said. "How are things in the Land of Nod?"

"Don't ask."

"Oh, that bad. Poor thing. What you need is tea and lots of it. You're undoubtedly dehydrated."

Roxanne spooned tea leaves into the pot and moved the kettle closer to the front of the stove. Within a minute the water came to a rolling boil.

"You could roast a turkey in here without putting it in the oven," I said. "Crack open a window before I suffocate, will you?"

"Sit still and behave," Penny commanded, leaving the room.

She returned with a blanket which she put over my lap and bare legs. Before I knew what she was doing she shook a thermometer and jabbed it under my tongue, then told me to be quiet while she took my pulse.

Roxanne stood by, fascinated. "Taking notes?" I mumbled.

"She's got your number, I can see that."

"Aw, shaddup, and gimme some tea."

"You're running a temperature of a hundred and one, Jack, but if your sarcasm is any indication of recovery then you're over the worst," Penny said, "Mind if we smoke?"

"Not at all." I started to take one myself but she confiscated the package. "Aw, come on."

"Tomorrow, perhaps. Try a sandwich." She pushed them toward me.

There were at least fifty tiny triangles without crusts on a tray. And no two exactly alike. I chose a devilled ham but it just wouldn't go down. The tea was good, though, and made me feel half-human.

Stubbing out her cigarette, Penny said, "I'm going to strip your bed and change everything. When we looked in on you you were practically sleeping in a pool of water."

"When did you get here?" I asked. It registered that Penny was dressed entirely in black except for a McPherson tartan scarf criss-crossed round her neck.

"About two o'clock," Roxanne said, putting more wood in the range. "Leonard had a half-session at school so we came early. Lucky for us Penny showed up because I couldn't get you to answer the bell."

"Yeah, I was down for the count."

"I telephoned Lincoln from the drugstore, then I went around back and got the key," Penny said. "We've been having a marvelous time."

Roxanne nodded. "It's been great. I don't get much chance at girl-talk. The other waitresses are kind of rough around the edges, you know?"

I pointed to the sandwiches. "What's with these?"

"Dorothy Sullivan insisted," Penny said. "I went to her house after the funeral."

"Oh, Jesus, I slept right through it."

"Dorothy said don't worry. She understands. Honestly, she confessed that it would've been too much for her to take if you had been there. She told me it would have brought back the old days."

I got emotional and put a hand over my eyes to hide the tears. Recovering, I reached for a cigarette and lit it before anyone could protest. "I'm glad you were there, Penny. Thanks for attending."

"Don't mention it. Have more tea. I'll tell you all about the funeral and the aftermath later. Now, excuse me, I'm going to change your bed and air out the room."

Roxanne sat in Penny's chair. "She's really nice."

After two puffs I crushed out the cigarette. I could hear Penny whistling while she worked. The Blue Danube. It gave me visions of skaters skimming arm-in-arm past the Lily Lake pavilion. Snow banked high…

"Hello in there," Roxanne said, passing a hand before my eyes.

"Sorry. My mind keeps wandering."

And wondering. Penny seemed very relaxed. Not behaving like she knew anything at all. Was she so practiced in the art of deception?

No matter what, I would have to confront her about the footprint at Sully's. Maybe she didn't remember being there? Perhaps she deliberately blanked it out. I didn't like what I was thinking. I didn't like the way I was thinking.

Roxanne went to the stove. "Soup's here when you feel like eating."

"Thanks, Roxy. Maybe later. I'll see what the tea does. That cigarette tasted like an old rubber boot."

"I think me and Leonard better be going. Don't get up."

"Okay. Here, finish the rest of these smokes. And let Leonard pick out a dozen copies of the *Post* to take home. I'll never get through these sandwiches. Grab a bag under the sink and make off with about half of them."

Roxanne stood to attention. "Yes, master."

"Hop to it, now. None of your sass."

When Roxanne was ready to leave she guided Leonard in to thank me for the magazines. He was pale and somewhat peaked, but otherwise looked fit enough. They were both wearing long-tasseled stocking hats and hand-knit mittens. I gave them bus tickets so they could ride back home. The side porch windows were covered with ice, a sure sign that it had turned freezing overnight. Finished with the job in the bedroom, Penny showed them to the door with a promise that they'd meet again.

I rearranged the blanket and eased my feet up onto a chair. Now that I'd been vertical for a while, I wasn't quite so dizzy. But, oh, how my bones ached.

"Try some chicken broth," Penny said, placing a bowl in front of me.

It was piping hot. I sipped at it gingerly. My stomach reacted with a few minor spasms but all in all it was easy medicine to keep down.

Watching me all the while, Penny ate a couple of the fancier sandwiches. "Better?"

"H'mm. But I'm weak as a budgie bird."

"You've been under a great deal of pressure lately. Your resistance is probably low. You want to be careful, Jack. People have died from this strain of influenza."

"That's encouraging."

"Don't be grumpy."

"I feel more like Dopey."

Penny laughed. "That might be an improvement. More tea?"

TERRY CRAWFORD

"Thanks. And tell me about Sullivan's funeral."

Penny settled and lit a cigarette. Staring at the ceiling, she began, "Let's see? Where to begin? First of all, it was *huge*. Scads and scads of relatives. An astonishing number of redheads. And more freckles than there are stars. There was a police honour-guard attired in dress uniforms and white gloves. Very somber and dignified. The Mass seemed endless but maybe it was because Sullivan's sisters were crying so much. Fairly wailing, they were. Keening. I'm not accustomed to such open displays of emotion. Dorothy Sullivan remained impassive throughout. Afterwards I overheard some old biddies saying that she ought to be ashamed. Heavens, Jack, what do people expect? I'm sure Dorothy's had her hands full. Anyway, I expressed my condolences and told her you were incapacitated with influenza."

"How did you know that?"

"I was talking to Doctor Cromarty at the Cathedral and he introduced me to Tom Waterman. Tom told us you probably wouldn't be coming," she said. "I don't think I've seen such a handsome young man in years. Really dashing. If I were twenty years younger and better looking…"

"Oh, you're plenty good looking," I grumbled.

Penny gave me a quizzical look, and continued, a trifle flustered. "We three met again back at Dorothy's. I was glad to have their protection. The way the Sullivan men drink is frightful. You know, I believe there were several boys, mere youths of thirteen or fourteen, quite shamelessly drunk."

"Sully's nephews. A rite of passage. A good excuse as any to get them baptized. Did you see Hardfield?"

"The Deputy Chief? Oh, yes. What a cold fish. I could tell that he didn't want to have anything to do with the proceedings. Didn't prevent him from getting quietly plastered, though."

"What? You don't say? I've never known Hardfield to get drunk. He keeps a decanter at the station but he's sanctimonious about over-indulgence."

"Well, he wasn't drinking ginger ale. And that wife of his, she knows her way around a bottle of gin."

"Mrs. Hardfield? Never laid eyes on her. What's she like?"

"Ten years younger. Lovely figure but she was wearing more warpaint than Cochise. And she's a bottle-blonde. I shouldn't be so catty. She's really striking. Something peculiar, though."

"Yeah?"

"Jack, I've seen Mrs. Hardfield before but I just can't put my finger on where. It's been driving me to distraction all afternoon. I expect it'll pop into my head in the middle of the night. It's absolutely maddening."

I couldn't picture Hardfield with a beautiful wife. He was a strait-laced stuffed shirt with the personality of a block of wood. And he was a nasty piece of work.

"By the way, I had an interesting conversation with Doctor Cromarty," Penny said, eyes shining. I'd seen her revved up like this before but not for quite a while. It usually had something to do with the laboratory.

"Remember that blood sample you wanted me to analyze on the sly?" she asked. "If you recall, it turned out to be Group B. Roughly eight to ten per cent of the population? Out of professional curiosity, I mentioned it to Doctor Cromarty. He was rather astounded. Then he whispered in my ear that Sullivan was Group B."

"Maybe that's why Sully donated blood so often. He never did tell me why. I thought it was a quirk. Everything that's happened goes back to Eugene Robichaud. Begins with Robichaud. Don't forget, I found that blood sample near the scene of Robichaud's death."

"The fellow in the hold of the ship?"

"Yes. I had a gut feeling that Sully and Hardfield were implicated in some way but I kept denying it to myself. The day I broke Sully's jaw I knew my instincts were right. He deliberately threw me off the trail with that garbage about Lincoln."

"You don't think they killed Robichaud?" Penny blanched at the thought.

"I don't know what to think. But Robichaud, Sullivan, and Hardfield are connected. That's why Hardfield was so eager to have Robichaud's death declared an accident. The misadventures of an alcoholic."

"But what, Jack? Those three are worlds apart."

"I don't know yet, but when I get over the flu the first thing I'm doing is go back to Sullivan's place."

"Why?"

"Hardfield often visited there so maybe I'll discover something."

"Sounds dreadfully complicated. What about Sullivan? Was he…"

"I can't say any more, Penny. Officially, for entirely different reasons, I'm not permitted to say anything at all about Sullivan."

Penny stood and yawned. "My, this stove's got me drowsy but it is comfy in here. It almost makes one forget the confusion and madness of the world outside."

"Yeah, almost."

Suddenly all business, Penny said, "I really must be off. I'm behind at the hospital and should put in an appearance."

I started to get up but thought better of it when the room decided to rock like a boat.

"Jack, stay put. That's an order. Here, try another bowl of chicken broth. How about something to read?"

"Sure. First, turn the radio off. There are some books on the end table in the front room. Bring me *Brighton Rock*. I haven't had a chance to open it yet."

Before she came back, I could hear her rooting around in the closets and, a minute later, the wardrobe in the bedroom.

"I brought back the things I borrowed to wear the other day but I can't seem to find my ski boots."

"Behind the stove," I said, watching her face as she dug beneath my rubber boots and galoshes.

"I've got it!" she said, ski boots in hand. "Vermont!"

I dropped the soup spoon. She was losing her marbles.

"Vermont! Don't look so stunned, Jack. It's where I first saw Mrs. Hardfield. The winter before last on a skiing trip to Mount Killington. Only she wasn't using the name Hardfield. Let's see. What was it? It was very unique. Lorelei Krieger. I was sharing a room in the main building of the resort and she had one of the chalets. Oh, let me tell you, she was notorious. A different man every other night."

"Are you sure it was Mrs. Hardfield?"

"A group of nurses from Saint Joseph's and myself were part of a large charter. We travelled by bus from Saint John and crossed the border at St. Stephen. The agency overbooked the affair and had to lay on an extra bus. This Lorelei/Hardfield woman was on the bus ahead of us. At the rest stops she kept to herself and apparently slept all the way down and all the way back. Some of the girls who like to dish the dirt say she also *slept* the entire time she was at the resort. But I must admit I did see her on the slopes and at après-ski parties."

"Her hair was styled differently. Marcelled. And was darker. I think she's a natural brunette. To be honest, she looked better without all the make-up she wore today."

I sat back, relieved and filled with gratitude. My mind was following dangerous byways when it could suspect Penny of wrong-doing or withholding. She was right about confusion and madness.

"Doesn't that just take the cake?" Penny laughed.

I grinned. "Oh, yeah. A surprise cake."

CHAPTER FORTY-ONE

FOG OVER THE Channel. Dreams of England. Penny lost in the backstreets of Brighton. Where is she? Why can't I find her? I awake but am not awake. Awaking is struggling up through deep water toward a distant light.

A book tumbles off my lap and onto the carpet. The green carpet so far below. I open my eyes. The doorbell sounds ill-tempered. I unwrap the blanket bound around my legs and go to the head of the stairs and press the buzzer.

I didn't really awaken until Doc Cromarty took me by the shoulders. "Steady, Jack. We don't need you falling head over heels down the stairs."

We went inside where he led me like one of the Lost Boys into the kitchen and sat me down at the table. "What did you go and do? Sleep sitting up in the front room all night?"

"Yeah. I read a book cover to cover then drifted off."

Cromarty rattled around the stove until he had a fire blazing. The activity made me alert but I was parched with fever and my muscles ached.

"Where did you get this?" Cromarty said, emerging from the pantry, electric percolator in hand. "I thought you didn't altogether trust electricity?"

"I'm learning. It is almost forty years into the twentieth century. I got it at Sully's. Go ahead, use it, it's a dandy."

Cromarty grinned maliciously. "Sully's? So you aren't incorruptible after all. Frankly, I'm aghast."

I laughed. My head hurt. "Go jump in the lake. Besides, he owed me for the World Series last year. Double because the Yankees swept the Cubs."

Cromarty sneered. "Baseball. Haven't shown any interest since I was in high school. Won't bother either until they let the Negroes play."

"Don't hold your breath," I said, sad at the mention of Sullivan.

Cromarty sensed this, or maybe was also saddened, and busied himself with preparing the coffee. Without saying a word he rolled up his sleeves and washed the dishes in the sink.

I took the sandwiches out of the icebox. Penny had wrapped them in waxed paper and placed them in a big cookie tin with a picture of a Scottish castle on the lid. I hadn't used it since Grace was alive. How the dead go on living with us. Not through big things but the small.

Doc Cromarty gave me a steaming mug of coffee. "Are you all right, Jack? You're not depressed?"

"Somewhat. I was just thinking about Sully – then this cookie tin reminded me of Grace." I ate one of the little triangles. Cucumber and cream cheese. Not bad. "Coffee's good, isn't it, Doc?"

Cromarty nodded. After picking up and examining five or six sandwiches, he stodged his briar with tobacco. Striking a match off the sole of one of his brogues, he huffed and puffed until I thought he'd blow the house down.

I managed to eat another dainty and then lit a smoke myself.

Contented, Doc mumbled, "Coffee and tobacco – twin poisons."

"Yeah, ain't they lovely?"

We sat for a long time, a kind of peace between us. We had been through a lot together and knew without speaking that there were dangerous curves ahead.

Cromarty's wristwatch, always ten minutes slow, read ten to ten when I disturbed the quiet. I told him about my meeting with Deputy Chief Hardfield and the business with Wilder Hunter. Also, the matter of the lockers at the station and the forcible entry of the locker at the D.A.R. wharf. There were so many details to catch up on that it took me almost half an hour. I included a description of what I'd found out at Shorty Long's woodyard, which to me was verification that something serious was in the works. I even confessed that I had suspected Penny of some kind of involvement. That I'd erased what I thought was her footprint at Sully's.

Cromarty listened with rapt attention, occasionally touching a flame to his pipe. "Mrs. Hardfield. The mind boggles."

"It might be the link I've been looking for all along. A lucky break. So much for police procedure. Who'd of thought?"

"Careful, Jack, you're walking on thin ice."

"More like walking on water. When I get rid of this flu I'm going to Sullivan's first thing. Screw Hardfield and Wilder Hunter."

Cromarty removed his tweed jacket, and hung it over the back of a chair near the stove. He poured more coffee and sat down at the far end of the table this time, as if afraid of catching my germs. "I've already been to Sullivan's."

"When?"

"This morning."

"And?"

Cromarty ran a hand through his rusty hair. Immersed in thought, he peered into the distance. I'd seen Doc like this before and knew better than to hurry him. He took a Philip Morris out of the pack on the table and absent-mindedly lit it.

I went into the bathroom and soaked my face and neck with cold water, then I took my temperature. It was a shade over a hundred. Glancing in the mirror to survey the wreckage, I stuck out my tongue. It had more coats than a rummage sale. I retreated to the kitchen. Like most tough guys, I was a pussycat when it came to being sick.

Cromarty gobbled a couple of sandwiches. Brown bread, of course.

"Don't keep me hanging," I said.

"Sullivan's place was clean. Abnormally so. By any standard, almost antiseptic."

"But who?"

"Your Mister Hunter pulled my car over on Adelaide Street just past Victoria. He was in the company of Hardfield. Without much ado they made me sign a document swearing absolute secrecy."

"Secrecy? They *told* me to clam up but didn't make me sign anything. What reason did they give you?"

I lit a cigarette and took too deep a drag but it didn't matter. I was furious.

"National security," he said. "It's under the umbrella of the Official Secrets Act. I'm not supposed to tell you but given the circumstances that seems irrelevant."

I hit the roof. "Secrecy, my ass! The investigation's been stolen from us. They've got our hands tied. If we're nabbed poking around they could throw the book at us."

Cromarty agreed. "But," he smiled, a gleam in his eye. "There is something else."

"And what's that?"

"From what you told me I gather you're almost certain Werner Strasser and the Nazis from the *Bergensfjord* are responsible for Sullivan's death. Correct?"

"Yeah. But I haven't got anything that will hold up in court. I'm *not* supposed to have anything – circumstantial or otherwise."

"Exactly. Both of us have been ordered to cease any action. To disavow any knowledge. Where does that leave us?"

"Up Shit Creek without a paddle."

"Even though I'm inclined to agree, I wouldn't put it into gutter language. But..."

"But, what? You got me hooked, Doc. Pull me in."

"I did an autopsy on a body dragged out of the bay off Partridge Island."

"Yeah, I heard about him."

"I don't know how you could've heard about him, and I'm not about to ask, but he was from the *Bergensfjord*, Jack."

"What?" Flu or not, my head was jumping with ideas. And questions. "That man's body was weighed down with tires and ballast bricks."

"How do you know that?" Cromarty said. "I'm beginning to wonder if you're telepathic. Nobody..."

"I get around in person, Doc. I was in the wrong place at the right time. But you said he was from the *Bergensfjord*. What makes you say that?"

"A number of reasons. Irrefutable reasons." Cromarty hustled into the front room and came back with his overcoat. He took a manila envelope from the inside pocket. "This contains my autopsy report and a couple of photographs I want you to look at."

I wavered, repulsed at the thought of looking at Cromarty's photographs. They weren't exactly picture postcards.

"I'll save you the trouble of reading the report. My conclusion is that this man was dead before he hit the water."

"Already dead?"

"Yes. And the disposal of his body was a matter of haste."

"I'll take your word for it that he was dead before he was dumped in the drink. But the haste? You're surmising, aren't you?"

"I understand your skepticism but I'm about to change your mind."

"Oh? I'm all ears."

Cromarty handed a small book to me. I cracked, "What's this? His bank book?"

"Solid evidence. Feel free to peruse the contents."

I pulled the book out of its leather pocket. It was still soggy and smelled of the sea. The ink had run on most of the pages, creating a colourful blur. It was a passbook, the type required by foreign seamen to check on and off the Government Wharf. I couldn't find a name anywhere but it was possible to make out what looked like dates, smeared but legible. I turned to the last entry. The time and date made my hair stand on end. "Where did you find this?"

"In the fellow's left boot. He wasn't thoroughly searched. That's one of the reasons why I think he was dropped overboard in a panic."

"Go on, continue," I said, staring at the date.

"There weren't any identification papers on the body. Obviously removed. And there was a clumsy attempt to further hide the man's identity."

"Don't show me any pictures of dead people," I said, stopping Cromarty before he turned the photographs face up. "My stomach doesn't need any extra help throwing up."

"Fine. Remember what you told me after you returned from your cousin Marvin's in Nova Scotia? About the Navy man you met on the train and the story he told you?"

"Yeah. George Hudson. I should be hearing from him any day now. He's going to try and come up with the name of the sailboat the Nazis were aboard in the Annapolis Basin."

"Precisely. And what convinced him they were Nazis?"

"Tattoos of swastikas on their chests."

"Over their hearts?"

"Yes."

"These photographs are of the body out of the water. If you hadn't told me about the tattoos I might have missed it. Mistaken the damage for the work of the fishes or sea worms."

"Doc, *please*."

"Okay, I'll get straight to the point. There was a botched attempt to remove a tattoo from this man's chest. To flay the area with a rasp or a crude scraper. I used a common food dye to heighten the dis-colouration of the subcutaneous traces and, lo and behold, a swastika." Cromarty flashed the photo. I shielded my eyes. He had further enhanced the tattoo with a blue marker.

Cromarty sat back proudly. "Furthermore," he crowed, "I remembered you saying the *Bergensfjord* went into drydock the afternoon of February fourteenth. That's the final entry date in the book – 1:a.m. Feb/14/39. What I'm saying begins to make sense, doesn't it? This man was killed that very day but instead of being thrown overboard on the high seas where he would have never been found, the perpetrators had no other option than to get rid of him before they completed the U-turn from the harbour to Courtenay Bay where the shipbuilders awaited the berthing of the *Bergensfjord* for repairs."

"Go to the head of the class, Doc."

He gathered the autopsy report and the photographs together, returning them to the envelope. "I'd like to leave this here for safekeeping. Where's a good place for it?"

"The record cabinet. File it under A."

The body in the bay. Eugene Robichaud dead in the hold of the *Bergensfjord*. Deputy Chief Hardfield and Det. Sergeant Sullivan at the scene before me. All on Saint Valentine's Day. None of it mere coincidence. And what about Hardfield's wife? To say nothing of Sullivan's cleaned-up flat?

"I can tell you're chomping at the bit to get back in harness, Jack, but don't give it a second thought. You have to let this flu run its course or else you'll suffer a relapse and be twice as far behind. Believe me, it's a virulent strain of influenza. I've done autopsies on several elderly people who died from it."

"Okay, Doc, I get the message. I'm not going anywhere. Why should I? I can sit here like a spider and have all this information fly into my web. I should get sick more often."

Cromarty groaned. "Balderdash. And you shouldn't be smoking."

"Quit huffin' the butts?"

"Yes, but I know anything I say about smoking will fall on deaf ears. I rarely have a cigarette but you're like a damned chimney. You should let me take a look at you."

"What do you mean?"

TERRY CRAWFORD

"Give you a check-up."

"No offence, but you're a coroner. A doctor of the dead. I'll wait thirty or forty years, if you don't mind."

"Suit yourself, but I *know* what kills people."

"What killed Sullivan?"

"Loss of blood."

I had a vision of Sully's bloodsprayed dining room. Gobs of red in the dust on the mantel. "I could've told you that. That's not what I meant. Why did you go back to his place?"

"Your detective's mentality is rubbing off on me. After Penelope Fairchild told me about the Group B blood sample, I got to thinking. Putting a few things together. Not the least of which was Sullivan's blood type – Group B. We know he was on the *Bergensfjord* February 14th. He never made any attempt to hide the fact. And you've already determined that he was in Robichaud's office. You found the blood sample you gave Penelope beside the door of Shed 7. Some distance away from the *Bergensfjord* but handy to Robichaud's desk. Let's presume the blood from the pier was Sullivan's. What was Sullivan doing there? Perhaps the people who killed him were trying to find out. Follow me?"

"Sure. But you're surmising again."

"No, I'm not, Jack. I withdrew a syringe of Sullivan's blood before the funeral people arrived. At the lab I discovered a chemical compound in it. After running the usual tests, eliminating A.S.A., prescription drugs, et cetera… I was baffled. But one of my young assistants had done thesis research on anesthetics. He engineered a mock-up that was surprisingly close. Care to hazard a guess?"

"Moonshine. How would I know?"

"Thiopentone sodium. More commonly known as sodium pentothal. It's a general anesthetic and is also the so-called 'truth serum'. Sullivan was injected with it and something that closely resembled benzedrine – to use the vernacular – speed."

"Ugly. What would be the effect?"

"Once it started to work it would be terrifying. So much so, that it might be too unpredictable to be useful as a means of extracting information. However, in experienced hands…"

"It makes my skin crawl. Who are we really dealing with?"

"If I might be allowed to be melodramatic?" Cromarty said.

"Permission granted."

"Desperate men on a deadly errand."

"That's big news. How did you get in to Sullivan's?"

"With a set of keys I took from Sullivan's after you went home on the day we found him."

"Found him? We were *sent* to his place. I was taken off suspension. Sully always kept his locker key on a ring in his pocket. It was used to open the locker at the station. I'll bet the keys you found were left there by Hardfield. He's in this right up to his handlebar mustache."

"The Deputy Chief has all the earmarks of a man about to have a nervous breakdown," Cromarty said. "I agree with you that he is involved in something dastardly. But not Sullivan's death. At the funeral Hardfield looked like he had a sword dangling over his head. He's mixed up in something. I'll leave it to you to find out exactly what. In the meantime, he's got us strapped with this Official Secrets move."

"You think so, eh?" I said. "Well, I've got a few moves of my own hidden up my sleeve. Before you go, leave the keys with me."

"Can't do it. Wilder Hunter seized them."

"Oh, he did? Well then, that calls for a B and E at the earliest opportunity."

CHAPTER FORTY-TWO

AFTER SIX DAYS, wearing clothes instead of underwear and a bathrobe felt strange. I was all buttoned down and wrapped up. Confined. Strange, also, to walk around in shoes when I was still light-headed from lying down so much. Overnight I had become an awkward inch taller and seemed in danger of pitching forward onto my nose.

I opened the kitchen door and went into the storage area at the back of the house that I used for a woodshed. It was a rough, unfinished room without plaster or lathe, a single bare bulb hanging from the ceiling. There was a stump for splitting kindling beside the woodpile and a dartboard on the wall next to the window. To jazz up the place I'd tacked baseball and boxing posters between the studs. I liked it out here. In warmer weather Lincoln and I often played darts or just sat with coffee or a beer and jawed about nothing in particular. Shooting the breeze, as they say.

I pushed up the window sash and stuck my head and shoulders outside. It had turned milder while I was sick. In St. Peter's churchyard there were circles of naked ground around the trees where the snow had shrunk away from the trunks. Vinca, green and waxen in the sunlight, lay exposed along the fence. As always, it gave me a boost.

I was accustomed to seeing my Studebaker in the yard. It took a minute for it to sink in that the bright new Pontiac parked behind the house belonged to me. That cheered me as well. I had serious work ahead and didn't have any business feeling as good as I did but depression never did stick with me. It got in the way of getting things done. And there were things to do.

I pulled in the dish towels pinned on the clothesline. Lincoln had visited last night and cooked my first square meal in days. Against my protests he cleaned the apartment and laundered all the towels. The bath towels were on the drying rack above the kitchen stove. I replaced them with the damp dish towels and fixed a pot of tea. I'd had enough housework for one day.

While waiting for the tea to brew, I slapped together a substantial ham and cheese sandwich. I'd eaten a huge breakfast about an hour ago but now that I was feeling better my appetite was unstoppable, my body sending messages that I'd best heed. After I wolfed down the sandwich I polished off a couple of Cortlands and tossed the cores into the trash can.

Tom Waterman was in the front room reading Doc Cromarty's autopsy on the sailor from the *Bergensfjord*. He walked into the kitchen. "What's all the commotion?"

"Apple-core basketball. In grade school the nuns used to send me to the cloakroom for doing that. I could sink them from thirty feet like they had eyes."

"Sounds like you were teacher's pet."

I poured tea for us and lit a cigarette. It was the last of a half dozen that Wilder Hunter had left for me when I'd run out of Philip Morrises last night. Hunter joined Lincoln and me for supper, then spent the evening listening to records. He and Lincoln knew the music inside and out. Lincoln was guarded at first but after an hour or so he let his defenses down. He was too often treated with outright prejudice by whites to trust them easily. On the other hand, he had once said he would rather cope with bald-faced bigotry than contend with tolerant, even kindly, condescension. There was no condescension in Wilder Hunter. If anything, there was a kind of familiarity that might have made me jealous.

"What's that you're smoking?" Tom asked, carving a slice of ham off the leftover roast. He slathered mustard on it then wrapped it around a pickle and a finger of cheese.

"Wilder Hunter's special tailor-mades."

"Distinctive smell. Can't quite place it."

"H'mm. Me too," I said, lazy from eating too much. Hunter had worn a Notre Dame cardigan with a shawl collar that had absorbed the aroma of the expensive blend. The sweater made him look collegiate even though he was close to thirty-five.

"Did Hunter say anything?" Tom said, dipping a pickle into the mustard jar.

"What about?"

"Anything. You know."

"No. Said it was a social call. That he was bored. So in a way, I suppose, he was admitting that everything was quiet."

"Or so he wants us to think."

I nodded. "He's crafty. A couple of times he dropped hints about Werner Strasser and the whereabouts of his henchmen to see if I'd nibble at the bait but I played dumb. Not too dumb, but dumb. If Hunter wants to relieve me of my ignorance, that's up to him. He's the one who put us under a shroud of secrecy. I did come right out and bluntly ask him about the Canadian Secret Service."

"And?"

"He said they'd given him *carte blanche*. I liked that. Told him it showed me he had *savoir-faire*. I think it galled him. He wants to be taken seriously. Anyway, Hunter carped that the Canadian Secret Service are too secret. Even worse than the British. Our people wouldn't let him bring his pistol across the border."

"Aw. Too bad," Tom said, digging the last pickle out of the jar.

"Hunter said he felt naked without his gun." I checked the clock. It was almost eleven. Soon time to hit the pavement. I wanted to break into Sullivan's house before it evaporated in a mist of cleanliness.

"Jesus," Tom said.

I'd never heard him utter so much as a mild oath. Now here he was taking the Lord's name.

"Jesus. Americans and their obsession with firearms. Hunter probably figures he's Wild Bill Hickok."

"More like Melvin Purvis," I said. "G-man with a mission."

"I'd like to know more about Hunter," Tom said.

"Like?"

"He appears out of the blue in Hardfield's office, and from what you've said, with unrestricted authority handed to him through some co-operative arrangement with our government…"

I interjected, "Secret Service. It's akin to government within government."

"Yes. I never thought of it that way. Anyhow, because of this arrangement we accept him at face value. I'm just saying I'd like to know more about him. Correct me if I'm wrong, but you're not exactly an open book where Hunter is concerned."

"Just giving him tit for tat," I said. "All right. You want to know more about him? Fine. Any ideas?"

"My father's brother Manfred is a physics professor at Fordham. Catholic institutions maintain affiliations. Manfred could make some polite inquiries to Notre Dame if I asked him."

"Physics? I'm impressed. Sure, contact your uncle. It couldn't do any harm and it might prove interesting."

I walked to the hall closet and reached into the back for my red and black hunting jacket. I wanted to wear something that could be easily recognized at a distance. The jacket was musty and a bit moth-eaten. I hadn't hunted in years. Animals, that is.

I put on my old felt hat.

Waterman chuckled. "Nice lid."

"There's method to my madness. If you're finished eating me out of house and home, let's go."

On the sidewalk, I pulled up the floppy collar of the hunting jacket. It was grand to be outdoors. "Did you put that autopsy report back where you found it, Tom?"

"Yes. Sickening. Doctor Cromarty's taking a big risk by replacing that report with one that's been modified. I take it that he's with us one hundred per-cent?"

A city bus rumbled past, spraying slush over the curb. I leapt out of the way. "Yes. It's not too late, Tom, for you to back out. We could, will be, in serious trouble if we're caught obstructing a government investigation. Especially where it involves national security."

We crossed the street at the corner and climbed the wide steps to Welsford's Drug Store. An elaborately dressed window displayed various cold remedies and preventatives. A three-foot porcelain statue of a fisherman with a codfish slung over his shoulder stared out at us.

Tom blocked the door. "Back out?" he said. "I'm in till the bitter end. This is why I joined the police force. To do something more than help old folks and kids cross the road. Don't forget, it was *me* who phoned you on Valentine's Day."

I had to smile at Tom's utter seriousness. "Yes. You did drag me into this quagmire, didn't you? Now, out of my way. I need smokes."

There was a cluster of girls loitering around the magazine stand. Every one of them clutched a bottle of Coca-Cola with lipstick-smeared

TERRY CRAWFORD

straws sticking out of the neck. A buxom brunette of seventeen or eighteen, in a sweater a size too tight, spoke sweetly to Waterman. Tom blushed and grinned at me.

"Lofty McMillan's daughter," he said. "Met her at the police picnic last summer. Pesters the daylights out of me." Tom tipped his hat. "Morning, Maggie."

"I should be so lucky," I said. "How come girls weren't that fetching when I was your age?"

"Careful, old-timer. Every generation says that."

I purchased a pack of Philip Morris and eased onto a stool at the fountain. Under close scrutiny from the girls, Tom hardly dared look sideways. From where we were seated we could see straight up Douglas Avenue. Welsford's was at the high point of Main, a long snake of a street that began at the bank of the St. John River in Indiantown, climbed uncertainly and crookedly to its peak, descended through a busy commercial strip, curved, then rose again at Fort Howe, before it dropped steeply toward the railyards flanking the harbour.

People griped about finding it so hard to get around Saint John but I liked the haphazard layout of the streets, the roads trailing the contours of the rockbound land, riding the ridges and taking the direct route up and down the hills. What my grandfather used to call, "An altogether fine mess!"

I ordered a large Cherry Coke. But Tom had ants in his pants. I took pity on him and slurped down the Coke in the blink of an eye.

"Whew, am I glad we're out of there," he said, glancing back through the display window.

McMillan's daughter waved alluringly and tittered with the other girls.

"Yeah, I thought they were going to break into a chorus of *Embraceable You*," I said. "How are you with a cuestick?"

"An honest opinion?"

"That's the best kind."

"Better than average."

"Good."

Gillespie's Poolroom was two blocks away on Main toward the river. It occupied the fourth floor of an old clapboard house. Parrtown

Plumbing and Heating was on the ground level. A pair of cold-water flats were sandwiched between it and the clacking of the pool balls.

I steered Tom into the alley and up the outdoor staircase to Gillespie's. On the top landing, I surveyed the neighbourhood for a minute. Nothing out of the ordinary. A mouthwatering aroma wafted up from the luncheonette next door. I almost succumbed to the temptation. Two burly men in striped coveralls appeared below and started hefting cast-iron radiators onto a truck. The flatbed groaned under the weight of the load. The men cursed good-naturedly at one another, turning the air blue. Deep blue.

Across the street, a tall gent in a cinnamon-brown overcoat and gray fedora stepped into a recessed doorway next to the Sunbright Drycleaners. I lit a cigarette and watched him out of the corner of my eye as he jotted down something in a notepad. He slunk back further, periodically stamping his feet on the checker-board-tiled entryway, even though the day wasn't cold.

I went inside. Tom was rolling a cuestick on top of one of the snooker tables. "It's not the stick, it's the shooter," I called. He laughed and continued searching from rack to rack for a straight cue.

Derek Gillespie was perched on a stool beside the cash register in a cubbyhole at the rear. A gooseneck lamp illuminated the book he was absorbed in. Gillespie was a goner on whodunits, a taste I'd never acquired.

"Snooker balls, table six," I said.

Without taking his eyes off the page, Gillespie reached under the counter and handed me a basket of balls. Consulting his wristwatch, he wrote down the time on the day-sheet then flicked the light switch to his right to VI. The lights came on over the table by the front windows.

"Nice to see you, too," I said.

Gillespie poked a finger into the middle of a sentence and glanced up. "Hello, Jack. Same here. Hercule Poirot. Can't put it down."

I was about to say something obvious but he nose-dived right back into the book. "Gee, and you don't even move your lips," I said in jest, but he didn't hear a word. About my age, Gillespie had a skeletal face and perpetual black circles under his eyes. He looked old before his time; it didn't help that he was stoop-shouldered.

TERRY CRAWFORD

I dumped the snooker balls onto the table and put the basket underneath. Tom racked the cherries and positioned the coloured balls while I selected a cue.

The only windows, three in all, overlooked Main Street. They were tall and wide with four panes each, the bottom two painted white and protected with chicken wire. Hardwood shelves with built-in ashtrays divided the windows horizontally, and provided a good spot to lean on with your elbows.

We played a couple of games. Tom was a pot-shot artist: terrific at nailing difficult shots but reckless on position. I had him beat in both matches long before we reached the coloured balls, which we potted just for practice. It was then that I took the opportunity to show him the basics about high and low stuff. "A little 'English' goes a long way," I said. "Get command of high/low and follow through/pull back on the cue ball and in no time you'll be a shark."

Tom laughed. "Instead of a fish? You're too good. You make it look easy."

"Patience and position. Instead of taking risks, play it safe. Otherwise you leave your opponent with too many chances." Pretending to check the weather, I scanned the skies. The brown overcoat was eating a sandwich. He saw me, because he stiffened and tilted his head upward. I couldn't see the guy's face under the brim of his hat but that didn't bother me. There'd be time for that later. I turned my back and leaned against the window shelf. Tom was practicing left-and right-hand "English" with a steady, smooth stroke. "Set 'em up again," I said. "You're getting the hang of it."

Except for the cone-shaped fixtures over our table the only other light on in the room was Gillespie's reading lamp. I walked through the darkness to the Coca-Cola cooler beside the pinball machine. I lifted a Coke out of the water, dried it with a towel, and tossed a nickel onto the counter. Gillespie raked in the coin with his fingers and deposited it with a clink in a tobacco can. He was on the last page of a chapter. I lit a cigarette and waited.

Gillespie folded a corner of the page, set the book aside, and squinted at me with unfocused eyes.

I reached over and stuffed a two-dollar bill into his shirt pocket.

He took it out and carefully examined both sides under the light. If it had been a coin he would have bitten it. "A deuce? What gives?"

"Nothing much. It's a snap. I want you to shoot snooker with Tom for forty minutes or so."

"There must be a catch."

"I can see your 'little gray cells' are in action," I said.

Gillespie liked that a lot. He sat up straight, as if he were Hercule, the Belgian wonder, in person.

"The catch is you have to wear my jacket and hat," I said.

"Why?" Gillespie asked in an excited whisper.

"Never mind. That's a secret," I whispered in turn. "Keep your back to the windows. Don't look out under any circumstances. Got that?" I gave him my jacket and hat, then stood back to see the effect. "Don't slouch. That's better. Keep your shoulders back."

I gave Tom a brief explanation, introduced him to Gillespie, then went out the fire exit. It led me to a catwalk on the roof of a three-storey annex which in turn led to a single flight of stairs down to the street above. Up there, I scurried through someone's backyard, went between houses, and arrived on the sidewalk across from the convent.

I transferred the screwdriver and putty knife from my pants pocket to Gillespie's raincoat, tugged on his Brooklyn Dodgers cap, and headed for Sullivan's. The street curved sharply at the bottom of a ravine where it ran into Main. But Main had already swerved away from the brown overcoat's watchful eyes so I didn't hesitate to beat it across the road and run up the hill opposite.

Then I calmly strolled the four blocks to Victoria Street.

TERRY CRAWFORD

CHAPTER FORTY-THREE

I T WAS THE late morning lull, the neighbourhood so quiet you could hear bedsheets flapping on the clotheslines. Two old men stood gossiping in front of Sullivan's walkway. When I passed by I heard, "And such a young fellow he was," from one, and, "A cop's life must be terrible, people hating you left and right," from the other. And then from both, "A thankless job." They nodded and parted. I retraced my steps, made sure no one was looking out of a window, and went quickly around to the back. A path had been neatly sculpted out of the snow, then swept with a broom. I climbed the stairs to the second floor. The sweeper had swept backwards, taking the broom with him. Smart. It was impossible to estimate how many were in on the clean-up.

I emptied Sullivan's clothespin bag onto the landing. His reserve keys and lucky shamrock chain were missing. I grimly acknowledged the thoroughness of the men I was pitted against. Putting the clothespin bag back as I'd found it, I took the tools out of my pocket and set to work on Sullivan's door. It was a piece of cake. No wonder break and enters were on the rise.

I secured the lock behind me. The shed was neat as a pin, not the jumble of odds and ends Sully called a workshop. Duke's bowls sat empty beside the welcome mat, his collar and leash fastened to a leg of the sawhorse. It gave me a major case of the creeps.

The kitchen would've won a gold medal from the *Ladies Home Journal*. So would the rest of the place. Everything had been washed and dusted. The linoleum gleamed, its true colours revealed for the first time in years. I sat on an arm of the chesterfield and lit a cigarette with Sullivan's table lighter. It was a thirty-fifth birthday present from me, a substantial item encased in blue granite. I wanted to swipe the thing but thought it best to leave everything intact.

With no one to stoke the furnace the house was cold as a barn. To stay warm I wandered in and out of the rooms, now and then poking into a drawer or searching a closet. It might be wrong to speak ill of the dead but Sullivan was a slob. A born slob. And yet every nook and cranny was arranged as precisely as a showroom. It was all wrong.

I'd sweated day and night in bed for almost a week, delirious most of the time but not so out of it that I hadn't thought certain things through. Sullivan had been tortured, and not just for sheer spite or wicked enjoyment. They'd wanted information. That was as obvious as the nose on Jimmy Durante's face. I'd concluded that Sullivan had screamed out whatever he knew. Now I wasn't so sure.

Before or after Sullivan was killed, the apartment had been turned inside out. Maybe it was the awful shock and nauseating dread I felt when Doc Cromarty and I first saw the murder scene that had thrown me off. It was obvious to me now. I'd been stupid. They were after some thing. And so were Wilder Hunter and the C.I.C. crew. Why else would they have meticulously fine-toothed every square inch of the place? But what was it? And why did it possess such deadly importance?

I was in a quandary. Officially, my hands were tied. I was unable, forbidden, to stir things up the way I'd like. And what about Deputy Chief Hardfield? Why did he often visit Sullivan? And what about the bottle-blonde, Mrs. Hardfield? I made a decision to visit her someday soon. The Pontiac could develop radiator trouble near the Hardfield's house, a pretext so transparent she shouldn't question it. Anyway, she was an alleged flirt and I was considered handsome. Getting in the door might be easier than getting out.

All of a sudden there was a racket down below. My heart jumped. I went to the window and peered out from behind the drapes. There was a coal truck in the driveway. A man in workclothes covered with black dust was gravity-feeding coal down a tin chute and on into a bin in the basement. The rattling reverberated through the backyards. I watched as the coalman off-loaded a half ton, climbed down off the truck, retracted the chute, stuffed the bill through the letter slot, and drove away.

I opened the door to the front stairwell and went down and got the bill. It was made out to Sullivan. It gave me an idea.

As usual, the basement door was unlocked. I turned on the light switch. There was a coco mat at the bottom of the steps. It was quite new. I stood on it and looked at the footprints in the coal dust on the floor. There were enough tracks for five or six men, all wearing identical overshoes. They had conducted a systematic search but there wasn't

TERRY CRAWFORD

much to see: the coal bin, an apple basket full of old shoes, a tidy shelf of illustrated magazines, a rack containing hockey sticks, baseball bats, and fishing rods. Sullivan had a phobia of fire. He could let bananas rot into a cloud of fruitflies in his kitchen, but he faithfully cleaned the basement every Saturday.

I followed the footprints but they didn't reveal anything much. There was a congregation in front of Sully's Vargas pin-ups but that didn't surprise me. I knew I wasn't on the trail of a band of fairies.

I wiped my feet on the coco mat and then I went up and sat on the bench inside the front door. The outcome of events might have been otherwise had Sullivan not been the only tenant. If only there had been someone to raise the alarm. The landlord's mother had lived on the first floor. In fact, died there in her sleep three years ago. The blinds were drawn and everything left as it was, so deep was her only child's grief. She was a jovial busybody forever watching out for people. Sully and the old lady had gotten along, always exchanging favours and running errands for one another. He used to take care of her tabby cats while she was away on vacation. I'd helped him clean the litterboxes. I eyed the brass nameplate mounted on her door. If you pressed the lower right hand corner the plate popped open on springs and the door key fell into your left hand. I did it.

The flat was in darkness. I tried a light switch but the electricity was disconnected. I lit a match and stood there gawking until the flame burned my fingertips. The windows were heavily curtained and the room was devoid of furniture. Sully had lied to me. I ran upstairs and got his flashlight from a drawer in the kitchen.

On the wall over Sully's telephone there was a list of numbers. One of them was mine – with a line drawn through it. Apparently Sully had dropped me from his social register. The phone was still in order. I dialled 3-8494. The raspy voice of Sullivan's landlord answered. I introduced myself as Detective Sergeant Ireland, an unnecessary formality considering we used to bowl together on the same team at St. Peter's Lanes, but it underscored the seriousness of our conversation. Five minutes later I slowly hung up the receiver. Sullivan had been paying rent for the bottom floor over the past two years. Each payment was in cash, six months in advance. He was paid up until the end of May. He claimed he wanted the privacy, especially in the winter when the woman upstairs was down south.

The sun edged over the roof of the house next door and flooded into the kitchen. I stared at the trick-of-the-eye geometrics on the linoleum for a while then I snapped out of it and hurried downstairs.

The brightness of the flashlight was exaggerated in the dark. So was the flowered wallpaper and the pastel woodwork. There were cigarette butts rudely squashed on the bare floors. They were Sweet Caporals – Sully's brand. The front rooms were empty.

I pushed open the door of what I presumed was the bedroom. Shining the flashlight high and low, I whistled softly in amazement then cursed out loud. Cursed long and hard.

Stacked to the ceiling were car tires, so new the paper was still on them. They were top-of-the-line imports. Dunlops from England. Crammed between the walls of tires were cartons containing Sparton radios – table and console models. And General Electric appliances – coffee percolators, automatic toasters, Mix-Masters...

I was too incensed to bother taking a further inventory. There was money here. And if stolen goods had been trafficked in and out for two years, there had been money made. Plenty of money.

I left everything as I'd found it and trudged upstairs in a state of severe shock. I'd had my suspicions. Strong suspicions. But now that they had been proven true I didn't want to believe my own eyes.

I put the flashlight back in the kitchen drawer. Before I really knew what I was doing I had Dorothy Sullivan on the phone. She inquired about my health and informed me that her mother was hospitalized with the flu and was not expected to survive.

"I guess I caught you at a bad time, Dot."

"Never. What is it, Jack?"

"Are your brothers still slinging freight?"

"Yes. They work for Donovan's Transfer."

"Do you think they can borrow a big truck the day after tomorrow?"

"Yes. Why?"

"I want them to go to Sully's and remove every single thing in the place. Furniture, appliances, pictures off the wall. Don't leave so much as a spoon. Got that? It's all yours, Dot, to do with as you please."

TERRY CRAWFORD

"You saw my house, Jack. It's as frayed around the edges as I am. I'll take whatever comes my way. But is this on the up-and-up?"

"Sully didn't leave a will. It's all yours, Dot."

She hemmed and hawed. "Aw, I don't know."

"Dot, you and Sully were separated, not divorced. You two couldn't have gotten a divorce if you wanted one, thanks to Holy Mother Church."

"Don't mention that bitch," Dot said bitterly. I could smell the Boodle's Gin over the phone. "I wanted. I *wanted.*"

"Then telephone Sandy and Red and instruct them to do as I say. And after the job's done phone Deputy Chief Hardfield and tell him so he won't think there's been a B and E. Promise?"

I heard ice clinking in a glass.

"Yes, I promise, Jack," Dot said, then laughed. "I don't mean to sound ungrateful, that money you gave me, dirty or not, was a godsend, but… you're not using me, are you, Jack?"

I always said that Dorothy would've made a better detective than Sully. "Naw. What makes you say that?"

"Because the trouble with you, Jack Ireland, is that you can be a devious bastard."

I sloughed off the compliment. "Listen, the back door will be unlocked. Sandy and Red can go to the front once they're in, and move stuff out that door. Just remind them to lock both doors when they're done. Okay?"

"Yes. And Jack?"

"*Yes*, Dot." I was anxious to vacate the premises.

"The trouble with you, Jack Ireland, is that you're also a nice bastard."

"Why, thank you, sweetheart. Now, bid me adieu."

"So long."

I exited via the back stairs. The coast was clear so I walked as fast as I could back to Gillespie's Poolroom.

On the catwalk I startled a crow with a piece of burnt toast in its beak. I was watching it fly over the rooftops toward St. Peter's Church when Gillespie pushed open the fire door.

I hung his raincoat and cap on a nail and got into my own clothes.

"Tom beat me two out of three. He's got potential," Gillespie said, returning to his post beside the cash register.

A pair of retired gents who were shooting eight-ball on one of the small tables looked at me with mild curiosity.

The guy in the cinnamon-brown overcoat was still across the street.

Waterman and I went outside. Tom protected his eyes until we were down on the sidewalk. Blinking, he asked, "How did it go?"

"Better than good. Let's take a stroll over to King Square. Give our tail a chance to warm up his feet. I've got lots to tell you, Tom. We can discuss it over lunch at the Silver Rail. They've got a great juke box."

Tom poked me in the ribs. "You must be hollow. How can you be hungry?"

"Hungry? I could eat a bowl of wax fruit."

CHAPTER FORTY-FOUR

I PARKED THE Pontiac on Winter Street, grateful to escape the radio. The news was depressing. The appeasement of Hitler had reached the level of ridiculousness. I wasn't a warmonger but there was such a thing as being too gun shy. Neville Chamberlain was probably having a heart attack every time a car backfired.

I walked around the corner to Stanley Street and over the steel-plated bridge that spanned the railyard. A caboose rolled underneath at the end of a long line of freight cars on its way to McAdam and destinations further west. Black soot settled on the snow as the locomotive disappeared around a bend a mile away.

I checked the specials printed in Bon-Ami on the windows and went into London's General Store at the foot of the bridge. Old man London was spreading fresh sawdust on the floors while a clerk swept the old stuff into a carton. They looked up when the bell on the door jingled.

"Morning," I said, waiting for them to finish their daily task. "Not a bad day out there at all."

Mr. London consulted the weather as if he'd forgotten blue sky and clouds existed. "Aye. Three or four weeks I'll be able to go out again. Never could abide winter."

Some of the dust from the wood chips got in my nostrils. I sneezed hard enough to drive nails.

Mr. London offered me a Kleenex. "Sensitive honker."

Eyes watering, I sneezed again.

"You must be a veritable sleuth-hound," he added dryly.

He took a fresh apron off a peg behind the vegetable stand. It was dazzling white and stiff as cardboard. He primly patted the part in the middle of his head with his fingertips. Then he adjusted his bow tie in the Black Cat mirror that faced the street. I watched as a car went in one ear and out the other. Penny Fairchild described Mr. London as the very personification of neatness. I said, "Mr. London, you're the personification of neatness."

He smiled into the mirror at me, smug as the Black Cat, trim gray moustaches twitching. "What'll it be today, Jack?"

I gave him my grocery list. "No need to deliver this. I'll pick it up later this morning."

He glanced at the slip. "Last night I made some of those sausages you like. How about a pound?"

"Make it two," I said, going to the cheese block and opening the lid. I lifted the blade and sliced off a wedge. "I'll take this now."

Mr. London placed the cheese on the scale and wrapped it in paper. Neatly, with a perfect bow on the string.

"What do you have for roasts? Good beef?"

I followed him into the meat locker and let him select a hefty one for me. "That's ideal, Mr. London. Do you mind if I go out through the storeroom? I'd like to see something along the tracks."

"Go right ahead, Jack."

The clerk tapped on the door with a coin. "Telephone, Mr. London."

"While you're at it, in your capacity as a policeman, you might have a look at my signs. Someone's been pelting them with rocks."

"Sure thing, Mr. London." I dropped the cheese into my jacket pocket and went through the storeroom and down an open stairwell to the basement. It was below Stanley Street but with a door opening onto the railyard. Standing on the loading dock, I could hear the low thunder of boxcars shunting in the distance. An old man on the lookout for bottles walked past, burlap sack clinking with riches. A woman opened a window in one of the houses opposite and shook out a dry mop.

From the middle of the tracks I looked at London's wall. His enameled signs had taken a severe beating. Some of them had more dimples than a golf ball. A fairly new Player's Navy Cut sign showed streaks of rust where the metal was punctured. It was a shame but there was nothing I could do about it unless I caught the culprit red-handed. It was the sort of assignment Hardfield yearned to see me fritter away my time and energy on. I'd already had a couple of piddling jobs directed my way from his desk. He was keeping Ireland out of trouble, but I had lots of trouble in mind for him.

Hugging the retaining wall, I went in under the bridge. Pigeons, restless and numerous, thrummed on the girders. I came out into the

TERRY CRAWFORD

sun, surprised by its warmth after the dank shade. A hundred feet further on I slipped between a row of boxcars and the Robin Hood flour mill.

At the four loading bays men pushed hand carts laden with sacks of flour across ramps and into the boxcars. I ascended a ladder at door 3 and swung into the mill, sidestepping a hand cart manned by a sullen worker who didn't return my greeting. Plainclothes railway cops, dressed as I was, were known to pay unexpected calls on the factories and warehouses along the railyard. Because of such tactics they weren't on anyone's list of popular personalities.

I kept to the right and wound through a maze of sacks piled to the rafters. Eventually I reached the front offices, housed in a pillared, ivy-covered brick façade. There was zero activity in the main corridor so I casually sauntered out the street door.

Traffic along City Road was heavy. I leaned against the mass of ivy vines hiding one of the pillars and waited for a chance to cross over to the White Rose filling station on the sunny side.

High above the station, on a steep slope, Hospital Hill dominated the valley. The General with its dome and ivory-coloured brick resembled a capital building more than a hospital, an impression dispelled by the approach at the emergency entrance of an ambulance crying forlornly through the neighbourhood.

I zig-zagged in and around the stalled traffic to the gas pumps. Rainbows of gasoline shone on the pavement, the fumes slightly intoxicating. A young mechanic in greasy coveralls with a small White Rose on the breast and a huge White Rose on the back hauled a water hose out of the garage and sprayed the spill.

I did a quick check of the tire racks, noting the prices, then climbed Ritchie Street opposite the flour mill gates. Stopping at the hospital heating plant, I listened to the dull roar of the boilers and stared up at the smokestack. It appeared to be toppling, a dizzying illusion on a day of swiftly moving clouds. I closed my eyes and the vertigo stopped. There was a promising smell on the breeze, of spring just around the corner. A scent of the earth thawing, ice and snow melting in a hurry. I was in the dreamy, slow mood that always overcame me when winter finally withdrew its icy fingers.

I opened my eyes and continued up the hill, passing over a wide expanse of rock that gave the adjacent street its name: Rock Street.

At the top I turned around in a grove of stunted poplars, some of them dead for want of sustenance, and scanned the valley for signs of someone following. Not that I was doing anything wrong but whatever the powers-that-be didn't know, wouldn't hurt them. And, I hoped, wouldn't hurt me.

The laboratory building nestled in the shadow of the hospital. It was connected by a tunnel to the morgue. An intern who looked young enough to be a high-school student held the door open and followed me inside. I watched as he read the directory. He kept unconsciously picking at a colony of pimples on his neck. I almost mumbled, "Physician, heal thyself," but thought the better of it. One day he might find me on the operating table and I didn't want to lose anything unnecessarily.

The hallways had the piney smell of Dustbane and a hint of another, more volatile cleanser. Behind the frosted glass of his office door, Doc Cromarty was watering the plants he usually tortured with neglect. He was in a gay frame of mind. I could hear a lively whistled rendition of *Swanee* floating through the open transom.

I went downstairs to the cafeteria and returned with paper cups of coffee and a bowl of soda crackers. Balancing the tray in one hand, I rapped sharply on the door.

The happy whistling ceased on a high note. Doc said, "I asked not to be disturbed until ten o'clock. Who is it?"

"The last of the Mohicans."

"Come in, Jack."

I turned the knob and with a flourish placed the tray on his desk. Then I took the wedge of cheddar out of my pocket.

"It's a good thing you came bearing gifts," he said, offering me a chair.

Cromarty unwrapped the cheese and sliced it into a dozen pieces with a surgical knife he used as a letter opener. I suppose coroners have an inherent right to act ghoulish.

We ate the crackers and cheese like a couple of greedy kids on a picnic. I lit a cigarette and sipped coffee. "How come you gave your plants a drink? They threaten to revolt?"

"Part of my spring house-cleaning. I also washed the foliage."

The office was spic and span. Cromarty had even applied lemon oil to the desk, bookcases, and wooden filing cabinet. The place would've passed a white glove test. He got up and took the T.B. poster of the rosy-cheeked children tobogganing off the wall. A moment later he replaced it with another of the same threesome bicycling along a country lane on a summer's day. He rolled up the tobogganing poster, inserted it into a cardboard tube, and handed it to me. "Here, take this. It'll save me carting it to your house."

"Ah, you remembered. Thanks, Doc. This is too nice for the shed. I think I'll hang it in the hall by the bedroom."

Cromarty complained to an invisible witness, "First he wallpapers his flat with jazz and cinema posters, now these. I swear, the man's turning Bohemian."

"A dozen posters do not a Bohemian make," I said. "But speaking of foreigners…"

Cromarty hooked his thumbs into his vest pockets and sat down, tilting the chair back until he could put his big brogues on the desk. It was his listening and thinking posture. He gazed toward the ceiling where an ornate light fixture from his grandfather's house on Leinster Street had been installed a week after his appointment as coroner.

"The man pulled out of the water," I said "We know he was one of Werner Strasser's henchmen. You established that and no one knows we know. You were out on the tug and saw him. I know he was weighted with car tires. This is important. Do you remember what kind?"

The Doc closed his eyes. "They were bound in paper, some of it torn away. Dunlop. They were Dunlop tires."

"I could've told you that, Angus, and here's the reason why…"

Doc Cromarty looked at me, not only out of curiosity, but because I seldom used his Christian name. I told him what I discovered in the empty flat below Sullivan's. I also mentioned the man in the cinnamon-brown overcoat. "But he's not the only mystery man," I said. "Wilder Hunter paid me a visit. He got along like a bosom buddy with Lincoln Drummond. Nice enough fellow. But, in his own way, Hunter's a mystery, too."

"I'm in complete agreement," Doc said. "I didn't say so before because I didn't think it was important, but Hunter was at Sullivan's funeral. In the background but there nonetheless. The only man in a light-coloured suit."

"Yeah. See what I mean? It might be part and parcel of Hunter's job but there's something too sure-footed about him. It's as if he's holding a royal flush and he wants us to think it's a nothing hand. Anyway, Tom Waterman's uncle is a professor at Fordham. He's going to do a discreet check via college channels. It might help steady my nerves. Hunter didn't like the suggestion I made that Americans should tend the weeds in their own garden. Weeds like the Nazi bund rallies in New York and the Ku Klux Klanners parading by the thousands up Pennsylvania Avenue."

"I don't imagine. You're not exactly the soul of diplomacy."

"The diplomats are giving in to the jackboots. Somebody's got to take a stand."

Cromarty sighed and smiled. "So it's Ireland versus the world."

"All right. Okay. I deserved that. I'm going astray so let's get back to something I can directly affect. I telephoned Dot Sullivan. As we speak, her brothers are loading Sully's entire possessions onto a moving van. That's guaranteed to get a rise out of a certain Deputy Chief of Police."

"And maybe a few other big fish?"

"Time will tell. A couple of Shorty Long's men are cleaning chimneys in the neighbourhood. No one gives them a second thought but they're all eyes and ears. Nothing slips by them."

A worry-line creased Cromarty's forehead. "What will you do, if and when?"

"I don't know. I'm flying by the seat of my pants as it is. What's the date? March the what?"

"Twelfth."

"It's almost a month since Eugene Robichaud *fell* into the hold of the *Bergensfjord*. He had the word TIRES tacked to the bulletin board over his desk. The biggest clue of all was hiding in plain sight. We've established a connection between Robichaud and the man in the water. They were both on the *Bergensfjord* the day they died. And we've connected Robichaud/Sullivan/Hardfield. I'm sniffing too close to something to suit Military Intelligence or they wouldn't blow their cover to put a clamp on us. Hunter admitted that I've been watched since Valentine's Day. Why? And why not let me in on it? I'm not the enemy. Look at the horrible way Sullivan died and the subsequent cover-up. And we're not supposed to do anything? We're not even permitted to ask questions? Bullshit! If they want clandestine activity, I'm happy to oblige."

Cromarty nodded, worry-line deepening. The phone jangled at his feet. He dropped them to the floor and stood. "Yes, Tom, he's here. Of course I'll relay the message. You're welcome. Good-bye."

I opened a fresh deck of cigarettes. Cromarty took one and lit it with his pipe-lighter. He didn't look well. "I told Tom where I'd be. What is it? You look godawful."

"You think you know somebody…"

"What?"

"Waterman phoned from the station. That letter you were expecting arrived a minute ago. The yacht that was in the Annapolis Basin with the Nazis on board was the *Vulpecula*."

"The *Vulpecula*? No wonder Hudson couldn't remember the name. Now to find out who owns the vessel."

"I already know. It's owned by Barry Stratton."

I nearly applauded. Wildly. Stratton was the landlord of the cathouse the Higginses operated on Station Street where Werner Strasser and his thugs got their jollies. It was close to where Randy Murphy was beaten out of shape by the same creeps. I was going to enjoy the living hell out of paying Barry Stratton a social call.

Doc Cromarty took off his tweed jacket and replaced it with a lab coat. In a barely audible voice, he said, "I've got an appointment with a dead man. You can let yourself out."

I watched as he left the office. For some reason the news about the *Vulpecula* had brought him low.

I picked up the T.B. poster and went outside. The sun was warm on the pavement, and high in an elm a song sparrow trilled. But my heart was cold as ice.

CHAPTER FORTY-FIVE

B ARRY STRATTON LIVED on the outskirts of Lancaster, Saint John's twin city across the river. I got the groceries from London's, stored them in the icebox at home, then drove up Douglas Avenue and across the Reversing Falls Bridge. It was noontime so I dropped into Pepper's Diner for a bite and a talk with Roxanne. Her son Leonard had seen the bearded man again. This time the man spoke to him and tried to give Leonard money. When Roxanne told me her face flushed with rage. It was a sinful thought but anger made her all the more beautiful. I was ashamed. Guiltily, I believed she could tell and averted my eyes.

She laid her check pad on the counter and asked, "What's with you?"

"It's terrible, but sometimes you're extra lovely to look at. I apologize, that was ignorant."

"Don't be sorry, you big lug. I can stand a compliment."

I shrugged like a kid caught with his fist in the cookie jar. We both had a good laugh. It really is the best medicine. I said earnestly, "Tom Waterman and I will force the issue with this bearded gorilla first chance we get. You can take that to the bank. All right?"

Roxanne's shoulders straightened. "Aces. Now, what'll it be?"

"A grilled cheese sandwich, cherry pie, and tea."

"Gotcha." She went to the kitchen, stuck her head through the swinging doors, and yelled my order.

A mob of New Brunswick Breweries workers streamed through the revolving door, jostling one another in a friendly way for space in the booths. Roxanne and the other waitresses grabbed menus and descended on the tables. A number of outside workers had sunburn on their noses and cheeks.

I'd already seen one sure sign of spring; little girls still in winter coats gamely skipping rope and singing rhymes.

Enjoying the crowded diner, I ate slowly. And, just as slowly, chewed my thoughts. Barry Stratton loomed large in local affairs. Like certain other bigwigs in the province he'd made a great pile of money rum-running during Prohibition. He was expert at smuggling contraband. It was claimed Stratton's boats were the fastest in the Maritimes and that he had the best coastal charts. I'd seen Stratton myself in one of his speedboats streaking across the waters of Grand Bay.

Intelligence was the man's signature. Clever beyond reckoning, Barry had gone legitimate years ago – the whorehouses on Station Street a holdover from the old days. And legally the houses belonged to old lady Higgins, so he was even covered on that score. In a twisted way I was tickled pink that the yacht the Nazis were seen cavorting on belonged to Stratton. It gave me a chance to disturb the calm surface of his existence. He had secretly and serenely amassed a fortune. I was going to get major satisfaction out of upsetting his applecart.

I tucked a five-spot under my cup and saucer for Roxanne. It was a thank-you for the restorative powers of the chicken soup she'd brought me when I was flu-bitten.

Brewery and lumberyard smells pervaded the neighbourhood, mingling with the salty tang pushed inland by the flood tide. To my way of thinking it was much too nice a day for serious business.

I sighed a spring-fever sigh and sped out of the commercial district and onto Manawagonish Road, a tree-lined street with fancy houses and clipped hedges. It was a far cry from the cramped slums of the East End where I grew up. I had the familiar uneasy feeling of being somewhere I didn't belong. You can take the boy out of the slum but you can't take the slum out of the boy.

Leaving the trees and houses behind, I rolled the Pontiac along a bald windswept ridge that faced the ocean about a mile distant. The waves shimmered, a shining sea in the golden sunlight.

The road veered then nose-dived suddenly into a dark and boggy forest of evergreens from which Barry Stratton's estate rose on a landscaped hilltop carved out of the woods. It was a modern two-storey place with a four-car garage. A stable at the edge of the clearing was surrounded by a paddock where a pair of shaggy-coated horses watched while I got out of the car.

Crows cawed a warning. Otherwise, it was so quiet you could hear your eyes blink. A burgundy Packard waited under the carriage porch at the front entry. I went up the limestone steps and lifted the door-knocker.

The sound echoed in the silence. One of the horses snorted then galloped behind the barn.

A thin elderly woman, dressed in dungarees and a flannel work-shirt, answered the door. She wore gloves and had a trowel edged with dirt in her free hand. "Good day," she said pleasantly. "I didn't know we were expecting company." Her accent was Old World and cultured, worn a bit smooth by this side of the Atlantic.

"I came to see Mr. Stratton," I said, stepping into the vestibule.

She wasn't at all flustered. "I see. In that case, you must have made an appointment. Who shall I say is calling?"

I showed her my badge. "Detective Sergeant Ireland." This made the woman definitely nervous. "Don't be alarmed," I said. "It's a minor matter." It wasn't, but I didn't have a gripe with her. The sooner she went back to potting plants, the better.

She ushered me down an oak-panelled hallway. There were paintings massed on the walls like a private art gallery. I recognized one by Miller Britain, a Saint John artist. It was a realistic depiction of dockworkers at quitting time. I didn't know any of the others. Most of the names were foreign. Eastern European or Slavic. The pictures were wild. One large canvas was a kaleidoscope of colours and shapes floating in the ether. Incomprehensible, but I liked it. There was a power in each painting that spoke to me in a language I didn't understand. Maybe Doc Cromarty was right, I had some of the Bohemian in me.

The old lady patiently stood by. "Do you like those?" she asked, leading me into a side room.

"Yes. Or maybe they like me. I can't figure it."

She smiled to herself. "Then you must be a fearless young man."

I liked the 'young man'. She mustn't have noticed my gray temples. "Hardly fearless and not so young."

"Oh, you *are* young," she said. "Please be seated. Mr. Stratton is reading a story to the twins before their afternoon nap. He should not be long. I will tell him you are in the smoking room."

I sat down on a leather sofa in front of a stained-glass window. Dozens of daffodils in clay pots bloomed on a side table watched over by a massive painting of a moonlit alpine valley.

I helped myself to a cigarette from a crystal box. Ten minutes passed. Barry Stratton's inner sanctum gradually worked a spell on me. I was losing the resolve to be hard-nosed and unrelenting in my investigation of his involvement in the whole complicated mess. The soothing quiet was lulling me into a sense of false peacefulness that I found hard to resist. Something inside me craved sanctuary.

Shaking it off, I walked back and forth on the Persian rug, reminding myself of my ultimate purpose – to find the killers of Eugene Robichaud and Sullivan. And to foil, thwart as Cromarty said, whatever plans Werner Strasser and his Nazi stooges had in mind.

There were doors on either side of the fireplace. I opened one on the off chance that it was a washroom. It wasn't. I now understood why Doc Cromarty behaved the way he did when he heard about the *Vulpecula*. I stepped into a storage closet that had been converted into a small tabernacle. Like Doubting Thomas, I was struck dumb. I flicked the light switch and closed the door. A pale yellow light shone from two flame-shaped bulbs affixed to sconces. A Star of David, woven out of willow twigs, hung on the wall along with a prayer shawl and a yarmulke. An elaborate brass menorah, polished to a high brilliance, surmounted a simple altar of white marble. Holy books that looked too old and fragile to open leaned against one another on a shelf. I pulled a long matchstick from a container on the floor and lit the candles on the menorah.

I knelt, honest to God knelt down, on a prayer bench and thought about Barry Stratton. He was about my age and height, which made him taller than most men of our generation. I'd observed him close up without his knowing. It was in the Admiral Beatty Hotel during a holiday weekend. Victoria Day, I think, not that it matters. We were crammed into Salon A with a bunch of mucky-mucks attending an I.O.D.E. convention. I was on duty, pretending to be one of the hoi-polloi. In reality I was after a pickpocket who specialized in Imperial Daughters of the Empire.

Barry Stratton was there with a woman I'd mistaken for expensive high-class fluff, someone kept in reserve for clients with deep pockets. She turned out to be Mrs. Stratton – a foreign-looking, alluring lady who knew how to wear a stole and walk in high heels. Barry didn't look out of place with her. He was an impeccable dresser with a suave manner I imagined was more suited to Monte Carlo than Saint John. He was vain though. It was said that Barry Stratton never looked into a mirror he didn't like. It was a flaw I'd planned to use against him. But now the menorah and the candles had me confused. Instead of finding answers here in Stratton's house I was uncovering more questions. Deep and unsettling. I pinched the candles out one by one, switched the lights off, and backed out of the room.

"I see you've discovered my tiny synagogue," Stratton said.

Startled, I spun on my heels. He was seated in a stuffed armchair to the right of the fireplace. A wisp of smoke trailed past his elegant head and toward the moon in the painting.

Caught unawares, I reached for a cigarette and said nothing until I had a drag. Even then it was all sign-language. I nodded, shrugged, and opened my hands. A half-minute ticked by. Stratton was self-possessed. I coughed into my fist and muttered, "Guilty as charged."

He laughed in a sophisticated way. With a dismissive wave of the hand, he said, "I don't mind one iota."

"Glad to hear it."

Eyes narrowing, Stratton said, "As long as it remains our secret."

"And Doc Cromarty's."

"Angus has been good enough to remain silent all these years. I'm dismayed that he betrayed a confidence. He must've had a compelling reason."

"The Doc didn't say anything to me. I was looking for a toilet."

Stratton pointed. "Other door."

I wasn't sure he believed me. "Cross my heart and hope to die."

"Then why have you come?"

It was my turn to laugh. "Not for religious reasons, Mr. Stratton."

"Barry will do."

"I'm Detective Sergeant Ireland. Detective will do."

A woman wearing a blue uniform under a gingham apron entered the room. She placed a tray beside the crystal cigarette box. Stratton ignored her as he leaned over and poured tea from a Bakelite teapot into Bakelite cups. The tea service was canary yellow with electric blue saucers and sugarbowl. It was too futuristic and splashy for the room. The maid departed as silently as she had arrived.

"Detective? Then this isn't a friendly?" Stratton sat back and put his feet up on the edge of the table. He was too damned sure of himself.

I went to the heart of the matter. "Cut the crap. I'm here about certain customers at your Station Street *house*."

TERRY CRAWFORD

"Station Street? Before my father died he bequeathed that dive to Mrs. Higgins and her offspring."

"Oh? Why was that?"

"Old man Higgins and my father met overseas during the Great War. It was Higgins who convinced Dad to emigrate to Canada. He helped us tremendously in the beginning and then we went our separate ways."

"And what *ways* were those? As if I didn't know."

Stratton put a hand over his eyes. He might have been dealing with an impertinent servant. Recovering, he smiled. "Modesty forbids."

I made a point of elaborately exhaling a trio of perfect O's. I had all the time in the world. Pouring more tea, I sipped contemplatively. Stratton observed me with the blank intensity of a mind-reader. I let him ask the question. "What customers at Station Street?"

I glanced over the teacup, bright as a flower in my hand, and said one word. "Nazis."

Barry Stratton's hand trembled when he put a cigarette to his lips. Taking a shallow, nervous breath, he repeated, "Nazis."

I nodded.

"Are you sure they were just customers?"

"What do you mean by that?"

Stratton rose then stopped in mid-stride. "You're an honest cop..."

I interrupted, "How do you know that?"

"It's my business to know. You're an honest cop so I might as well tell you. With your lowlife connections you'll find out sooner or later anyway."

"Find out what?"

"I've been helping, assisting, German Jews relocate to this country."

"Illegally relocate?"

"What other way is there? There isn't time to go through the normal channels. Besides, most of them are closed. It's difficult for Jews to be granted asylum here on political grounds. They're not really considered refugees. As absurd as that sounds."

"For Christ's sake, I know that. Sit down and stop pacing."

Stratton sat beside me on the chesterfield. I had two days' growth and he was as clean-shaven as a movie idol. Even under pressure he seemed to assess my clothes, scanning my steel-toed wing-tips, gabardine trousers, corduroy windbreaker, and plaid shirt. I said calmly, "I follow events in

Germany. The plight of Jews there is very precarious. I think they're in mortal danger. It's almost a year now since The Night of Broken Glass. Hitler should've been stopped when he occupied the Rhineland. Long before. Now he's got Austria and Sudetenland. But I'm getting off the track. Listen to me – I wish you every success in what you are doing but as of this moment I know absolutely nothing about your activities with illegal aliens. Understood?"

"Understood. And I'm thankful beyond words, but what about the Nazis on Station Street?"

"Be honest," I said. "Do you have any involvement with the operation of that whorehouse?"

"No. My father and I had a falling out when it came to prostitution. He found other things for me to do."

"Other things?"

"More suited to my talents," Stratton said, still shaken and unsure whether or not to trust me. I'd heard he was tight-lipped so I was bowled over when he revealed the business about the Jewish illegal aliens. I took it as a measure of his profound concern. *Someone* had to be concerned. Who better than an ex-smuggler? I thought about the menorah and the simple Star of David. And the peace of that hidden closet. I'd heard about closet poofs, but closet Jews?

"What's with your name?" I asked.

"My father's idea. He didn't want any of his children to suffer the overt prejudice his family endured. My real name is Ancil Bermann."

Waterman and now Stratton. I wondered how many other people had name changes. Wilder Hunter, for instance. "Ancil Bermann. That's not bad, but unless you owned the hotel you might have trouble getting a room. How did you come by Barry Stratton?"

Stratton smiled. "Why not? With my father's obsession with machinery it could just as easily have been *Briggs* Stratton or Massey Harris. Mother once told me that our surname almost became Chevrolet."

"Yikes. While we're on the subject of names – how does *Vulpecula* strike you?"

"What about it? Are you asking me as a detective?"

"Yeah."

"It's the name of a yacht I own. Though I don't know why, I hardly ever go sailing anymore."

"How about last August?"

"Yes. I sailed the *Vulpecula* on the Kennebecasis. It's tied up in Renforth."

"You didn't sail across the Bay of Fundy and through the Digby Gut?"

"Not for several years. Why?"

"Someone did. It was sighted in the Annapolis Basin."

"Conner Higgins, I take it you're familiar with him from Station Street, had a seven-day charter. Believe it or not, that cretin is a superb sailor. Used to win regattas all the time. Why are you interested in the *Vulpecula*?"

"Conner Higgins?" I leaned forward and took a cigarette from the crystal box. "That slimy son-of-a-bitch."

My vehemence alarmed Stratton. "What is it?"

"Conner's got some dubious clients. The whorehouse I can understand. Chalk it up to circumstances. But the *Vulpecula*, that's another matter. And the Annapolis Basin. It's rumoured that in the event of war it'll be the site of a naval training base. It all makes sense now."

Stratton stood and smoothed his trouser legs. He went to a cabinet and poured two large whiskies. We touched glasses. "What makes sense?"

"I came here in the mood to skin you alive, Stratton. But I discover that you're Jewish. That we have enemies in common. Major League curveball, all that. But because of the *Vulpecula* and its passengers I had to persist despite the obvious contradiction."

"Contradiction?"

"You sailing with the Nazis in question plus an unidentified older man."

Stratton drained his glass in one slow swallow. "You are absolutely right. Conner Higgins is a slimy son-of-a-bitch."

"Does Conner know that you're Jewish?"

"No. That secret died with his father."

"And his mother?"

"Doesn't know. Never knew. She was a two-dollar whore when Higgins first met her. Bought her, I should say."

Stratton fixed another drink. I covered my glass. The whiskey was a single malt Scotch called Glenmorangie, as close to divine as liquor gets. He took a phone out of a mahogany box and dialled a number.

"Who are you calling?" I asked.

"That idiot Conner."

"Hang up."

He hung up. "Why? I was going to find out the identity of the older man."

"Asking Conner is too risky."

Stratton laughed bitterly. "Conner. Do you think I'm afraid of that moron? He's so stupid he thinks a policeman is someone from Poland."

I grinned. "I'll have to remember that one for the Policemen's Ball."

Stratton glanced into the mirror over the fireplace and ran a hand through his dark wavy hair. He automatically adjusted his French cuffs and necktie. He was handsome in a civilized, aristocratic way.

I stood and faced the mirror. Without false modesty, I suppose I was handsome in a Celtic, wild sort of way. My grandmother used to say that when angered I resembled a wolf at bay. A green-eyed wolf. "Barry. Look at me." He looked further into the mirror. "Turn around." Stratton turned and leaned an elbow on the mantelpiece. "These Germans are dangerous. Doubly dangerous for you. I believe they tortured and murdered my ex-partner."

"Sullivan?"

I nodded.

"Why?"

"I don't know but I aim to find out. I came here thinking you were part of the equation. Evidently, you're not."

"I thank you for that," Stratton said quietly. "But I want to help if I can."

"Then get the name of the older man. That might help."

"No sooner said than done." Stratton picked up the telephone. He had a conversation with someone named Max. It was short and to the point. He put the phone back in the box and closed the lid. "Max is a retired shipwright who moors the *Vulpecula* for me and does repairs. I've never heard him swear before. He said the young Germans left the *Vulpecula* in a filthy state below decks and treated him like shit under their feet."

"And the old man?" I accepted another splash of the Glenmorangie.

"Brace yourself, Ireland. He was one of yours. A pillar of the Catholic community. None other than Doctor Patrick Kinsella."

I sat down to let the name sink in. I never liked Kinsella. In his own way, he was as much a dictator as Hitler or Mussolini. But he was an out-and-out big shot with unassailable credentials. Oh, I'd heard stories about Kinsella and young women for years but always wrote them off as ugly rumours spread by disgruntled Orangemen.

"Sorry, Ireland. I didn't mean to desecrate…"

"Forget it. Kinsella is a self-important windbag and I haven't taken the sacraments in years. I seem to be going around in circles. About three weeks ago I paid a call on the house at Station Street at the behest of Prudence Reilly. A minor thing – her husband likes to drink and play cards there and *lost* his wallet containing some tickets for a church fund-raiser."

Stratton anticipated what I was about to say. "Prudence Reilly? Dr. Gallagher's daughter, of Doctors Gallagher and Kinsella?"

"One and the same. Prudence never liked Kinsella. She might be able to shed some light on this. She owes me a favour so I think I'll see her tomorrow. Kinsella? I can't get over that."

Stratton admired his reflection light a cigarette. "Why not? Kinsella is anti-Semitic. It's well known that he won't treat Jewish patients."

"Or Frenchmen, Negroes, Lebanese. For the love of God, he tried to keep the Syrians out of the Holy Name Society. If he had his way the Vatican would be moved to Dublin."

"So you know him then?"

"I wish to hell I didn't. Catholics create enough trouble for themselves without representatives like him. If you checked, I'll bet you'd find that the good doctor chartered the *Vulpecula*."

"Likely. What do you think is Kinsella's connection with the Nazis?"

"He's probably a Fascist sympathizer. You'd be surprised how many of those are hiding in the woodwork."

"No, I wouldn't, Ireland. You know I have certain… resources at my disposal if you need them."

"Are you suggesting an alliance?"

"Yes."

I got up and without saying anything went into the bathroom. There was an eerie tinted photograph of the pyramids on the wall over the toilet. A sandstorm, like a dry tidal wave, was blowing in from the desert. A man dressed in a burnoose and carrying a whip stared distressfully toward the camera. I filled the tiny sink with hot water then applied a cloth to my face and neck.

When I reentered the smoking room Stratton was leaning against the mantelpiece, one foot resting on an andiron.

I didn't mince words. "I came here with the full intention of declaring war on you, Stratton."

"I didn't think it was to deliver the bagels."

"Just so you know where I stand."

"On the side of the angels. Your reputation precedes you, Ireland. I even understand that you're someone who believes virtue is its own reward."

I groaned. "Something like that. And I've heard that narcissism is *its* own reward."

Stratton laughed. "Ouch, that hurts."

"Sit down, Barry, and bring the bottle. I've got a tale to tell and it's going to take time."

And it did. I told him everything.

Everything.

CHAPTER FORTY-SIX

RATHER THAN GO immediately into the house I decided to have a cigarette outdoors on the Reillys' wraparound verandah. It was one of those dark, wetter-than-wet Saint John days with the streetlights still on at ten in the morning. A thick, warm fog had come in with the tide and was consuming the snow at an amazing rate. I could hear people climbing Garden Street on the sidewalk opposite but couldn't distinguish anything other than indistinct shapes moving in a shroud of gray.

Strolling the length of the verandah, I thought about Barry Stratton. He had been a revelation. And perhaps an ally in time of need? Or accomplice? Tight and elated, I telephoned Doc Cromarty after I got home to reassure him that all was well with Stratton. That I now understood why he had reacted so strangely at the mention of the *Vulpecula*. Cromarty was greatly relieved, muttered something about being able to sleep that night, and hung up in a good frame of mind. As for me, I ate a huge meal, went to bed early, and slept the sleep of my dreams for almost twelve hours. When I awoke, the neighbourhood was muffled in fog, traffic creeping on all fours.

The front door opened and James Reilly stepped out in dressing gown, pyjamas, and slippers. "Come on in, Jack. There's no one home but me. I'm just now fixing coffee."

I left my toe-rubbers on a mat in the vestibule and hound-dogged a trail of aftershave and shampoo to the kitchen. The room was large and airy with an oriel window looking out onto a dormant garden. Hydrangea bushes scratched the panes beyond the sink.

James Reilly's face was as shiny as a new penny. He placed a coffee pot on the green enameled range, shook the grate, and said somewhat formally, "Excuse me for a few minutes. I'm going to dress."

I buttered one of the scones wrapped in a tea towel on a plate in the centre of the table. There was also a bowl of hard-boiled eggs. I ate two of those, three scones, and drank a glass of milk. Reilly had the newspaper folded open on an article entitled "Storm Clouds Over Europe". I wondered when the thunder and lightning would start, a sudden clear image in my mind of Cromarty and me hailing the troop ships at Market Slip in 1914. There was a celebratory, festive mood with bands playing and tri-colour bunting festooned on the buildings. We were hanging off a telegraph pole, ever the daredevils, as war-mongering and blood-thirsty as everyone else. We had Union Jacks clutched in our fists. I still had my flag rolled up in the sock drawer at home.

"Lost in thought?"

I sidled around in my chair and beheld James Reilly framed in the doorway. He was attired in pearl-gray slacks, a white linen shirt, and brightly patterned jacquard vest. Gone was the dissipated and defeated Reilly I knew.

The coffee pot, percolating furiously, spattered and hissed on the stove. I picked up a potholder and removed it to a trivet on the table.

"James, you've been through a sea-change. I've never seen you look so good."

Reilly smiled and sat down. He filled two mugs, added brown sugar and milk, then offered me a cigarette. We smoked in silence for a time. Somewhere upstairs a clock chimed like a glockenspiel.

"In a way I guess I owe the change to you, Jack."

"Come again?"

"Maybe you didn't change me on purpose, but you did tell Molly Higgins to sit next to Prudence at Mass."

"I was just stirring up trouble."

"No doubt. However, your little shenanigan backfired. The holier-than-thou crowd *was* suitably scandalized – a whorehouse madam rubbing elbows with Prudence the Pure in the house of God was judged unendurable. Some of the protectors of the true faith arrived here one evening and made the fatal mistake of trying to tell Prudence what to do. Prudence sat in the front parlour and took it for about an hour, then called them a bunch of double-dealing hypocrites and turfed them out into the street."

"Sounds like the actions of a human being."

James laughed. "Exactly. And, get this, Prudence and Molly are out now distributing pots of shamrocks to the elementary schools. It's good for them both."

TERRY CRAWFORD

"And what about James?"

"I've been miserable, we've been miserable, for years. Prudence was not *well*. My happiness depended upon hers. Maybe that's weak but that's the way it is."

"That's not weak. What do you mean, 'not well'? You said that the last time I was here."

"Prudence always had her ups and downs. I knew that when I courted her. But not long after we were married she became despondent, seemed to lose interest in life. Then overnight, she got immersed in church work in a sour, determined way. There was no joy in it. It was a kind of self-flagellation."

"Beating the sins out of herself? If you don't mind me playing the theologian, that's an ugly path to redemption."

"I thought so. It depressed me. I withdrew into my workroom upstairs. Let me tell you, I've bound a lot of books in the past years. Awarded a first prize under an assumed name in Toronto. I attended a bookbinders convention in New England intending never to come back. But I did."

"I'm glad you did, James. Tell me about Dr. Gallagher."

"Prudence's father?"

"The one and only."

"I never liked him and he never liked me."

"Is that it?"

"What do you want to know?" James said uneasily. "He treated me like dirt under his sacred feet. If I was the sort I would've grown to despise him."

"How come you didn't?"

"It's just not in me. Anyway, he died before I could develop an enduring hatred. Why the sudden interest in Dr. Gallagher? He made his grave, let him lie in it."

"Okay. Amen to that. I'm curious about his partner, Dr. Kinsella."

"Another paragon. He's still alive, unfortunately for the general populace. What is this all about?"

"Can't say. It might turn out to be nothing. I'll have to ask Prudence about Kinsella."

"Why not go directly to Dr. Kinsella?"

"That won't do. Kinsella is involved with some people I'm investigating. Some people I'm not supposed to be investigating."

James Reilly laughed under his breath. "Jesus Christ, Jack, you always did move in mysterious ways," he said, then he harkened to a sound behind the house. "That must be Prudence. She took the Nash."

"The Nash? I didn't know she could drive."

"Better than most men. She used to go driving up to Hampton and Sussex all by herself. Disappear for hours on end."

Prudence said, "Hello?" from the back hallway. Moments later she entered the kitchen, a Glencheck Burberry draped over one arm. She flung the raincoat onto a chair. "Oh. This is a nice surprise. How are you, Jack?"

"Grand."

She rubbed her hands together and stood next to the stove.

"The heat feels lovely. It's not cold but it is damp. And so foggy. I had to turn the headlamps on and drive like an old maid."

It was a wild notion, but Prudence seemed to have reverted to the way she was in her early teens. In those days she was cheerful, out-going, and obviously bright. I was happy to see the change. I felt like saying welcome back.

"What became of Molly?" James asked.

"I dropped her off," Prudence said, eyeing me.

"On Station Street?" I said.

"Of course not, Jack. I may be working at rekindling a childhood friendship but I'm not about to commit social suicide."

"Haven't you already done that?"

By now the old Prudence would've bitten my head off and spat it out. Instead, she blithely sing-songed, "What of it? Who cares? I certainly don't."

"Wonderful. But a word of caution – it would be best if your car wasn't seen anywhere near the Higgins abode."

"By whom?"

"Conner, for one."

"Molly's brother?"

"Yes. Among others. Particularly the others."

Seeing my worry, she explained, "I pick up and drop off Molly on Lombard Street by the footbridge. She comes and goes over the train tracks all by her lonesome. Satisfied?"

I took my time lighting a cigarette. It was a stalling tactic. I poured coffee, slowly adding milk and sugar. The Reillys never took their eyes off me. In cashmere sweater and pleated slacks Prudence looked as vivacious as Katherine Hepburn.

James broke the loud silence. "Jack wanted to ask you a few questions, Prudence."

She slid onto a chair and chirped, "Oh? Did one of the C.W.L. ladies accuse me of skimming the Christmas Bazaar profits?"

I couldn't help frowning. "If only it was that simple, Pru."

"Pru? You haven't called me that since Grade Nine."

Yesterday I'd given Barry Stratton the complicated lowdown on everything from Eugene Robichaud's death to finding stolen goods in the flat below Sullivan's. I decided to give the Reillys a sanitized version. One with murder but without the blood and horror. They grew solemn, hardly breathing. The lack of telling detail seemed to fill their imaginations with dread. Sometimes it's better not to have to guess. Now and then Prudence and James would share a cigarette, passing it back and forth like kids hiding behind the garage.

When I finished James commented, "I know German U-boats have been sighted in the Bay of Fundy and up and down the Eastern Seaboard but I never gave much thought to espionage activity right here in the Maritimes."

"With our harbours and shipyards, why not?"

"Do you think if there is war that it will reach this far?" Prudence asked. "It will really affect us? Involve us?"

"The last one did. The war to end all war," I said.

"What did you want to ask me, Jack?"

"I mentioned the *Vulpecula*?"

Prudence nodded.

"The older man who went along on that cruise to the Annapolis Basin was none other than Dr. Patrick Kinsella."

Prudence slumped forward, burying her face in her hands. An anguished moan came from somewhere deep inside. Alarmed, James put his arms around her trembling shoulders. He shot a look of protective inquiry at me. I shook my head, at a dead loss for words.

Abruptly, Prudence sat upright, jaws set, eyes afire.

"Maybe you better leave," James said.

Prudence croaked, "No. It's time the truth came out."

I waited. Five, maybe ten minutes. James squirmed endlessly. I had the patience of Job when it came to the truth. There was so little of it around that I could wait hours. Days. Weeks.

Prudence was in torment. A couple of times she started to say something but fell mute.

I tried to help her out. "Why would Dr. Kinsella be on the *Vulpecula*? Is he a Nazi sympathizer?"

"Nothing that simple, although it wouldn't surprise me if he was in league with the devil," Prudence said in a firm voice. "You said the women were young enough to be taken for girls, teenagers?"

James gasped, "Oh, Prudence."

"Let me go on, Jim, it's all right. I've kept it bottled up for too long. The family used to have a summer camp on the Kennebecasis River near Renforth. My father would often entertain his cronies there. Dr. Kinsella was a frequent visitor. The year I turned fifteen it was a hot, dry summer. I swam constantly. Some of my father's friends would watch me dive and talk to me while I sunbathed. I was flattered. Until one sweltering August afternoon I'll never forget. My parents and a party of guests went sailing. I stayed behind. So did Kinsella. He said he had a headache and wanted to rest. No one cared. He was a heavy drinker and could be a huge bore. I was on the jetty getting a suntan when he brought me a Coke. Then he went away and sat in the shade. A while later I felt woozy and stunned as if I'd had too much sun. I made my way very unsteadily to the cottage and lay down in my room. My head was pounding like a tom-tom. I fell asleep. More like passed out. When I awoke I couldn't move my limbs and I was completely undressed."

"Prudence, you don't have to continue," James said. "We get the picture. I'll kill the filthy bastard."

"No, you won't. It isn't worth dirtying your hands on him. And I will continue. I have to get it out."

I lit a cigarette and gave it to her. She took a drag and handed it back. James was livid. My guts were crawling with revulsion and anger. "Did he rape you?"

"That depends on your definition of rape. He molested me with his hands and his mouth. And he was naked. I was helpless." Prudence shuddered. "What he did to me was far worse than forcible intercourse."

"Did you tell your parents?"

"Yes. They were incredulous. My own mother said I was wicked and hysterical. My father put me under sedation and had me cloistered for two weeks in a home for wayward girls. It was operated by nuns outside Trois-Rivières, Quebec. Oh, it was quite the production. I was the only English-speaking person there. When I was brought home my father said I was to give up my delusions or he would commit me to an insane asylum. I was adamant. He confronted Dr. Kinsella while I was in the front parlour with them and my mother."

"And?"

"Dr. Kinsella protested to the high heavens. The very soul of outraged indignation. Oh, he was convincing. He said the most hateful things about me. How I was a temptress. A secret tease. He *shamed* my parents and then emotionally blackmailed them until the day they died."

I glanced at James. Tears welled up in his eyes. Prudence had spoken in a straightforward monotone as if long since resigned to the crushing injustice of it all.

She broke the silence with a bitter laugh. "Kinsella used to come here every year for my father's Christmas splash. My parents forced me to serve canapés and hors d'oeuvres. Show off my latest party dress. Kinsella always contrived to catch me alone in the kitchen or on the stairs. He would whisper the most lascivious things in my ear. Mr. God-Almighty-Respectable. For the longest time I was very confused. I felt I was somehow to blame. But I eventually got over that and began to despise myself. I was just so angry."

"And now?" I ventured.

"You know, Jack, I feel kind of queer. Light in the head. Like laughing right out loud. I've carried a burden of heinous secrets for so long I thought I'd suffocate. Seeing Molly again has been a help. Don't get me wrong. I don't approve of the business she's in, even if she did inherit it. Molly reminded me of a time before Kinsella. There was a glimmer of hope. Without your instigation I don't know if I would've ever come out with the dirty truth. But here I sit. The truth is out. And the truth does set you free."

James Reilly began to sob, head in his hands. Prudence held him close. I got up to leave before I started bawling.

In the vestibule I discovered an emerald green leather-bound volume of W.B. Yeats poetry in my raincoat pocket. I put my toe-rubbers and hat on and opened the door.

"Don't go just yet," Prudence said. "I have to thank you for giving me a new lease on life."

"I didn't do any of the work. I'm just stumbling along in the dark. I'm glad you're out of the woods, Prudence. Truly."

I lit a cigarette so that I wouldn't have to look her in the face. We were children together and a lot of memories of the better sort were beginning to crowd in on me.

"What are you going to do about Kinsella?" she asked.

"What do you mean?"

"Well, don't you want to find out what this Werner Strasser is up to? Maybe Kinsella knows."

"And if he does, what am I going to do? Beat it out of him?"

"I'll talk to Molly. We'll figure something out."

"Whoa now, hold your horses. Molly's brother Conner has to remain ignorant of anything you're scheming. He'll squeal. Don't forget we're dealing with violent men. Killers. In fact, I don't want you to do anything."

"Too late. I'll telephone you in a couple of days."

"No. Don't phone me. I'll call you. Be more than careful, Pru. Do not take any chances."

"I won't. Not to worry, Jack."

I walked up Garden Street in a fog in more ways than one. Without even trying, I'd enlisted the aid of people outside my usual circle of misfits and ne'er-do-wells.

I wandered as far as King Square. It was too bad the park benches weren't out yet. I needed to sit down and think. I was lost all right – in thought, word, and deed.

CHAPTER FORTY-SEVEN

I TRAMPED THE crosses and diagonals of King Square at least a dozen times. As I did, the fog became thicker, full of echoing sounds. I was trying to gather my thoughts, penetrate a mystery, but I was getting nowhere. Nowhere that made much sense. Everything led back to the *Bergensfjord*. Eugene Robichaud's body in the hold. The German nationals who turned out to be National Socialists. Sullivan and Deputy Chief Hardfield and the stolen goods. Something that Werner Strasser and his creeps were looking for that was so important they'd commit murder. Deliberate, slow murder. What? Something seen, heard, or taken from aboard the *Bergensfjord*?

I stopped and tried to assess the situation objectively. I wasn't even supposed to be thinking about any of this, let alone skulking around the city trying to piece it all together as if it was some kind of crazy-quilt. Maybe I should just lock horns with Wilder Hunter and risk the wrath of the secret powers that be. Or maybe I should hand in my badge and raise chickens. That would be the easy way out. But the trouble with me is I've always been compelled to finish something I've started. Quitting is not in my vocabulary.

I ran across Sydney Street to King Street East and the station. I had made up my mind to take the path of least resistance. Under a false pretext I'd pay that visit to Hardfield's wife. She had to know something about her husband's underhanded activities. You couldn't live with someone and not have some inkling of their comings and goings. If the kid who was shovelling snow at Sullivan's was right, then Hardfield had made quite a few night visits. Disappearances at odd hours that the wife would surely remember. If not question outright. And there was that footprint at Sullivan's. Was Mrs. Hardfield there in person?

Devlin was desk sergeant on duty. He handed me a couple of messages. The first was a phone number that I recognized – Pepper's Diner. It said call between 12 and 12:30. That would be Waterman with news of the bearded man who might be stalking Roxanne's son Leonard.

The second message, another phone number, struck the alarm bell. It was Shorty Long's. He never contacted me at the station. I sat down at the switchboard and dialled. Shorty picked the receiver up on the first ring. "Long's Coal and Wood."

"Shorty, Jack here. What's up?"

"My chimney sweeps gave me a jingle and said a large moving van, very legit looking with two guys in spiffy overalls, hauled into Sullivan's about an hour ago and cleaned out that bottom flat."

I nodded while I took notes. Shorty gave me the license plate number, the company name (probably fake), and the route they took out of town. "Great job," I said. "Tell the boys there'll be an extra something from Santa."

I swivelled the chair away from the tangle of phone-jacks. "Devlin, is Hardfield in?"

"Yeah, but he's keeping a low profile these days. Doesn't do the inspection tour like he used to. Tell you the truth, suits me fine. I retire in a year. Don't need anybody tellin' me I got a button undone."

"I hear you. Do me a favour? Take these wet things up to my office and exchange them for the dry ones on the coat rack? I'll man the desk."

After Devlin disappeared up the stairs I telephoned Pepper's Diner. Tom Waterman must have been sitting next to the phone booth. I waited while he shut the door behind him.

"I'm calling from the switchboard at the station, Tom. Make it quick."

"Okay. I haven't seen our man yet today but he'll show sometime after lunch."

"Then why did you want me?"

"I got a letter from my uncle Manfred, the professor at Fordham. He inquired through university channels about Wilder Hunter. Well, Wilder Hunter is for real, but get this, Manfred was given the third degree by a pair of F.B.I. agents. They claimed there was a possible breach of national security."

"Oh, no. Is Manfred in hot water?"

"Manfred's a cool customer. He convinced them that it was a misunderstanding. The result of a typographical error. That he was really interested in a thesis written by Wilber Hunter and was inquiring as to his whereabouts. I warned Manfred in advance to cover his tracks. Lucky he did."

"Luck has nothing to do with it. Intelligence must run in your family. See you later."

F.B.I.? Wilder Hunter was C.I.C. It sounded like the left hand didn't know what the right hand was doing.

Devlin passed me a raincoat and salt-and-pepper cap that had seen better days.

"Been cleaning your office, Jack?"

"No. Why?"

"Somebody's been going through your files."

"Surprise, surprise. What's the Deputy Chief doing?"

"Starin' into space. I asked if he wanted lunch sent up but he just waved like I was a fly buzzin' around his head."

"Hardfield's got things on his mind. Did Dot Sullivan phone him yesterday?"

"About her brothers picking up Sully's stuff?"

"Yeah."

"Sure did. Lemme tell you, that lit a fire under Hardfield's old hard arse. Took off out of here like a banshee was chasin' him. Said he had to supervise the movers."

"And I'll bet he did. See you, Devlin."

I went outside and sat on the balustrade in front of the jail. Dressed in the fog's mournful garb, the sooted granite of the old clink looked older than a century. It seemed medieval. So did the court house and the police station. For that matter, I felt like I was embroiled in a medieval plot. A plot so entangled, so filled with dark angels, that I wondered if I would ever unravel it.

I took a last drag and flicked the butt over the railing, then I walked down the wide steps. Medieval plot or not, I didn't feel much like a knight errant. Even if I was on a quest.

The snow in the Loyalist Burial Grounds had almost vanished since nine o'clock, when I left the car at the Golden Ball Garage on the other side of the graveyard. I wound in and out of the headstones and slid the last ten feet on the slippery grass.

The Pontiac was parked over a grease-pit. Louis Cormier, the mechanic, walked up the stairs from underneath the car and switched off the trouble-light in his hand. He had oil smudged on his forehead and down the side of his face. He hooked the light over a wire and said in a thick Acadian accent, "Don' know why you wanted me to check dis car. It's bran' new."

I shrugged. "Better safe..."

"Dan sorry, eh?" Louis said. "Every'ting good. She revvin' bit fast. I fix the timing. Okay?"

"Swell, Louis, how much?"

"One buck."

I paid him and asked if I could use the office phone in private while he moved the Pontiac.

"Sure. Leave a nickel in the cup, eh? It's our coffee fund."

Louis' office was behind the grease-pits. There was a girly calendar on the back of the door that would've made the most jaded sailor wolf-whistle. The phone was on top of an orange crate.

I thought for a few minutes, consulted the woman with nothing on but fur boots, gloves, and earmuffs, then I rang the number. I lowered my voice, rasping, "Take this down."

"Who is this?" the R.C.M.P. officer on the other end said.

"Never mind. Got your pen ready?"

He seemed uncertain. Someone picked up an extension and listened in. I was brief. I told them the license number of the truck, the trucking company, the route, and what time they could expect to intercept the thieves who cleaned out Sullivan's stolen goods.

An older voice, one of command, said, "This is all well and good, but we don't make a habit of responding to anonymous tips."

"Like hell, you don't," I growled. "If the police didn't have stool-pigeons they wouldn't catch half the crooks they get. I gave you the inside dope on this — now nab the bastards."

"Just *who* is this?"

"The Green Knight, that's who." I slammed the receiver down. The Green Knight? I don't know where I got that. But, at least, it made me feel better than Willie the Weasel.

I dropped a fifty-cent piece into the cup beside the phone and didn't bother fishing out the change.

Louis was washing up in a sink outside the door. His face was scrubbed clean, almost raw. "Jack, I seen you wit' a guy by the station one day. Guy wit' a accent like a cowboy?"

"Wilder Hunter?"

"Yeah. Tell him his car's fixed five days now. I need the room. Pretty soon I have to charge him for parking space."

"Didn't he leave a telephone number?"

"No. Said he'd come back. Nice car. Maybe I keep it, eh?"

"I forgot, but he did mention to me that he had a vehicle. Where is it?"

"Round the corner in the lot. Next yours."

I went and had a look. It was a green Plymouth. I got the keys from Cormier and opened the trunk. Nothing unusual met the eye. I lifted the mat and found a set of Illinois plates wrapped in brown waxed paper. I put them back.

Then I made a thorough search of the inside of the car. The upholstery reeked of tobacco and long drives. The floors in front and back were scattered with debris tracked in by footwear. I inspected it with my penlight. It consisted mostly of sand, dried clay, pebbles, gravel, and evergreen needles.

I locked the Plymouth and returned the keys. Drawing Louis aside from the other mechanics, I said, "When Hunter picks up his car I want you to let me know. Okay? And don't tell him I saw it. Phone the station and leave a message for me."

"What message?"

"Just say, the Plymouth sailed. And give the time."

Louis smiled. "Is it police work?"

"Yes. And it's damn important. Can I count on you?"

"Friggin' right."

I went out to my own car, but before I got behind the wheel I wanted another look at the Plymouth. Standing on the running board, I ran a hand over the roof. There was a depression on the driver's side in the back. It was about a foot wide and an inch deep. About the size of the dent the chunk of ice I lobbed onto the roof of a car in front of Lincoln Drummond's on the night of Valentine's Day would have made. I didn't think this indentation was a coincidence.

I sat in the Pontiac and pondered the situation. It was a three-cigarette ponder. I recalled seeing the green Plymouth on Erin Street just after I'd interviewed Billy Moffat, Eugene Robichaud's best friend. And I remembered thinking that I saw Werner Strasser and a pal in the back seat.

Also, it was probably a green Plymouth that tailed Penny Fairchild the day my Studebaker almost wound up at the bottom of the St. John River. Until now I didn't have a reason to connect the drive-by at Lincoln's with the Plymouth.

So where did that leave Wilder Hunter? Playing both sides of the fence? And whose side was he on? No wonder I was ordered to stay clear of the case. Somehow I didn't think Hunter's hands were clean. I felt that almost from the start in Hardfield's office when Hunter arrogantly told me I'd been under surveillance since Valentine's Day. One thing was irrefutable — I'd established a direct link between Hunter and the people we were supposed to be against. I don't know if I hate anything more than double-dealing.

I eased the Pontiac into traffic. The radio was dishing out some awful blarney about Saint Patrick. I rotated the dial and tuned in Benny Goodman's *Christopher Columbus*. It was time to give Mrs. Hardfield a visit from over the horizon. Maybe I'd discover uncharted territory.

CHAPTER FORTY-EIGHT

T HE HARDFIELDS LIVED on Hawthorne Avenue not far from Lily Lake. Instead of taking the Wall Street bridge then climbing Rockland Road past Holy Trinity, I decided to go to Haymarket Square. The long way around. It was a mistake. No wonder truckers called it Haywire Square. There was an endless freight train rolling through the Square. Before I could detour away and avoid the mess by snaking through the backstreets, I was boxed in by a snarling traffic jam. Car horns honked in the fog like enraged geese.

I managed to squeeze the Pontiac over to the curb. I got out and walked a few yards to England's. Old Joey England ran a tobacco shop and snack bar on the Square. He brewed his own root beer. Foamy brown/black stuff that you could smell from across the room. Joey always joked about England and Ireland getting together. After exchanging pleasantries I got him to draw off a pint. For a soft drink the root beer was bracing – a refreshing pick-me-up.

I snuggled into a small booth at the back, took a long swallow and wiped the suds off my lip. The world outside might be obscured by fog but inside my head the weather was beginning to clear. And I knew enough by now to stir things up. The anonymous tip to the R.C.M.P. was a good start. It made me feel a little bit in control, as if I was pulling a few strings instead of acting the puppet in somebody else's twisted scheme.

As for Prudence Reilly's revelations, I was shocked and sickened but not surprised. I hoped for her and James' sake that they'd do better now that the awful secret was out. I also hoped that they wouldn't do anything rash. At least, without first letting me in on it.

Then there was the car with the dented roof that turned out to be Wilder Hunter's automobile. Was he a snake-in-the-grass or a guardian angel? Or both? I decided to put him on the back-burner. Besides, I had a feeling that Hunter would soon have to lay down his cards. What he didn't know was that I'd be ready with a hand of my own.

So, first things first. I stepped into the phone booth and dialled Hardfield's home number. After four rings a woman answered with a curt, "What is it now?"

I placed my handkerchief over the mouthpiece. "Mrs. Hardfield?" "Yes???"

"Good Day, Ma'am. Name's Ned Mulrooney, your local Hoover rep. I'd like to demonstrate our new upright vacuum cleaner for…"

Mrs. Hardfield said, "I am *not* interested," and hung up.

I tipped my hat to Joey England and went out to the car. A caboose appeared out of the fog, a brakeman jumped aboard, and traffic started to move. In no great hurry, I waited a couple of minutes. Mrs. Hardfield was at home. That was fine. It would make nosing around a little trickier but I did want to talk to her. She had some explaining to do.

I drove slowly toward Hardfield's, not minding the Irish music on the radio. It was a bittersweet reminder of Sullivan and better days. I still couldn't fully accept the fact of his corruption. It wasn't a free-lunch-here-and-there corruption but a larger thing; serious and willful. Something which took planning and a craftiness that wasn't like Sullivan. I couldn't help thinking that it got to him, that it bothered his conscience and turned him against me. He knew how I hated crooked cops or anyone in authority who betrayed the public trust. To Sullivan I would've been a reminder of lost values, a prickly thorn in his conscience. Looking back, I should have been more aware of the signs. The gradual erosion of confidence. Little things. The little things.

I motored past the Public Gardens, barely able to make out the greenhouses, usually easy to see from the street. Further on, I stopped above Lily Lake. Here on the high ground above the city the fog was patchy. The ice had begun to melt away from the center of the lake, leaving a black pool of open water where a flock of gulls quarreled and shrieked. In a few months time the lake would be swarming with throngs of day-trippers: swimming, sun-bathing, rowing rented boats.

Overlooking the shallow end of the lake where lily pads grew in profusion, a dirt road connected with Hawthorne Avenue. I took it, careful of the deep ruts. The avenue was at the outer limits of the city. Beyond it lay woodland, scattered ponds, and outcroppings of bald rock. Most of the houses were on spacious lots with room for large, park-like gardens. There were no houses on the steep, brambly south

TERRY CRAWFORD

side of the street. That and the fog made it easier for me to sneak around undetected.

I parked the Pontiac on the dirt road and ran across the pavement to Hardfield's property. Out of curiosity I'd driven by the place once last summer. Now, without foliage on the lilac hedge, I could see a couple of outbuildings near the avenue and the house beyond in a grove of white birch. All in all, a nice layout.

I tried the side door of the first building. It was unlocked. I went inside and closed the door behind me. I was standing in a two-car garage. The only light came through the small panes in the sliding doors. Aiming it at the floor, I clicked on my penlight and explored. There was a maroon Chevrolet coupe with a ski-rack attached to the trunk parked in the far space. At the back a gas-powered lawnmower that looked like it could eat whole forests sat perched on wooden blocks, a pair of garden gloves folded over the throttle. Various rakes, shovels, trowels, and shears were clipped to the wall in holders as if on display rather than ready for use. Hardfield's mania for "everything in its place and a place for everything"? That was part of his standard lecture to the men on the beat. Well, if this was a sign, he at least practiced what he preached. On a shelf, watering cans were arranged in descending order of size. So, too, were bottles of bug-killer.

I turned my attention to the car. Presumably it belonged to the missus. It certainly screamed look at me, look at me, right down to the white-wall tires. I knelt down on the running board and shone the light inside. The keys were in the ignition. I eased the passenger door open. The interior smelled of oil of wintergreen. It didn't quite mask the odour of stale cigarette smoke. Checking the glove box I discovered that the car was indeed registered to Mrs. Hardfield. Her Christian names were Helena Ardith Grace. H'mm, fancy.

The ashtray was chock-a-block full of corktip butts. Millionaire butts smeared with lipstick. The back seat appeared to have never felt the warmth of a human rear end.

I took the keys and opened the trunk. Oil of wintergreen again. Also, two tartan blankets, a wicker basket containing woolen mittens and stocking hats, and a pair of ski-boots on a newspaper. I picked up the boots. They had the same tread I saw imprinted on Sullivan's living room floor. The tread didn't mean so much, it was pretty well standard.

Penny Fairchild's boots were identical. That's why I went through some guilty misgivings about Penny until she told me about Mrs. Hardfield. Even at that, all I really had was coincidence. Until now. I focused the penlight on the newspaper. Cigarette ashes had dried and shaken onto the paper. I tapped the boots into my palm. More ashes. I pried a mashed cigarette end from between the treads of the right heel. It was a Sweet Caporal, Sullivan's brand. Circumstantial, yes, but it was enough confirmation for my sake. I replaced everything as I had found it and went outside. I was perspiring, so the foggy air felt good on my face and hands.

After waiting a few minutes I stepped watchfully between the patches of snow toward the building nearest the house. It was a two-storey affair, possibly a converted carriage house.

When I was inside and my eyes had adjusted to the light I unfolded a garden chair. There were windows on either side with the shades drawn down. I peeped around the edge of the blind that faced the house. Not twenty feet away behind a picture window a woman gyrated wildly to music that I thought I could hear if I strained my ears. She was dancing alone and with incredible abandon. An almost maniacal energy pulsated through her limbs. I'd seen newsreels of Josephine Baker filmed back in the 20's in Paris that were steamy enough, but this woman had some motions that'd melt an igloo. Embarrassed even in solitude, I backed away from the window. From Penny's description, the woman was Hardfield's wife. How did he wind up with her? Or she, him?

I nosed around, now and then turning on the penlight to see something in detail. There was a mildewed photograph on a shelf beside some strawberry boxes. It was of a man in military uniform posed rigidly in front of a Sopwith camel. The hawk-like glare unmistakably belonged to Hardfield. He cut a dashing figure even though he was never in the Air Corps. The cardboard frame was inscribed, To Helena, fondest regards, Hardfield. A memento relegated to a cobwebbed corner of the storage shed. Trouble in Paradise?

Satisfied there was nothing of interest on the ground floor, I climbed the narrow stairs to the loft. A trap door stopped me. Secured with a combination lock, it wouldn't budge. I went below and found a pinchbar propped against the wall. With one twist I pried the hasp loose, leaving the lock dangling in the staple. Combination, zero.

TERRY CRAWFORD

The loft was pitch black. The penlight probed the darkness. There was plenty of headroom even for someone of my height. A linoleum square in a Cubist pattern popular ten years ago covered the floor. In the far corner I counted a dozen Dunlop tires wrapped in shipping paper. But that wasn't all. Hidden beneath a waterproof tarp I found eight factory-sealed cartons marked Steward-Warner. Opening one for verification, I covetously fondled a beautiful table-model radio and phonograph combination. As much as I'd like to have one I put it back. Every box was stamped with the same overseas destination and all were part of the same consignment.

I placed the violated carton behind and beneath some intact ones and repositioned the tarp. Then I lowered the trap door and did my best to fix the lock and hasp so that from the foot of the stairs it didn't appear to have been jimmied.

Not wanting to press my luck I retreated to the road, mindful not to leave any footprints. I'd had a worthwhile snoop in both buildings.

Brazenly, I marched up the center of Hardfield's driveway and rang the doorbell. I don't know what kind of phonograph the lady had but it was loud enough to wake the dead. Which was good, I guess, because I wanted to resurrect the dead in her presence. I pressed the bell long and hard. The music stopped. I stood there cooling my heels for several minutes before the door opened.

Mrs. Hardfield had covered her hair with a turban and changed from her sleeveless dress into slacks and a turtle neck sweater. Her oval face was flushed with exertion. It gave her a breathless, bright look not unbecoming.

I showed her my badge and introduced myself.

She squinted, crow's feet spreading from the corners of her eyes.

"I've had a spot of car trouble, Mrs. Hardfield, and realized you were nearby…"

Apparently relieved, she interrupted, "Oh, do you need the telephone?"

"No, Mrs.. A couple of quarts of water would do the trick. I just had work done at the garage. The mechanic must've drained the radiator and forgot to top it all the way up again."

"I see. Won't you come in?"

"No, thanks. My feet are muddy."

"They're fine. Step in on the mat and I'll fetch the water."

I stood at the entrance to a long hallway. There was a gleaming kitchen painted ivory and yellow at the other end. Mrs. Hardfield stared over her shoulder at me while she ran tap water into a scrub bucket. It was a searching stare, in a way as penetrating as her husband's. Maybe it was just a habit she picked up from him. I hoped so.

When she handed me the bucket her manner became more hospitable. "I hope that's enough. Are you far away?"

"That's plenty. I'm over on Arrowhead Road by the lake."

"Oh, lovely. Tell you what. Come and have tea with me after you've tended to your car."

"Thanks, that'd be nice."

Like a good Boy Scout I lugged the water across the road and over the blind knoll where I'd tucked the car. I actually lifted the hood and after a suitable intermission slammed it down. Then I raced the engine a couple of times, letting it roar in the silence of the dull afternoon. All this in case Mrs. Hardfield was waiting and listening on the front stoop. I emptied the bucket into the ditch and cruised over to the Hardfield's and parked in front of the second building. The one with the hot goods in the loft. It was a very bold thing for Hardfield to do. Too bold.

I lolled behind the wheel. Pertinent questions buzzed like angry wasps inside my head.

A fair bit of time must have passed because Mrs. Hardfield called, "Hello, hello?" and waved from the front steps. She'd changed her clothes again, discarding the turban, slacks, and sweater for a dress, a blue and white item that looked summery and out of place on a foggy day in March.

I returned the bucket and slipped my rubbers off. I'd left my scruffy coat and hat in the Pontiac. I followed Mrs. Hardfield's curvaceous figure into the kitchen.

"I thought coffee instead of tea," she said. "Extra stimulation for such abominably gray weather."

"Good idea, Mrs. Hardfield."

"Please, Detective, I prefer Helena." She led the way into a comfortable living room.

I sat in a rocking chair. "Nice room," I said. There was an ashstand beside me so I lit a cigarette without asking permission. "Kind of old country."

"You like? Thanks for saying so. My husband doesn't care for it. He wanted brass, leather, and mahogany. Something like an officer's clubroom."

I frowned. "This is heaps better."

Helena rose and went to an antique cabinet with carved wooden doors. She removed a bottle of Chivas Regal from a top compartment. There were at least ten bottles of the same brand keeping it company. She must've noticed my noticing because she explained, "My brother's a sales representative for several distilleries. I'm not a souse. Honest Injun."

I held up a hand. "I believe you. It must be nice to be so well stocked. You know, in case of an emergency."

"Such as?"

"I don't know. Forty days of rain. A famine?"

"You *are* a wry one. Are you on duty?" Helena asked, brandishing the bottle.

"More or less."

"Which is it?"

"Less."

"In that case." Without hesitation she poured whiskey straight into both cups of coffee.

Dubious, I tasted the mixture. It was good. Damn good.

Helena Ardith Grace Hardfield settled down on the chesterfield, her legs folded beneath her dress. Penny Fairchild had said she was attractive, a looker even. All of it was true, but what Penny didn't know or had only guessed at was Helena's personal charm. This was a self-assured and relaxed woman: easy to be with and easy to like.

Before I fell under her spell I reminded myself of some ugly truths. Her husband was a thief. Part of an organization of thieves. He may have committed thievery even before the bastard blessed us with his arrival in Saint John. And if he wasn't himself a murderer, he kept company with old man Death. There was a broken bottle of Chivas Regal beneath Eugene Robichaud's body in the hold of the *Bergensfjord*. I always figured it was a prop that didn't fit the scene. As obviously out of place as a fur coat in Jamaica.

Sullivan and Hardfield were on the pier the morning of Robichaud's death. That was a matter of police record. All above board. What wasn't so clearly evident was Hardfield's eagerness to close the book on Robichaud. That had been a sore spot with me from the very beginning and above all else had raised my suspicions. I now believed, and I'd been denying it all along, that Hardfield had hands-on involvement in the cover-up. So did Sullivan. His accomplice. His partner-in-crime. His partner in a box in the ground.

Helena interrupted my dark memories. "You know, if I was insecure I'd swear I was being ignored."

I took a deep breath. It was like coming up for air. For something to do I offered her a cigarette, lit it and mine, then went to the window. A couple of bluejays were squabbling over sunflower seeds strewn over a boulder. They were oblivious to a cat pressed to the earth maybe ten feet away.

"I've heard you like to ski," I said, turning.

"Why, yes. I like to get away from here. And I ski on the trails in Rockwood Park whenever the conditions are right. How did you know?"

"A friend, Penny Fairchild. She teaches chemistry at the General. Quite a skier herself. Sometimes travels to Mt. Killington with a group of nurses."

"Oh? I don't believe I know the lady. Do you ski?"

"Not intentionally."

Helena winced humourously. "Then what *do* you do for excitement?"

"I work out at the Monarch Boxing Club and play baseball whenever I get the chance."

"You move like an athlete," she said matter-of-factly.

For a woman who rendezvoused with men at ski-resorts, Helena didn't behave anything like a vamp. I guess I expected to meet a seductress.

Sitting down, I helped myself to the Scotch. This seemed to alert her to a change of mood. She watched me nervously. She knew something. But what?

Without intending to, I found myself asking, "How did you and Hardfield ever get together?"

Helena closed her eyes for a few seconds. "I was young. Twelve years his junior. And my family had ambitions for their darling daughter. I was an only child. My father, a bank manager and mayor of the town we lived in, pushed me to excel in everything. His Worship, Mayor MacKenzie, practically flung me at *Major* Hardfield. A case of Hail the Conquering Hero. There was a whirlwind courtship, and suddenly, a honeymoon. I was a sheltered child. I hardly knew what hit me. Oh, I'd received a crackerjack education but nothing prepared me for married life. Especially to a cold fish like my husband."

She gave me more than I bargained for but the admission seemed to take a weight off her shoulders.

She smiled wanly. "There, I've said it and I'm not sorry."

I nodded. "How'd you end up in Saint John?"

"My husband's investments were wiped out in the crash of '29. It forced him to seek gainful employment. He was awarded the preferential treatment former military officers receive. I've often thought it ironic that as a veteran of the Great War he *heard* the action at the front but never *saw* it. But never mind all that. He had a couple of appointments – Regina, Waterloo – before we landed here." Helena glanced toward the window. "There's a patch of blue. Gawd, I do hate the fog."

"Regina and Waterloo. Nice postings. Sinecures, really, considering what little he has to do." I jabbed a finger toward the floor. "I sound like a broken record, but why end up here?"

Helena unfolded her legs and stood. "Rumours. Whispered innuendos."

"Concerning?"

She stared down at me, for the first time her eyes acquiring something like fear. Or worry. "He wouldn't tell me. And, let me tell you, I screamed bloody murder about it. In the final analysis it was liberating. On the surface we live together as man and wife but that's as far as the charade goes. But you know that if you know about Vermont," she added, accusingly.

"I'm not making any judgments," I said, my mind on the phrase bloody murder. What did she know about bloody murder?

Helena went to the liquor cabinet, poured Chivas into a glass, topped it up with Canada Dry, and lit one of her corktips with a table lighter. She was on edge.

"Come and sit down," I said, "and tell me about Sullivan."

Her knees wobbled and Helena just about collapsed. I started to help her into a chair but she wouldn't have it.

She took a while to regain her composure, then she looked at me and said quietly, "I'm ready."

"Bloody murder," I said. "How come you were at Sullivan's the day he was murdered?"

Beneath the rouge the colour drained out of her cheeks. "You know I was there? How could…?"

"Detection. I'm a detective."

"I was in the North End on my way to the dry goods store when I chanced to see a car that belonged to an acquaintance of my husband."

"Acquaintance? Who?"

"I don't know. I've only ever seen the man's car. A big green thing. Quite a distinctive shade of green that you don't often see around here except in summer when the American tourists arrive."

Tourists. An American car. She wasn't a bad detective herself. "Do you remember the make of the car?"

"Why, yes. It was a Plymouth. Sullivan's driveway was the first opportunity I'd had to see the car at close range instead of at a distance."

"Was the Deputy Chief's car there?"

"No."

"So why go into Sullivan's?"

"My husband's car was out there in the garage. The green car had picked him up at the end of the driveway at sunrise that day."

"Was that common? Weren't you suspicious?"

"I *was* suspicious. His surreptitious behaviour had become habitual."

"Did you say anything about it to him?"

"I confronted my husband about the odd hours he had been keeping for months on end and he said it was a matter of national security. That he was sworn to secrecy. He condescended to show me a few official letterheads and that was that."

"And you believed him?"

"Yes. He seemed to be much busier than usual. Intent on something."

"The green Plymouth – was that a months-on-end thing?"

"No."

"Correct me if I'm wrong. The Plymouth showed up around Valentine's?"

"About a month ago, yes."

"Okay, you're at Sullivan's. Why go in?"

"I needed extra money for material. I'd discovered I was out of cheques. It was almost closing time so I thought I'd get cash from my husband."

"Had you ever been to Sullivan's before?"

"On one occasion last summer. I delivered a parcel to Sullivan for my husband."

"Front or back door?"

"Back door. I had to hand the parcel to Sullivan. He was about to go on vacation and was doing my husband a favour. Or so I was told."

"Describe the parcel."

"A large, fat, manila envelope."

I noticed Helena's hands shaking. The pupils in her gray-blue eyes were as large as saucers. There wasn't much sense torturing the woman any longer. "Did you go in through the back door?"

"No. I'm frightened of dogs. That thing of Sullivan's barked its head off at me the first time. Scared the life out of me."

"Did you ring the bell?"

"No. I tried the door. It was unlocked so I went into the hall. From the foot of the stairs I could hear voices coming from Sullivan's apartment. I went up, afraid with every step that the dog would leap out at me. When I got to the landing the door was open a little bit. I pushed it and went inside, still afraid of the dog. At first I could barely see. The curtains were closed and the only light was from the kitchen. Oh, Jesus, Lord help me…" Helena said, completely atremble.

"Everything happened at once. I heard a muffled scream from behind the dining room doors. Those sliding doors. At the same instant I could see that the room I was in was a shambles. Things tossed and turned everywhere. And a horrible burnt smell. I put my fist between my teeth and fled. Oh, God, I should have phoned the police but I didn't know what I'd stumbled into. I didn't know Sullivan was dead until the next day. I assailed my husband with questions but he said it was top secret. *Top secret*? Can you imagine? That it had to do with German agents and that I wasn't to utter another word about it to anyone. He even forced me to attend the funeral and that insane wake. I was so frightened I didn't know what to do or where to turn. I was certainly silenced. But now, I'm relieved it's come to light."

Helena looked at me with sudden horror. "My God, the dog."

"Dead. Killed before you arrived. And a good thing it was or you would've never come out of there alive."

"What am I to do?"

I stood and stretched. "First things first. I'm going to impose on your hospitality and get you to fix me a couple of sandwiches and a glass of milk. Then, we'll talk."

"Fine. What would you like?"

"Anything. Butter and jam's okay."

The sandwiches would give Helena something to focus her attention on and allow me a few minutes to scheme.

We moved into the kitchen. I finished the coffee while she prepared the sandwiches.

I ate in silence, the kitchen clock ticking toward two. I'd decided that Helena was an innocent bystander. Trapped in a failed marriage, her worst sin was that she'd been blind to what was going on around her. Practically underneath her nose.

"Listen, I want you to pack an overnight bag," I told her. "Get yourself a hotel room and don't come back until tomorrow or the next day. There are going to be some visitors here this afternoon."

She started to leave the room.

"Hold it. Don't worry. It's not who you think. But I don't want you here when they arrive. Do you trust me?"

"I have scant choice. It appears I can't trust my husband."

"I don't think he would willingly endanger you, Helena, but he's stepped off into the deep end and can't swim."

"You have a way with words," she said, attempting a smile. "If you will allow me to continue the analogy, I think he's been treading water for a long time."

"You can say that again."

At the door I peered up at the deep blue sky.

"Was there anything really the matter with your car?" Helena said, folding her arms and shivering.

I shrugged, "Naw. I had to determine your innocence."

"Or guilt?"

"Or guilt."

"Thank you for caring. I'd like to buy you a drink sometime."

"Sounds fine. See you."

I pulled the Pontiac onto Hawthorne Avenue and headed back to the station. Helena waved farewell from the stoop. I thought back to this morning and Prudence Reilly's revelations. Two women in one day. Both with disturbing stories about respectable men.

I clicked on the radio and turned it up loud. Bing Crosby sang, "When Irish eyes are smilin'..."

CHAPTER FORTY-NINE

T HE DESK SERGEANT had draped my wet raincoat over the office radiator. It was baked dry. I shook out the wrinkles, hung it on the hatrack, and removed the book James Reilly had secretly placed in the right hand pocket.

It was a collection of poetry titled *The Winding Stair and Other Poems*. My father read Yeats. He even telephoned me on the last day of January to say, "W.B. passed away on the twenty-eighth."

Dad treasured an autographed copy of *The Wanderings of Oisin and Other Poems* that he received from his family when he graduated from high school. Ever since then – a rainy, blustery day in 1891 – he faithfully collected each new volume of Yeats. When I was a kid the old man force-fed me at least a poem a week. They were like doses of medicine that had a lingering aftertaste.

I reread *Spilt Milk* four times, then set the book aside. The green leather binding made it seem too grand an object for the dreariness of my office. But maybe that's what the joint needed: a few books, magazines, a pot of shamrocks. A new lamp for the desk. A bright red blotting pad. Travel posters from the Canadian Pacific Railway: The beauties of Chateau Frontenac, the Rockies, the Royal York…

Oh, hell… I pushed my hat back and kneaded my forehead with my fingertips until the pounding stopped. I was postponing the inevitable – a trip to Hardfield's office.

In a cold fury I thought about Eugene Robichaud. A small, crumpled body at the foot of a ladder. And Sullivan: I didn't want to think about Sullivan.

Picking up the phone, I called the R.C.M.P. This time I was immediately switched through to the senior officer.

"Is this *alias* the Green Knight?"

I grunted.

"I would sincerely like to know who you are. We successfully apprehended the moving van. The drivers have provided us with several names. We could use your further co-operation. Why don't you come in and see us? We guarantee absolute anonymity."

"Can't do it," I said.

"Then will you answer a few questions?"

"Depends."

"We think that you're an insider. But which side of the law are you on? In or out?"

"In."

"Excellent. Then why don't you talk to us face-to-face. There's a hefty reward involved."

"Forget it, I won't come in. Send the reward to, write this down, Marie Robichaud, twenty-seven St. Patrick Street, Saint John."

I could hear a bustle of activity at the other end. "Robichaud is one of the names. Eugene Robichaud is deceased. Officially, death by misadventure. Why should his wife benefit as a result of her husband's criminal activities?"

"Marie is Robichaud's sister. She's as poor as a church mouse. She could use the money to defray his funeral expenses. Robichaud was coerced."

"Coerced? Are you a lawyer? Or a police officer?"

"I'm gonna hang up."

"Don't, please. We'll see that Marie Robichaud receives the reward. There's another name. Perhaps you can help us?"

"Try me."

"Detective Sergeant Sullivan, also deceased. Officially, a victim of a heart attack. Any comment?"

I thought about that one. But not for long. I took the handkerchief off the mouthpiece and declared, "Robichaud and Sullivan were murdered."

It was as if a bombshell went off in the R.C.M.P. Headquarters. There was a shuffling of feet and a clearing of throats as the dust settled. In the silence that followed I heard a minute squeak repeated at regular intervals. The conversation was being recorded.

"That's extreme for a ring of thieves."

"They didn't do it."

"If not, who did?"

"I'll tell you in a couple of days."

"Why not now?"

"Don't interrupt. If you want my help in future tell me the rest of the names you were given."

The Mounties hesitated. They held a short conference then listed eight names. Two of them belonged to local connivers. A pair of scrap metal dealers who made a tidy sum in the junk business. And in whatever else happened to fall off the truck. Four names were French, probably Montreal underground, more than likely Teamsters. One name was Polish, maybe he was the fence, or another scrap dealer in Quebec. The final name clanged like a saucepan dropped into a bathtub – MacKenzie.

I told the R.C.M.P. what I thought. "As for that last name, MacKenzie, he's a liquor salesman. Runs the roads for whoever handles Chivas Regal. Try the United Commercial Travellers, he might be a member."

"You're very well informed. Why don't you come in? We could forge a mutually beneficial alliance. You may need protection."

"I'm not ready for that. Not yet. Take down this address: one-three-three Hawthorne Avenue. Look in the loft of the carriage house. You'll find a truckload of incriminating evidence. I'm sure you're going to want to talk to the man of the house since his name isn't on your list."

I ended the conversation without another word. The R.C.M.P. could carry on without me. I'd given them plenty. They had cross-Canada jurisdiction and were, if anything, thorough. And tenacious to a fault.

I reached into the bottom drawer of my desk. Out of a viper's nest of old neckties I selected the most garish, a bronze and purple satin number with flying silver V's.

I walked down the corridor to Hardfield's office. The janitor was sleepily pushing a broom along the hardwood floor. Dust rose into the air and made me sneeze. It sounded like a gunshot in the silence. Whispering, I asked the janitor if Hardfield was in.

"Yeah, I emptied his wastebasket a minute ago. All he does lately is stare out the window. He looks rough for a guy who used to chew the hide off me if I didn't mop his office every day."

I put a finger to my lips. "Sssh. Do me a favour? Take a break and tell the desk sergeant to hold any calls for me or Hardfield. I need ten or fifteen minutes. Okay?"

The janitor angled his broom against the wainscoting. I gave him a dollar so he could go around the block to the Cozy Corner for coffee and a snack and have money left over for cigarettes. When he disappeared down the stairwell I stepped over to Hardfield's door and went in, neglecting to knock.

Hardfield was leaning with both elbows on the high windowsill. He turned and regarded me despondently. The hawkish glint in his stare was reduced to a dull glaze. He slumped into his chair and rocked back and forth on the springs. His tunic was unbuttoned, a traitor to his awful fastidiousness. And he hadn't shaved or slicked his hair with Brilliantine.

"What is it?" he said in a hoarse voice.

Drawing attention to it, I adjusted my necktie. Hardfield sighed impatiently. I lit a cigarette and exhaled luxuriously. "You look like the Hounds of Hell have you at bay."

The Deputy Chief's firm jaw sagged. He straightened up and began buttoning his tunic. Carefully. Brass button by brass button. Then he realigned the articles on his desk: letter opener, pen and pencil set, note book, cast-iron lamp.

I let him finish. He looked at me with the eyes of a condemned man contemplating the hangman. Under a different set of circumstances I would have felt sorry for him.

Now that the moment of truth had arrived I hardly knew where to start. An old rule came back to me: Keep It Simple. "Tell me about Eugene Robichaud."

Hardfield folded his hands like a schoolboy. "That case is closed. You were given strict orders…"

"Cut the comedy, Hardfield," I said, putting the noose around his neck. "Tires, radios, kitchenware, moving vans, Montreal, *MacKenzie*. Need I say more?"

"I haven't the vaguest idea what you're talking about," he said, already defeated. "Nor am I obliged to answer any of your questions. You can't force me…"

"Force? I'd gladly knock your teeth out but I'll let your German buddies have that pleasure."

Hardfield's throat constricted. He lit a cigarette unsteadily with a wooden match, inhaling all the sulphur. Avoiding my eyes, he swivelled his chair and presented his profile to me. "You seem to know everything. Why bother me?"

"Tell me about Eugene Robichaud."

"Under threat of arrest and imprisonment he altered documents, bills of lading, fixed inventory counts. We had other people inside the system. It was all too easy."

"We?"

"Myself and Sullivan."

"Sullivan was a late-comer. How did he get entangled?"

"He was investigating an assault and battery case on the West Side and crossed paths with me. The sneak doubled back and caught me in the act."

"Yeah? What act was that?"

"I had a midnight rendezvous with two of the distributors in the upper echelon. Sullivan saw me with them and added it up."

"Distributors? That'd be Ritchie and Thorne. Correct?"

Hardfield nodded.

"Nice company you keep. No wonder Sully smelled a rat. The boob must've figured he won the sweepstakes."

Ritchie and Thorne were the scrap metal dealers on the R.C.M.P. list. The railway had spur lines right into their yards. Who bothers sifting through a hopper car full of junk? I stopped thinking about all that. I wasn't interested in the details of the operation. "Why did you and Sullivan kill Robichaud?"

Hardfield glared. "We didn't kill Robichaud. What in God's name?"

"God's got nothing to do with it. Sullivan had a rare blood type. He left a trail of it in the snow next to the shed door. The door that sticks. You and Sullivan killed Robichaud inside his cubicle…"

Hardfield kept shaking his head. "No, no, no."

I persisted. "Inside his cubicle. Then you moved him onto the *Bergensfjord*. It was low tide, remember? No steep gangplank to negotiate. Step across to the *Bergensfjord*, open the hatch, and lower him into the hold. Of course, you got too smart and dropped a bottle of Chivas Regal down first to make it look like Robichaud was drunk. Sure, he liked to drink but not liquor he couldn't afford to dream about. And then you got really lucky, it snowed for a couple of hours. But it didn't drift in under the overhang where Sully had the nose-bleed. Good old Sully. If it wasn't for his doughnut addiction and his tender nose, I wouldn't have guessed you knew Robichaud. Why go through his desk if you didn't think there was something there that would incriminate you? You took

TERRY CRAWFORD

some big risks. Moving Robichaud was playing with fire but if there *had* been any kind of investigation there would've been stevedores who could've placed you in the shed in Robichaud's cubbyhole. Talk about returning to the scene of the crime, but who would've thought the police were murderers?"

"No one, because we weren't. I've scraped the bottom but I'm not homicidal."

"Look at me, Hardfield."

Hardfield rocked forward and stood up with his back to the window. Moments later he leaned against the wall for support. The veins on his temples pulsated as the colour rose to his cheeks. I'd seen him like this before; barely able to contain his contempt.

"Explain," I said. "Enlighten me."

Hardfield murmured, "We moved Robichaud just like you said but the man was dead, dead at his desk, when we arrived."

I didn't like what I was hearing. "Then why did you go there in the first place?"

"Robichaud phoned Sullivan and said he had something important to show us."

"Yeah? What?"

"We'll never know. Sullivan did a quick search and found nothing."

"Sullivan? Where were you?"

"Watching outside the door."

"Watching for what?"

"Robichaud's body was still warm. We thought he had fallen asleep. There was a cup of coffee beside him with steam rising from it – I can see it now as clear as day. I shook him by the shoulder and discovered he was dead. There wasn't any sign of a struggle. We thought he might have drunk poison."

"Suicide? Try again, Hardfield."

"Robichaud was the sorriest individual I ever met. Sullivan was always worried that he would jump off the Reversing Falls Bridge."

"I don't buy that for one second," I said. "If you didn't kill him, why not just leave him and scram?"

"We wanted to make his death look like an accident. It was known that he went aboard the ships and drank with the sailors. We took him aboard the *Bergensfjord* and disposed of him."

Disposed. At that point I felt like hauling off and belting Hardfield in his sanctimonious yap. But I resisted because just about now the R.C.M.P. would be parking on his doorstep. "And you didn't see anyone standing watch on the *Bergensfjord*?"

"No."

"You didn't think that was strange?"

"I didn't think about it at all."

"But you must've thought you had a horseshoe rammed up your arsehole."

Hardfield reached for his hat and swagger stick. "I've had enough. I'm going home."

"Not yet. Sit down and behave," I snapped.

Hardfield tucked the swagger stick under his arm, put on his hat, and sat down stiffly.

"Sullivan's dead. Dead at the hands of Werner Strasser and the *Bergensfjord* Nazis. And it was covered up. Why?"

Hardfield flinched at the name Strasser. "I don't know. It's a matter of national security."

"Which brings us to Mr. Wilder Hunter. He must've been the answer to all your prayers. An umbrella of secrecy to hide under. Official, at that."

"That's a matter of national security, Ireland. You don't know what you're getting into. Leave it alone."

"Or I'll suffer the same fate as Sullivan. Is that it?"

"You were ordered to leave it alone, Ireland. There are powers beyond me."

"I never signed any documents. You and Cromarty did that."

The air in the room was growing stale. I worked my shoulders and lit a cigarette. "Secrets. Secrets. Secrets. What does Helena make of all your secrets?"

Hardfield was electrified. "You keep Mrs. Hardfield out of my affairs. She knows absolutely nothing."

"She went to Sullivan's looking for you the day he was murdered."

"What? That's impossible. I was here from eight until six."

"I know. I checked. But you left your house that morning in Wilder Hunter's green Plymouth."

"Damn you, Ireland. If you've been meddling..."

"You'll what? Sue me? So sue. What is Helena's role in your crooked dealings?"

"None. She knows nothing. She's too busy out traipsing... never mind. We don't exactly live in Holy Matrimony."

"So I've gathered."

"Gathered?" Hardfield raised his swagger stick, thought better of it, and strode out of the office.

As he went by me I said, "Nice talking to you."

From the window I observed him while he got into his car and swerved away from the curb.

His telephone rang. I answered. It was the desk sergeant. "Jack, young Waterman just called in one helluva state. Said he was tailing somebody and lost him near your place. He wants you to meet him at Welsford's Drugstore."

I ran into my office, snatched my dry raincoat and hat, and made a dash for the Pontiac. I wonder who first said, "*Tempus fugit*".

CHAPTER FIFTY

WATERMAN WAS SITTING on a stool at the end of the fountain. He was slurping a milkshake through a straw and looked drained, not energetic like the rosy-cheeked youths on the ice-cream advertisements above the mirrors.

I sat beside him and ordered a vanilla Coke. "What's up, Tom? You look beat."

He waited for the soda jerk to leave my drink. "I followed this guy Roxy's been worried about all the way from Simms Corner," he said then. "He was outside Leonard's school earlier, but with the fog there was no recess today. Anyway, he wandered from the school down to Simms Corner where he loitered by the bus-stop letting bus after bus go by. I got the impression he was keeping an eye on Pepper's Diner from a convenient vantage point."

"Why would you think that, Tom?"

"Leonard goes there on Tuesdays and Thursdays to have lunch with his mother. The guy is working himself up to something. That's why I sort of flipped when I lost him."

"Where did you lose him?"

"That's just it, Jack. It was on Douglas Avenue not far from your place. Up from St. Peter's Church grounds. I was on the other side of the street, back a distance. A couple of buses and a delivery truck passed and he was gone. I ran to catch up with him but he'd vanished."

I glanced past Waterman's shoulders. The pharmacist waved hello as he came out through the swinging doors of the dispensary. He gave the delivery boy half a dozen prescriptions in white paper bags with typewritten labels. There was a skull and crossbones on one of the bags.

"It's not like you to panic, Tom. How come?"

"Panic?"

"Maybe that's too strong a word."

Waterman tipped back the rest of the milkshake and wiped his mouth with a napkin. "No, it's not. I guess with all that's happened I jumped to conclusions. Sorry."

I nudged him in the ribs. "Don't be sorry. What conclusions?"

Tom's weariness disappeared in an instant. "All we've had to go on so far is an uneasy feeling young Leonard has whenever he's seen this guy hanging around. Right?"

I nodded.

"That could be easily explained. Some kids are scared of men in beards, for instance. Granted, the guy spoke to Leonard one day and tried to give him money. But for the sake of argument, even that could be innocent enough. It isn't a crime to say hello to someone. And Leonard's a bashful kid. Downright shy. Right?"

"So far, so good," I said.

"Okay, I'll get to the point. This guy was watching for someone at Pepper's Diner. Leonard's in school. That leaves who? *Roxy.*"

Doing a slow revolution on the stool, I absorbed the thought, and stopped.

"Yes, *Roxy*," Tom said. "Then I tailed this guy across the bridge and up Douglas Avenue almost to here before I lost him. Or he loses me. How do I know? Then the idea hits me like a ton of bricks – Leonard, Roxy, *Jack.* You sometimes walk home from Pepper's Diner. You could've been followed. Or you could've been seen with Roxy and Leonard uptown."

I weighed it all in my mind. "So what are you saying, Tom? That the guy went into my place?"

"No, but I figured he might be lying in wait for you somewhere and I wanted to warn you. Do you think I went overboard?"

"Not by a long shot. What you say makes sense. But why didn't you think he actually went into my house?"

"Your lights were on."

"Not when I left this morning."

"But Lincoln Drummond's there, isn't he? I mean, it's the day he fixes supper."

"It is, but Lincoln's aunt went into the hospital for an emergency appendectomy last night. He's practicing his bedside manner instead of cooking."

I tossed a quarter on the counter and went outside with Tom on my heels. We took the crosswalk to Douglas Avenue. My house was only seven doors away. We approached cautiously, wary of anything out of the ordinary. But it was like any other foggy day in Saint John. People walked unhurriedly through the gray while the houses moped in the dampness.

I stepped into the vestibule of the house where I lived. The door to the upstairs was unlocked, but the tenants above me often did that when they went out to the markets. We tiptoed up to the landing. Tom and I traded glances as we listened, ears pressed to the wall. Silence and more silence.

There was such a thing as erring on the side of caution, so I unlocked the door and let it swing open. Wishing for once that I was wearing the revolver that as a detective I'm permitted to carry, I entered. The floor lamp and the ceiling lights were on. Down the hall, the bedroom and kitchen lights. Otherwise, nothing seemed out of place.

Still, I didn't like it. I signalled quiet to Tom and we crept toward the kitchen. Outside the bedroom, Tom pointed to footprints on the linoleum runner that were visible only at a certain angle. Nodding, I went into the bedroom while he continued onward. The bedclothes were stripped and the mattress askew. The bureau drawers were empty, contents scattered over the floor. At first glance nothing was missing. Then I noticed my wife's jewellery box. Her wristwatch and brooches were gone along with the forty dollars I kept there for emergencies. The money was nothing, but Grace's belongings were sacred. I started to call Tom when he cried out, "Jack, here quick."

I frantically dug into the back of the closet where I kept my .38 wrapped in a shammy cloth. I'd cleaned and oiled the thing and loaded five chambers last week, but rather than tote it around I had returned it to its hiding place.

Tom was standing beside the kitchen table. In a chair, as if asleep on his folded arms, was the bearded man. I felt his pulse, knowing there wouldn't be one. He felt warm. Warmer than I did.

"Can you use one of these?" I said, handing the .38 to Tom.

He cleared his throat. "If I have to."

"Check the woodshed, then go down the back stairs and search the yard. Don't let anyone see the gun."

I didn't seriously think that the killers would still be around. But I wanted to be left alone to search the body. I leaned the fellow back in the chair. His head wobbled unnaturally like it was mounted on a broken coil. Dead arms fell to his sides. This just wouldn't do.

Doc Cromarty would be mad as hell but I laid the guy out on the floor anyway.

I knelt down beside the corpse, mouth suddenly dry as scorched sand. I uncrossed his plaid scarf and unbuttoned his shirt. There were no bruises on his neck. I looked for tattoos, particularly over the heart. There were none. I then felt his pockets for a wallet, keys, anything that would help identify him. I came up empty.

I redid his clothes and crossed his arms over his chest in a semblance of funereal dignity. Despite the beard the fellow couldn't have been much older than thirty. I didn't think it would be hard to give him a name. Somebody would know him at the Seaman's Mission, but I had a feeling it would be an assumed name.

Quiet as a cat, Tom came back and sat down at the table. He avoided looking at the body, not questioning the change of location. I took the gun from him and pocketed it in my raincoat.

Tom spotted something on the floor beneath the table. He retrieved a piece of notepaper, a pencil stub, and the key to the back door.

Tom's eyes widened. "Read this, Jack."

The note was written with the careful penmanship of a striving pupil. It was addressed to me. I read:

Dear Mr. Ireland,

Excuse me for coming into your house. I rang the bell but there was no answer. I saw a woman get the key from the garbage bin one day so I took the liberty. I don't know what to do. I need your help in a very important matter. It's nothing bad. Could you please meet me whenever and wherever you want

That's as far as the writer got to before he was cut short. Forever.

I looked down at the dead man. It would've been easy for him to spy on Penny from St. Peter's walkway. The guy should never have entered my flat. But it wasn't a capital crime. I would have to find out what his murderers were looking for when they were interrupted. Sullivan had been killed for it. And maybe Eugene Robichaud.

They had searched my locker at the station, broken into the locker on the Dominion Atlantic Railway wharf at the ferry terminal, and had now violated my home. Penetrated the walls of my castle. As far as I was concerned this was a declaration of war. But I only had an educated guess as to who was the enemy. At least, it was a highly educated guess.

The break-in convinced me of one thing – whatever they were after they had reason to believe it had been in my possession for quite some time. What was it? Evidence of some sort? Information? Or both? And if I had evidence or information, why hadn't I acted upon it?

Because it was *unknowingly* in my possession and *someone else* had placed it there. The someone else would have to have been Sullivan.

I was beginning to see the light. Deputy Chief Hardfield told me Eugene Robichaud was dead when they found him. Sullivan moved Robichaud's body to cover up his and Hardfield's crookedness. Sullivan was alone with Robichaud while Hardfield stood look-out. Sullivan could've found something, hidden it, and returned to claim it later on. Or stuffed it under his belt.

Robichaud wanted to show them something. Something so serious that he lost his life over it. What? Robichaud went aboard the ships, had definitely been on the *Bergensfjord*. Had he stolen something from Werner Strasser and the National Socialists? My guess was a resounding yes. And someone went to Robichaud's with a sense of daring impunity – maybe planning to dump the body overboard on the high seas. But he hadn't counted on the arrival of Hardfield and Sullivan. When he witnessed their removal of Robichaud, the killer must've had extremely mixed feelings. On the one hand his murderous act was erased, but on the other hand unwanted attention was drawn toward the *Bergensfjord*. Not just in the form of Sullivan and Hardfield, but also from Detective Sergeant Jack Ireland.

Ever the young gentleman, Tom had been silently watching me. "What do we do now, Jack?"

I revealed what I'd been thinking. "…and, don't forget. It had to be the Nazis who forced the Studebaker off the road," I said. "Jack Ireland's interference should've ended there and then with a convenient 'accident'.

After they muffed that escapade it wasn't so easy. Rubbing out policemen attracts too much heat. It just isn't done.

The demolished Studebaker was all too much for Sullivan – he was coming apart at the seams. The Robichaud thing alone must've given him no end of guilt pangs. It's starting to make sense."

Tom voiced skepticism. "But wouldn't murdering Sullivan, obviously a policeman, attract unwanted attention?"

"Usually, but by then they had the complicity of Wilder Hunter. He had the authority to sweep everything under the rug in the guise of national security. And I think they killed Sullivan because they suspected he knew something that could damn them all to hell. They couldn't afford to let him live. With Hunter's protection they were in effect sanctioned by both the American and Canadian Secret Services. Talk about a sweet arrangement; it stinks to the high heavens."

"How can that be?" Tom said, shaking his head.

"Wilder Hunter is a double-agent. *He's* the man the Americans have got inside. *He's* the infiltrator he told me they had to protect. And I think the bastard's more on their side than ours."

"The Nazis'?"

"Sssh, they might hear you," I said, lighting a cigarette.

"How long have you known about Hunter?"

"Since this afternoon. But I've been wary since we first met. That's why I was so interested when you got your uncle at Fordham to check Hunter's background. And look what happened. Manfred came under scrutiny. From the F.B.I., no less. Hunter seems to have a blank cheque. He can have things done. The clean-up at Sullivan's for instance, and no questions asked."

"But a double-agent, Jack? It's hard to believe."

I plugged in the coffee pot and told Tom the history of the green Plymouth. He let it sink in, nodding as he made mental notes. Convinced, he said, "So, what do we do?"

"Not a thing. Hunter doesn't know I'm in the know. If he wants to be secretive, he just might've met his match."

"But, Jack, you're probably still under surveillance."

"No doubt, but I've been watching my step. Who ever killed this man on the floor probably knew I was at the station. This guy walked in out of the blue and straight into eternity. They're not after me, they're looking for something they think I might have."

"Which is?"

"A mystery to me. Whatever it is it'll shed light into some dark corners."

I fixed two cups of coffee and gave one to Tom. "Let's go into the front room. I can't take sitting here with a corpse on the floor any longer."

We went inside and sat on opposite ends of the chesterfield. Tom was young and not used to death at close quarters. I could tell that he was badly shaken. Contending with the feeling of unreality around a homicide isn't easy to overcome. At first it seems like so much playacting. But it's acting for keeps.

I picked up the phone and called Doc Cromarty. He was as gruff as a bear rousted in mid-hibernation. "What is it, Jack? I'm up to my armpits in pathology reports."

I didn't beat around the bush. I told him exactly what happened and what we found waiting for us in the kitchen. As I expected, he didn't appreciate me moving the body.

"Couldn't be helped," I insisted. "Something's in the works. I wanted to know who or what he was. Can you come right away?"

Cromarty released a flood of expletives that almost melted the telephone. Tom burst out laughing. I did, too.

"Okay, now that you told me what you really think, can you come right away, or not?"

"Why? You're not going to move him again, are you?"

"No. Scout's honour."

"All right. I'll be there in ten minutes."

"Come alone, Doc. I don't want anyone else in on this, okay?"

"Christ, Jack, what about Hardfield? I'm already in his bad books."

"Hardfield is no longer in the picture. I'll explain later. If you bring an unmarked wagon and park it in the alley, Tom and I will load the victim after your examination."

"You're asking a lot, Jack."

"There's a lot at stake, Angus. I'll bring you completely up-to-date when you get here. There are some shockers I haven't even told Tom yet."

We drank coffee and waited. I went to the record cabinet and took out the autopsy on the Nazi dredged out of the depths near Partridge

Island. He had been anchored down with Dunlop tires. Maybe he blackmailed Sullivan and Hardfield and was paid off in goods. But was that reason enough to kill him? One thing was certain – it was intended that he disappear without a trace. Drastic measures. For what?

Cromarty clumped up the backstairs and burst into the kitchen. Grunting in our direction, he pulled off his raincoat, tossed it over a chair, and immediately set to work, kneeling down and opening his black bag. Without looking, he reached out and closed the hall door.

I went into the bedroom with the intention of straightening up the mess but I didn't bother. After I changed into more comfortable clothes, I harnessed my shoulder holster and put on a tweed jacket to hide the extra bulk.

Tom had his nose buried in a stack of *LIFE* magazines. He showed me several articles about the Nazis. What bothered him most were the bloodless conquests. The appeasement.

"There'll be bloody conquests soon enough," I said. "And the next war won't start with the assassination of an archduke who wears plumed hats. It'll be total war like the burning of Atlanta."

Doc Cromarty sat down in the armchair, struck a match on the woodwork, and started puffing his pipe. Smoke billowed above his head. He looked irritable and overworked. He had helped himself to coffee and in a short time appeared calm, less worn-out. His bad temper gradually went up in smoke.

That was a relief because I was in no mood to pussyfoot around Angus or anyone else. "What do you think, Doc?"

Tugging it toward him with his toes, Cromarty put his feet up on the ottoman. "Death was instantaneous. The result of a broken neck."

"How come there's not a mark on him?"

"I suppose because he was killed by an expert. I doubt if he felt anything. Lights out. That was all there was to it."

"Does it remind you of somebody else?"

Cromarty had a thoughtful puff on his pipe. Frowning, he said, "By coincidence, Eugene Robichaud. Same vertebra snapped. Mind you, Robichaud was banged up as a consequence of falling partway down the ladder in the hold."

I shook my head. "Lowered, then dropped into the hold."

"What makes you say that?" Tom asked, moving closer.

"Hardfield confirmed it this afternoon."

"What?!"

"I'll second that," Cromarty said. "What?"

I told them the story, the whole rotten story of Sullivan and Hardfield. Then I told them about Mrs. Hardfield and her visit to Sullivan's on the day of his torture and death. Lastly, I recounted my morning call at Prudence Reilly's. Cromarty and Waterman sat with the awed stillness of children listening to ghost stories. When I finished they got up and stretched, overwhelmed by the significance of what they had heard.

Cromarty raked his fingers backwards through his hair. "Whew. What do you think Prudence has up her sleeve?"

"Besides a hatchet? I shudder to think."

Tom was serious and quiet. He looked out the window just as the streetlights blinked on. "It'll soon be dark enough to make a move. I'll get the stretcher."

Cromarty and I stood over the body of the bearded man.

"Who is he, Jack?"

"Other than what Tom and I told you, I don't know. I'm going to bring someone in tonight to have a look at him."

Tom came in with the stretcher. We unfolded it and placed the body on the canvas. Then we covered the man with a blanket and fastened the buckles on the straps.

He wasn't very heavy. We got him downstairs and into the wagon without incident. Before Cromarty got behind the wheel, I took him aside. "Do something right away, will you? Have an orderly give the corpse a shave."

"Why?"

"You'll find out later."

The tail-lights of the wagon disappeared up the alley. I turned toward Tom, "You've had one helluva day. I'll buy you supper at someplace nice uptown. I parked the Pontiac over on Harris Street. Why don't you go warm it up and I'll meet you in a few minutes. Meanwhile, I have to make a phone call and lock up the house. Not that it seems to do much good."

Tom nodded and took the car keys.

I went back inside. Using a quart milk bottle, I watered the plants on the windowsills and the bookcases. Then I pocketed the spare key and turned out all the lights.

In the dark, I dialled Penny Fairchild's number at the General. She was happy to hear from me until I asked her to meet me at the morgue at nine o'clock.

"Is that your notion of a date?"

"It's important, Penny. I'll explain then. Okay?"

Reluctantly she agreed, and said, "Then can we *please* get together afterward?"

I said, "I don't see why not," and rang off.

I yawned.

It was a long day getting longer.

CHAPTER FIFTY-ONE

IN A SPARKLING white, crisply starched lab coat Doc Cromarty was the High Priest in his Temple of Final Answers. He pushed a metal table mounted on rubber wheels into the farthest corner of the autopsy room. Before I could read the last lines of its grisly information, he erased the blackboard behind the scales. I shivered in the thirty-seven degrees Fahrenheit. This place was one of my worst nightmares. I'd seen too many John Does end up here on the slab; chests ripped open, vital organs weighed one by one...

I lit a cigarette and turned away from the luminous white light reflecting off the examining table. It was too much like an incandescent altar where diviners sought to unlock the secrets of death. I was so lost in thought I hardly heard Cromarty say, "Put it out, Jack."

Taking a deep drag, I said, "What does it matter?"

He switched off all the lights except one. I could see his shoes coming toward me out of the dark. He reached into my shirt pocket and shook a smoke out of the package. "Then give me one."

He put a flame to it with his pipe lighter. "When did you start wearing a gun?" he said, backing into the darkness.

I shrugged inside the shoulder holster. "Since today."

Cromarty smiled and shook his head. "You're *supposed* to wear it. You're a goddamned detective, Jack."

"Yeah. What's so funny?"

"You. Following orders. *That's* what funny."

"Hilarious. Now where would we be today if I followed orders?"

"On our way to a nice, safe retirement," Doc said, walking into the pool of light where I stood.

"Sounds awful dull to me, Doc."

"I'm beginning to appreciate dull. Is Penny here?"

"Upstairs in the waiting room with Roxanne. The commissionaire will send them down when he hears from you."

"Well, I think we're ready. Shall I phone now?"

"In a minute. Did you do a further examination of the bearded fellow?"

"We stripped him. Didn't find anything in his clothing, but you know that. I did a preliminary. No bruises or signs of trauma. I didn't open him up. I'll let an intern do that tomorrow. We're not going to find anything out of the ordinary other than the broken neck."

"You said at my place that the guy's neck was broken the same way as Eugene Robichaud's?"

"Same vertebra."

"Could the bearded man and Robichaud have been killed by the same person?"

"Yes. But more importantly, they were likely killed by the same method. Quick. Expert. Deadly. It's a special knowledge and takes someone who's cold-blooded and willing to commit murder."

"Someone trained."

Cromarty nodded. "Highly." He bent over and shoved his cigarette into a drain-hole in the ceramic tile floor.

I did likewise. "Is the guy clean-shaven?"

"Yes. Did it myself. I wanted to see if there was any bruising under the chin or along the jawline but, as I said, nothing."

Cromarty stepped into the darkness. A moment later I heard him speaking on the phone to the commissionaire, then he reappeared at my side. We entered the next room where the bodies were stored in vaults. Cromarty went to a vault and pulled it open. I felt queasy. It was one thing to deal with dead bodies in familiar surroundings but entirely something else in this netherworld. I took several deep breaths before I joined the doc.

"Bit green around the gills, are we, Jack?" Cromarty said, smirking like Bela Lugosi about to perform a vivisection.

The body lay between us, covered with a sheet, a sheet as white as snow. A shiver went up my spine.

I gave a start when the commissionaire rapped on the door. Glum as an old goat, he ushered Penny and Roxanne in and left without so much as a glance.

Penny put an arm around Roxanne's waist even though Roxy seemed to be the more composed of the two. Roxanne hadn't said much when I'd told her how the bearded man had met his demise. She was more worried about me than him. It touched me when she revealed that. In the past month we'd become pretty good friends. I guess I looked forward to stops at Pepper's Diner more than I liked to admit. These things kind of creep up on you and hit you on your blind side.

Cromarty bowed neatly, professional mask firmly in place. "All set?"

Roxanne freed herself from Penny and stepped forward. Staring at the sheet, she said, "Yes, I'm ready."

Doc Cromarty uncovered the man's face and shoulders. In death's repose the fellow's features had perceptibly sagged, gravity pulling them back to earth. He looked much younger without the beard.

I studied Roxanne's reaction. She squinted, closed her eyes, and upon reopening them gasped. Not in dismay, but surprise. Beyond a doubt, she knew the man. She stared at him not with revulsion but an almost childlike curiosity. Perhaps wonderment. To my shock, she touched him, giving him a slight shove as if to confirm not only his dead state but his actual reality.

She raised her eyes toward Cromarty and nodded. He replaced the sheet, pushed the body into the chamber, and sealed the vault. Then he gathered us into a group and escorted us to his office.

Roxanne was silent, a contagious condition. I sat beside the Christmas cactus, crazily in full bloom the day before St. Patrick's Day. For some reason it arrested my attention and soothed my nerves, something we must've all felt because when I glanced around everyone was gazing at the crimson flowers.

Tom Waterman quietly opened the door and slipped into the room. He raised his eyebrows inquisitively but didn't say anything in the hush. We had all come too far to be in a rush now. Those of us who smoked lit up and puffed meditatively.

Roxanne French-inhaled, and said, "Rupert."

Our heads turned toward her, beseeching more.

"Rupert Lawton. My *late* husband. Can you beat it? He was already declared legally dead. I caught a glimpse of him from a distance a couple of days ago. I wouldn't have recognized him in a hundred years. The Rupert I knew was a big moon-faced man, not that skinny bag-of-bones down there. I can see why Leonard was nervous, not that he ever really knew his father. I mean, Rupert disappeared without a trace when Leonard was only two and a half."

Doc Cromarty wrote down the name. "Are you positive it's your husband?"

"That zig-zag scar on his chin? He got that when he tripped and fell on a bucksaw one night when he was drunk. It's Rupert – I'd swear on a stack of Bibles, it's him."

"Fine, Roxanne," Doc said. "I presume you don't want the body so I'll need his date of birth in order to make out a death certificate and notify his next of kin."

"Next of kin?"

"Parents. Are they alive?"

"Yes. They live in Newcastle. They disowned me after Rupert walked out without a word of farewell."

"So there's no love lost between you, is that it?"

"That's one way of putting it."

"And another?"

"I hate them both. They won't even admit that Leonard is Rupert's son. Their own grandson."

"I know it's difficult, Roxanne, but the other option is to let the City bury Rupert in a pauper's grave."

Roxanne shook her auburn curls from side to side. "That would be wrong. I'll tell you whatever you want to know."

I stubbed out my cigarette, clutched Penny's hand, and stood.

"You don't need us so we'll take off. Tom will drive you home, Roxy. Thanks for the I.D…"

Roxanne got up and kissed me on the cheek in a sudden display of emotion. "You don't have to thank me. I'd do anything for you, Jack. You've been so decent to us."

"Glad to help," I said, getting out of there before I got sentimental. It had been a long grind since six o'clock in the morning and I couldn't take any more wear and tear.

I held the door for Penny as we went out into the night. She was dolled up in her finest. Best coat, velvet gloves, high heels, and the Robin Hood style hat I liked so much. We strolled arm in arm over to Waterloo Street and headed uptown. A big three-quarter moon hung over the Cathedral, casting Gothic shadows into the darkened churchyard.

Penny steered me up Cliff Street and past St. Vincent's School. The silhouettes of shamrocks were glued to the windowpanes of the lower classrooms. Through the main door we could see a pair of nuns hanging green and white streamers along the corridor.

Cliff Street wasn't the easiest route to Penny's house. "Where are you taking me? I'm too tired for detours."

"I received a telephone message from Prudence Reilly. She wanted me to come by earlier but your call intervened," Penny said, sounding more English than usual. "You could've knocked me over with a feather."

"Prudence? Is that why you've got your glad rags on?"

"Precisely. You do know that women dress for other women, don't you?"

"Never thought about it," I said, shoving my hands further into my tweed jacket. "Makes sense, I suppose."

We stopped under a streetlight on Garden Street a few doors up the hill from the Reillys. It was as far as I was willing to go. I could see Penny safely to the door from there. "Now, I've come full circle today," I said. "The old mansion looks like it's got more life than it's had in years." Lights shone through the big windows, for once unshuttered. "Looks inviting instead of haunted. You better go in, Penny."

"You don't want to join me, Jack?"

"I can't. I need sleep in the worst way."

"Surely you're not going back to your flat."

I shrugged. "I thought we were going to your place, Penny."

She smiled. A grand, beautiful smile. "Goodie. You know where the key is. I'll take a taxi home. Won't be late."

I watched her fly with wings on her heels to the Reillys' front door. Once she was inside I circled the block. Then I ran a few back alleys and jumped a couple of fences until I was behind Penny's.

In the house, I didn't waste any time getting into bed. The mattress felt like a cloud. I drifted off into a deep, dreamless sleep.

Sometime after midnight, moonlight streaming through the window, Penny crawled in beside me. I awoke in her warmth. She had gin on her breath and love on her mind. We got lost in the land of forgetfulness.

CHAPTER FIFTY-TWO

I WALTZED PAST the headwaiter and on into the dining room of the Admiral Beatty. A party of sleepy hotel guests chatted over a late breakfast; otherwise the room was empty except for the busboys. I collared one of them and asked for a pot of coffee on the double. Then, plunking down my fedora on the spare seat, I occupied a table for two by the cut-glass windows. In the soft light the atmosphere was sedate and refined. Not my present mood.

I had received an official summons, not in writing but by word of mouth. You might even say, straight from the horse's mouth, the horse being none other than Chief of Police Gordon S. Delaney. I'd slipped out of bed around eight without waking Penny, who was sleeping like an angel, and phoned the station for messages. Under orders, the desk sergeant put me directly through to the Chief.

You'd think they were gold nuggets the way Delaney rarely wasted words. I never objected to that quality because the Chief was always evenhanded and fair. And honest beyond reproach. But today he sounded as grim as the Reaper, his commands like a dirge over the telephone line.

I'd hastened to the hotel but wasn't in any great hurry to meet the Chief. I lit a cigarette and stared at the gray and burgundy carpet. A cloudburst of thoughts rained in my head. If I could just calm down. Not think.

The headwaiter himself placed coffee in a silver pot in front of me. "I regret to say that breakfast is no longer being served," he said. "However, if you would care to return for lunch we will gladly accommodate you. As it is, sir, we are closing the dining room in a few minutes' time."

I looked from the AB engraved on the coffee pot to the AB embroidered on his vest. Picking up the pot, I said, "Do you want me to drink this in the kitchen? I don't mind."

Taken off guard, the man stammered, "Why, ah, no."

I poured coffee into the monogrammed china cup and emptied it in one swallow.

Regaining poise, the fellow said, "Why, you're Detective Ireland, aren't you?"

I grinned. "Yes, Michael, one and the same."

"Sorry, I didn't recognize you right off. You've really gone quite gray at the temples. I used to work up above in the ballroom and the salons. As I recall, you used to do extra security for some of the society bashes."

"Yeah, that was a while ago. Seven, eight years."

"You just missed Chief Delaney by a whisker."

"Oh? Tell me, Michael, was he alone?"

"Yes, but a couple of gentlemen asked for him at the front desk and sent a message in. I delivered it personally. The chief went upstairs with them after they sat waiting in the lobby for a considerable time while he ate."

I could easily picture it. I grinned again. "Delaney likes his grub."

"I'll say," Michael said, touching me on the sleeve. "Well, must go, duty calls. The coffee is on the house."

"Grand. Give the Admiral my thanks."

The headwaiter tittered. "Oh, very good, excellent." I watched him scurry on tiny footsteps toward the swinging doors of the kitchen. He must have shared my little joke because moments later I heard the kitchen staff laughing in there among the pots and pans. Michael was one of a number of small, effeminate men who worked uptown, mostly in the hotels and department stores. They were hard-working, solid citizens who wouldn't jaywalk if their lives depended on it, but they were harassed and beaten on a regular basis by so-called real men.

I poured the last of the coffee and had another cigarette. I was trying to do something about some other so-called real men: self-proclaimed supermen who didn't hesitate to maim or murder the defenseless. It angered me to the depths of my soul.

I went to the kiosk in the lobby and purchased an extra deck of cigarettes. I had a hunch I'd soon be chain-smoking.

At the front desk I asked for a bellhop named Arthur. He was to guide me to Delaney. The clerk sent me to the luggage room via a short corridor beside the elevators.

Arthur was sitting on a steamer trunk in the cage. He looked up at me with the palest blue eyes I had ever seen. Stockily built, with the big fists of a boxer, he chipped the cigarette he was smoking and put the butt in his pocket. He locked the cage door behind him then smoothed the front of his slate-gray uniform. "What can I do for you?" he said pleasantly.

"Take me to the Chief."

"Name?"

"Ireland."

"Follow me."

We wound our way through a maze of narrow hallways to the rear of the hotel. Arriving above the underground garage, we got into a cramped service elevator. It hoisted us slowly to the ninth floor. Arthur stuck his head out and peered up and down the passage before ushering me toward the Charlotte Street side of the building. He was whistling musically under his breath and seemed to get a kick out of the obvious subterfuge. He halted in front of 914. I noticed there was no 913.

"Enjoying all this, Arthur?"

"The chief told me to bring you here on the sly."

I flipped a quarter into the air which he let fall into his palm.

"Well, slyly done."

Arthur smiled foxily and bowed at the waist. I watched him return to the elevator and waited to hear the whirr and squinch of the winding cables before I rapped on the door.

Chief Delaney yelled, "One minute!"

I cupped an ear to the door. Besides the Chief there were two other voices, neither of which I recognized. As he strode toward the door, Delaney irritably said, "Yeah, yeah, *yes.*"

I stepped back onto the hallway runner and gazed innocently out the window. The early morning fog had dissolved, skies now a brilliant blue. Within an hour it had turned bitterly cold. A sharp northerly blew litter along the street. Pedestrians bustled with hat brims pulled down, collars turned up.

"The guest of honour," Delaney muttered, leaving the door open. He turned his wide back on me and went and sat behind a desk that had been moved catty-corner to face out into the room. He pointed toward a chair. "Might as well be comfortable, Jack. This is going to take a while."

"This?"

"Your story."

I took off my jacket and fedora, tossing them on the bed. Under Delaney's watchful eyes, I looked round the room. We were alone, but the door to the adjoining room was open a crack. The other room was dark; the blinds drawn down. Someone clicked on a lamp and began clacking on a typewriter.

A pair of Dictaphones squatted like ugly insects in front of Delaney. He folded his hands over his cumbersome belly. "Whenever you're ready, Jack."

I knew better than to ask Chief Delaney for explanations. Moving an ashstand so that it was within easy reach, I lit a cigarette and sat down.

"You know how to use one of these contraptions?"

I nodded.

"Before we start," the Chief said. "Deputy Chief Hardfield is nowhere to be found. You know the reason why. The prime reason. It throws a different light on his association with Official Secrets, and secret activity he ordered you to steer clear of. I authorized Hardfield to pull the reins in on you because the orders came from an unimpeachable source. But you've exposed Hardfield for the thief that he is. And I applaud you for it. However, the dictum pertaining to secrecy still applies regardless of Hardfield's criminality. Obviously, as it turns out, Hardfield used the secrecy stratagem to hide his dirty laundry. You persevered and nailed his rotten hide, Jack. I'll give you the benefit of the doubt – you couldn't come to me with the facts because you weren't supposed to be investigating the Germans. You were caught between a rock and a hard place, so I'll let bygones be bygones."

I had never heard the Chief talk so much at one sitting. It wasn't like him to run off at the mouth. I suspected it was mainly for the benefit of the unidentified listeners in the next room. Anyway, what he said more or less let me off the hook.

"All right, I'll take care of the machines. When you finish a recording, go to the next," Delaney said. "Meantime, I'll remove it and put in a blank. Any questions?"

I picked up the mouthpiece. "Where do I begin?"

"Valentine's." The Chief switched on the first Dictaphone. "Don't omit anything but don't elaborate unnecessarily. Stick to the facts." He clenched his fist and gave me a thumb's up. "Do not speculate or interpret events."

I'd done a lot of thinking about the past month during the last three days. It had helped me to review everything, turning it over and over in my head. I gave them a clear, step-by-step report.

It took a long time. I left out a few names. I lied more than once about details important only to me. Whenever I started a new recording, the Chief would pass the completed sleeve into the other room. The typewriter never stopped clacking. One of the men stationed himself close to the door and listened to every word, smoke from his cigarettes drifting in and mingling with mine.

Around twelve-thirty we took a break. Chief Delaney, grouchy and red-eyed, ordered coffee and a tray of sandwiches.

I wandered over to the window. The fish-shaped weather vane at the top of Trinity Church's steeple glinted in the sun. The wind blew fiercely, hurling down from the north.

Arthur arrived with the food. He collected a healthy tip from everyone and departed a foot taller. The typist and friend sent in American bills with the Chief, which he unsuccessfully tried to hide. It didn't help when the bellhop commented about the denominations before he pocketed them in jubilation.

We ate in disgruntled silence. All the talking had given me an appetite. When we finished eating I continued where I left off. Now and then Chief Delaney shook his head in disgust.

"That's about it," I said. I had taken the story to just after the visit with Mrs. Hardfield and my anonymous phone call to the R.C.M.P.

The Chief put the brakes on the Dictaphone and went into the next room for a conference. He returned and said, "Tell us about the Plymouth."

I hadn't said a word about the Plymouth. I was glad of it. I now knew how tight the surveillance was on me. In a way, the guys in the next room had blundered into a trap.

The Chief restarted the Dictaphone. I gave them the dope on the green Plymouth. I didn't say anything about the Illinois licence plates hidden in the trunk. But I did admit that I knew the vehicle's driver was none other than Wilder Hunter, a fellow who figured large in my report.

"And now the man with a beard," the Chief said.

"What man with a beard?"

Delaney sighed. "The one you found dead in your house yesterday."

"Oh, that one," I said. "His name's Rupert Lawton. He went into my place to leave a note for me. His timing was wrong. My educated guess, and it would only take a kindergarten diploma, is that the Nazis who entered our sainted city on the *Bergensfjord*, and who seem to be anointed with immunity, killed him."

"Enough already with the sarcasm," Delaney said, too exhausted or fed-up to bother even shrugging his shoulders. "Is that it?"

"Yeah. They're doing an autopsy on the poor sap today. He was an innocent bystander. A drifter. A seaman who wanted my help with a personal matter. He was due to set sail last night."

I let it go at that, not wanting to involve Roxanne. She had reestablished her maiden name after having Rupert declared legally dead. The Chief seemed satisfied. If anything, he acted as if he'd already heard too much.

The typist ceased pecking words; the silence, a relief. Between the coffee and the cigarettes I was too jumped-up to sit still any longer. I got up and went into the bathroom. I flushed the toilet and ran the taps into the sink. Kneeling, I peered through the keyhole. A man in an overcoat handed a sheaf of typewritten pages to Chief Delaney. Before I could get in position to catch a glimpse of the guy's face he shook hands with the Chief and left in a rush.

I rolled up my sleeves and soaked my hands, arms, and face. In the mirror my eyes looked sunken and strained, as if I'd been reading fine print for hours in a dark room. The colour of the guy's overcoat was cinnamon-brown. A distinctive brown, fashionable and in style elsewhere in the big cities. Conservative Saint John, always behind the times, was still mired in grays and blues. Odds were that he was the same guy who tailed me and Waterman to Gillespie's Poolhall the day I found stolen goods in the flat below Sullivan's. I gave him the slip that day but apparently not on others.

Chief Delaney pounded on the door. "Did you die in there? Get a move on, Jack."

Grabbing a towel, I jerked the door open. The Dictaphones were gone but the door to the adjoining room was still ajar.

"Read this. If there's anything you want to add or change, now's the time. Otherwise, sign it and forever hold your peace."

I sat down at the desk. The first page was stamped TOP SECRET in red ink. There wasn't any indication as to who was garnering the information. It could've been the Royal Order of the Purple Moose for all I knew. I glanced at the Chief. He cast his eyes heavenward then turned his back and went to the window. While I poured over the pages – a verbatim transcript of what I'd spoken into the Dictaphones – Delaney stared out over the rooftops.

I read slowly and carefully. Words in plain black and white had the effect of coalescing my thoughts. By the time I was through reading I had a solid idea as to what Werner Strasser and his thugs were seeking.

Chief Delaney handed me his fountain pen. I hesitated, not wanting to sign anything on the dotted line. Something I'd avoided until now. Especially a document that swore me to secrecy, that under promise of prosecution forbade me to ever speak of the matter again.

"What's the problem?" the Chief said.

The fellow in the next room had been pacing for the last ten minutes and Delaney himself was itching to leave.

I lied. "Nothing."

The names of Werner Strasser and Wilder Hunter were blacked out. I didn't like that one damn bit. Also, the document neglected to mention anything about the green Plymouth. Odd. Was the query about the car merely a test? And, if so, of what? My veracity?

I scratched down my name. Delaney witnessed the signature. The other gentlemen hadn't as yet signed the testimony of Det. Sgt. Jack Ireland. They'd put the date in though and it struck me – March 17, 1939. Could it be possible that I was almost forty years old? That just yesterday I'd joined the police force? That twenty years had passed away into the ether? The world had changed a lot since 1919. And changed too damned fast.

I tightened my shoulder holster. Putting my jacket and hat on, I said, "If that's all, I've got things to do, people to meet."

Chief Delaney's considerable belly jiggled as he laughed, "Yes, I'll bet you do."

"Happy Saint Patrick's Day, Chief," I said, stepping into the hall.

"Blarney to you too, Jack," he said, closing the door to 914.

Instead of retracing the bellhop's circuitous route I walked round to the main elevators, which would take me directly to the lobby and King

Square. The hotel was quiet, napping in the doldrums of late afternoon. I was watching the arrow on the floor indicator arc toward 9 when Chief Delaney caught up to me.

We got on the elevator as if we didn't know one another. I said, "Lobby," to the operator and we started down. After a few moments spent rubbing his jowls, the Chief threw up his hands. "I can't stand it – STOP."

Startled, the elevator girl almost jumped out from beneath her pillbox hat. Recovering, she eased the lever forward and we glided to a standstill on the sixth floor.

Guiding me out of the elevator, Delaney said, "A word?" He waited for the stainless steel doors to slide shut. "I can't abide these Third Reich spooks polluting our city," he went on. "And I can't abide our governments on this side of the ocean letting them do it. Hang that sworn to secrecy malarkey. Damn it all, we've got American police running undercover operations on our soil. And for what? Some secret agenda that God the Father Almighty doesn't even know about. Horsefeathers! Nothing can be so important that you can let these Nazi sons of bitches get away with murder. If you can get to the bottom of this, Jack, do it. And with my blessing."

"Glad to oblige."

His outburst over, the chief went on calmly in a low voice. "I can't give you any official help. After all, we just signed up for a case of permanent amnesia. I know you've got your own methods. And resources. And I've always known that if you have to, you'll play offside. But you score goals so I've never blown the whistle."

"I've appreciated you understanding, Chief Delaney."

"Yeah, sure, Mr. Green Knight. Cripes, Jack. What next? Your own comic strip in the funny papers?"

The poing-ping of the elevator bell alerted us. A swarm of men wearing green ties and shamrock boutonnières disembarked.

The Chief and I got into the elevator, strangers again. I hadn't said a word about the Green Knight in my report. I guess we all have our little secrets.

TERRY CRAWFORD

CHAPTER FIFTY-THREE

I LEFT THE Admiral Beatty Hotel in a better frame of mind than when I'd entered. Chief Delaney was not only in my corner but had sanctioned my clandestine ways and means. Probably out of necessity because there was no other approach left to me now. Or to him for that matter. The Official Secrets Act made sneaks of us both.

I turned right and strolled toward Sydney Street in not much of a hurry to get anywhere. I'd expected the Chief to give me the third degree then hand me my walking papers. Instead, Delaney gave me a mission. Ironically, one I was already on and would've stayed on come hell or high water. I felt a whole lot better knowing that someone else knew. Especially someone in authority I respected and trusted.

I stopped under the marquee of the Capitol. An icy blast of wind nearly stole my hat. The theater was showing a couple of reruns. *A Yank at Oxford* and *The Saint in New York*. I checked the schedule. I could see *The Saint* and *The News of the Day*. And catch forty winks if I sat in the balcony. I looked at the photographs flanking the poster. The suave and debonair Louis Hayward wore suits as impeccable and tailored as the mysteries he solved. Ah, if only drollery and dry wit were the answer. Instead of beating the pavement and depending on informants – a policeman's best friends.

I could use a few hours' escape, and the silver screen usually acted like a tonic, but I tugged my hat on tighter and kept going.

At the corner, I decided to go down Sydney Street to Vulcan and Shorty Long's woodyard. I wanted to visit a couple of my best friends to see what they had to say.

The north wind pushed me down the hill, a freezing reminder of winter's reluctant grip. Icicles clung along the rooftops and above the window ledges where yesterday's fog had melted the snow. Without gloves or a scarf, I wasn't dressed for the weather. By the time I passed Mecklenburg Street I was shivering in my shoes. I ducked into a doorway to get out of the wind. A car cruised up the other side of Queen Square.

It stopped and circled around to the Sydney Street side. Trying the brass knob at my back, I slipped into the front hall and watched through the glass panels of the door. It was the green Plymouth. Hunched over the wheel, Wilder Hunter twisted his head furtively from side to side.

He jammed on the brakes and pulled over to the curb across from the apartment house I was hiding in. Aggravated by some inner turmoil, he lit a cigarette and tossed the spent match into the road. He sat with the window rolled down, letting the arctic air cool his perspiring forehead. His manner was high-strung and skittish. Where was the easy-going American I'd first met in Hardfield's office?

I was about to saunter over and wish him a happy Saint Patrick's Day when I heard a bosun's whistle. From beyond the car, where a lawn sloped steeply up toward flowerbeds, came another shrill blast on the whistle. A figure dressed in a black duffel coat with the hood up stepped out from behind the plinth of the Samuel de Champlain monument. Oddly, he struck the same pose as the statue of the explorer and pointed with an outstretched arm toward the mouth of the St. John River.

Wilder Hunter rolled up the car window and peeled away from the curb, screeching the tires when he rounded the south side of the square. I waited until the duffel coat got into the Plymouth before I came out onto the sidewalk. The car sped up Charlotte Street and toward King Square. If anything the wind was colder and the sky an even frostier blue. I ran as far as the Armouries, slowing down for traffic when I crossed St. James and Broad Streets. Resting in the lee of the Armoury Building, I looked out over the parade grounds at the waves rolling in toward the rocky shore. There was a heavy sea, wild in the wind. Gulls pitched and reeled in the high sky.

Certain I hadn't been followed even though I was uncertain who would be doing the following, I went over to Vulcan and stopped in front of the woodyard. At the other end of the street the ironworks was just knocking off, men with lunchboxes under their arms heading in small talkative groups for the bus stop. Further on, a train chugged across the trestle toward the grain elevator and the piers. A ship with red stripes on its funnels steamed out of the harbour, deckhands running to and fro in the cold.

I opened the door and stepped through the gate. There was no one in the yard. It smelled of wet sawdust and split kindling. Shorty's ever-present gang of diligent derelicts must have vamoosed early. Expecting a beehive, I didn't like the ghostly quiet.

I climbed the icy stairs. Brightly painted chairs lined the porch in anticipation of the arrival of spring. I listened for voices then went into Shorty's office. It was empty but the pot-bellied stove had a stomach full of coal glowing behind the isinglass. I warmed my front and then my behind in the circle of heat.

Footsteps stamped up from the kitchen. Shorty flung open the door. Catching his breath, he said, "Thought it might be you. I'm on my lonesome. I was scoffing a devilled ham sandwich when I heard you march across the floor." He wiped mustard off his lips with a polka dot handkerchief and issued a champion burp. On the blackboard behind his desk, Shorty had copied down the words to *Molly Malone*. Picking up an eraser, he wiped the words off with the exception of Alive, Alive, O.

I was too drained from the interrogation at the hotel by Chief Delaney and the unknown quantity to interpret the significance of the message. If it was a message and not just another one of Shorty's affirmations of life. We'd known each other for too many years for me to feel I had to break into song.

He sat down and put his size twelves up on the desk. There were brand new rubber heels on his black oxfords. Shorty's shoes were buffed to a brilliant shine, a persistent habit since boyhood, beaten into him by his father.

I found the silence comfortable after being forced to talk for most of the day, but I was beginning to wonder where Shorty's motley crew had disappeared.

"Where is everybody, Shorty?"

"I thought you heard."

"Heard what?"

"We shoved Randy Murphy into a General Hospital ambulance not more than a half-hour ago. Beat to a friggin' pulp he was."

I immediately thought of the man in the black duffel coat. And the friend to one-and-all, Wilder Hunter. "News to me. Tell me more."

"A couple of the boys were delivering a cord of wood when they spotted Randy on Britain Street a few houses up from the corner of Sydney. He wasn't too steady on his feet. Anyway they dumped the load of wood off on Pitt Street and circled back. They found Randy face down in an alley. His eyes were beat shut and he was spitting blood. They hoisted him onto the back of the truck and brought him back here. I couldn't do much for him other than clean him up. I think he had busted ribs the way he was breathing."

"Did Murphy say anything?"

"Tried, but his jaws are still wired together from the last licking he took."

"So he didn't say who attacked him?"

"In a way. He kept passing out so I phoned for an ambulance. It was after he was gone and I was outside on the porch when I happened to look down at the truck. Randy must've used his fingers to scrawl a message in the sawdust. It was the sign of the swastika. Once I saw that I gave the men money to eat out and catch a movie. I wanted to be alone."

I sat on the end of Shorty's desk. He poured two large sherries. The good sherry, not the bad. I drank mine slowly. So Randy Murphy had gotten too close to the fire once again and got himself burned. Randy tended to be reckless, and since he was bent on revenge he probably threw caution to the winds. But I wanted him to gather information, not get pounded into silence.

"Hand me the phone, Shorty."

I dialled Penny at the hospital.

She purred, "Jack, wherever did you get to? I thought you would be lying next to me when I woke up. For round two?"

Aroused, I turned my back to Shorty.

He laughed and said, "Oh, *romance.*"

I tried to think of a can of worms but it didn't do much good. Fumbling with the matches, I managed to light a cigarette. "Penny, I've got an important job for you."

She giggled at my serious tone. "Oh? What kind of job?"

"Penny."

"Right-O, Jack. I'm all ears. Fire away."

"A man named Randy Murphy was delivered by ambulance a short while ago. He was brutally assaulted. I want you to find out his condition and tell him for me that I'll get the perpetrators."

"Murphy? He's probably in Emergency."

I gave Penny the phone number of Long's Woodyard.

"I've got other news for you, Jack. I didn't have a chance to tell you this morning."

"Hold off till you phone back. I'm not going anywhere for the time being."

"If you insist. But, Jack, *stay* there."

"I'm stuck like glue."

Penny rang off. In case he said something in a delirious state, I wanted her to get to Murphy before a possible visit to the O.R. If Randy was spitting blood he might be hemorrhaging and only have a short time before going under the knife.

I stretched out on the cot beside the stove and pulled the quilt up to my chin. Shorty was muttering to himself behind one of the six or seven journals he read in the run of a day.

I grunted, "Stop talking to the papers," and turned my face to the wall. It was cozy and warm. The sherry had given me a minor glow. I fell into a dreamless slumber. The kind I had when I was a boy and played hockey all day, chasing a puck across the lake from sun-up till dark.

Forty minutes later I awoke with a start. The telephone jangled. Shorty was asleep, head resting on his arms, mouth opening and closing like a fish. He opened his eyes when I scrambled for the telephone, but he just lay there yawning.

"Jack, where have you been?"

"Nowhere, Penny. I was asleep on the cot."

"I looked in on Randall Murphy. His condition is stable but could change for the worse. The interns pumped his stomach. He drank something caustic. So strong it ruptured blood vessels."

"Caustic? Murphy's a booze-snob."

"That may very well be, Jack, but he ingested some sort of solvent. Perhaps even a drain cleaner. Was he suicidal?"

"Suicidal?" I almost laughed. "No. He was beat up, then probably had the stuff poured down his throat."

"How absolutely appalling. That's ghastly," Penny said. "What kind of fiend would do such a thing?"

"The two-legged variety. Did you give Randy my message?"

"Yes. He kept repeating something about a number. Scott somebody's number."

"Scott Joplin?"

"Joplin could have been the surname but Mr. Murphy's speech was garbled. He was in great pain. His incisors were broken off at the gums."

I felt a hot wave of apprehension. I had given Lincoln Drummond's phone number to Murphy but with the code-name Scott Joplin. Lincoln occasionally accepted messages for me from informants. Messages that I didn't want sent to the station.

I muzzled the phone. "Shorty, go warm up the truck. Make sure it's got plenty of gas."

Shorty gave his head a shake and slowly got to his feet, towering over me as he snatched his Burberry off the coat rack. He swept out of the office and left the door wide open. I welcomed the fresh air.

"Jack, don't you dare go away. I've got news for you," Penny said. "Are you there?"

"Yes, but you'll have to tell me later."

"No, that won't do. Right now, do you hear me?"

I'd never heard Penny get the slightest bit hysterical. It wasn't in her nature to lose her aplomb.

Down in the yard, Shorty revved the truck engine. Seconds later, I heard the squeal of the rollers as he slid open the high gate. Then he drove the truck out into the street and pulled the gate noisily closed. He honked the horn twice.

"All right, Penny. I don't want to be ignorant, but make it quick."

"Good news or bad news first?"

"The good."

"Your cousin Marvin is in town. His wife gave birth to a healthy baby boy at three-fifteen this afternoon. Mother and son are both doing well. So is Marvin, for that matter."

"I knew Marvin was bringing Peggy to Saint John when she was getting close but I didn't think she was due yet."

"She was overdue, Jack. It's a wonder she didn't have the baby on the boat on the way from Nova Scotia."

"Where's Marvin now?"

"Here in the hospital. He said to tell you the *Barbara Ellen* is moored in Indiantown at the wharf at the foot of Main Street."

"That's swell," I said. "Be a sport and go to the gift shop and buy Peggy a pot of mums for me? Now, give me the bad news."

"Prudence Reilly is hosting a Saint Patrick's Day party tonight."

"What's so bad about that?"

"The guest list. Let me finish. Prudence has put her head together with that Molly Higgins woman who runs the, the *house* on Station Street. They've invited Dr. Kinsella and those German fellows you told me about. Apparently, Kinsella knows them. And Molly's two Montreal *friends*."

"Cancel the party! I haven't got time to go and talk sense to the Reillys. Telephone Prudence and tell her to suddenly take sick. She's insane if she lets those people into the house."

"It's too late, Jack. They'll be there in an hour or so. I've been invited and Roxanne is going with me."

"Whose bright idea was that?"

"Mine," Penny said sullenly. "Safety in numbers. Roxanne said her husband was a rat to desert her and Leonard, but that he didn't deserve to end up like he did. She just wants to help, that's all."

"Penny, I'm disappointed."

"Sorry."

"It's too late, the horse is out of the barn. I love you, you idiot, and I'd go nuts if anything happened to you."

"Oh, Jack, I've been secretly in love with you for years."

"I guess I knew that but let's save the sweet nothin's for later. Promise me you won't – and this goes for Prudence, Roxanne, and Molly Higgins's two ladies of the night – go anywhere alone. If you have to go to the powder room take one of the other girls with you. Prudence is playing with fire."

"Yes, but she's confident she can get the information you need."

"Which is?" People tell me migraines are hell on earth but they couldn't be much worse than the headache I was getting.

"Whatever it is the Germans are looking for."

"That's just dandy. What's Prudence going to do? Slip them a truth serum? Forget I said that, it'd be just like her. I have to go – Lincoln might be in trouble."

"Before you hang up will you tell me again?"

"What's that, Penny?"

"That you love me."

"I love you madly, Penelope Fairchild."

"Do be careful, Jack."

"Look who's talking."

I clicked off the desk lamp, throwing the room into darkness except for the amber light coming through the windows of the stove. I sat on the cot to finish my cigarette. I could send a squad car around to Drummond's but if someone was there it might mean the end for Lincoln. I poked the butt through the grate and went back to the telephone. I called his number and let it ring seven times. It was an old signal. If he was busy and couldn't come to the phone, chances were it was Jack on the line. There wasn't any answer, and sick aunt or no, Lincoln was always home at this time of day. I didn't like it. I hoped he realized help was on the way.

I locked the door and took the stairs down to the woodyard three steps at a time. Shorty had a tight grip on the stick shift, his knees splayed to either side of the steering wheel.

He gunned the engine and we lurched ahead, the huge buggy of a truck backfiring like I-don't-know-what.

TERRY CRAWFORD

CHAPTER FIFTY-FOUR

W E MADE GOOD time rattling and banging through town, Shorty tense and silent behind the wheel. He didn't like the motor backfiring and glanced at me apologetically whenever it shotgunned. I didn't care as long as the old pile of nuts and bolts didn't break down. When we crossed the railway tracks at Union Station I told him to take Main Street all the way to the river. It was the simplest and most direct route and would give me a chance to think instead of pointing out go-rights and go-lefts.

We swerved around the final few curves on Main and dropped into Indiantown. I directed Shorty to pull over to the curb. I would walk the rest of the way. If there was someone at Lincoln's I didn't want them alerted by us banging like gangbusters barreling up the road.

Taking the bullets out of my pocket, I unholstered the pistol and loaded all six chambers. Shorty inhaled at the sight of the gun. He knew I ordinarily didn't bother to carry a sidearm. I gave him a few seconds to calm down. We were parked next to a corner grocery that was closed but had a big clock with an illuminated face in the window. "See that clock? Give me five minutes to get to Lincoln's, then ten minutes later come and pick me up. If there's a car there, keep going and phone the station. The house is the third one up the road. Don't forget, turn right after you go over the little bridge. And don't worry, it might be a false alarm."

Shorty laughed nervously. "And if it isn't a false alarm?"

"Then you have my permission to worry."

I jumped off the running board and onto the sidewalk. The neighbourhood was quiet except for a couple of dogs yapping in the distance. Across the street the ACME shipyard was idle, night watchman smoking a pipe at the end of the wharf. An almost full moon was rising over the water, the river so wide it was difficult to see the bluffs on the other side. Marvin's *Barbara Ellen* was moored near one of the harbour dredges. You could easily step off the street and onto her deck.

I clicked the flashlight I'd taken out of the truck on and off. Then I went over the steep knoll ahead and down to the bridge. Across the creek the streetlights ran out. The roads were potholed and unpaved.

From the bridge, I shone the flashlight into the darkness along the creek. The wind had died to nothing but it was bitterly cold. Chunks of ice and snow clung to the bank among the alders but Lincoln and I fished along here enough to know every step blindfolded. I climbed down and started up the hollow. It only took a minute to reach the path behind Lincoln's house.

Elbows thrust forward to shield my face against thorns, I went up and through overgrown blackberry bushes and knelt behind Linc's compost bin. I listened but couldn't hear anything but the steady beating of my heart. There was no car in the driveway but that didn't matter. Something wasn't right. The backyard light wasn't on as it should have been and the kitchen was in darkness. I didn't hesitate. Crouching low, I drew my gun and ran around the corner of the bin. The shadow of a man fell across my path. Spinning, I nearly shot Lincoln's scarecrow. I paused and took a deep breath, infuriated at the stupid thing because it looked so lifelike in the dark.

I crept up to the back porch and peeked over the windowsill. All was silent. Also not right. Lincoln either practiced playing the piano or listened to the radio for a couple of hours after supper. Each and every night. Unless he had company.

And he did have company. A tall, broad-shouldered man walked through the living room and on toward the front hall.

I unlocked the porch door and slipped inside. Back pressed to the wall, I slid over to the window above the kitchen sink. I could see Lincoln sitting under the bright glare of the floorlamp in the front room. He was bound and gagged, fastened with ropes to one of the pressed-back chairs.

I was filled with a murderous loathing for the man who did this to Lincoln but now wasn't the time to lose my head. I waited until I was convinced he was without accomplices. Just before I made my move, the man returned to the living room and knelt at Lincoln's feet. He jabbed Lincoln with something I couldn't see. Moments later he stood up, a hypodermic syringe in his hand. It was filled with Lincoln's blood, which he proceeded to squirt around the room, all the while demanding in a menacing voice, "Where are the photographs? Tell me, you black

TERRY CRAWFORD

mongrel. Next I break your fingers one by one. You not play the piano so good then, yes?"

Lincoln struggled wildly. I had seen more than enough but I didn't dare fire a shot that might go astray. I put the skeleton key into the kitchen door, counted to three and flung the door open. The devil had stacked empty tin cans on the other side. They made one hell of a racket when I charged through the door.

The man bolted behind Lincoln and was gone. The front door opened and slammed shut before I passed through the kitchen

"Are you hurt bad?" I yelled.

Linc shook his head.

I rushed outside in time to see the man clambering up the hill across the road. There was nothing in that direction except rocky scrubland and the limestone quarries. I knew the footpaths well. He would have to circle back toward the lights of the city or risk getting lost in the woods.

I went back inside to free Lincoln. The floor was covered with broken records, the music Lincoln and I had collected since we were boys. Almost all of the sheet music had been torn to shreds. There were bloodstains everywhere. On the curtains, the wallpaper, the ceiling. I looked at the piano bench and my heart stopped at the sight of an array of surgical instruments. I picked up a gleaming silver knife and cut the ropes binding Lincoln. Some of the knots were in the form of a noose. The surgical blade did its work with zero resistance. It could've severed a muscle as easily as a straight-razor slicing through butter.

Lincoln gulped air and shakily got up on his feet. His right foot was naked. There were puncture marks in the big veins above the ankle. I took bandages and Mercurochrome out of the medicine cabinet and made him sit while I dressed the wounds. When I looked up he was weeping quietly, tears streaming down his face. I was unable to speak.

There was a bottle of cooking brandy in the cupboard. I poured a couple of stiff drinks and handed one to Lincoln. He tossed it back and wiped away the tears. Then he did an incredible thing. He smiled at me as if everything was right in the world. It nearly broke my heart.

"I'm going after this sub-human, Lincoln," I said. "Shorty Long should be here in about five minutes. His truck backfires so don't be afraid if you hear it coming up the road."

"Afraid? If you hadn't have phoned I would've died of fright. The things that man threatened to do. But when the phone rang seven times it was like a cavalry trumpet. I hoped and prayed you knew something was wrong."

"How did he get in?"

"I was practicing my piano when he rapped on the door. He told me he was Randy Murphy and showed me the note you wrote with my phone number and Scott Joplin's name on it. I didn't know any different. His English is really good. It only slips when he gets riled. He pulled a gun on me and tied me to the chair with those ropes with the nooses on them. Didn't take more than twenty seconds."

"What did he want, Lincoln?"

"Photographs. Somebody stole photographs off of their ship."

If I hadn't been so sapped I would've kicked myself. Photographs. Werner Strasser had a darkroom aboard the *Bergensfjord*. At the dry dock I'd seen some of Strasser's photographs pressed inside copies of *LIFE* magazine stored beneath his bunk. There were only two issues that didn't have photographs inside. The issues were so recent I didn't give it any thought. They had probably contained the missing photographs. Eugene Robichaud had been known to go aboard the ships and drink with crew members. He must have gone onto the *Bergensfjord* when the Germans were on shore leave. In a drunken ramble he went to the officers' quarters and got too curious for his own good. Or maybe innocently wanted to read that week's *LIFE*. He must have stolen the photographs and fled back to his office to phone Sullivan and Hardfield. But when they arrived he was dead. In a panic they moved his body into the hold of the *Bergensfjord* to deflect suspicion away from their stolen goods racket. What they hadn't counted on were the Germans: all card-carrying members of the National Socialist German Workers' Party. And no one counted on Jack Ireland. But *where* were the photographs? Did Sullivan have them after all?

I thought it best to give Lincoln something to do. "Fix a pot of coffee for Shorty will you, Lincoln? I'll be back."

There was a duffel coat hanging on a coathook behind the kitchen stove. Searching the pockets, I found a packet of Aspirin and a Luger.

It was the first time I'd seen one in real life. I gave the pistol to Lincoln after I demonstrated how to use the safety. "If he comes back, ventilate the son-of-a-bitch with his own weapon."

I left by the back door and crossed the road two hundred feet from the house. The way was almost straight up, but it would take me to the high ground. I went boldly, not caring about the noise. I was the one with the gun.

It didn't take long for me to get to where I wanted to be. I squatted on a granite outcropping at the edge of the treeline from where I could survey the barren headlands above the limestone quarries. Nothing much grew there except the wild blueberries Lincoln and I had picked for pies ever since we were kids. The path the man climbed up to would've led him directly into a criss-cross maze of trails winding in and out of the blueberry bushes. He would soon find himself running in circles. And unless he really was a superman he would have to stop and rest. Maybe even lie in wait for me. Either way, all I had to do was bide my time.

I lay in the dark on my rocky mattress and watched. Between craving a cigarette and wishing it wasn't so cold, I almost missed seeing his head bobbing and weaving not more than three hundred feet away. I was above and behind him. He kept looking in the direction of Lincoln's place, his white head a spectre in the moonlight.

I crawled off the rock and moved stealthily toward him, making sure I could dodge out of sight if he turned around. He straightened up suddenly at the sound of Shorty's truck backfiring. It was a bad moment for me because my prey turned halfway around as if to flee. I crouched low but he seemed to think the better of running and remained stock still.

I kept to the paths and wound my way toward him. He was concentrating on the racket echoing from below when I came out from behind a bald dome of rock about twenty feet away from him. Leveling the .38 on his back at the spot where I estimated his evil heart resided, I clicked on the flashlight and yelled, "*Achtung!*"

He spun round and rushed at me. I squeezed the trigger and sent a bullet a lot closer to his head than I intended. I think it might've singed his hair. He stopped and raised his hands, gibbering a mile a minute in German.

"On your knees," I said, waving the .38. He pretended not to understand. "On your knees, *schweinehund.*"

He knelt down and in a calculated voice said God-knows-what to me in German. Although it wasn't necessary, I cocked the pistol. He shut up. I aimed at his mouth. "One false move and I'll blow your brains out."

I could see his breath now and heard him whisper, *"Mein Gott."* I only knew about ten words of German but I could guess what that meant. Up close, he looked like any other blonde sailor you see around the harbour. He could've been Swedish or Dutch: clean-cut, healthy, athletic in appearance. Someone you'd think was straight as an arrow.

I got right to the point. "What photographs are you after?"

He glared and spat, "I tell you nothing. I am a German citizen. You have no authority…"

"Fuck off. A German dead man is what you'll be if you don't answer my questions."

"You cannot…"

"Why not? I'll shoot you and leave your body for the wolves. You'd be no more than a light lunch for them."

His eyes widened and his lips trembled. The last bounty paid for wolves shot in New Brunswick was in the 1860s, but like many Europeans he probably believed Canada was overrun with snarling carnivores. The land of fang and claw.

"Yeah," I said. "The wolves around here are ravenous after a long winter. They'll eat your soft parts first."

I didn't expect any of this Big Bad Wolf stuff to scare him, but it terrified him. I let out a long howl that would have made the grandfather of all timberwolves proud. He started in with the *"Mein Gotts,"* again, then began pleading for his life.

"Tell me what I want to know and I *might* let you go."

He nodded, teeth clenched.

"What's your name?"

"Bernard Koenig."

"There, that wasn't too hard was it?" He was shivering, sweat beading on his forehead. "What photographs?"

"I do not know."

"All right, have it your way. Say another prayer. I'm going to kill you in ten seconds."

"Our mission."

"What mission?"

"I do not know, *mein Gott,* I do not."

He could've been telling the truth and if I pursued the question I'd get nowhere. I changed course. "Who murdered Eugene Robichaud?"

The blonde head raised toward me; face a mask of incomprehension. "I do not know this person."

"The body in the hold of the *Bergensfjord*? A month ago?"

He nodded.

"Well? Spill it. Come on." I waved the gun at him. He closed his eyes as if expecting a bullet in the brain. I hated the thrill that went up my arm. "Who?"

"Heinrich Gottlieb."

"And where can I find Heinrich Gottlieb?"

I no longer gave a tinker's damn about official secrets, intelligence agencies, and government skulduggery. I wanted to haul Eugene Robichaud's killer in front of a judge and charge him with homicide.

"Where? I'm losing my patience. Will he be at the Reillys' party tonight?"

Mention of the Reillys shook him. He must've smelled a trap.

"Is that where Gottlieb's going to be?"

"*Nein.*"

"Forget the *nein*. It's *yawvol*. Correct?"

"*Nein.*"

"Then where?" I shouted.

My voice carried toward the quarries and disappeared into the darkness. I took a quick glance over my shoulder. The moon had slid behind a cloud bank, the sky beyond was black from horizon to horizon. "Where?"

"I do not know. You have Gottlieb."

I kept the flashlight trained on him and stepped back a few paces. Kneeling there on the path, naked blueberry bushes on either side, Koenig looked like a frightened school boy. But I knew better. He was as cold-blooded as a cobra. I thought about Sullivan and the knots. The knots in the form of a noose. And all the blood. The blood. The blood and burnt flesh.

I held the flashlight between my legs and took a cigarette and a wooden match out of my jacket pocket. When I scratched the match with my thumbnail and lit the cigarette, illuminating my face, it paralyzed Bernard Koenig. Perhaps murder was written there in large letters.

"I have him? Explain."

"Heinrich was dragged out of the water by the tugboat men. You know he was one of us."

"That was Heinrich Gottlieb? How do you know he was identified as a Nazi?"

Even on his knees, Koenig came to attention. A proud Nazi. "We read the autopsy."

"Oh? At my house?"

Koenig snickered. It was a tacit admission that they'd killed Roxanne's husband after he walked in on them. Would've killed me.

"Are you telling me Heinrich Gottlieb murdered Eugene Robichaud?"

"Yes."

"And Gottlieb. Why was he killed and thrown in the bay?"

"He did not follow orders."

"What orders?"

"To stay awake."

"Is that all? I don't believe it."

"Heinrich killed this Robichaud man for stealing photographs."

"Werner Strasser's photographs."

Koenig seemed shocked by my knowledge.

"How come you didn't recover the photographs?"

"Those two policemen come so Gottlieb went back aboard ship to hide. We question Gottlieb in the morning and find out what he did."

"Did?"

"He fell asleep. Drunk. Robichaud stole photographs then Gottlieb went hunting for them."

"And killed Robichaud?"

"Yes."

"How did Gottlieb know Robichaud stole the photographs?"

"Nobody else visit ship that night. That dumb little man left cigarette ends in Werner's room. Cork-tips. And he upset the *LIFE*s."

I contemplated my own, plain-tipped, cigarette. "Cork tips. And for that he was killed? Jesus Christ."

"What do you do with me? You let me go now. Yah? You are police. You cannot harm me. In this country, the police…"

"Shut up or you'll have your picture on the cover of *DEATH* magazine. You're worse than an animal. Get on your feet. Up. Up." I signalled with the .38. "Up. Before I shoot you right now."

Koenig sneered at my apparent weakness. He stood and flexed his knees; one then the other as if preparing for a sprint in a track and field event.

I sneered back. "Who do you think you are? Jesse Owens?"

He went stone-faced and spouted something in his native tongue with the word *schwarz* in it. I knew the word. There was a factory on Union Street with the name *Schwartz* on the roof in six-foot letters. Schwartz's produced foodstuffs famous all over New Brunswick and the Maritimes. Items found in every kitchen. I quoted Koenig the company slogan, "Say Schwartz and be sure." The bastard fumed as if he was going to argue racial superiority. "I guess Owens upset your Aryan applecart. Yah?"

Resorting once again to German, he screamed something about my "*mutter*".

"Bernard, drop dead," I snarled. I flicked the cigarette at him. "Get the hell out of here before I *do* shoot you."

I could tell he didn't believe me. He hesitated, then began running up the path to his left. "Stop," I shouted. "You'll get lost in the woods with the wolves. Go toward the lights in the distance and don't ever come back to Canada. If you do, I'll shoot you on sight." I shone the flashlight up the path behind him.

He ran to the end of the light and stopped. "Tomorrow you die," he yelled. "Stinking nigger-lover."

I aimed toward his feet and pulled the trigger. A bullet ricocheted off the rocks. He hurtled off at top speed, running for his life. I trained the light in his direction and listened as he crashed headlong through the blueberry bushes.

I shut off the flashlight and waited in the pitch black. I lit another cigarette. It was at that moment that I heard the scream, the scream of Bernard Koenig running into thin air and falling, falling, falling, into the limestone quarry.

CHAPTER FIFTY-FIVE

AFRAID OF THE height, I didn't dare go to the edge of the precipice and shine a light down on Bernard Koenig. I knew exactly where he would be lying – at the deepest end of Quarry Five amid a rubble of boulders the size of automobiles. The thought didn't trouble me. The quarries didn't reopen until May 15th and with any luck Koenig wouldn't be found until then. The property was posted as private, and the fines were stiff and always levied. Not even the North End kids, a lot of them hard as nails, ventured this far away from home. It didn't matter anyway. All I needed was a few more days to scuttle the master plans of the master race.

I followed the path down that the late Herr Koenig had come up. I soon reached the crag overlooking Lincoln's place. Shorty Long's spidery frame threw a giant shadow across the front lawn. He was peering upward in my direction and had what looked like Lincoln's bird gun cradled in his arms. I hollered, "Shorty!" as loud as I could and blinked the flashlight. The last thing I needed was a buttock full of buckshot. I shone the light on my face and Shorty nodded then turned and went into the house.

Lincoln was busy sweeping when I entered the front room. There was a dustpan full of broken records in his hand. The blood-spattered curtains and tablecloths were in a heap on the floor. The linoleum and the hard surfaces had been washed clean. A scrub-bucket of crimson water with a crimson rag sat beside the piano bench.

After all he had been through Lincoln was as calm and dignified as a prince.

"I wanted new wallpaper in here before 1940," he said. "Instead of waiting until October to do it, I'll do it now. Maybe that old-fashioned pattern you like with the willows on it."

"Grand. I'll help you hang it. You okay, Lincoln?"

"Right as rain," he said bravely. I could tell that he wanted to stay busy. "Coffee's ready, probably."

I went into the kitchen and moved the percolator onto the table. Shorty was outside in the backyard. Flames leapt into the dark above the barrel as he fed the sheet music into the trash burner. He came in and bundled the curtains and tablecloths together and added them to the fire. The scarecrow watched from the corner of the garden, dancing in the flickering light in his hand-me-down clothes.

I poured Carnation milk into a beer mug and topped it up with coffee spiked with an ounce of brandy.

I found the Reillys' number in the phone book and dialled it. To my surprise, Penny answered, "Good evening, Reilly residence."

"Penny, Jack. If anybody asks, just let on it's the Knights of Columbus reminding James about the next Holy Name Society breakfast a week from Sunday."

"Yes, sir. I'll tell Mr. Reilly."

"Can't you talk now?"

"A week from this Sunday? I'll jot it on the calendar."

"I know what the Germans are after, Penny. Don't let anybody take any chances. And tell Prudence not to tip her hand by asking leading questions. No risks. Understand?"

"It's all right, Jack. He's gone."

"Who?"

"Dr. Kinsella. He was raiding the canapés, that's all."

"Are you on the hall phone or in the kitchen?"

"The kitchen."

"Okay. I won't keep you long. Tell Prudence to lay off. I found out what I need to know."

"Will do."

"What's going on? Who's there?"

"You mean men?"

"Yes."

"The doctor, Werner, Herman, Gustav, and Ernst. They're expecting someone named Bernard later."

I didn't tell her Bernard was a scratch. "Is everything okay?"

"Actually, it's quite a civilized affair. I don't know if James is doing it on purpose, but he's playing Brahms and Beethoven on the phonograph."

"So?"

"By Paderewski."

"Good for James. Listen, Tom Waterman parked my car on Dorchester Street parallel to where you are on Garden. The keys are under the seat in case you need them. How's Prudence?"

"Fine. She's a trifle tight but ever the gracious hostess. That Dr. Kinsella keeps undressing her with his eyes, though."

"He's a lecherous old fool."

"Jack, I *must* go. I'm supposed to be fetching a tray of hors d'oeuvres."

"All right. I'm going to come by and stay undercover just in case."

"Oh, someone to watch over me?"

"Something like that. Be careful. I mean it – walk on eggs."

I sat down at the table opposite Lincoln and Shorty. Shorty had a band of sooty black freckles across his nose and cheeks. I soaked and soaped a dishcloth and handed it to him. He scrubbed his face with a circular motion, rubbing so hard I thought he'd wear his nose off. He tossed the cloth over my shoulder and into the sink.

He stretched his legs under the table till his feet poked up on the chair beside me. "We heard shots," he said, taking a Philip Morris out of my pack and lighting it.

"Must've been a truck backfiring."

Shorty took a pull off the bottle of brandy. "Yes, that must have been what I heard."

Lincoln spoke up. "Seriously, Jack. Did you shoot that guy?"

"No."

"But we did hear shots."

"Target practice. I shot at a couple of boulders."

Lincoln said, "Then you didn't shoot him?"

I stared at the Luger lying on the table between us. "No, Lincoln, that would be cold-blooded murder."

"Then what happened? Where is he?"

"He wouldn't heed my warning shots and ran away from me. He won't be back. He disappeared into the dark and ran right off the top of the quarry. Screamed all the way down. I didn't bother looking to see if he was finished or not. It's at least a hundred-foot drop."

Shorty slapped the table. "Good riddance to bad rubbish!"

"Then I did hear a scream," Lincoln said. "Jack, I'm so rattled I thought it might've been you. I came straight back into the house and started cleaning up."

I got up to leave. "You know I only scream on Halloween."

Tense to the breaking point, Lincoln laughed, eyes shut tight. Shorty shook his head but soon joined in, nearly falling out of his chair.

Myself, I was in a strange mood. Keyed up but with a sense of elation mixed with dread. At the center I was calm, knowing I had to keep on an even keel.

I tried the duffel coat on for size. Even over my jacket it was too big but the sleeves were just about right. There was a black watchcap shoved into one sleeve and an expensive silk scarf in the other. I shelved my fedora and tugged on the watchcap. In the mirror, I put up the hood of the duffel coat. It was roomy and would protect my face from the wind and prying eyes.

I went back to the kitchen where I gave Shorty and Lincoln a fright. "Whoa boys, it's only Uncle Jack."

"Don't do that," Lincoln said. "Lord Almighty."

"Sorry." I tossed the scarf to Shorty. "A souvenir. Fascist moron had taste."

"And money to burn," Shorty said. "What next, Jack?"

"I want you to take Lincoln back to the woodyard for a couple of days. You'll be safe, Lincoln, and you can make whatever telephone calls you have to from there."

Lincoln nodded. "I'll pack a suitcase. I could do with a vacation."

"That's the spirit. I don't think anybody will come back here looking for what's-his-face." I almost blurted Koenig. "It's too risky."

I walked into the front room and looked at the surgical instruments on the piano bench. My appendix scar flinched at the memory of the knife. "Shorty, take this garbage and throw it into the trash burner."

"Isn't it evidence?"

"Of what? Get this, you don't know anything. And I hate to say it, Lincoln, but the same goes for you too. Nothing happened. Nothing."

Shorty shrugged. "Whatever you say. You're the boss."

"No, I'm not. But the bosses aren't the only ones who can play cover-up."

"Yeah, this is for Sullivan," Shorty said with enthusiasm. "Friggin' right." He rushed to the back porch and returned with a burlap sack. He dumped the instruments in one by one. "I'll throw some kindling into the barrel and then a shovelful of coal. That'll melt these into one ugly lump."

"In the meantime," Lincoln said, "I'm going to see if I can do something about the truck. I'll be damned if I'll ride through town with that thing backfiring like it does."

"Good enough," I said. "I'm going to leave on foot. Talk to you tomorrow."

I went out the front door and stopped, looked, and listened.

An owl hooted on the hilltop. Otherwise, all was quiet. The wind had shifted direction, foretelling a change in the weather. By midnight it was supposed to turn balmy. A windstorm full of rain and bluster was sweeping up the Eastern Seaboard.

I walked down the pot-holed, rutted road. The homes of Lincoln's nearest neighbours, cousins one and all, were scattered far and wide along the slope. About now the kids would be doing schoolwork while their parents relaxed around the radio or did household chores. Without streetlights the area was as dark as a backwoods settlement. Satisfied there were no cars around that might contain Bernard Koenig's cronies, I clicked on the flashlight and ran as far as Bridge Street and turned left toward Indiantown.

Instead of going all the way to the foot of Main I hurried up Victoria Street and into the North End. Some of the local toughs were hanging around the corner of Adelaide and eyed me aggressively but because of my size glanced away when I met their stares. All except Bomber Logue, a sawed-off middleweight with a flattened nose, one cauliflower ear, and baby-blue eyes. He trained at the Monarch Boxing Club. He knew me but didn't let on in front of his friends. He also knew I could pulverize him with one uppercut. But Bomber didn't know how to spell f-e-a-r. That's why he got slugged so often and carted around a face that looked fresh out of a meat grinder. I flashed my badge. Bomber knew I was a detective but I didn't want to show him up to his friends.

"Did you see anything out of the ordinary tonight?" I asked.

Bomber hooked his thumbs over his belt. "That depends, copper. What's it worth?"

"Ten days off in Purgatory."

Since they were all micks from St. Peter's parish the boys had a good chuckle.

"Maybe we seen something. What are you looking for?"

"Say a strange car with strangers?" Not many people could afford automobiles in this neighbourhood so I thought the question wasn't too far out in left field.

Bomber held a whispered exchange with the others.

"Yeah, we seen a car," he said then. "Big green job with a couple of guys in it. We made it for a Plymouth."

"When and where?"

"Just after dark over at Jerry's Lunch."

"What did they do?"

"Nothing much. Got two orders to go."

"Describe them."

Bomber lit a cigarette. Watching his every move, his friends shuffled under the streetlight, their youthful faces more curious than threatening. They should've been home brushing up on the three Rs.

"One of 'em was a yellow-haired hound with…," a kid who was as thin as a rake started to say.

Bomber drew a hand across his throat. "Cut. Lemme tell the story will ya?"

The skinny kid froze.

"Like blabbermouth was saying," Bomber went on. "One of them was a giant blonde guy wearing a coat same as yours."

I nodded. Oddly, all the boys nodded along with me. Except Bomber, whose pretty blue eyes had a washed-out, disturbing quality. "And the other fellow?"

"Nervous geezer. Kept biting his thumbnails."

"Was he tanned?"

"Yeah, that's what was funny about him. Wasn't it?" Bomber turned to his friends.

There was a chorus of yeahs.

I stepped in close and looked at each one of them. "Thanks, fellows," I said. "You've been a great help in an important investigation."

I reached into my wallet. "Here's a five-spot. That's a buck a piece."

I handed the bill to Bomber, who passed it on to a jug-eared kid with no front teeth. He must've been the gang's treasurer. I wasn't interested in bribing them or buying their loyalty. But I'd seen them in a queue in front of the Regent enough times to know they liked the movies. A dollar would keep them off the streets for a few nights. And if they saw the *Movietone News* enough times they might learn something you can't pick up on a street corner.

I said, "Good night, gents," and before I got twenty feet I could hear them arguing about the double-bills at the Mayfair and the Empire. Uptown theatres. Already their world was expanding. I didn't have much to smile about but I grinned anyway.

I took the roundabout way home, going through the church grounds and hopping over the stone wall into my backyard. The moon was out again and gleamed off the façade of St. Peter's. I surveyed the area, then went up the backstairs and into the woodshed.

The duffel coat and watchcap were too warm to wear. I hung them on a nail beside my catcher's mitt. Then I telephoned Chief Delaney at his home on Princess Street. I told him I'd solved the murder of Eugene Robichaud but that Robichaud's killer had himself been murdered. That I had been hunting for a dead man. I gave Delaney the name Heinrich Gottlieb and the pertinent details. I confessed that I had the sole proper copy of his autopsy. The Chief took this in stride. He said he would phone Doctor Cromarty and tell him to dispose of the body either in a pauper's grave or on the dissecting table. I didn't tell Delaney about the other body in the quarry. That corpse would, and could, wait until it too was found by accident.

Chief Delaney didn't ask me any questions. I suppose as much for his own protection as for mine. Before he rang off he said, "Report to me again when you can, Jack. You did the right thing by calling me at home. Be careful. Extra."

I slid off the arm of the sofa and onto the soft cushions. There was a photograph of Lincoln and me on the wall over the radio. It was snapped in 1917 during the Great War when I was in grade eleven. That didn't seem nearly as long ago as seven-thirty this morning. Forcing myself to rise, I switched on the radio and listened to some schmaltzy dance arrangements while I washed, shaved, then changed clothes.

Rain began pattering against the windows and the wind rattled the loose sash in the kitchen. I put a new pack of cigarettes in my trenchcoat and phoned a taxicab.

On the ride over to Garden Street I sat in the back seat and pretended to slumber. Photographs were much on my mind. Missing photographs

TERRY CRAWFORD

of a mission so important to the Germans that Heinrich Gottlieb killed Eugene Robichaud. *Silenced* Robichaud because he had seen the photographs.

I cast my mind back to the dry dock and the day I went aboard the *Bergensfjord*. The pictures dealt exclusively with harbours, docks, naval yards, seacoast installations. Locales accessible by water.

We drove along Paradise Row and over the Wall Street bridge to the foot of Garden where I had asked to be dropped. I knew the cabbie. For the sake of something to say I inquired, "Doing anything for St. Paddy's, Brendan?"

O'Brien collected the fare and shrugged. "Nix, Jack," he said. "I'll be too busy ferrying drunks around. Might grab a pint at the bootlegger's later on. Whoops, shouldn't of said that, you being a dick and all."

"As long as the bootleggers don't do business with minors I turn a blind eye."

"Yeah, I know. What we need is a change in our ridiculous liquor laws. You should hear the tourists whining about not being able to get a drink at a restaurant or a hotel. We need the bars and saloons back again. Taverns, anyways."

"I couldn't agree more. A lot of things could do with changing. See you around, Brendan."

I watched the cab go down City Road toward Haymarket Square until I could no longer see TAXI on the roof. Something Brendan had said made me walk down Station to Dorchester Street and go up the hill to my car.

It was still relatively early in the evening. Even if Penny bothered to use the Pontiac she wouldn't need it for at least an hour. What I wanted to do wouldn't take any longer than fifteen minutes. I didn't dally. I gunned the motor and did a U-turn into the middle of the road.

At five miles above the speed limit it didn't take long to get uptown to the police garage. There was always a grease monkey on duty to pump gas and check tires. I got him to unlock the gates to the yard where we kept impounded vehicles and anything smashed-up in a recent accident. He threw on the switch to the arc lights and left me alone. I lit a smoke and waited for my eyes to get accustomed to the sudden brilliance. My Studebaker sulked in the corner like a battered old dog.

On Valentine's Day Sullivan had written "Nix on Dicks" in the snow on the windshield. Afterwards he ribbed me about it. Maybe in his clumsy way he was trying to tell me something. Making it obvious without making it obvious. Hide something serious behind a joke. Until now there wasn't any reason for me to think there would be anything in the old crate. At the time the Studebaker was found wrecked I was too busy searching for Penny to think straight. And then Sullivan was dead. And Penny surfaced. And hardly a moment's peace since.

I pried open the door on the driver's side. The one that had popped, throwing Penny clear before the car pitch-poled down to the river and through the ice. When we were beginning detectives and still partners in good standing, Sully and I would conceal messages in the springs under the front seat. I groped underneath and found nothing. Then in a fit of rage I tore the rearview mirror off and held it at an angle, reflecting the arc light's glare. There was a soiled manila envelope compressed against the jute matting of the seat's lining. I removed it and looked at the contents. Two water-stained photographs. Both taken from a sailboat and clearly showing part of the craft's rigging. The subject was a large house with a mansard roof and mowed lawns. A seaside cottage? Its identification would have to wait but it did seem familiar. Had I possibly seen it on postcards?

I rushed back to the Pontiac and tucked the envelope under the floor mat beneath my feet. Including the recently dispatched Bernard Koenig, five deaths had resulted either directly or indirectly because of these photographs. For starters, Eugene Robichaud and his killer – at least that chapter was closed. But the book was still open on Sullivan and Roxanne's husband whether the Secret Service liked it or not. And I wasn't about to forget Penny's brush with death and subsequent escape across the ice. If it hadn't been for her resourcefulness she'd be dead. And now Lincoln… I didn't want to think about Lincoln and those cursed surgical instruments.

I drove back to Dorchester Street, windshield wipers beating like metronomes in the warm rain. I parked the car under the same streetlight and took the alley cat route to Garden Street. The neighbourhood was still; curtains drawn against the weather. From above, on the ridge that was Coburg Street, other streets descended every which way like the spokes of a broken umbrella. It was part of my territory. Every inch

TERRY CRAWFORD

known to me. The rain started to pelt down, bouncing noisily off the pavement. I welcomed it. Even though I was wearing rubber heels and soles it would muffle my footsteps.

There was only one vehicle near the Reillys' house and it was parked around the corner on Hazen Avenue. I went and had a look. It was a big Buick with a doctor's insignia beside the plate. Kinsella's land yacht. I hid behind the car and scanned the house. On the ground floor the shutters were closed, some of them leaking little bars of light. Upstairs all was in darkness except for the turret on the third floor that James used for his book-binding workshop. There a light shone like a beacon.

As I watched, the lights on the wraparound porch were switched off. Perhaps Penny with her thinking cap on? She knew I preferred to conduct surveillances from up close. I scaled the stone wall, ran along the hedge, and hoisted myself over the railing.

It was too late to complain, but I heartily wished Prudence Reilly hadn't set up this damned set-up.

CHAPTER FIFTY-SIX

RAIN WAS SPILLING over the eavestroughs, cascading like a waterfall off the verandah. It was so dark I had to light a match to make sure I didn't trip over anything. Shielding the flame with my hat, I crouched down and walked crablike toward the windows. There was a shovel and a pair of pruning shears leaning against the wall. And just past them a wooden stepstool with a handhole cut into the top. I sat down before I burned my fingers. The pounding of the rain was hypnotic, a rhythmic trance-inducing drumming...

I jumped when the outside light came on then went off. A few seconds later I heard Penny calling, "Here puss, puss, pussy," in a high voice. I sat still, unable to hear her walking toward me. I hoped to hell she was alone.

She came along the curved outer edge of the wide porch, looked toward Garden Street, then turned and leaned out and gazed up Hazen Avenue, all the while mewing, "Puss, puss." A car drove up the hill and swung around the corner, momentarily freezing her in the headlights. She was cradling an enormous fluffy gray and white cat. Holding it out into the rain, she gave the animal a good soaking then hugged it again. Lying on its back, the cat craved the attention even if it did yowl at getting wet. Penny released the thing but it followed her into my dark end of the porch.

I took a drag off my cigarette to show my face. Penny came close and whispered, "My guardian angel. I saw you from upstairs." She was wearing a perfume that could launch a thousand ships. I buried my face in her bare shoulders then kissed her beautiful lips. She started to hug me tighter but said, "Oh, you're drenched."

"Just the trenchcoat and hat. Smart move with the porch light."

"That was Prudence's little brainstorm. She let the cat out. Silly animal won't leave me alone."

"Must be the perfume," I said, floating on the scent. "What's going on? Did you tell Prudence to scotch her plans?"

"Yes, Jack, but she's intent on Dr. Kinsella for some reason. She actually flirted with him a few times."

"You mean, 'teased him'?"

"That's what a man would say," Penny replied evenly. "Why would you say that? It's not like you."

"Prudence initially set out to help me uncover the big mystery about what Werner and his crowd are after, but now I think she's bent on revenge. And I mean *bent*."

Penny took my cigarette and puffed daintily. When she handed it back I could taste lipstick. I thought I'd kissed it all off. "Whatever do you mean, Jack?" she said.

"We've got to be quick. Didn't she tell you last night?"

"She said you brought to light something about her past for which she and James would be eternally grateful. And by way of thanks she hit upon the idea of this party in order to help you."

"Is that all?" I threw the cigarette out into the rain. I was tempted to send Penny directly to my car but that would imperil the Reillys and the other women inside the house. Reluctantly, I said, "You'd better go back in, Penny."

"What did you mean, 'Is that all'?"

For her own protection, I decided to tell her. "When Prudence was fifteen, Kinsella drugged and raped her."

"Dear God," Penny gasped. "Jack, Prudence *is* going to do something. It makes sense now."

"What makes sense?" We had been whispering, the rain almost drowning out our voices, throats now dry and rasping. "What?"

"I had a headache earlier this evening. There was nothing for it in the downstairs medicine chest so I went upstairs to the bathroom off the master bedroom. Without intending to, I surprised Prudence. She was sitting at her vanity muttering oaths at a pill bottle. The top suddenly flew off and spilled pills all over the place. I glanced at the label on the bottle while she gathered up the pills. It was from a veterinarian. Prudence explained that it was worm medicine for the cat. I hadn't the chance to read the prescription, but I accepted the explanation. Why not? But I realize now where I've seen those kind of tablets. They're horse tranquilizers. I used to administer them at the riding club."

Penny had been outside for at least a couple of minutes and I was anxious to send her back in before she aroused suspicion, but I had to know more. "You think Prudence is going to slip Kinsella a Mickey Finn?"

"Did that cat look like it had worms?"

"No. It's healthy as a lion. You better go back in before they miss you."

"Prudence and Molly are singing Irish ditties. No one will miss me for a while yet."

I thought about the Mickey Finn. "Wouldn't Kinsella taste the drug in his drink?"

"No. It's tasteless. With animals you don't want them tasting anything strange that by instinct they'll spit out. With humans it's a different case – it's sometimes the other way round. Offensive tastes are purposely added to otherwise tasteless medications to prevent too much being ingested. Indeed, some medications contain additives that will cause vomiting in the event of an overdose." It was the professional, scientific Penelope Fairchild, B.Sc., M.S., speaking.

"You're a veritable fountain of information," I said, kissing her again.

"Always at your service," she said dreamily.

I held her close and did not want to let her go. Only a few feet away were men who had killed and would kill. "Penny, get Molly aside and tell her to get her girls to entice a couple of the men back to Station Street. Divide and conquer."

"All right, I'm getting chilled. Time to take kitty and go back indoors."

I watched her outline disappear, that intoxicating perfume still in my nostrils. When she'd gone inside, I got up on the footstool and found a peephole in the shutters.

No one even turned a head as Penny entered the parlour, cat fussing for affection at her feet. I had chosen my spot well. Everyone was visible and I was far enough away so that they couldn't see the glint of my eyes. The window was up a few inches and the sound carried from the inside out.

Prudence was occupying the limelight, her mezzo-soprano barely audible above the rain. She was wearing a green satin gown that accentuated her long legs, slim hips, and full bosom. Her hair was unfastened and fell onto her flawless shoulders. Dr. Kinsella, corpulent and red of face, was seated in an armchair. He was pouring Guinness into a tankard and drooling like a country squire smitten by a comely handmaiden. Prudence was singing to him as if serenading no one else but the good doctor.

I couldn't find Molly Higgins. But her two working girls, Hannah and Abby, were standing by the fireplace with a pair of young men I had never seen before. Werner and Herman were lounging on the chesterfield as if they owned the house, so I guessed the other two men must've been Gustav and Ernst. All four Germans were dressed elegantly in white evening jackets and black bow ties, outfits for infiltrating society. Or impersonating respectability.

There wasn't much I could do but watch and wait, let the party run its course and hope everyone went home peaceably. Gustav and Ernst behaved politely toward Hannah and Abby, replenishing their drinks and offering them eats from the plates on the sideboard. Except for the slovenly Dr. Kinsella, who occasionally roused himself long enough to grab the air in the direction of Prudence's lovely legs, the affair seemed genteel enough. Even with whores and Nazis in attendance.

As surveillance it was a snooze but I was too worked up to get bored. An hour passed. Molly came into the room once or twice to monitor Hannah and Abby. She liked kitchens instead of fancy parlours and I imagined she was out there playing cribbage with James. Penny tended the gramophone, spinning platter after platter of syrupy love songs with ricky-tick arrangements. I'd have to teach her a thing or two about jazz.

I had a smoke break and relaxed a little in the darkest corner of the porch. The rain didn't want to stop. Earlier, I had major misgivings about the party, fearing it would get debauched and out of control, somehow lead to violence. But so far it was almost dull. Hannah and Abby were steering clear of Werner and Herman. Small wonder considering the threats they'd received from them after Randy Murphy was first beaten up. As for Prudence, she kept plying Dr. Kinsella with food and drink. Drink. Now that did make me nervous, but short of crashing the party I couldn't prevent Prudence from drugging the old boy senseless. I just hoped he would pass out soon so James could stuff him into a taxi and send him home.

My biggest worry had been reserved for Penny. I figured Werner or Herman would zero in on her but they were more interested in one another. And the nose candy they were snorting out of a snuffbox when they thought no one was looking. Werner was one of the handsomest men I'd ever seen. Maybe too handsome. He knew the effect he had on people and appeared to wallow in it. Something like a spoiled aristocrat. Perhaps that's what made him seem all the more sinister, as if he had an unseen power that placed him above the law. Herman, his fellow conspirator, was dark and bulldoggish with eyebrows like toothbrush bristles.

A taxicab pulled up in front of the house and honked. I leaped over the railing just as the outside lights came on. A moment later Prudence's voice, slurred and a bit silly sounding, bade "Good-night, all," to four figures huddled under a couple of umbrellas. Someone said, "*Danke, auf weidersehen*," then the taxicab sped away. Prudence went back inside and the verandah became dark again.

I climbed back up over the railing and returned to the window. The occasion had turned downright solemn. Dr. Kinsella had regained his senses somewhat but was staring fixedly into the fire as if he was contemplating eternal damnation. Werner and Herman were leisurely sipping wine and listening to the music while Prudence and Penny wandered around looking gorgeous. I could hear John McCormack's plaintive tenor stalking its way through a heart-rending aria. At the climax everyone stopped moving and remained motionless until the release, then they simultaneously slumped their shoulders. All but Kinsella, who wore a bewildered expression as he struggled to his feet and began cursing Prudence. Unable to walk, he stood weaving on the spot and let go a torrent of invective.

After he railed abuse upon abuse at Prudence, the likes of which I'd never heard, he staggered backwards into a Windsor chair beside the chesterfield. He fell so heavily the chair legs splayed and some of the railings splintered like broken bones.

Werner and Herman laughed uproariously, to the point where I couldn't help snickering myself.

Prudence sedately absorbed it all and stood defiantly over the doctor. "Why, Dr. Kinsella," she said, "you amaze me. I thought you were fond

TERRY CRAWFORD

of drugs. Especially when they take you by surprise." She was icy and stone sober.

Penny looked aghast and retreated to the double doors where Molly and James stood awestruck. At Prudence's feet, Doctor Kinsella flailed helplessly on his back amid the debris of the demolished chair. The obscenities pouring out of his mouth were growing more and more confused by the second.

Still laughing, Werner and Herman disappeared into the hall and reappeared a minute later in black duffel coats with the hoods pulled over their heads. Together they bowed from the waist and backed out of the room. I listened as they went down the front steps and walked up Garden Street, their laughter eventually drowned out by the rain.

I started to go indoors but stopped cold when the small form of Molly Higgins came out into the darkness. She was wearing a rubber slicker and sou'wester and resembled a grade school youngster as she hurried down the hill toward Station Street. She was probably worried about leaving her house of business in her brother's hands for too long. Then again, never mind the racket she was in, Molly always avoided real trouble.

I let myself in without ceremony and tip-toed to the foot of the stairs. The doctor was alternately lucid then incomprehensible. And now he just lay still, staring bug-eyed at the ceiling as if Prudence hovered up there like a witch. All of a sudden he started screaming then kept going on and on with threats of sexual degradation, acts so hideous that I couldn't believe he ever really liked women. There was a hate in him that I couldn't understand. Didn't want to understand. Didn't want to hear.

Penny looked over her shoulder and saw me. At that moment someone came down the stairs. I turned and in a single motion unholstered my gun. It was Roxanne in stocking feet. She had a red shoe in each hand. I shoved the gun back and said, "Don't do that," with a grin. I'd forgotten about Roxanne. When I didn't see her with everyone else I figured she couldn't get a sitter for Leonard and stayed home.

She stopped on the stairs and stared in at Dr. Kinsella. "He doesn't sound human." she said.

She was dressed in basic black, a choker of imitation pearls round her neck. She'd pinned up her hair and looked older. Sophisticated.

"Where have you been?" I asked.

"Up in James's workshop. I was reading *Lady Chatterly's Lover*. That shocked me. But this is from another planet."

"I saw the light in the turret," I said. "But how come you were up there?"

"Werner."

A shot of fear went through me. "Werner? Why?"

"He was nice to me at first but then he acted funny. Claimed he knew me from somewhere. I didn't say a word. But after awhile he asked me how my friend was. Did my friend still have a job?"

"And?"

"I didn't say nothing. I shrugged it off, you know? But later when I was getting something to eat he whispered in my ear."

"What did he say?"

"At first I didn't get it. *Polizei*. I went and told James and he said it's German for police. I should've known. Jack, Werner's seen me waitressing at Pepper's and he must've seen us together. I didn't feel comfortable so James fixed a tray of goodies and moved me up above. I was enjoying myself until I heard that excuse for a human being screaming his lungs out."

Roxanne no sooner said it than the excuse started screaming again. Screams from a sick imagination.

Prudence sighed and folded her arms. The doctor abruptly sat upright. Clutching his chest, he began clawing at his rib cage as if trying to dig his heart out. His face inflated and went ashen then bluish-purple.

Penny quietly announced, "He's going into cardiac arrest."

Dr. Kinsella swung his head toward her and opened his mouth. Foam drizzled over his lips and his eyes rolled back. He wheezed and then the wind went out of him. It was the first time I'd ever seen a person die.

Prudence turned and placidly stoked the fire even though the room was already too warm for the mild weather. James sat on a hassock beside her, holding her free hand. Roxanne mumbled, "These people are nuts."

My thoughts were travelling a mile a minute. I hadn't counted on anything like this happening. Penny walked over to the body and checked for a pulse. She shook her head, then closed Kinsella's eyes.

I felt a queer sense of relief. I suppose out of nerves or sheer exhaustion. The episode at Lincoln's earlier in the evening had just about done me in. Strange to say, it seemed distant and irretrievable. Gone forever.

I made for the liquor cabinet and poured a stiff belt of Jameson's. It burned all the way down. Everyone was staring at me as if waiting for me to lead them out of the wilderness. It was getting late, way past the average citizen's bedtime. The city would be quiet and without much traffic. I came to a quick decision.

"James, find the keys for Kinsella's Buick and back it into your garage. Ladies, help me get this bag of guts into his raincoat, then into his car. I'm going to take the doctor for a drive."

I dragged Kinsella by the armpits onto the chesterfield. He was as heavy as Ali Baba and the Forty Thieves. "Don't everybody move at once," I said.

Roxanne fetched the doctor's hat and raincoat. Meanwhile, I found the car keys in his vest pocket. I tossed them to James. He hesitated to leave Prudence but at my insistence went out the back door and into the garage.

"I don't approve of this, Jack," Penny said. "By rights, you should telephone the department."

Aiming a fat arm into the left sleeve, I forced the raincoat onto the body and around the other side, then held the doctor in a sitting position. Prudence snapped out of her dream state and calmly inserted the right arm then did up the buttons. Roxanne put the depraved monster's homburg on his bald head. I grabbed the hat brim with both hands and pulled it down tight, almost enough to burst the sweatband.

"What are you going to do with him, Jack?" Penny asked in dismay. She was getting shrill. "Will you please tell me that?"

I peered through the shutters. I glimpsed the Reillys' Nash parked across the street. The doctor's Buick was moving in reverse toward the garage. I had to move fast. We would all have to move fast.

"Put your coats on," I said to the women. Prudence and Roxanne did as they were told but Penny stood firm. I held her by the shoulders. Her bare arms were trembling. "We haven't got much time, Penny. I'm not phoning the station. You heard Dr. Kinsella. Do you want to repeat that at an inquest? Kinsella's done enough damage already without ruining all our lives even after he's dead. Besides, they'd never let the smut leak out and besmirch the name of the almighty doctor. Him being a pillar and all."

Penny remained unconvinced. I didn't have time to draw a complete picture of how she and the other women would be humiliated under rigorous questioning and cross-examination. They'd be stained forever. I wasn't going to let that happen. "Look at him, Penny. Look at the bloated slug. He's seventy-three years old. Old men get drunk and have accidents."

"Accidents?"

James came into the room and gave me the high sign. "Yes, accidents. After we get Kinsella into his car, I want you to drive Roxanne home. Maybe stop off at Pepper's Diner for pie and coffee. Show off your party dresses. Be *seen*."

Penny nodded.

"James, you take Prudence with you in your car and park across the foot of Sewell Street by the rail sheds. I want you to signal with your headlights when the coast is clear. No traffic either way. Then you hightail it out of there. Take Prudence dancing at the Royal Hotel. The orchestra will be in high gear by then and everybody who brown-bagged it will be loaded. They'll think you dropped in from another party in the hotel. Make yourselves visible. Laugh and be gay. Do you figure you can handle that?"

I glanced from face to face. Satisfied that panic wasn't on the loose, I added, "All right, let's get to work."

I wrestled Kinsella into a half-nelson and stood him up. Penny had dressed for outdoors and seemed prepared to go along with my plan. I started to back out of the room. Kinsella's heels dragged. Penny urged Roxanne to carry one leg while she toted the other. James and Prudence went ahead and opened the doors.

The garage was attached so we didn't have to go outside. It was difficult getting Kinsella's dead weight into the Buick but we managed. I reminded everyone that Kinsella was a widower, lived alone, and hadn't practiced medicine in ten years. In the unlikely event that anyone in authority asked, namely my own department, they were to say that the doctor had visited briefly and then insisted on driving his own car home.

I sent the Reillys to their car, waited a minute, and then had Roxanne and Penny leave by the back door. I found a chock for the car tires and threw it in on the seat beside Kinsella. He was slumped against the door on the passenger's side. A fat old man sleeping the big sleep. He reeked of booze. It's too bad there isn't a hell because right now he'd be at the gates. I turned the downstairs lights off before I opened the garage door. Easing the Buick outside, I parked at the curb and made sure the emergency brake worked. It was perfect. I ran back and pulled down the garage door with a slam.

The rain had changed to drizzle. The Buick sailed up the hill and cruised the two blocks to Sewell Street. I hung a right and went down past Dorchester. Sewell had one of the steepest hills in Saint John. On the bottom third there weren't any houses on either side and it was too much of an incline to permit parking.

I stopped in the middle of the road about three hundred yards up the hill and pulled on the emergency brake. Sewell was a sidestreet and because of its steepness not used much. I got out and put the chock under the left front tire. Behind me a barren hillside rose almost straight up to the Old Stone Church, medieval in the wind and rain. Across the way, a wooden guardrail protected the unwary from falling over a rocky cliff.

I pushed Dr. Kinsella's sagging bulk across the leather seat to the driver's side. Picking up his floppy arms, I positioned his fingers around the steering wheel at ten and two o'clock.

Down below, James was parked by the railway sheds where Station Street dog-legged toward Union Station. I turned on the motor and blinked the headlamps. James gave me the signal then drove off, screeching his tires on the cobblestone.

I placed Kinsella's foot on the accelerator. Once the Buick got rolling his sheer weight would step on the gas. Not that it was even necessary. Merely coasting, the car would be speeding toward fifty by the time it reached bottom. I released the emergency brake, pushed down the lock button, closed the door, and kicked the chock from under the tire. At first, the Buick seemed to move in slow motion with the doctor slouched behind the wheel like an overstuffed ragdoll but then the engine roared and the car hurtled downward.

The hill was so steep the car went straight as a bullet along the centre of the road. At the bottom it zoomed across Station Street, sparks flying from the undercarriage, then it glanced off the corner of a loading dock and cart-wheeled, crashing spectacularly against the brick wall of the railway freight sheds.

It lay on its roof in a crumpled mass, one tire spinning crazily, the terrific bang of the impact echoing through the valley. I began walking up the street. Lights blinked on here and there on the far hillside. There were shouts in the railyard to the other side of the freight sheds. Halfway up the hill I turned to have a final look. Tongues of fire licked along the twisted frame, lighting the intersection and a row of boxcars on the siding.

It startled me when the Buick's gas tank exploded. It was something I hadn't foreseen but, of course, the late doctor would've travelled full-up.

I stepped into a cellar doorway at the corner of Dorchester and Sewell. By now there was quite a commotion on the street, silhouettes of men running back and forth. There was a blazing inferno inside the car as the upholstery caught fire. The heat of the flames must have been fierce because no one was getting close. I heard the clanging of fire trucks and looked down Dorchester in time to see the City Road brigade fly past.

I continued on up Sewell to Coburg and went over to Garden Street then headed down toward the Reillys' house. I thought it best to clean up the damage in the parlour. And have a quiet drink by the fire. I had done a wrong thing but it was right.

CHAPTER FIFTY-SEVEN

I PUT MY drink on the mantelpiece and looked at myself in the mirror. Spent, used-up, ready for the loony bin. I fed parts of the broken chair to the fire and stoked the coals with one of those fancy brass pokers movie aristocrats use to brain unwanted relatives.

I was warm but wetter than a wharf rat. The fire blazed. I backed off and did a slow spin, heat penetrating to the bone. Then I tuned the radio to the dance at the Royal Hotel. The band was performing a workmanlike foxtrot. I imagined Prudence two-stepping in her emerald gown. She and James now had a chance at happiness after the years of anguish.

I hoped Penny and Roxanne were making a big splash at Pepper's Diner. The New Brunswick Breweries' graveyard shift would be set to go on soon, a lot of the men stopping at the Diner for a snack before work. They'd get a pleasant eyeful. Something to beat the gums about all night. Which was just what I wanted, the more they talked, the better.

A siren wailed on the street above. When I looked through the shutters, a black- and-white went screaming past on the way to the accident. Otherwise, the neighbourhood was quiet, the asphalt glistening with rain.

I went to where the food was laid out and nibbled, suddenly hungry. I devoured some sliced ham with spicy mustard and a couple of devilled eggs, yolks dyed green. There were sandwiches cut into shamrocks that were just too cute to eat but I dug in and downed a dozen anyway.

After mulling it over, I decided not to phone Chief Delaney and tell him about Doctor Kinsella. Kinsella drove drunk all the time and had been stopped by the department damn near every month of the year. His end was predicted eons ago. The only sorry thing was that we didn't toss the blessed doctor in the drunk tank with the other souses when we should've instead of granting him special dispensation. It was the kind of blight on the force that bothered me, but unless the world went topsy-turvy the privileged would always be the privileged. Anyhow, in this case, Kinsella's driving record provided me with a ready-made cover-up. Maybe there was justice after all.

I broke the last of the chair rungs over my knee and added them to the flames and put the firescreen back in place. On the radio the band's chanteuse was crooning a version of *Blue Moon* that was sadder than a map. Before she gave me nightmares I turned the travesty off.

It occurred to me that I could bed down on the chesterfield. The Reillys could wake me when they got home or let me sleep. Either way, it would make them feel more secure to find me in the house. And if I was lucky, Penny would put two and two together and wake her sleeping prince with a kiss.

On that thought I climbed the stairs and retreived a blanket and a pillow out of a cedar chest. Returning to the parlour, I set the gun on the end table, arranged myself comfortably, and drifted off in the firelight.

With my head sunk deep into the pillow I dreamt someone quietly opened the front door and walked into the house. A man with a hoarse voice who rasped, "Berndt, Berndt," stood alone in the foyer.

I awoke in a cold sweat. It wasn't a dream. The fire had burned down to embers blinking lazily in the hearth. I lay still and tried not to breathe. A figure advanced toward me and whispered, "Berndt." I could make out the bushy eyebrows and hard glint of Herman's eyes. Berndt must've been the German equivalent of Bernard. Before Herman discovered that it wasn't Bernard sacked out on the chesterfield, I made a move for the gun. Throwing off the blanket, I reached toward the end table beyond my feet. I should have shot Herman when he was caught by surprise. Instead, I began to stand up and said, "Don't move."

Something came out of his sleeve and into his hand. I'd made a mistake. He lunged forward and slashed upward. I felt a searing pain in the thigh and then a numb kind of stinging in my wrist as the gun flew out of my hand and skittered across the hardwood floor. Herman glanced sideways, watching as the gun struck the baseboard and spun like a top. I swung with my good hand, smashing him with a left hook that caught him squarely between the eyes. I couldn't tell whether my knuckles or his nose broke. He fell backwards but in a second came up with the .38. I had no choice. It was run or get plugged.

I ran into the foyer and made for the kitchen. A flash lit up the room behind me as a bullet zipped past my hips. It struck the bronze cavalier and caromed into a picture at the bottom of the stairs, shattering the glass. Herman was spluttering through his nose and cursing furiously. I went through the darkened kitchen, out the garage door, and onto the street. Hardly aware of the pain from the wounds, I ran up Hazen Avenue faster than I thought I could ever run.

I stopped to catch my breath in front of St. Joseph's convent. My leg felt sticky and warm. Blood flowed freely. Taking off my belt, I fashioned a crude tourniquet. Whatever cut me had sliced cleanly through my trousers and opened a gash about six inches long above my right knee. My guess was that Herman was after my wrist, which he missed, cutting instead the meaty part of my hand. It was bleeding like crazy but when I made a tight fist it slowed to a steady drip. I wrapped it with my handkerchief, all too aware now of the burning pain.

I was standing at a Y in the road, able to see down Hazen Avenue and along Coburg Street. When we were kids we used to trespass in the convent garden for a lark, hiding under the verandah as the nuns went to and from the hospital. I climbed onto the spear fence and dropped on one leg to the lawn. Limping past the statue of St. Joseph, I found a gap through the hedge and fumbled for the bolt that secured the door in the lattice work. The door was still there and hadn't changed, but I had. I scrunched my shoulders together and squeezed through the small opening. I remembered the thrill of running along the south and west walls beneath the verandah. The sand piled against the foundations would slip under my feet as I ran toward the other hidden gate. We were barbarians invading God's own harem. Stooping as I walked I felt quite barbarous now. Caught between the blood and the pain, and without a weapon, all I could do was play cat and mouse. And hope the cat didn't find me.

I sat down in the sand and leaned back against the brickwork. It was dark and without shadows where I lay watching and waiting, ears alert to every sound. After a minute or two I heard someone running. Beyond the lattice and the leafless hedge, Herman hung onto the spear fence and panted. His aquiline nose was shoved to one side. He snorted in an attempt to clear his nasal passages, failed, tried again, then began swearing loudly and gutterally in German. He was staring in my direction but I had a hand over my eyes and was peering between my fingers.

A door opened and somebody stepped out onto the verandah above me. Herman reached into his coat, gripped the gun, and held it at his side.

"Young man, what is the problem?"

Herman looked up and grinned, his face a graven image with bushy eyebrows. "*Nein...* pardon. Nothing, Sister."

"Then why are you venting your spleen?"

"I'm hunting for my dog. He made me angry by running away," Herman said in stilted by-the-numbers English.

"This is a hospital zone. Control your language *and* your temper if you know what's good for you."

"What's good for me is to kill that dog," Herman said, spitting gobs of blood on the sidewalk. "That is what is good."

The nun stamped her foot and said sternly, "That's enough out of you. Now be off before I summon the police. Shoo, go away."

Herman slunk away from the fence, then hurried along Coburg Street. He turned left at the nurses' residence and went down Cliff Street toward Waterloo. I was thankful that he was moving away from the Reillys' house. And me.

My leg was becoming numb and difficult to manoeuvre. Satisfied Herman hadn't backtracked, I hobbled toward the other door. Poking a finger through the lattice, I pushed the bolt open and came out from under the verandah and onto the deliveryman's driveway. There was that peculiar stillness in the air that only seems to happen before or after a storm.

I did something I'd been wanting to do for the last twenty minutes - I lit a cigarette and took a drag. It didn't really help but it gave me a sense of doing something normal, something ordinary and innocent.

I grimaced as I loosened the tourniquet and felt the circulation easing the numbness in my leg. But it also increased the bleeding. I would have to get the wound stitched. And soon. I wasn't that far away from the General. It would be better to go there rather than St. Joseph's Hospital, which was close at hand. St. Joe's had a small staff that would ask too many questions and fill in too many forms. At the General I could get Doc Cromarty to sew me up with a minimum of fuss.

It would be easier to travel on the streets but I couldn't risk getting caught out in the open. Herman might be lurking in any doorway. The end of Jack was an event I wasn't ready for and wasn't about to assist via stupidity. I'd already been careless and had the wounds to prove it.

Keeping one eye over my shoulder, I went the short distance to the head of Hazen Avenue and hid behind a massive elm tree at the entrance to Hazen's Castle.

There were lights in some of the windows of the rambling green mansion. Candles mostly. Now and then a shawled figure moved past the high bay windows.

I wriggled between the castle's stone gatepost and its cedar hedge, a tight fit that squirted me out the other side. Avoiding the house, I limped down a gravel path that traced the eastern edge of the gardens. It had a tall wooden fence that I could lean against if I needed to rest. Over the fence, a wild bramble-infested hillside descended to the Thistle Curling Club behind the Cathedral grounds.

Like a spotlight the moon came out of hiding and startled me in its embrace. I entered a gazebo constructed of laths further along the ridge and lay down with my bad leg elevated against the herringbone pattern of the wall. The position alleviated the pulsating throb at the wound-site.

I watched the mansion. Upstairs, an old lady floated past a quartet of double bay windows.

I left the gazebo. The moonlight was dangerous. A sundial on a hillock encircled by stone benches actually read one o'clock. I hurried as best I could to the barns at the rear of the premises. In the shade of the dark side, I found a bundle of beanpoles. I broke one and made it into a walking stick. It helped me negotiate the last fifty feet of fence that marked the jagged northern perimeter. Unable to open the swollen door in the fence, I sidled up a cross member and lowered myself over, landing where the grounds-keepers dumped garden refuse. Mercifully, it was soft and spongy, composed of mouldy leaves and grass clippings.

The old lady must have seen me sneaking through the garden or climbing over the fence because I heard a dog growling as it raced toward me. Judging by the way the beast shouldered the fence and snarled through the cracks it was a lucky thing I was free and clear. But the damn animal set to howling like the hound of the Baskervilles. I used the pole to battle through a tangle of brambles and fought my way down to the flat in front of the curling club.

No sooner did I pass the rink and start up Golding Street than I heard someone running. Herman had doubled back through St. Vincent's schoolyard behind St. Joseph's Hospital and was headed toward the barking dog. Before he could catch sight of me I went straight ahead to Waterloo. I didn't dare go the back route to the General Hospital over the rough terrain where Herman might apprehend me.

I reached Waterloo Street and looked back. Herman came to the top of the rise on Golding and fell to his knees. I was too far away for a shot but he took aim anyway. He had been running fast and was fagged out. Instead of firing, he retched violently into the gutter.

I crossed the street and ran down the lane between the houses to Exmouth. I was desperate. Less than a month ago I'd trailed Penny to Exmouth Street and the home of Jimmy Quinlan. I hoped he still had his brother's Colt .45 hidden in the kitchen cupboard. The thing was so ancient it might explode in my hand but I figured at least one shot from a cannon like that would scare off my pursuer and give me time to get to the hospital.

Exmouth was a curved street that descended sharply downward at the bend. Pressed shoulder to shoulder, the houses crowded the sidewalk with only a few covered alleyways between them. I went around the curve to number 48 and almost passed out trying to remain upright on such a steep pitch. I sat on the steps for a moment and listened but could hear nothing. Maybe Herman had stopped up above somewhere and was himself listening. I opened the door as quietly as possible and was hit by the ripe stench of alley cat, damp wallpaper, and rotted linoleum. I went inside and unscrewed the lightbulb hanging in the stairwell. It left the hallway, which listed to one side, in darkness. Taking the beanpole to the door, I wedged it crossways under the knob. If someone tried to get through he would make quite a racket.

I climbed the stairs to the third floor, gripping the railing hand over hand and pulling myself up. There was a slit of light coming from under the door of number six and caterwauling hillbilly music inside. I knocked hard. The hectic music stopped.

"Who is it? It's late," a quiet voice asked.

"Quinlan, it's Jack Ireland, let me in."

Jimmy Quinlan opened the door and was taken aback by my hatless, bedraggled appearance. He looked a bit drunk but otherwise was neat as a pin in white shirt, gabardine pants, and green tie. Noticing the state of my trousers, he said, "Holy Mother of God."

Offering an arm for support, he helped me into the kitchen. The room was as sanitary and bare as I remembered. And there was that icebox painted white. The table had little towers of coins on it and a wad of bills. Quinlan was calmly studying me, his bright eyes scanning from head to toe. I nodded toward the money. "Sell a lot of cider today, Jimmy?"

Quinlan shrugged. "Well, you know, Saint Patrick's. Can't stop an Irishman from drinking."

I wiped the sweat off my forehead. "Speaking of which."

Quinlan went to the icebox and returned with a pint of cider in a corked beer bottle. I drank while he put the cash into small envelopes with the amount written on each. He placed the haul into a cigar box and disappeared into the next room. He returned with a mop and swabbed the floor where I had tracked blood into the flat. "Put your leg up on this," he said, moving a chair. "You're bleeding like a stuck pig."

Quinlan was steady as a rock. I watched as he put a basin on the floor to catch the drips. I didn't like the sound of the plop, plop… it was too steady. "Have you still got your brother's Colt here?" I asked. "I've got a score to settle."

"So I gather," he said, kneeling. He tore my trousers open and studied the wound. "But you won't get far with this."

I looked. It was a long incision with blood seeping steadily out. "Christ. You wouldn't have a telephone?"

"No. There isn't one in the whole house."

"Could you bind this leg for me? Make bandages out of a pillow case?"

Quinlan rubbed his chin. "No, sir. Wouldn't do any good. Needs sewing."

I guzzled the remainder of the cider and grinned. "How are you with a needle and thread, Mr. Quinlan?"

The small, trim man folded his arms and looked me in the eye. "I've sewn up many a horse gored by a cow or ripped by barbed wire. I don't see how this would be a whole lot different."

"Have you got the right equipment?"

"I tie flies with the best of 'em, so I can do a delicate knot. How's about fishing line?"

"As long as you sterilize it."

Quinlan went into the bedroom and came back with a tackle box and an assortment of tobacco tins. I didn't want to watch but I couldn't take my eyes off of him. After he got everything ready he went into the bathroom for rubbing alcohol and iodine. Reminding me not to worry, he cleaned the wound with a cloth and dabbed it with the iodine. I thought the top of my head was going to come off. He removed the belt from my leg and told me to clench it between my teeth. Pinching the skin together, he started. Two stitches were all I could watch. He was adroit and fast but it stung so badly I decided to close my eyes until it was over.

The ice-cold facecloth Quinlan draped over my face made me release the belt. I'd almost bitten through the leather. The slash didn't look much different than other suture jobs I'd seen. Except that in my case the stitches were a flamboyant aquamarine, garish against the bright orange stain of the iodine.

"That's stopped the bleeding," Quinlan said. "I don't know what you were cut with but it's the cleanest slice I've ever seen outside of a hospital. No ragged tearing at all. Was he a professional?"

"No. A fanatic."

"Religious?"

"You could say that."

I tried flexing my leg to get the circulation going. My toes were tingling as if asleep but in a minute they came back to life. I stood. The stitches hurt but really didn't feel all that bad. At least I had confidence that my leg wasn't going to come apart. "Good job, Quinlan."

"Get out of those pants," he said, indicating my exposed thigh. "I'll lend you a pair."

"Thanks, but I haven't been your size since I was twelve."

Quinlan laughed. "I'll bet. My brother leaves some city clothes here for when he comes from up country. Fred's not as lanky as you but they'll fit."

I got out of my trousers and emptied the pockets. Out the window, the East End was a jumble of flat rooftops and darkened houses, lifeless beneath the drifting moon. But Herman was out there and he was very much alive.

"Here, try these," Quinlan said. "But first, let me bind those stitches."

While I stood he took a strip of sheeting and dressed the wound. I pulled on the pants. They were brown flannels with wide cuffs and roomy pockets. My argyle socks were showing.

"You are tall," Quinlan said.

He reached into the cupboard, took out a box of Corn Flakes and handed me the Colt .45.

The pistol was bigger and heavier than I recalled. I plucked the bullets from Quinlan's outstretched hand and pushed five slugs into the cylinder. I left the top chamber empty. I didn't want the damn thing firing off accidentally and blowing a hole in some poor citizen's house.

Quinlan sat me back down at the table and applied iodine and a bandage to the cut on my hand. "You're somewhat expert at this," I said.

"I was too small for the army but they let me in the Ambulance Corps," he replied. "I served in France from '15 to '18."

"Ah, so you've seen wounds worse than this before."

I lit a cigarette and gave Quinlan one, which he tucked over his ear. He had been concentrating on the first-aid but now his thoughts seemed far away.

"I've seen things no human being was ever intended to see," he said.

"Amen."

There was a noise from downstairs at street level. Not loud, but an insistent rattling at the door.

"That's my wake-up call," I said. "Where's the back exit?"

"Right down the hall from the front. You can't miss it."

"Okay. Turn out all your lights. I'm going to lead him away from here. He's got my police revolver so don't try any heroics."

"Don't worry. I did my good deed for the day."

"I'll say. Thanks a million, Quinlan."

I went down the stairs two at a time and screwed the lightbulb all the way back into the socket. Herman had almost broken through the barred door. He was swearing in English. I opened the back door and let it bang against the wall. It silenced him. I yelled, "Temper, temper," and escaped down a rickety staircase into the yard. Herman had no way of knowing I'd been repaired and was carrying a lethal weapon.

I clambered up to a grassy knoll the local kids called Green Hill. As I did I could hear the beanpole splinter and Herman bust noisily into number 48. I kept climbing up through back yards until I reached the Baptist Church opposite the lane from Exmouth to Waterloo. I wanted to lead the enraged German away from Quinlan's. And if I could, I wanted to get back my .38. The last thing I needed was to have Herman or one of his goons shoot somebody with it and have the gun traced to Det. Sgt. Ireland.

I found a couple of garbage cans and positioned them at the rim of the hill. Crouching down between them, I waited. Herman came out onto the landing behind Quinlan's house and stood there bold as brass in an oblong of light. The intervening yards were pitch dark. I sent the garbage cans tumbling down the rocky embankment. Herman lifted his head and peered toward me. I stepped back into the moonlit churchyard and staggered out of sight.

As soon as I knew Herman could no longer see me I broke into a run, crossing the street and into the lane. Herman was clever. He didn't bother stumbling blindly through the backyards but went out the front of Quinlan's and charged up the middle of the pavement. He was so quick that I was sure he caught a glimpse of me. But that was all right. The lane was narrow and unlit with plenty of hiding places. This was one of my childhood hide-and-seek territories. Before he could hear me, I climbed the wooden fence beside the St. Vincent de Paul Society building, then stepped off and onto the overhang protecting their back door. It was level with the top of the fence and enough out of the way to provide cover.

I'd tucked the Colt in my belt. I took it out and felt its heft. The butt was almost too big for my hand. It was a firearm fit for Tom Mix and the Texas Rangers. Something impressive to sport on one's hip. A peacemaker to reckon with.

Herman entered the bottom end of the lane, his breathing wheezy and laboured. I was standing about eight feet in the air and not far from Waterloo Street. He would have to come past me. I hoped he was angered and frustrated enough to think I was still on the run.

Car tires screeched somewhere near the Cathedral. Moments later, another screech. Much closer this time. It worried me. Herman quickened his pace. When he was almost below me I threw a handful of pebbles, scattering them at the base of the wall behind him. He reeled around. I used my good leg to vault off the fence and jumped. Clutching the barrel of the Colt, I swung hard and cracked Herman on the head before I even touched ground. He fell headfirst in a heap. I landed on my good leg, pitched over, and rolled up against a shed.

I got up, scared but none the worse for wear, and lit a match so I could have a close look at Herman. At first, I thought I'd fractured his skull, but most of the blood was from his broken nose and not the gash on the top of his head. He was breathing the way men knocked out breathe. Hardly at all. I picked up the .38 and holstered it. I lit another match. At that moment I felt like killing Herman. He was wearing my wife's stolen watch, the one Grace used on her rounds when she was a nurse. A car went slowly by the lane, jammed on its brakes, then reversed. I removed the wristwatch and raised the Colt at the vehicle, its headlights nearly blinding.

The driver honked the horn and opened the passenger's door. I heard Penny's angelic voice scream, "Jack, get in."

I didn't waste a second. I got into the Pontiac and kissed Penny as if she issued the breath of life itself.

"Did you kill him?" she asked, backing the car onto Waterloo Street.

"No. But I gave him a couple of souvenirs."

"Gawd, Jack, I've been frantic. I went back to the Reilly's, found your hat and coat and saw the blood. When I couldn't find you I didn't know what to do. I got back into the car and drove around in a state. Finally, I saw that man but then I lost sight of him when he went into St. Vincent's schoolyard. He must have been insane the way he chased you."

"That about sums it up," I said. "Could you do a fellow a favour and drive him to the hospital?"

"Only if he promises to let me nurse him back to health."

"Gladly," I said, as lightheaded as the moon high in the sky.

CHAPTER FIFTY-EIGHT

VOICES MURMURING ABOUT Jack. Somewhere in a haze miles above. If I could only rise and go. But where? I seem to be nowhere and everywhere at once. I'm trying not to be afraid although something in me wants to panic. I'm about to scream.

My eyelids open, heavier than lead. The light hurts. I turn away but the sunlight slanting through the window is even more painful. There is a needle stuck in my arm. A bottle of blood, so red it looks black, hangs over me on a hook. My tongue is made of sand and my right leg is on fire. I try to get up but a firm hand restrains me.

"Easy does it, Jack. You've had enough excitement…"

I squirm, for some dumb reason believing Werner or Herman has got hold of me but it turns out to be Doc Cromarty. He's standing there in a lab coat with his name on it. That's how I'm sure it's really him. He's got a stethoscope dangling from his neck. For a pathologist, that's weird.

"I didn't know dead people had heartbeats," I say, sounding like I'm moaning through a megaphone. My ears pop and the fuzziness disappears. Noises in the room suddenly become piercing. Everything shifts gears.

"Cheap sarcasm," Cromarty said. "He'll survive."

For the first time I noticed Penny at the foot of the bed and Tom Waterman leaning against the bureau. Penny was dressed in a lab coat and Tom was attired in plainclothes, if you could call a snazzy dark suit plain. Penny smiled a smile that could melt a million hearts.

"Crank me up, will you, Penny?" I asked.

Doc Cromarty gave the okay.

Penny brought me up forty-five degrees. "That's better. I feel like I was flattened by a steam-roller. I don't remember drinking all that much."

"Drink be damned," Cromarty said. "We gave you enough medication to knock out a bull elephant. You weren't supposed to wake up for another hour or two."

I glanced out the window. The sky was an incredible blue but to save my soul I couldn't tell whether it was morning or afternoon. "What time is it?"

"Quarter past four," Waterman said.

I didn't believe him. "What? I've gotta go. Get me out of this contraption, Doc."

"Behave yourself," Cromarty said. "While you were asleep we checked up on your Germans."

"And?"

"Waterman will give you a report by and by. I want you to stay in this room, in that bed, for at least another twenty-four hours. And don't roll your eyes at me. As it is, you're lucky you weren't killed yesterday. And who the hell sewed you up? Doctor Frankenstein?"

I rubbed my leg. There was a new dressing on it and I was wearing one of those backless Johnny shirts invented to drive hospital patients insane. "Is it that bad?"

"It's illegal to practise medicine without a license, Jack," Cromarty said, so angrily it gave Penny a jolt. Then he laughed and said soothingly, "No, it's not that bad. It'd get a B+ in surgery. Whoever did it probably prevented you from bleeding to death. I left the fishline in place. But I wish you'd stop thinking you're invincible and ask for help on these escapades you embark upon without so much as a how-do-you-do?"

Embarrassed, Penny and Tom studied the shine on their shoes.

I said, "Nice lecture, Doc, but you know me."

"Yes, and I'd prefer to know you a good deal longer. Don't push the luck o' the Irish too far, Jack."

There was an uncomfortable silence. Finally, Penny snuck a peek at me. "Got a cigarette?" I asked.

Cromarty sighed and nodded. Penny took a pack of Black Cats out of her lab coat. "Will these do?"

I took one and tore off the cork tip. It didn't taste too bad.

"Do you need anything?" Cromarty asked.

"An ice-cold quart of Alpine."

Cromarty laughed along with Tom and Penny. "I meant pyjamas, toothpaste, a razor, change of clothes?"

"Thanks, Doc. Tom can do that."

"What about me?" Penny said.

"Food. I'm starved."

Penny consulted Cromarty. "What do you think?"

"Try him on some consommé and a poached egg later on before bedtime."

"Him? I'm right here, Doc. See? Me. The guy in the bed."

Cromarty ignored me. He glanced at his pocket watch. "Nothing more solid than that until tomorrow." He gave me a pat on the shoulder. "Now, I have to go. I'm scheduled to perform an autopsy to verify the identity of the charred remains of an automobile accident victim. One of our more illustrious citizens went up in flames last night. You might even say he was the guest of honour at a pig roast."

Shocked, Penny busied herself with the sheets at the side of the bed. Tom frowned at Cromarty's lack of respect but stepped forward. "Oh, that'd be Dr. Kinsella. I heard there was a hell of an explosion and fire after he crashed his car."

"*The* Dr. Kinsella?" I said, pretending surprise. But Cromarty didn't notice, merely going with a backward wave out the door.

"Yes," Tom said. "Must've been pie-eyed. He was notorious for drinking and driving. I guess it finally caught up to him."

Wanting to change the subject, I said, "Speaking of catching up, what have you got to tell me?"

"I'll find you something to eat," Penny said. "That way you two can conspire together. After last night I don't believe I want to know any more about anybody doing anything."

Tom took a notebook out of his vest pocket, flipped through the pages, and began, "Werner, Herman, Gustav, and Ernst left Wellington Hall shortly before dawn this morning. The landlady told me Herman was in need of medical attention. He wasn't treated in any of the local hospitals or clinics."

"No big surprise. What about Wilder Hunter?"

"I'll get to him, Jack. Apparently, there was a fifth guy name of Berndt Koenig who didn't show last night."

I shrugged. What Tom didn't know…

"Anyway, the others took this Berndt's gear with them. The landlady was a talkative old biddy. Said they were all fine, upstanding gentlemen even if they didn't come home till all hours of the night. I think her opinion was influenced by the twenty-dollar tip they gave her to keep mum about Herman."

"Oh? How did you find out about him then?"

"I gave everybody's room the once over. In Herman's there was a towel with a lot of blood on it in the hamper."

I helped myself to another one of Penny's Black Cats, not bothering to tear off the cork tip. "How come she spilled?"

"I told her to get her hat and coat and come to the station with me. Poor woman almost burst into tears. I reminded her that I was a detective and that it was best for her to reveal everything."

"Did you actually say, 'reveal everything'?"

"Yes. Why?"

"It could've been taken to mean something else. I wouldn't try that approach on a young woman."

"I never thought of that. You know what I meant."

"Yes, never mind, Tom. I'm only joking. But you did tell her you were a detective?"

"Yes."

"Great. What if she phones the station and asks for Detective Waterman?"

Tom smirked. "I told her my name was Parker."

"M'mm. You're learning. Now, Wilder Hunter?"

"Hunter checked out of the Ten Eych Hotel at six-oh-five last night."

"Did anyone notice his car?"

"Yes. The desk clerk doubles as a bellhop there. He helped Hunter put his luggage in the trunk. Big Plymouth. Green."

"Was anyone else with him?"

"Matter of fact, yes."

"How many of them?" I was hoping Penny would come back soon with some food. Even if it was a measly broth.

"Them?"

"Yeah, the Germans."

"They weren't in the car, Jack. And the clerk never saw any of them with Hunter. Ever."

"Then who?"

"A woman."

"A woman? Did you get a description?"

Tom turned a page in his notebook. "Not her face. She was wearing a hooded raincoat."

"Raincoat. That doesn't fit. It didn't rain until later in the evening."

"I know. I made a note of that."

"Sorry, Tom. Go on." My leg had stopped burning but was itching like crazy. Maybe that was a good sign. A healing sign. "Continue."

"A hooded raincoat and kept her face hidden."

"Was the clerk sure it was a woman?"

Tom gave it a moment's thought. "Yeah. But I never considered that before. If she hadn't left the car and gone for cigarettes, she could've just as easily been a man."

"Why do you say that?"

"She was tall. Desk clerk estimated five-nine, ten. He also said great legs. Custom made for high heels."

"Hunter and a woman. H'mm. Did you go to the smoke shop?"

"Yes. She went along the street to that snack bar on the corner of Dorchester and Union. She bought a carton of Gold Flake cigarettes. The soda jerk was extra busy at the time. You should've heard the jive that came out of him. He said she was a barbeque and was wearing cogs."

"Cogs?"

"Dark glasses," Tom explained. "Also she had a bandana pulled up around her chin."

"And probably wore gloves."

"Yes. She took the bills and left the change."

"Great. The Invisible Woman."

"Did someone mention my name?" It was Penny with what looked like a tray of real food. "Tea time, gents." She served Tom cookies, sandwiches, and tea, then sat the tray on the bureau.

Watching Tom eat made me salivate. "What about Jack?" I begged. Penny handed me a bowl of broth with a few strands of shredded carrot and three floating peas. "Is this Cromarty's idea of torture?"

"Offer it up, Jack," Penny said archly. "It'll benefit your soul."

"Forget my soul and think about my body. I need something that'll stick to my ribs. Something to go on."

"That's the trouble with you, you're always on the go. For once, follow orders and stay in bed until tomorrow."

I tipped back the bowl, draining the entire contents. When I proferred the empty bowl Penny placed half a sandwich and two ginger snaps into it. It could've been a king's ransom, I was that happy.

"With the Germans gone you shouldn't be in any hurry anyway, Jack," Tom said, handing me a cup of tea.

I grabbed the I.V. pole and swung my legs over the edge of the bed. I was a bit dizzy but otherwise felt strong. A second later I was standing barefoot on the cool floor. Penny wheeled a chair over and forced me to sit down. I let her put a blanket over my bare legs. A willing convalescent I would never be. She knew me only too well and seemed resigned, but she looked strained, ready to throw in the towel. Last night's insanity had been too much for her. A heroine in my eyes, she would see herself as having strayed into the underside of life. An innocent who stayed too long at a carnival of freaks.

Tom caught my eye. "The Germans are gone. Let somebody else deal with them. You did all you could. Remember, you were never supposed to involve yourself with the Nazis, Jack."

"Does that mean you're through, Tom?"

"We set out to solve Eugene Robichaud's murder. To be exact, to *prove* that he was murdered. You did and…"

"Whoa! Wait a minute, hold your horses. I solved Robichaud's murder? Where did you get that notion?"

"Chief Delaney stopped me on the street this morning and dragged me into Carmen's Restaurant."

"Interesting."

"Delaney told me you telephoned him at home last night with the news about Heinrich Gottlieb."

"The news? Oh, yeah, a front page exclusive." I guess I felt cheated because I wasn't the first to tell Tom. Gone was the opportunity to feed him the cock-and-bull story I'd fabricated to cover my tracks.

Tom reflected for a minute. "Who would've thought? A dead man dredged out of the harbour."

I wondered what connivances Chief Delaney was up to. It was a large wonderment. "Yes, Tom. Dead men do tell tales."

"Well, it's over. At least for now."

"What about Sully's murder?"

"We aren't supposed to know about Sullivan. Dr. Cromarty even signed papers to that effect."

"I can't deny that what you said about Sullivan is true," I said. "But the document Cromarty signed was witnessed by Deputy Chief Hardfield and Wilder Hunter. They might've had the backing of legitimate government agencies but they don't cut any ice with me."

I hadn't had the chance to tell Tom about my interrogation yesterday morning at the Admiral Beatty Hotel and my subsequent signing of documents stamped TOP SECRET. I decided not to tell him. He was right. He was out of it and it was best that he remain out of it.

"You're right, Tom, we've accomplished what we set out to do. It's over. And you've done yeoman service. But since I'm temporarily out of commission, could you do me a couple of favours?"

"Name it," Tom said. "Providing it's on the up-and-up for a change."

Penny was sitting on the end of the bed, her slim legs dangling. There was a nasty bruise on her left shin. She was smoking a cigarette and had turned a deaf ear towards us. "Penny, what did you do with the Pontiac?"

"I parked it in my spot."

"Your spot? You don't even own a car."

"But I have a parking space with my name on it. I'm a tiny bit important around here, you know. You should have seen the kitchen staff hop to it when I went in there and got the tea thingies."

"And good thingies they were, too," Tom said.

"Thank you, sweetheart. The Pontiac is about twelve spaces away from Outpatients. Some of the nurses were oohing and aahing over it this morning."

"Aces," I said. "Tom, run down and bring back a brown envelope hidden under the floor mat on the driver's side. And stop in the magazine shop and get me a pack of Philip Morris."

"Gotcha."

Careful of the I.V. pole and my injured leg, Penny came and knelt beside me. "How are you?" I asked.

She sighed. "Worn to a frazzle."

"My heroine." I gave her a long kiss.

"Jack, I've aged ten years in the past month. I don't think I can keep up the pace."

"How much do you think Tom knows?"

"Perhaps, like you, a lot more that he lets on."

I laughed. "Yeah, he is a fast learner. You should go home and get some rest, Penny. I'll see you tomorrow."

"Oh, you won't get rid of me that easily, Jack. I'm here to ensure that you don't pull a runner."

"How could I do that? My clothes seem to have disappeared."

"Part of a diabolical plot. Those things that weren't blood-splattered I sent to the laundry. The trousers are at the dry-cleaners. Your wallet and house keys are in the nightstand. The pistols are in the closet beneath the winter blankets."

"My girl Friday."

"If we could only be on a desert island. Just the two of us."

"Find the island and I'll meet you there."

"What I'm going to find is a suitable meal for you. Now, get back into bed. When your transfusion is done I'll have something sent in. What would you like?"

"Meat and potatoes. Nothing ground, pureed, or diced. No baby food."

When I was settled back in bed, Penny gave me the afternoon paper.

"There's an article in here about Dr. Kinsella. I didn't want you to read it on an empty stomach."

I set it aside. Nazis dominated the headlines again. "Good idea."

"I'm going home, after all. I'm exhausted."

"Another good idea. See you tomorrow."

We kissed. I didn't really want her to leave.

"Jack, what are moon-dials?"

"Beats me. Why?"

"After the sedatives took effect last night you were murmuring about moon-dials and moon clocks as you went under."

"I don't know. Dope always did put me in another world."

"M'mm. Tell you what. There's a desert island in my bedroom with two pillows on it. Meet me there?"

"As soon as possible. Say tomorrow at four?"

"I'll have the wine on ice."

Tom returned. He looked askance at finding us locked in an embrace. Penny took her time disengaging. She could be languorous even in a lab coat. She said her good-byes and sauntered out the door in a vain attempt to act casual.

I indicated the envelope. "Have a look, Tom." He tossed a pack of cigarettes to me and sat down in the vacated chair. "Tell me what you make of those."

I enjoyed my first honest smoke of the day while Tom studied the photographs. He stared at the pictures, a finger pressed against his lips, for maybe five minutes. At last, he said, "What's the significance of these?"

"You tell me. Those are what Werner and company have been after ever since Valentine's Day."

Tom stood up and tugged his vest down. "Cripes, you know where it is, don't you?"

"It's drivin' me. It seems so damn familiar. But don't keep me in suspense."

"Campobello Island. It's the Roosevelts' summer place."

I lay back and closed my eyes. F.D.R. The President of the United States. The God Almighty United States of America. The road trips along the coast that Werner's men had taken made more sense to me now. But, besides supplying a vehicle, where did Wilder Hunter fit in? And what were the Germans scheming? Roosevelt wouldn't be anywhere near Campobello. As far as John Q. Public knew, F.D.R. hadn't been on the island in ages. But Werner must be spearheading something to do with Campobello. Why else torture and kill to get the photographs back? And where were Werner and the others now?

When I opened my eyes Tom was standing over me. "Are you okay?"

"I'm fine. Did you check the *Bergensfjord*?"

"I'm way ahead of you, Jack. Werner Strasser took his belongings, photographic equipment and all, off the ship after it came out of the dry dock yesterday morning. So did the rest of them. The captain, who wasn't too happy about talking to me, said he had to sign on six new crew members. He did admit that he was glad to get rid of the Germans, though. Get this, he blames them for the damage to the ship's underside. Claims they changed course in the middle of the night and were doing depth soundings off the coast of Nova Scotia and scraped the bottom on a shoal."

"Depth soundings? For what?"

"He doesn't know. He put them on report but the ship is owned by a German family named Koenig. One of their sons, the above mentioned Berndt Koenig, was Chief Navigator."

"Nice arrangement." I thought about the vicious and unrepentant Berndt. He could navigate Hades for an eternity for all I cared. "Anything else?"

"Penny introduced me to your cousin Marvin. We had lunch with him right here in the hospital. I loaned Marvin my key to your apartment. He's going to bring you a change of clothes tomorrow."

"First-rate. You're rapidly becoming indispensable."

Tom beamed. "Glad to be of service."

"Above and beyond, Tom. Above and beyond."

Blushing crimson, Tom got into his overcoat and hat. "Gotta go. I have to meet my uncle for sauerkraut and sausages at Aunt Lena's."

"I wish I wasn't indisposed. It sounds delicious."

"*Wunderbar.* You should taste Lena's streudel. Fit for a king."

"Or a Kaiser?"

"I suppose. You know, Germany's given a lot to the world. Music, science, literature," Tom said defensively. I kept forgetting his parents were born and raised in Germany, that Tom could speak the language, read the books. "Not to mention great beer."

"I know, Tom."

"This fascist thing won't last."

"Hitler says the Third Reich will last a thousand years."

"Well, it's got nine-hundred and ninety-four more to go. I don't think it'll make it. On that note, I'm off. Aunt Lena's home cooking will make me forget all about the planet's sorry state for a few hours at least."

"Stop it, you're making me hungry. See you, Tom."

I picked up the newspaper. Penny was right. It was a good idea that I didn't read the article about Dr. Kinsella on an empty stomach. Words like revered, esteemed, widely respected, would've given me the dry heaves. I took a terrible, guilty pleasure in the charred remains bit, though. That was the news that was fit to print.

I slipped the photographs out of the envelope. Now that I knew, it seemed obvious that the place was the Roosevelt retreat on Campobello Island. I had premonitions, of what it was hard to say, but I knew in my bones that I would go there. And, foregoing the slower-than-molasses land route through the endless evergreen forest, I would go by sea. Marvin didn't know it yet, but the voyage would be aboard the *Barbara Ellen*. No one would think twice about a fishing boat. It would be just another vessel working the bountiful waters of the Bay of Fundy.

I turned the photographs over. At a certain angle under the light I could make out a faded inscription in pencil. Straining my eyes, I stared fixedly at the tiny numerals. Three slash twenty slash thirty-nine. March/20th/1939. The day after tomorrow. I suppressed a strong desire to pull the I.V. needle out of my arm and leave the hospital. But I didn't really have the strength. Besides, the commissionaires would nab me trying to get to my car if I was dressed only in a hospital robe and slippers. I had time. I'd need to take time. My leg flinched spastically, a reminder that I'd already made a mistake. There was no sense being foolhardy and running off half-cocked, compounding the error. When I gave it further thought I realized I had the element of surprise on my side. Werner and the others had no way of knowing I was in possession of the missing photographs. Anyway, they were apt to be concerned more about the missing member of their gang, Berndt Koenig, than me.

Tired, I placed the photographs in the nightstand and shut my eyes. I dreamt about the ocean, fog and fish in a net. And a landfall below the horizon.

When I awoke the I.V. was gone. It was like being set free. Sleepily, I looked about the room. It was after dark but I had no idea how late in the evening. I rang the buzzer and a nurse responded within a couple of minutes. She asked, "Ready to eat?" and disappeared when I nodded.

A volunteer in a candy-striped apron brought in a tray. "Miss Fairchild gave us strict instructions," she said. "I hope you like what she chose for you."

I did. Two juicy pork chops with mashed potatoes and carrots. Apple pie a la mode for dessert. I washed it down with a glass of milk. Then I had a cigarette with tea. I wasn't quite ready to go out dancing but I could conduct the orchestra.

TERRY CRAWFORD

CHAPTER FIFTY-NINE

U NDER A SILVERY gray sky, the water on the St. John River was as smooth as a mirror. I heaved the duffel bag onto the deck of the *Barbara Ellen* and stepped over the gunwale. Sure no one had followed me, but with the uncanny feeling someone had, I watched the pedestrian traffic in Indiantown. It was just past suppertime and people were out strolling, enjoying the mild weather at the end of winter.

I bent over and peered into the wheelhouse. The boat's stove, a cast iron article no bigger than a foot square that I'd ordered from the Lunenburg Foundry, was pushing out enough heat to form condensation on the windows. I went in and took the coffee pot off the stove before it blew its lid. Then I turned the damper down.

Marvin turned over on the bunk and stared at me with sleepy eyes. "Where've you been? We don't soon get going, it'll be too rough to get through the falls." He looked at the time on his wrist. I'd given him Grace's watch for safekeeping until he could pass it on to his new son. "Jumpin', it's ten after six."

I poured the coffee while Marvin undid the hawsers and set us adrift. Half a minute later he fired up the Chevrolet engine he'd scavenged from a car wreck and we were chugging comfortably downriver toward the Reversing Falls. I stood beside Marvin as he steered the course.

"This is close, Jack," he said. "Can you feel the river? The tide's coming in and the river's gonna start running backwards at the mouth."

I glanced out to portside. At the top of a shaly slope ran the green outfield fence of St. Peter's ballpark. Further along, the back of the New Brunswick Museum hovered over the wooded trail the Micmac once used as a portage around the rapids to get to their encampment in Indiantown.

"How's the leg, Jack?" Marvin asked.

"Not bad. I walked down from the house to the boat through the back alleys. It's not burning like it was yesterday. Cromarty gave me some extra strong Aspirins for it. I never take pills so they seem to be working. I was always a fast healer."

"True. True. Did you get to see Peg?"

"Yes. And the baby. He's handsome, Marvin."

"You must've had a long visit."

Marvin squinted at something ahead. "We'll keep to the right of that island. Way the river's flowing we'll have to struggle through the rapids," he said.

"No. I was only there ten or fifteen minutes. Margaret was tired after feeding the baby."

"Oh, yeah? Well, where'd you go?"

"A desert island. Got lost for a few hours."

Penny wanted me to stay overnight and was miffed when I said I couldn't. And angry when I wouldn't explain. I didn't like leaving her place under a cloud but it couldn't be helped. She was already in too deep. Knew too much.

"Wouldn't be an English lady on that island, would there be, Jack?"

I elbowed Marvin. "Shut up and keep your eyes on the road."

"Hey, I'm the captain here. I give the orders."

I could feel the tide now, an invisible force pushing in through the narrows. We navigated across the current at an angle, then Marvin brought the *Barbara Ellen* around, into, and against the flow. We plowed along, rising a few inches when we negotiated the rapids. Raising his eyebrows, Marvin sighed.

High above us, spanning the gorge, the steel girders of the bridge showed black against the sky. Eddies and whirlpools swirled around us. Marvin increased the power, shoving the throttle all the way forward. We went through some turbulent water directly beneath the bridge then came into a calm inlet at the final bend in the river. Black ducks skimmed the surface, running on webbed feet before they took to the air. We seemed to be drifting now, but it was only because Marvin had eased back on the throttle.

"That was a near thing, Jack," Marvin said. "Don't let me do that again."

The heat in the cabin was getting to me. I was wearing Koenig's duffel coat and watchman's cap. I'd intended it as a disguise but it was too damn hot. I stripped them off and went out on deck. We were

TERRY CRAWFORD

approaching the harbour and the West Side piers. The winter port wasn't so busy now that spring was almost here. I made my way aft, aware that I was limping, and sat down on a crate. The *Barbara Ellen* was towing a dory that swayed and bobbed in its wake.

We rounded Navy Island and headed southerly. I gazed over at the Dominion Atlantic Railway wharf where the Digby ferry was berthed. Market Slip was a beehive of baggage carts, freight handlers, and passengers milling around in organized confusion. When she was released from the General Hospital, Margaret and the baby were going to board the *Princess Helene* and steam home to Nova Scotia. Margaret's sister had come over to help her on the return trip. It was all prearranged because Marvin didn't want the newborn to ride a rough sea on the *Barbara Ellen*.

We passed a tugboat. The deckhands waved. Beyond them, the mooring place of the *Bergensfjord* sat deserted except for gulls fighting over someone's leftover sandwiches. I thought back to the drops of blood in the snow. So little, yet so much.

I stood up, turned around, and scanned Saint John's skyline. My eyes were arrested by the steeple of Trinity Church, and beyond it, the Admiral Beatty Hotel. It was a city I loved and wanted to protect. Maybe that's why, down deep, I seemed gripped by an obsession I didn't quite understand. That I couldn't put into words.

Entering the Bay of Fundy, Marvin kept the *Barbara Ellen* well clear of Partridge Island. A heavy swell lifted then let us down in a long, slow sweep.

About a mile in the distance on the heights above the west side, the Martello Tower squatted like an overturned washtub, its single antiquated cannon a kind of historical joke.

I went in and stretched out on the bunk, head propped up on a pillow. I soon realized it wasn't a good idea to look out the window. I kept losing the horizon and then thought I'd lose my supper along with it. Queasy, I asked Marvin how far we had to go.

"Seasick, Jack?"

"Naw. I've had hangovers worse than this," I said, easing myself lower.

"Relax and don't get into a sweat," Marvin said. "All kidding aside, you'll be all right if you lie easy and don't tense up. Stop trying to hold on, and rock with the waves. Hell, this ain't even bad."

I tried to raise a smile. "How far?"

"By water it's less than from Saint John to Digby. If you were driving you'd be carsick by now and cursin' every monotonous tree alongside of the road."

I closed my eyes. My brain felt like a pile of slippery spaghetti sliding around inside a hot bowl.

"I can see the light outside of Chance Harbour already, Jack. And the Point Lepreau light down the coast. Once we pass that then it's a straight jog to Black's Harbour. Piece of cake."

"Don't mention food." The checkered red-and-black pattern on Marvin's coat was beginning to do strange things.

He glanced over his shoulder at me. "There's a bucket right under you with a clean rag in it. If you gotta heave, do it, and I'll dump the results over the side."

"How long?" I said, taking a deep breath to relieve the nausea.

"This ain't no speedboat, Jack. We'll be in sight of Black's Harbour in three, three and a half hours."

An eternity. I rolled over onto my side and tried not to hold on. After a while I managed to remain limp for longer and longer periods of time, the sensation not much different than lazing in a hammock. A hammock that made you mildly ill from swinging too freely. I'd given Marvin Black's Harbour as our destination because Werner and Herman were spotted there no more than two weeks before. A couple of Shorty Long's men, who sometimes worked piecemeal at Connors Brothers' cannery, had seen them and telephoned the woodyard. I knew it was somehow important. That it wasn't just a sightseeing jaunt. Not by a long shot. This afternoon I'd consulted the atlas and sat up so straight I thought I'd popped a stitch in my leg. Black's Harbour was situated on a point on the eastern shore of Passamaquoddy Bay. Near the western shore of the bay, a few miles from Maine, sat Campobello Island.

Black's Harbour was a company town where everyone knew everyone else. And everyone else's business. If Werner and the others were anywhere near the town, someone would know. And I would find out. With that in mind, I fell into an oceanic sleep and didn't awaken until the *Barbara Ellen* bumped against a row of car tires hanging off a barnacled wharf.

TERRY CRAWFORD

We were about a hundred yards to the lee side of the fish plant. While Marvin tied up, I sat on the edge of the bunk until I got my bearings. Darkness had fallen, bringing with it a steady onshore breeze that pushed the smell of rotting fish inland. I scaled a ladder and stepped onto the wharf's weathered planking. Then I put a hand to my nose.

"What's the matter, Jack? That's the smell of prosperity. Money in the bank," Marvin said.

I had a hard time catching my breath. "Whew. I'll never eat sardines again. How do you stand it?"

"Aw, you get used to it. After a while you don't really notice. Just like a lot of rotten things."

"Oh, now you're going to wax philosophical about it. Let's get away from this stench before the rest of my hair turns gray."

There was a lamp post at the end of the wharf. It was the only source of light in the blackness. An old-timer Marvin knew by name came out of a shed and spoke. "Marvin," he said. "Haven't seen you since last time. How you been keepin'?"

"Just grand, Everett. This is my cousin, Jack."

The old fellow nodded and inspected me from head to toe. He seemed wary but interested. Inviting us into his shack, he asked, "Been out fishin'?"

"In a way," I said.

Inside the shed a radio was playing Irish music left over from St. Patrick's Day. From a kettle that simmered at the back of a wood stove Everett poured tea, then laced it with rum. It tasted fine. I offered him a cigarette.

"Philip Morris?" he quipped. "You like Yankee cigarettes? I got lots. And American liquor. Real good price. Jamaican rum too."

Marvin scowled and cleared his throat.

Picking up the cue, Everett said, "Geeze, you ain't Customs?"

I handed Everett a two-dollar bill. "No. If you've got them, give me a couple of packs of Lucky Strikes. And a mickey of this rum."

He glanced at Marvin for the go-ahead. Marvin nodded and sat down on a wooden keg. I did the same but had to stretch my bad leg at an awkward angle.

The old man reached behind a stack of kindling and retrieved the smokes. "Chesterfields all right?" he asked.

I dropped a pack into each of the duffel coat pockets.

He gave me a pint of rum, liquor as black as ink against the brightly coloured label.

"I'm gonna need some gasoline, Everett," Marvin said. "Fill up the tank and stow an extra twenty gallons on board. You'll find some cans in the hold."

"Gotcha." Everett sprang to his feet with a spryness comical for a man of his accumulated years.

"Don't get your water hot, Everett," Marvin said. "No big rush. We're going up into the village for a little spell here. So just sit tight and rest easy."

I slipped Marvin five bucks for the gas. Without checking the denomination of the bill, he handed it to the old man. "This'll cover the fuel."

"Sure will. Anything wrong, Marvin?"

"Naw. Jack's hoping to meet up with some of his friends. He had a little accident. Hurt his leg and missed the ride. Now he's not even sure they're around here. Notice anybody from out of town, Everett?"

Everett removed his hat and scratched his pink skull. I had the impression that he was born mischievous and liked it. "You know, I does some smugglin'…"

We nodded.

"So I notice things. I saw a fellow at the general store with a coat like Jack's there. Them white ropes and wooden pegs always gets me."

I lit one of the Chesterfields and took a drag. They were well named. "And?"

"Nuthin'. Guy didn't say much. Figured he couldn't. Had two big shiners and head all bandaged up. Was he in the same accident you was?"

Marvin and I laughed. When we calmed down we said, "Yes," in unison.

Shrewdly, Everett didn't pursue the subject. "Still got the *Barbara Ellen*?" he asked. "Cape Islander's a good boat. Seaworthy, you know."

"Yeah. I'll always have a *Barbara Ellen*. Be nice to some day have a scallop dragger. Those boys in Digby make a fortune."

"Lobster fishermen too, but scallops and lobsters make men greedy. Stick to the herring, son. You'll never go far wrong with the herring."

"That's not what Jack thinks," Marvin said.

He pulled me out the door and we stood on the wharf in what felt like fresh air but smelled like God-only-knows. I followed Marvin up a dilapidated staircase that clung precariously to the side of a cliff.

Marvin shone a flashlight on the mossy forest floor. Everything was sopping from the previous night's rain. The scent of the evergreens surrounding us was ambrosia to me. We tracked a well-worn path through the woods and on into the lower village. We came out into someone's backyard and ducked under a couple of clotheslines, went round the house and onto the road. There were only a few lights burning here and there along the deserted streets.

"Early to bed," Marvin said.

The general store, which also served as a service station and post office, was situated on a prominent rise overlooking the harbour. It was dimly lighted as if not really open. Marvin was known hereabouts so I let him go in first.

Four old gents, nearly as ancient as Everett, were gathered beside a pot-bellied stove. All the men held their chins as they silently studied a checkerboard. When I looked I saw that the game was chess. The black king was cornered and a few moves away from toppling.

A young man came out of a stock room and stood behind the cash register. Marvin bought a can of apple juice and a large tin of beans. I bought six bottles of Coca-Cola. The clerk wore glasses as thick as the bottoms of the Coke bottles. His eyes now and then magnified hugely, giving him a scared rabbit expression. He kept looking at my duffel coat. I asked him if he had seen any of my friends and explained that they might be wearing the same coats.

"You're not British," he said, more in the nature of an accusation than a flat statement. "Not British at all."

"And proud of it," Marvin said.

"I go to all the J. Arthur Rank movies in St. Stephen and you're not British," he repeated like a self-important teacher's pet.

I was tired and on a short fuse. Annoyed, I showed him my I.D. and told him to move into the back where we could speak in private. The chess players paid no notice when I left Marvin at the counter and escorted the clerk by the elbow into a storeroom, then shut the door. He was nervous and started to sputter. I cut him short. "What's all this about Englishmen?"

He wiped his spectacles with a handkerchief and blinked blindly about the room. "Your friends. Three of them have English accents."

"Three?"

"Yes. There were two more but they didn't say anything."

"Two others? Describe them."

"One had two black eyes. The other was kind of a fancy dresser. He wasn't like the rest who were dressed the same as you."

English accents. Clever. "The fancy one. Did he have sandy hair and a dark tan?"

"Yes."

"Did you notice what they were driving?"

"I'd give my eye-teeth to have her. A big Plymouth – American model. You can't get them here. Not like that one," the young fellow said covetously. He had lost his timidity when speaking of the car. "No sir, a beaut. A real jim-dandy."

I sat down on a trunk beside a bin filled with rubber boots. The incision on my leg was throbbing with a pulse all its own. Wilder Hunter and the Germans weren't exactly acting in a clandestine manner.

"Did they say what they were up to?" I said, thinking aloud.

"Sightseeing along the bay."

"The bay?"

"Passamaquoddy."

"Anywhere in particular?"

"They mentioned Campobello Island."

"They did, did they?"

"Yes, sir."

I didn't know what to think. This was too blatant, as if they wanted to be remembered. Vividly. It was like leaving a calling card. "When were they here?"

"About eleven this morning."

"What did they buy?"

"About a day's supplies. Canned goods, mostly. And home-made bread and preserves."

"Anything out of the ordinary?"

"No. Unless…"

"What?"

"They bought a lot of Canadian cigarettes. Ten cartons."

"Sounds like they're leaving the country," I said quietly to myself. "All right, that's enough for now. I don't want you breathing a word about this interview."

"No, sir."

I opened the door. "See that you don't. Not unless you enjoy looking at the world from behind bars."

His eyes, already big behind the thick lenses, enlarged. *"No, sir."*

I shut the door behind us. "This isn't exactly Miami Beach," I said. "Where do you think they'd be staying if they were here overnight?"

"Only one place operating this time of year," he confided, pleased to be part of an investigation. "The Bayview Cabins, not far down the road. Salesmen and Fisheries Officers stay there. It's got a neon sign with a sailboat that rocks."

I stepped into the passageway. "Exciting."

The fellow nodded eagerly and returned to the cash register. The chess match was still in progress. The black king had evaded an easy checkmate and in two moves could turn the tables. I didn't have time to stand and watch. I tapped Marvin on the shoulder and motioned him outside. Without lifting their heads, the men said, "Night, boys."

We walked to the edge of town. Marvin observed my silence with puzzled glances. The sky was clear now, moon suspended above the treetops. Our shadows loomed on the road. I stopped out of earshot of the nearest house. "Are we headed in the direction of the Bayview Cabins?"

"Yes. They're about a half-mile. Me and Peg stayed there once. Why?"

"I have to go there. Tell me about the place."

"What do you mean? 'I'?"

"You're a new father, Marv," I said, placing my hands on his shoulders. "What you've done so far is risky enough. I'm armed. If I have to shoot every fucking one of them, I will."

Ill at ease around bad language, Marvin drew a breath. "What? You mean those guys you're looking for are at the Bayview?"

"They might be. I'm not taking any chances with you, though. Gimme your flashlight."

Marvin gave me the flashlight. I put a Coke in each pocket and handed him the bag with the other four.

"There's ten cabins, Jack. Tidy little jobs with their own bathrooms. They're arranged in a crescent on the side of a hill. The office is hard by the road. It's got a café where they serve breakfast and light lunches. Place is run by a couple by the name of Kynock – Vera and Raymond. Ray's a nighthawk. Never sleeps. That's why he keeps the cabins open year 'round. In the wintertime there's probably haunted houses do more business."

"Okay, I want you to go back to the *Barbara Ellen*. I'll meet you on board after I scout the cabins."

"You're not going to do anything, are you, Jack? I mean you're just gonna scare them off, aren't you? You're not gonna shoot…"

"Don't worry, Marvin. Only in self-defense. Now, take off. I'll see you later."

Only half convinced, Marvin hesitated, then turned on his heels and strode away toward Black's Harbour. I watched until he was out of sight then continued down the moonlit road. I was baffled. Sullivan was murdered because he allegedly knew something about Campobello. For all I knew, he did, and died without saying a word. But whether he or anyone knew, now seemed irrelevant judging by the way the "British" were telegraphing their every move. They wanted to leave an indelible impression on the locals.

I went over a hump in the road. Above the dark woods, the neon outline of a sailboat's white sails and red hull rocked back and forth on blue neon waves. A car spun out of a driveway, headlights spearing toward me. I ran for the bush and pressed myself into the moss. The Plymouth sped past, too fast for me to get a glimpse of the occupants.

I got up slowly, clicked on the flashlight, and threaded my way through the undergrowth, not stopping until I reached the cabins. There were no lights on in any of them. The only vehicle, a panel truck with the words BAYVIEW CABINS on the side, was parked in front of the office porch. A big man with a ruddy complexion and a paunch came out and leaned on the railing.

I circled around and came down the slope from between cabins 8 and 9. I took the big man by surprise. He started to go back inside but pulled up when I called out, "Mr. Kynock?"

He grinned affably and spat tobacco toward the truck. "Yessir. The one and only."

I had the .38 clutched in my right hand inside the duffel coat. With my left, I showed him my I.D. He inspected the badge for a moment and said, "What can I do for you, Detective?"

"Is there anyone else here, Mr. Kynock?"

"Ray, will do. No. Just the wife and she's asleep. It's a gift," he said, smiling. "A true blessing."

The man was so merry I almost laughed out of sheer tension. Discreetly, I holstered the .38 and climbed the stairs. Classical music was blaring from a radio on the reception desk. The Mrs. was truly a sound sleeper. A gifted sleeper. "Tchaikovsky?" I ventured.

"Yes. Toscanini conducting from Radio City Music Hall. Are you a fan?"

"I know the really famous pieces. I prefer jazz."

Kynock regarded me as if I had three heads and no ears. But his disposition was so sunny he shrugged and immediately offered me a cup of coffee.

"Sure," I said. "A quick one."

He disappeared indoors and came back with two mugs. After the first mouthful I figured this guy was a self-made insomniac. "Grand," I said.

"Yeah, I like it strong."

"You've got some guests."

"They just took off a couple of minutes ago."

"Are they returning?"

"Don't know for sure. They're paid up till tomorrow. They showed up yesterday morning. Been sleeping most of the time. Britishers, they are."

"Did they tell you that, Ray?"

"No, but they sound like it. And they say stuff like, 'Good show, old chap,' and 'bloody right', and 'rather' with about five A's."

I nodded. Vaudeville bloody Englishmen. What were they up to? "Did they sign the register?"

"Sure did." Without waiting to be asked he went and fetched the book. "Here you go."

I took out my notepad and pencil and copied the names: K. Philby, W. Stephenson, Harry Hensley, David Cornwall, and I. Fleming.

"Was there a woman with these blokes?" I said.

Kynock chuckled, his big paunch jiggling. "No, but funny you should ask."

"Why's that?"

"The wife, she said one of 'em smelled like *Evening in Paris*. She told me in the kitchen that he might be a pansy. I don't pay attention to that guff. She's from Edinburgh and hates limies."

"Which guy was it?"

"Tall, expensive clothes."

"Tanned?"

"Now you mention it, yeah."

"Could I see their cabins?"

Cabins 4 and 5 were spotless, the beds made after they'd been slept in. Refuse from chocolate bars and emptied ashtrays in the wastebaskets.

Kynock scratched his head. "Hardly know they'd been. I noticed they had a meeting in six."

Number 6 held the smell of stale cigarette smoke and the body odour of five men packed into a small room. Otherwise, it too had been housecleaned by its last tenants. The contents of the wastebasket was roughly the same with the exception of a New Brunswick road map. It was from an Imperial Oil station. I opened it and found the quadrant where Campobello Island was located had been ripped out. I put the map in my pocket. "Did you overhear them talking about anything?"

Ray Kynock considered the question while we walked back toward the office. "They had sandwiches and pie in the coffee room. I heard them say something about cryptography, cryptographers? What's that?"

I turned toward the road. "Don't know. Maybe they're archeologists and study crypts, ancient burial sites, Indian mounds, whatever. Thanks for your help, Mr. Kynock."

"A pleasure. Do you want a lift anywhere?"

"Thanks. I'd rather walk."

"Okay, then."

I marched straight down the middle of the road toward the rising moon. Cryptography. Was the secret writing on the wall?

CHAPTER SIXTY

CARELESSNESS WAS CONTAGIOUS. At the same moment as I lit a cigarette I heard voices from down below in the woods. It was dark enough on the road for someone to see a match if they'd been looking in my direction. I hid the cigarette behind my hand and smoked furtively. The talk was further away than it sounded. I stood still and listened to the give-and-take of activity and hastily spoken orders. The mood was one of elation, of unalloyed arrogance.

I thought about the cryptography bit. The business in the Bayview Cabins lunchroom was deliberate carelessness. A willful act that had nothing to do with concealed intentions but was clearly aimed at being remembered. Instead of ciphers and codes it was an open book written in plain English.

I found an opening in the trees, a rough but well-travelled dirt road. When I could hear waves slapping against the rocks I veered off into the woods. I didn't want to alert a look-out.

I needn't have bothered because they hadn't posted a sentry. I crouched behind a stack of lobster traps up the slope. Wilder Hunter's Plymouth was parked on the road out of sight of the water. He stood apart from the group while they loaded gunny sacks and cardboard boxes onto a fishing boat. Herman sat on a piling, head in his hands, unable to help. Werner barked at the two young fellows, Gustav and Ernst, to take care with the cartons because they contained his collection of *LIFE* magazines.

Herman started to bellyache about something in German. Hunter turned on him and said, "Confound it, old chap. English. There's a good lad," in a passable British accent. "Remember everyone, English."

Werner leapt off the gunwale and onto the jetty. Ever the suspicious one, he cast a look around, scanning for signs of movement.

Hunter passed out cigarettes. "Werner, relax for Christ's sake."

"I will when we have accomplished our mission," Werner said, then yelled at Gustav, "*Affenarsch*, my camera is in that satchel. Stow it forward."

Gustav bowed and scurried with the camera bag. Then he joined Ernst and the others near a ramshackle drying shed. Every one of them wore black turtle-neck sweaters and black stocking hats. A quintet of second-storey boys.

I gambled when their backs were turned and moved closer, slipping through the open door of an outhouse that faced away from the bay. I peeked through a cracked board. They weren't more than thirty feet away. Hunter had a bottle of schnapps and poured shots into juice tumblers arranged on a fish crate. They clinked glasses in honour of Adolf Hitler. If I'd had a tommy-gun I would've mowed them down on the spot and fed them to the fish.

Werner stiffened and spun around, peering out of the light into the dark.

"What is it now?" Hunter said testily.

"A feeling, that is all," Werner said.

I held my breath, heart pounding, while he stared into nothing.

Hunter poured a second round of drinks. "A feeling? Stop worrying. Nothing can go wrong at this stage."

"That is what you have said before," Werner hissed.

"If you're still concerned about Ireland," Hunter said in a flat drawl, "don't be. I've checked. He's in the General Hospital in Saint John. Don't forget that Herman knifed him."

"Yah, and look at Herman. Fortunate to be alive. And where is Berndt?"

"Koenig will show. That nigger friend of Ireland's dropped out of sight. I expect Berndt is dealing with him. He knows the contingency plan. Stop worrying, Koenig will join us in a week. You'll see. We'll all have drinks together at the Blaue Reiter on Kaiser Wilhelm Strasse."

"Yah, and German *liebchen*, not these Jew sluts," Herman spat from between gritted teeth.

Werner laughed and slapped Herman on the back. "*Ach*, Herman, you liked them well enough. Little Hannah and Abby. That is what they are good for – sex slaves."

Gustav and Ernst, who had nodded at the reference to Drummond, shuffled uncomfortably at the mention of Hannah and Abby. They were shy, inexperienced boys. But they were probably Hitler Youth, indoctrinated and ready to serve the cause without question. Dangerous children.

"Listen carefully," Hunter said. "Don't forget the sealed orders we opened this morning. We are to anchor close offshore to Campobello. I'll take one of the outboards and go around the inland side of the island. You take the other outboard directly ashore. The security men at the Roosevelt cottage know me and are expecting a report on your activities. I've got the codes with the outdated indicators. They are useless. But it will keep their cryptanalysts occupied while you approach from the rear. Await my signal. Green flare for GO. Red for ABORT."

"We'll have the Purple Analog in a matter of minutes. At oh-two-hundred hours you'll be aboard the U-27," Hunter exulted. "And there'll be an explosion on Campobello all the way to bedrock. Gentlemen, raise your glasses to the Third Reich."

They threw their heads back and drank, then like insane Prussians smashed the glasses on the wharf. Hunter tossed the empty schnapps bottle into the bay and jumped like Errol Flynn into the boat.

He was having fun, his pep-talk larger-than-life. But it was too much like play-acting, as if he had nothing to lose and everything to gain. The harried and distracted man I'd seen a couple of evenings ago was gone. Even under the present circumstances I found myself unable to place much faith in him. Which was ridiculous. I was hiding in a shithouse spying on him while he admitted to double-crossing his own government. And yet…

The men boarded the fishing boat. The vessel was similar to Marvin's but had an open-ended wheelhouse. Two rowboats with outboard motors trailed behind as it headed for open water. I waited until I could see the craft plainly outlined against the moon-splashed bay. I noticed it had the unlikely name of *The Flying Dutchman*. Well, so be it.

I walked down and had a look at the Plymouth. It was locked. For the hell of it I could smash the windows and slash the tires but I had a better idea. I took the two bottles of Coca-Cola out of my pockets, unscrewed the cap on the gas tank, and gave it a drink. The big tank sounded only half full and thirsty, in need of the pause that refreshes.

One of the shacks by the wharf had a stovepipe protruding through the roof. I tried the door and went inside. On a shelf beside the cookstove I found tea-bags, canned milk, and what I was looking for – a tin of sugar. I left a quarter on the stove and hurried back to the Plymouth. For good measure, I added two pounds of sugar to the tank.

I returned the tin and hobbled up the driveway to the road. When I was almost back to the *Barbara Ellen,* Marvin saw my light and met me at the foot of the stairs by the seacliff. I'd come across a discarded Christmas tree on the way through the woods and dragged it along. It still had tinsel on it and a single broken ornament. The needles were nut-brown, sharp and dry.

"What the hell?" Marvin said as I threw the tree onto the *Barbara Ellen*

"No time to explain," I said. "Let's get under way. Did you hear another boat?"

"Yeah, it sounds like it's heading up the northern arm. Do we follow?"

"Can you do it without being seen?"

"Depends," Marvin said, switching off the running lights. He put a chart on the deck and took a quick compass reading by the light of a match. "Any idea where they're headed?"

"Campobello."

"A breeze, Jack. Have a gander at the map."

I dropped a pillow on the floor and knelt down with the flashlight. Black's Harbour was deeply embayed. Something I hadn't known, having slept during the inbound voyage. Once clear of the harbour we could choose whatever channel we liked, keeping islands between us and *The Flying Dutchman*. When we gained the outer reaches of Passamaquoddy Bay it was open water across to Campobello. That worried me. I explained my fears to Marvin.

"Look again, Jack. About eight miles north of Grand Manan there's a bunch of tall rocky islands called The Wolves. If we go east of The Wolves and take the ferry route to Grand Manan we'll be able to see Campobello off to the west. Before we get to Grand Manan we can swing about and head to Campobello. You might as well call them sister islands, they're not all that far from one another. But I'll tell you, Jack, when the tide is running between Eastport and Campobello it's about seven knots in there. These are treacherous waters. I won't go to the leeside of Campobello."

"No need to, Marvin." I showed him a point on the chart. "My guess is if we stay within a quarter mile radius of here, we'll have *The Flying Dutchman* in easy view."

"The *Dutchman*? I know her. One of Everett's old boats. He told me he sold her about two months ago. She's got a secret compartment in the hold. She's an old rumrunner. Faster than she looks. We can lay back and let her go on ahead. One thing about the *Barbara Ellen*, she's quiet and we'll be downwind of the prevailing southeaster. Should be fairly easy to come up on them. Besides, we're just humble fisherfolk, ain't we?"

"Humble, anyway," I said, standing beside the wheel and staring through the windscreen. Lighted buoys to starboard and portside marked the outer channels.

We soon rode into a heavy swell that brought the stars suddenly closer, then farther away in a long slow decline. Marvin jerked a thumb toward the right. "There lies Campobello," he said.

I could see scattered lights way off across the waves. Somewhere beneath the surface a U-boat waited for an appointed hour. I decided that it was only fair to tell Marvin. All he said was, "In for a penny, in for a pound."

We smoked and drank the Coca-Colas. As for what I was going to do, I didn't have two clues to rub together. Create a diversion of some sort that would alert the people on the island, but beyond that I'd have to wait and see.

"What's that?" I said, looking out and up at a dark presence that blotted out the stars. I could hear waves crashing and the raking of stones along shingle. The *Barbara Ellen* rocked as she was gently broadsided by the wash.

"The Wolves," Marvin said. "We're about halfway to Grand Manan. I figured we'd change course once we got round the cliffs here, and make a beeline for Campobello. What say?"

"You're the captain, Marvin."

The Wolves projected up out of the sea like stone fortresses without windows. Blind towers hovered above boulder-strewn beaches. The place gave me the creeps but it had an eerie fascination all its own.

"Do you know what the Germans are after doing, Jack?" Marvin asked.

I didn't want to tell him more than he needed to know but he looked at me with such trust I couldn't help myself. "They're after a cipher machine."

"Come again?"

"It's an apparatus for encoding and decoding cryptograms."

"Gobbledy-gook. Gimme some English, Ireland."

"Cryptograms – hidden or secret messages." I immediately felt weary, fed-up to the teeth with secrecy. "Important to the military. Especially naval intelligence. If the enemy can break your codes it becomes a matter of life and death. A man named Yardley – an ex-secret service man – wrote a book about it in the early '20s. I read it about five years ago. Bought it for a dime at a church bazaar at Saint Malachi's. I've still got the book. I'll give it to you. It was called *Secret Service: The Black Chamber*."

Marvin cut back on the throttle. "Black Chamber? What's that?"

"A room in Washington on Constitution Avenue where the Americans intercepted wireless messages and decoded them. Big stuff during the Great War. They intercepted German messages that convinced Woodrow Wilson to send American troops overseas."

"Geeze. What was the message? Do you remember?"

"Yeah. It was from the German Admiralty – U-boats were to sink everything, including American ships."

Marvin glanced at me. "Hell, the Yanks should have been in the war before then. Tell me more. It'll help stave off the jitters."

"We can turn back."

"Not on your life. Keep talking."

"After the Great War, the Black Chamber listened in on the Japanese and found out how ambitious they were about building a navy. That's why when negotiations were held Japan only got about half the raw materials they wanted."

"And this Yardley character wrote this in a book?"

"Marvin, it was a best-seller, especially in Japan."

"Is it any wonder?"

"That's not the half of it. Yardley revealed that the Americans had been decoding messages from friendly powers like Britain. *They* were not amused."

TERRY CRAWFORD

"Can't blame 'em. Why'd Yardley spill the beans?"

"That branch of the Secret Service was taken over by someone else – the name escapes me – who disapproved of such behaviour. He came out with a famous quote, 'Gentlemen don't read each other's mail.' He fired Yardley."

"So Yardley was paying him back?"

"Something like that *and* making money off the book. In the end Yardley was right – there has to be a certain amount of secrecy and spying. Although I agree with his boss – you shouldn't spy on your friends."

Marvin pulled up the collar of his Mackinaw and tugged his hat on tighter. "How else you gonna know what they're doing?"

"Try asking them," I suggested.

Marvin clutched my sleeve. "There. *The Dutchman's* got a little show-off mast with a couple of lights on the spar and another atop the mast."

I could see a bobbing triangle of lights. They had made no attempt to land in complete darkness. We were within ten minutes of their anchorage, the wind in our faces. I lifted the binoculars and had a long look. A searchlight had been directed astern, illuminating the two outboards. Wilder Hunter was already in one and had just cast off, departing with a Nazi salute that precariously rocked the boat. He sat down, I imagined drunkenly, spun the boat in a tight circle, and was gone. The others had a quick head-to-head conference, slapped one another on the back, and got into the remaining outboard. They went straight for the island, according to Marvin, no more than fifty yards from *The Flying Dutchman*.

I limped out to the bow. I lit a smoke and hoped it wasn't my last. Using the glow of the cigarette tip, I read the time. It was already 1:40. They were on a tight schedule if they were to rendezvous with *U-27* at 0:200. I liked my chances. Time was on my side. And so far, the element of surprise. But what to do? What to do?

I rejoined Marvin. "I want you to put me aboard *The Flying Dutchman*," I said. "Can you do that?"

"I'll stand off and you can take the dory. You do row?"

"Yes. But just looking at that scares me to death. This isn't Lily Lake."

"Jack, men use dories off the Grand Banks. It ain't gonna sink."

"Can't you get close enough with the *Barbara Ellen*?"

"Sure, but they're apt to see us."

"We'll take our chances. They should be busy watching for Hunter's signal."

"Signal?"

"Green flare for go. I want to create a diversion so that they don't respond to the signal. If Werner and the others fail to show, then Hunter will have to abandon his plans. He'll be left to bluff it out or hightail it himself. What do you think?"

"There's a boat hook aft. You could use that to come alongside but you'll have to jump for it. Can you do it with that leg?"

"Yes. It's all right as long as I'm not just sitting."

We were getting closer and closer. I couldn't see any activity on the beach through the binoculars. Marvin cut the engine to a mere sputter. We seemed to be coasting more than running. I kept watching the shore. The outboard was pulled up on a sandy inlet edging the treeline. The moonlight showed driftwood, white and skeletal. They had to be hiding in the woods.

"Better wear a life-jacket," Marvin said.

"No. If they see me on board the *Dutchman* I want them to mistake me for one of the missing."

"The missing?"

"A guy they left in Saint John."

"Who?"

"Never mind." I dug into the duffel bag for the Colt .45. I gave it to Marvin. "A little insurance."

"Who do you think I am? Johnny Mack Brown? Cripes, Jack."

"Hang on to it, will you?"

We were almost on top of *The Flying Dutchman*, the sea calm beneath us. Still no sign we'd been discovered. I heaved the dead Christmas tree aboard the *Dutchman* then I grappled her with the boat hook. We bumped together, gentle as a kiss, and I jumped. Marvin swung about and hid as best he could, keeping the *Dutchman* between the *Barbara Ellen* and the shore.

I went forward and found the cardboard boxes with Werner's collection of *LIFE*. The photographs were still inside the magazines. I threw the magazines overboard, photographs and all. I watched for a few minutes as they drifted toward the beach. I dug into Werner's camera bag and stole his Leica. Then out of pure spite I tore open the cartons of cigarettes, pocketed four packs, and sprinkled the rest on the waves where they floated like white worms with rigor mortis.

Swivelling the searchlight, I spotlit the outboard, the long beam brilliant in the dark. Marvin cursed a blue streak and made to come alongside. A man appeared from out of the woods. It was Werner. I yelled, "*Achtung!*"

Werner shouted, "Koenig?" Then looked over his shoulder as the green flare rocketed skyward. I swept the searchlight over the *LIFE* magazines. The effect was instantaneous.

"Policeman? Is that you?" Werner screamed.

The others stepped out behind him. All of them had blackened faces. In their rage they looked like infuriated minstrels.

I found the toggle switches for the running lights and shut them off. Then I smashed the searchlight with the boat hook. I dragged the tree into the wheelhouse. Marvin almost knocked me off my feet when he came alongside, gunwale scraping gunwale. I tossed a handful of matches on the tree. It started to crackle, then the needles began exploding, showers of sparks flying everywhere. I threw the boat hook onto the *Barbara Ellen* and followed it with a poorly-timed leap that sent me tumbling against the railing.

I stayed flat on my back while Marvin revved the motor then gave it everything she had as we pulled away from *The Flying Dutchman*. Like an evil fireworks above me, the flare seemed to hang in the sky forever. Green. Green. Green.

Something zipped and whined over our heads. A second later I heard popping sounds from the shore. Pistol shots. We were out of effective range but it was still dangerous. Marvin yelped, "Jesus Murphy," after a bullet broke the glass in the starboard porthole of the cabin.

I scrambled inside on hands and knees. "Are you all right?" I yelled.

"She was pretty well spent but the damn thing pinged around in here and busted the radio," he shouted.

"That's too close for comfort, Marvin," I said. I took the Colt and knelt down astern. Holding the revolver with both hands I released a shot. The muzzle spewed a blaze of fire. I spaced the four remaining shots several seconds apart.

The Christmas tree burned completely in a matter of minutes but it set the deck and open wheelhouse afire.

"When the flames hit the gas tank, she'll blow," Marvin cried.

There was a muffled bang, then the explosion ripped through the vessel, sending splintered wood arcing above the masthead. I stood in sickened wonder at how fast *The Flying Dutchman* sank. She slipped under the waves with a final gurgle, flames seeming for a moment to light the depths.

The flare grew faint, hung above the trees for a moment, then disappeared. Marvin cut the engine and we floated as silently as a log.

"What do you figure?" Marvin asked.

"I hope they're captured and tried as spies," I said. "You know what that means?"

"The death penalty?"

I nodded. "Do you hear something?"

"From ashore?"

"No. Somewhere else."

I checked the time. It was almost two.

Marvin and I stared at one another as the *Barbara Ellen* lifted strangely then descended in an uneasy tremor. My insides quivered. It was as if something huge had swum beneath us and sighed. We could make out an aquatic whirring and a humming like dynamos heard at a distance. Marvin went to portside and shone a light into the ocean. I gasped. The U-boat passed so close beside us we could see the periscope, then the conning tower as it rose out of the water.

"It's surfacing," Marvin said in subdued awe. "Go and start the motor. We haven't got much time."

I did as I was told. Marvin stuffed a gunny sack into the duffel bag I'd brought aboard and put them in the dory. I clicked on the cabin light and the running lights so that he could see. And so I could see him. He was fiddling with the anchor and the steel cable attached to it. Beyond him, only yards away, the U-boat was rising out of the sea. He came and took the wheel, manoeuvering the *Barbara Ellen* in reverse. We struck the rear of the U-boat with a clang.

"Get into the dory, Jack, and hold it fast. And don't dally."

It wasn't the time or the place to ask questions. I grabbed the boat hook, latched onto the dory, then climbed in and held fast to the gunwale

TERRY CRAWFORD

of the *Barbara Ellen*. Marvin flung the anchor overboard, giving it about twenty feet of cable. He swished it back and forth and then let go when the cable started slithering wildly like an eel dropped onto a hot stove. He jumped in beside me and cut the rope attaching the dory to the boat.

"Remember the dory races in Digby?" he asked.

I dipped an oar into the water.

"Well, row like holy bejesus, Jack."

We put our backs into it and in a hundred strokes covered a good distance between ourselves and the *Barbara Ellen*. A light probed the darkness just off Campobello. That'd be Werner, Herman, Gustav, and Ernst coming in the outboard. We pulled in the oars, both of us in need of a breather, and let the dory ride the waves. A spotlight came on in the conning tower of the U-boat, blinked three times, and was extinguished. The *Barbara Ellen* floated free of the submarine. We rowed on, did several sprints, then laid the oars by.

I squinted into the binoculars. A hail of machine-gun fire raked the *Barbara Ellen*.

Marvin said, "We would've been dead ducks."

"What were you doing with the anchor?"

"I lowered it along their arse-end until it hooked onto the rigging. That's an eight-ply steel cable. It ain't gonna snap. That'll slow them up."

"But the *Barbara Ellen*? You'll lose her."

"Yeah, it'll be tough to explain to the wife. What the hell, it's a worthy cause. If the American Coast Guard is on the ball they should be able to corral those guys come daylight."

I trained the binoculars on *U-27*. As I did, the moon came out, half-hearted and dim. Marvin pulled a tarp over our heads. "They can't see us but just in case."

It was warm, almost cosy, under the canvas. The *U-27* took its passengers on board, swallowing them through a hatch. "Do you want a look-see, Marvin?"

"Naw."

The *U-27* got underway, swift in its stealth. The *Barbara Ellen* drifted quite alone for almost a minute then began moving erratically as if it was on a leash and didn't want to go. I watched as it plunged back and forth, tugged in the direction of the U-boat. We got out from under the tarp. Marvin had a compass on a leather thong round his neck. He took a reading and consulted a light on Grand Manan and another to our north. Meanwhile, I kept a vigil on the *Barbara Ellen* through the binoculars. All of a sudden she was gone.

I peered landward. Flashlights searched the beach. One. Two. Three. Four. A ground flare, whiter than white, lit the trees and the driftwood, making them stand out like a stage set. Four men dressed in get-ups identical to the Germans stood behind the light as if they were actors waiting to deliver lines.

"I don't suppose you want to go back to Campobello with that Hunter fella still there," Marvin said.

"No," I whispered, still shocked at losing sight of the *Barbara Ellen*. And wondering at the appearance of the four men. Somebody else could take care of Wilder Hunter.

"I figure we can make The Wolves by first light," Marvin said. "We'll lay over there till the flood tide, then make for the coast. We don't want to go to Grand Manan and attract a whole lot of attention, do we?"

"Not on your life."

I stroked the oar, thankful for a calm sea and the moon at our backs. "Marvin, that was quick thinking back there," I said.

"Runs in the family, Jack. Trouble is, so does stubbornness."

We fell into a steady rhythm, oars hardly making a sound out there under the stars.

TERRY CRAWFORD

CHAPTER SIXTY-ONE

THE EASTERN SKY had turned a hazy blue and was burnished copper along the horizon by the time we reached The Wolves. Awakening seabirds cried in the dawn, their raucous clamour echoing off the cliffs. We made for the sunward face of the dominant island, rowing out and around a rocky cape pungent with seaweed revealed by the ebb tide.

Seals bobbed in the water inshore, dark eyes big and curious. When I saw the first one I mistook it for a man and gave a start. Marvin, used to the sea, stared back and stroked on.

We shipped oars and let the dory drift toward an inlet. When he saw a suitable landing, Marvin stepped overboard and guided us through a sandy channel until we could beach. The periwinkle-encrusted rocks were slippery and still dripping wet below the tidemark. The tide had a ways to go out so we weren't worried about losing our transportation. We hoisted the dory out of ankle-deep water, and left it high and dry.

High tide in Saint John would be shortly after twelve o'clock. I knew high tide in Black's Harbour was fifteen or twenty minutes earlier than at the city so I figured we were safe until sometime before noon. By then The Wolves would be projecting straight out of the sea, waves crashing against the cliffs. But we would be long gone, heading on the tide for the New Brunswick coast.

Beaver Harbour was the closest inhabited landfall. With luck we could catch a bus or hitch a ride from there to home. I wanted to get back to Saint John with a minimum of fuss. Ideally, no one who could make trouble for me would even know I had gone anywhere of consequence. If everything went well, Marvin and I would be sitting down to supper at the Royal Hotel by five. With that in mind I followed him as he climbed, taking a precipitous route up a rockslide to a headland towering above us.

At the top the height frightened me. I moved back among some windblown trees, found a bare spot and stretched out, head resting against a stump. The island seemed to sway beneath me, rocking me to sleep.

I forced myself awake and sat up.

Marvin dropped the duffel bag to the ground. Seconds later he opened a can of beans with his hunting knife. We devoured the beans, neither of us bothering to chew.

"Afraid of high-up," Marvin said. "I dunno, Jack, whether you're so smart or not. You don't seem to know what to be really scared of. Jumpin', you go for those guys like a ferret after a nest of rats but a little high-up and your knees are knocking."

"Make no mistake, I get scared. Lincoln Drummond's got a record with a blues holler on it that goes, 'Man, if you ain't scared, you just ain't right.'"

Marvin nodded. "Yeah, I sort of know what he means. Cripes! We were reckless last night, though. I'll tell you something – I was right as right gets."

"Me too."

The events were still too close at hand to seem real. Even while they were happening it was as if they were happening to someone else. In more ways than one, so much of it in the dark.

Marvin gave me the last of the apple juice we had been drinking through the night. "I'm going to see if I can find some rainwater," he said. "Why don't you go back to sleep for a while? You really oughtn't to be out of the hospital."

"I'm not supposed to be anywhere," I said.

I lay back and yawned, too tired to think. The weather was mild, sun warm on my face. I snuggled into the duffel coat and slept.

I didn't dream. Four hours later I woke, warmed by the remains of a camp fire. Rubbing the stiffness out of my legs, I gazed skyward. We were under a blanket of clouds and the wind had changed. The taste of snow was in the air. Marvin was curled up like a dog on a bed of spruce boughs. I added some driftwood to the fire and jostled him with my foot.

Marvin stood up, Mackinaw coat covered with green needles. "Holy geeze," he said. "Did I ever sleep. Out like a light."

"You shouldn't have let me sleep so long. It feels like snow."

"So it does. We'd best be going. Don't want to get caught in a squall."

"Why did you let me sleep?" I said, worried and out-of-sorts.

"'Cause you needed it, Jack. And so did I."

"Okay. Sorry, Marv. Let's have a smoke and shove off."

I noticed the binoculars sitting on top of the duffel bag. "Why did you have those out?"

"I tramped over to the other side of the island hoping I'd find some fresh water. I didn't but I heard a boat so I came back and dug out the glasses. It's only a short jaunt from here to a pretty fair look-out. Anyways, I spotted this boat zig-zagging like it was searching."

That alarm bell in my head went off. I lit a Chesterfield and made a face. Bad weather closing in and now this.

"Could you see anyone?"

"No. But they were looking for somebody, Jack, I can tell you that."

"What about the fire?"

"It wasn't smoking that much and you looked dead to the world. I went and had myself a long look and came back and rested for a couple of minutes. Didn't mean to nod off for so long."

"When did you see the boat?"

"Shy of an hour ago. Jack, she's the fastest thing I've ever seen on water. One of them racing boats with an inboard motor."

"Where was it headed?"

"That's just it – towards Campobello."

"Come on. We'll see if it's still around."

We trekked along the cliffs to the other side of the island. Off to the south lay Grand Manan, according to the charts about seven and a half miles from The Wolves. To the southwest Campobello Island sat off the coast of Maine. We were more or less at the top of an isosceles triangle, a good vantage point from which to view both islands and the sea between.

Sure enough, there was a boat off Campobello. And a very fast craft it was too. It was scouring the area in more of a grid pattern than a zig-zag. As I watched, the boat slowed to a crawl and did a series of figure eights. Large at first, then diminishing in size. I wondered if they had found something floating on the water. Evidence of the explosion aboard *The Flying Dutchman*, perhaps. Or maybe the outboard Werner and the Germans abandoned. They were just too far away for me to tell.

The boat ceased its search and abruptly picked up speed and bore off toward Grand Manan. I handed Marvin the binoculars. Wisps of snow were beginning to swirl in the wind.

"That's her," Marvin said. "And here comes Old Man Winter. Jumpin' Jesus, we're gonna have to man the oars and take our chances. What do you think?"

"Let me have another look." I didn't like it. They were incredibly fast. For once, I was glad I was carrying a firearm. "If they catch us in the open we'll be at their mercy. Then again…"

"What? I don't like the sounds of that 'then again'."

"Why not hide the dory and send them a signal?"

Marvin grinned nervously. "Then what?"

"Commit piracy. I don't know. Improvise. That boat could get us safely to the coast in no time."

"You're happy right, Jack," Marvin said. "Let's get to it. It's worth a try."

I shook my head. "That's what I like, Marv, enthusiasm."

The stitches in my leg were giving me fits. I limped along behind him until we reached the camp fire.

We wove a sled of spruce boughs and moved the fire to a bald patch of rock visible from the sea. While I piled dead branches on the flames, Marvin scrambled down to the beach and camouflaged the dory with seaweed.

When he returned the flames were leaping high and giving off an intense heat that brought sweat to my forehead. A frigid blast of air swept across the island, sending a shiver through the trees.

"You got shoes on under those galoshes?" Marvin asked.

I nodded.

"Good. Give them to me."

Marvin took off his rubber boots and put on the galoshes, cinching the straps tight. "Cigarette time," he said, inhaling deeply. "We can hide behind those boulders."

I risked a head-spinning glimpse over the cliff. The dory had disappeared, hard to find even though I knew where it was hidden. Marvin glanced at me. There was the whine of a motor not far away.

"You're the gunman," he said. "I kinda wish now that you didn't fire off all the forty-fives."

We smoked and waited. Marvin winked and tossed one of his rubber boots on the fire. "Needed a new pair anyhow," he said.

A black column spiraled upward, acrid and foul smelling, discernible against the silver-gray sky. "Did this to Molloy's gumboots last year after he stole a couple of lobster traps. Stank up half the village," he said.

I leveled the binoculars toward the ocean. The boat came into view. Marvin dropped the other boot on the fire. I withdrew to the shelter of the boulders.

A white mane of spray flew out behind the speedboat. All at once it died in the water and swung about. Marvin was fanning the fire, passing a green bough over it that sent up black billows of smoke like an S.O.S.

"I'm beginning to wonder about you," I yelled.

The boat was approaching at full speed. Two men sat behind the windscreen. A Canadian Ensign flapped on a chrome standard at the bow.

Marvin took a handful of beach stones out of his pocket and threw a couple for practice. He gave me the O.K. sign and pressed himself flat on the ground.

The boat was speeding toward us dead on. I placed the .38 on a boulder and raised the binoculars. The fellow behind the steering wheel cut the motor. The man in the passenger's seat stood up.

They had seen the smoke. And where there's smoke...

I seized the pistol and squeezed off three shots. Straight up. The gulls started screaming for their lives. The fellow in the boat sat down. I jumped out of hiding and frantically waved the duffel coat over my head. Marvin thought I was cracked.

"It's Tom Waterman," I yelled. "Make a fuss."

Marvin beat it down to the shoreline, whooping and hollering all the way.

I leaned back and sighed, nearly overcome with tension and fatigue. Then I felt a burst of energy and went to the fire. I inserted a branch into the rubber boots one at a time and let them plummet over the cliff and into a tidal pool. I hunkered down and warmed my hands and feet.

Tom joined me, his face rosy from the climb. He poured coffee from a Thermos flask, the aroma more uplifting than a choir of angels. I drank two cups, savouring every drop. Tom watched wordlessly until I finished. Marvin was down below, talking excitedly to someone who couldn't get a word in edgewise.

"You don't look too great, Jack," Tom said, screwing the lid back on the Thermos.

"Too many late nights. Who's Marv talking to?"

"Barry Stratton."

I looked up in astonishment.

"Penny tried to find you last night. We went down to Indiantown to see if you were on Marvin's boat. It was gone and when it wasn't back this morning Penny got worried. I got worried. I remembered you telling me about Barry Stratton. About his speedboat racing. And his real identity and all. I know you by now so I had a good idea where you took off to. I telephoned Stratton and filled him in and here we are."

I got up and climbed down on stiff pins toward the inlet, sea legs not wanting to work on land. Tom grabbed the duffel bag. The weather was closing in fast. In a matter of minutes it would be hard to see more than a quarter mile. "You're a lifesaver, Tom," I said. "Dying of exposure has a bad ring to it. Not half dramatic enough."

Marvin and Barry had uncovered the dory and were lugging it to a ledge above the high-water mark. Stratton was dressed for a regatta in captain's hat, turtle-neck sweater, double-breasted blazer, gray flannels, and deck shoes. He was listening to Marvin's account of last night's events.

Tom laughed at Marvin's animation. "I see I was right to worry that you might not still be in this world."

"Then you did find debris on the water?"

We reached the beach, the smell of seaweed and salt air stronger.

"Yes, but I knew it wasn't the *Barbara Ellen* – wrong colour scheme. What about the rowboat with the outboard? Whose is that? And where is the *Barbara*…"

"Later. I'll tell you everything on the way home, Tom."

Flocks of gulls were winging toward The Wolves, seeking safe haven from the gathering storm. "Have you heard a marine forecast?"

"That's part of the reason we came after you and Marvin. Small craft warnings for the Bay of Fundy, Gulf of Magdalene, and the South Shore. Gale force winds."

"Lost at sea has a nasty ring to it, too," I said.

Even lightly dusted with snow the varnished mahogany on Stratton's boat gleamed. It had leather seats front and back like an expensive car and a dashboard with a cigarette lighter. It also had a push-button radio. "Deluxe," I commented. "Thing's fast, isn't it?"

TERRY CRAWFORD

"If it had wings," Tom said, stowing the duffel bag.

I reached in my pocket and took out the camera I'd taken from *The Flying Dutchman*. "Put this in there, too."

"A Leica? Where did you get that?" Tom asked, passing me a sandwich wrapped in waxed paper.

"It was Werner Strasser's. It's mine now. Still got a film in it."

I stuffed the sandwich in my face. Peanut butter and grape jelly. It was horrible but I ate the whole thing. And if he had another dozen, I would've eaten them too.

Tom looked incredulous. "Whew, you *do* have stories to tell."

Barry Stratton shook my hand. His thirty-dollar cologne added a strange note to the smell of the sea. "How are you, Mr. Ireland?"

"Never better now that you and Tom are here, but this isn't much of a place for a picnic."

Barry eyed the cliffs and the rockslide. "H'mm, I see what you mean. Difficult to find a decent cocktail. Shall we embark? I'll have you gentlemen home in time for a late lunch. I believe we can outrun the storm."

"Aye, aye, captain," I said.

Marvin beckoned me aside for a private word. "Is this guy Stratton the genuine article?"

"Yes, why?"

Marvin took off his hat and ruffled his curly hair. "He says he'll replace the *Barbara Ellen* and with a better boat to boot. No strings attached."

"If Stratton promised you a new boat then it's as good as launched."

Marvin guffawed in disbelief. "I didn't even have the *Barbara* paid for."

"Doesn't matter. Stratton is on your side. My side. I'm tired. You know what I mean. Just name the new boat after the baby, will you?"

"Done."

"Let's kiss this place good-bye."

We climbed into the speedboat, Marvin up front beside Stratton, and Tom and I behind. The seats were as comfortable as club chairs. The sea was choppy, white caps tumbling in toward the rocks.

Stratton steered away from The Wolves and brought the boat up to maximum speed, prow out of the water as we skimmed over the waves.

He made a straight run for the coast and then angled off, landfall never more than a few hundred yards from portside.

Tom and I huddled while I told him the whole truth and nothing but. He nodded once or twice but didn't ask questions, whether out of innocence or wisdom it was difficult to say. I hardly believed the words falling off my own tongue.

The bell-buoy aligned with Partridge Island appeared out of the snow flurries. We slowed and entered the harbour, our sleek speedboat dwarfed by the ocean-going vessels moored at the piers. Gliding smoothly, Stratton delivered us all the way into Market Slip at the bottom of King Street. We waved farewell, then watched as he motored at high speed toward the mouth of the river en route to his boathouse at Ketepec.

After the mournful silence of the Bay of Fundy the noontime traffic seemed a din. I hailed a taxi and we went to my place. Marvin asked for a raincheck on dinner and went immediately to bed, flopping fully clothed onto the cot in the kitchen. I pulled off his hat and threw a blanket over him. He was sound asleep and didn't so much as bat an eyelash.

I'd slept on The Wolves and was still exhilarated by the sea voyage. I snapped the caps off a couple of quarts of Alpine and padded on sock feet into the living room.

Tom was listening to the international news. Things were bad all over. It didn't require a soothsayer to predict a heavy mortality rate for his generation.

"Franco is bound to win. The Civil War will be finished before Easter. Maybe sooner," I said, turning the dial until I found music.

Tom arose and poured his beer into a glass. We listened to the radio and drank. "Chopin," he said.

"Yeah, at the gallop."

Tom changed the station, tuning in a number by Artie Shaw, who was popular enough to run for President. It was a swell arrangement of *Begin the Beguine.*

Elegant even in casual clothes, Tom swayed in time until the tune ended. "I've been thinking about the loose ends," he said.

"Ah, yes, those loose ends. They're like telephones ringing in an empty house."

On the radio, a trio of songbirds sang a jingle about RINSO, promising that everything would come out in the wash.

CHAPTER SIXTY-TWO

I PARKED THE Pontiac beside the City Market and walked across Germain Street to Manchester, Robertson, and Allison's department store. Roxanne was moving to Restigouche in a week and I wanted to send Leonard some books on science for young readers. It wouldn't be quite the same at Pepper's Diner without Roxanne but I couldn't blame her for wanting to go back home.

It turned out that her ex-husband had a life insurance policy worth $25,000 and Roxanne was the sole beneficiary. Doc Cromarty made sure there was no problem collecting the money. His autopsy report stated 'Accidental Death'. No one argues with the Coroner, least of all the deceased. Anyway, the dead man's ultimate wish had been fulfilled and not thrown out the window on a mere technicality, a trifling matter like murder.

I chose six titles, the last a big picture book on the history of architecture. The clerk promised delivery before noon of the following day. Satisfied, I rode the elevator down two floors and browsed around Men's Clothing. I ordered a fedora in my size in shingle green. A new shade. Maybe Tom Waterman's sartorial habits were rubbing off on me. The salesman tried in vain to interest me in a tasteful necktie. And a pair of shoes that didn't look like clodhoppers.

Before he could annihilate my fashion sense I fled to the Music Department. I was in pursuit of a thank-you present for Jimmy Quinlan, semi-pro surgeon. I rubbed my leg, still smarting and a little itchy from the recently removed stitches. Penny did the job and it was just as well. I didn't want my regular physician asking embarrassing questions. Questions like, "Who was the interior decorator who sewed you up?" After their removal, Penny disinfected the aquamarine stitches and put them in a test-tube with a rubber stopper and a label marked: Break in Case of Emergency. The stitches were in the glove compartment of the Pontiac. One never knows.

I quit trying to select hillbilly records when I came across a number by Roy Patterson and the Lightnin' Pickers called *Two Possums for-a-dime*. Exasperated, I purchased a ten-dollar gift certificate and instructed the young lady at the counter to mail it to Quinlan. I left before I got depressed at the thought of replacing the records the late Berndt Koenig had destroyed at Lincoln's.

I took the elevator to the top floor. It was the middle of the afternoon and the Rose Tea Room was empty except for a quartet of old dolls who each looked too much like Wallis Simpson.

A waitress in a frilly apron and a gingham frock escorted me to my favourite table. It was tucked behind a latticework screen intertwined with paper roses. I ordered a pot of tea, a ham salad sandwich, and two slices of orange-vanilla cake.

I sat back and relaxed. It had been over a week and still nothing in the papers about Campobello Island or the *U-27*. Marvin had headed out across the Bay of Fundy yesterday at the helm of his new boat, the *Patrick Ryan*, bought and paid for by Barry Stratton. Tom Waterman and Stratton had pored over the papers, particularly *The Boston Globe* and the Maine weeklies, but there was nothing. They thought this curious but I didn't. I was through being curious. Somehow the *U-27* had gotten free of the steel anchor line from the *Barbara Ellen*. For all I knew, Wilder Hunter had escaped and was probably hoisting a beer stein with Werner and the others in Berlin. Or sipping bourbon in Washington. Who really knew? His green Plymouth was gone from Black's Harbour. I had ideas as to where but so far didn't have the time to check.

One story did surface in the papers. Our own newspaper. The corpse of an unknown man was discovered in the limestone quarries north of the city. The body was badly ripped apart, the face unidentifiable. It was ironic that Berndt Koenig, terrified at the mention of wolves, should've been eaten by their domestic cousins. Birds and small animals had done further damage. Apparently the dear departed had almost completely departed. Doc Cromarty was called to the scene to view the scattered remains. His statement to the press – dog owners shouldn't allow their animals to run loose lest they revert to roaming in packs – reignited an annual controversy. Cromarty didn't say a word to me even though he knew Lincoln Drummond lived only a quarter mile distant. A fact not lost on Tom and Stratton, who pointed it out and let it go without further comment. That is, if you didn't include sly grins as potent signs.

I removed *The Winding Stair and Other Poems* from my pocket. Reading at the table was a lifelong habit my father tolerated despite Mom's protests. Dad had seen and coveted the specially bound copy James Reilly had given to me but it was mine as a keeper. When I telephoned Reilly to order the same emerald green binding for Dad, James volunteered to do Yeats' complete works. My father was ecstatic.

Prudence spoke to me over the phone. She sounded cheerful, almost young again. She and James were leaving on a Caribbean cruise on the Cunard Line on Holy Thursday. "It's a new beginning, Jack. A chance to forget the past and start living again." I thought, easier said than done, but wished them a bon voyage. They had the essential ingredient – love for one another – to sort out their problems. For them, I could see nothing but blue skies.

I brushed the cake crumbs off my vest and reread "Spilt Milk" for the umpteenth time. The waitress, who had always seated my wife and me in our favourite corner, brought the check. I left a tip that would afford her the luxury of a new hat for Easter. It was my way of ending a ritual I'd performed every spring since Grace died.

I wandered through the store and lingered over the pipes at the tobacco counter but bought cigarettes after all. Then I went out one of the King Street entrances.

The day was bright. Mountains of clouds scudded along the horizon. March going out like a lamb. I loitered under the striped awning and smoked, content to watch the passers-by walking up and down the hill. Too warm for overcoats, it was still scarf and jacket weather. A toddler, dressed in jodhpurs and a knit sweater, toddled by in a harness and leash. His mother smiled the way strangers sometimes do on sunny days.

I took the crosswalk to Canterbury Street. Chief Delaney was standing on the corner by the Bank of Montreal. He was out of uniform and looked like a retired gent uptown on errands.

"I was waiting for you, Jack. The bastards wanted to go in and search all eighty-four departments to find you but I wouldn't let them."

I stiffened and glanced around. "Them?"

Two men in overcoats rounded the corner of Germain by the Royal Hotel. Jaywalking, they crossed the street towards where we were standing. Delaney put a hand on my sleeve. "At ease, Jack. These jokers are what pass for friends nowadays."

The pair were big fellows and reminded me of Military Police. I wasn't too far wrong.

"These guys are with Naval Intelligence," Chief Delaney said, watching them approach. "South of the border."

"What do they want with me?"

Delaney laughed bitterly. "Damned if I know. Maybe you should ask the Green Knight. Sufferin' Jesus. Don't make any sudden moves. These characters wanted to shanghai you to Kennebunkport but I wouldn't allow it. I gave my word that you'd talk to them on the condition that it's in Canada."

I watched them slow down to a snail's pace. They were sweating and looked like they were carrying heavy iron under their coats.

"Why should I talk to them at all, Chief?"

"Because, Jack, I got a phone call from someone placed high up."

"Yeah, how high?"

The bigger man stopped ten feet away and opened his coat. He had a .45 automatic in a canvas holster strapped on his left hip. I nodded and smiled. He was grim.

"How high? How about the right hand of God," the chief said.

The men stood, one on each side of me. I was tall but they were taller. And big as Clydesdales.

Chief Delaney snorted, "Return this man to the pavement safe and sound or there'll be hell to pay. I don't want any double-crosses."

The men regarded Delaney without a trace of emotion. The Chief turned on his heels and went down Canterbury. He got in behind the wheel of an unmarked car and opened a newspaper.

I was escorted down King Street to Prince William. Neither usher was in the mood for small talk. Three addresses from the corner, beside the Canadian Pacific Steamships Agency, we entered a black door into a dimly lit stairwell and climbed to the fourth floor. The black door had been unlocked with a key. Till today it was just a door in a doorway.

I was left by myself in an office at the front of the building. Large windows overlooked Market Slip and the intersections at the foot of King Street. A long table with a desk lamp and three chairs sat back in the shadows away from the sun. I lit a cigarette and perched on a stool near the window. That was it for furniture. Not even an ashtray or a wastebasket.

A door opened at the rear and a man with the whitest hair I've ever seen walked into the room. He wasn't old, maybe forty-five, but he seemed tired. Or bored. Sighing, he took the middle chair and opened a file folder. He riffled through a stack of photographs and papers, ignoring me the whole time. Finally, he gazed at me and said, "You may smoke if you like," even though I was already smoking.

Maybe he was used to giving permission and couldn't help himself. It didn't matter to me. I said, "What's this hugger-mugger about?"

"Patience," he said calmly. "The others."

A minute later two other men and the giants in the overcoats filed in, their shoes clumping on the hardwood floor and resounding in the emptiness. The sun was warm on my back but I didn't move.

Two official-looking types flanked the white-haired man. He spoke to the big men who were standing at the end of the table. "Gaskin," he said. "Pull the blinds. Ireland's going to roast. Withers, coffee all round. And sandwiches. I haven't eaten since Bangor."

Not until the coffee and sandwiches arrived did the white-haired man turn on the lamp. Meanwhile, the four of us sat in the muted green light cast by the drawn shades and stared at one another. If it was supposed to be a war of nerves the only one addled was Gaskin, slouched against the wall and sweating inside his heavy overcoat.

I declined the coffee. Withers and Gaskin withdrew, the last I was to ever see of them. The interrogation began, for it was that, the three of them plying me with questions and me chain-smoking. This time there were no Dictaphones or stenographers.

The white-haired man introduced himself by rank. He was with the O.S.S. The others were Naval Intelligence. They wanted to know about Werner Strasser and the Germans.

"Where do you want me to start?" I took off my suitjacket and hat and unbuttoned my vest.

The white-haired man closed his eyes and leaned back, fingertips pressed together in an attitude of prayer. To what strange god I'll never know. "Begin at the beginning."

I looked from face to face to face. The elder of the Naval men prompted, "Valentine's Day."

I started. It took a very long time. Whenever I prevaricated, they tripped me up. Whenever I evaded, they cornered me. Whenever I strayed, they pushed me back on the path.

The part about the stitches put them in stitches. I wanted to see if they could laugh.

I finished sarcastically with the details of my pick-up and delivery to three secret agents, one of them prematurely white from a life of burrowing in the dark.

The white-haired fellow rose and came around the desk. He sat on the edge and lit his first cigarette. "Ah, Ireland. What are we to do with you?" The man's face was in darkness. All I could see was the white halo of his hair.

"With me? With you," I countered. "Sullivan, my former partner, is dead and you covered it up, cleaned up that mess in his apartment for those Nazi bastards just so you could gather information on them. And Wilder Hunter, he's playing you for a patsy."

"Wilder Hunter is a double-agent who had no choice but to go along. He couldn't have prevented Sullivan's murder. He didn't get there until it was too late. In fact, Hunter stopped them from eliminating you on several occasions, if you must know."

Unconvinced, I said, "Remind me to light a candle at the altar. Where's Hunter now? Or do you have any idea?"

There was a long pause. "In Berlin, attempting to salvage some credibility after the shambles you've made of the situation."

"Grand. Feel free to blame me. What situation is so important that innocent people can die for it without any say in the matter?"

The men whispered together behind their hands. "Tell him," the Naval men insisted.

The white-haired man spoke quietly, smoke streaming from his nostrils, "Ireland, you're an idealist. A political anachronism."

"Anachronism? Since when has simple justice gone out of date? All I ever wanted was to find out who killed Eugene Robichaud. A little man in the hold of a ship. Someone you would probably consider a nobody. Well, that little man brought me all the way here."

"Tell him," the older Naval man said. "Let him know what he's done."

The white-haired man returned to his chair, turned it around, and sat with his elbows resting on the back. He removed a single sheet from the folder. I picked up the stool and carried it to the table. No one objected.

The man to my right wore a tie clip with the coat-of-arms of the Glengarry Rifles on it. His accent had sounded like the prairies, western and flat. Naval Intelligence, be damned. He was probably Canadian Army Intelligence. The other had a U.S.N. briefcase and the unmistakable pronunciation of a Bostonian. I'd been to Red Sox games at Fenway enough times to know the Massachusetts accent by heart. The Canadian casually secreted the tie clip in a shirt pocket.

"Read these names," the white-haired man instructed, sliding the sheet toward me across the table top.

I read: Thomas Waterman, Cornelius Long, Lincoln Drummond, Marvin Halliday, Dr. Angus Cromarty, Penelope Fairchild, Roxanne Doucette, James Reilly, Prudence Reilly, Ancil Bermann. "What is this?" I said. "A threat?"

"Interpret it however you choose," the white-haired man said. "If you reveal what has been discussed in this room or what we are about to tell you, each and every one of these persons will be arrested and summarily convicted under the Official Secrets Act. Furthermore, you are to convey to these persons, and make it abundantly clear to them, that if they so much as breathe a word regarding their knowledge of the Strasser/Hunter liaison the above conditions apply. Do you understand?"

I felt like asking the guy if he'd ever heard of the Magna Carta. I nodded instead.

With eyes closed, the white-haired man sighed and said in a low voice, "Campobello was a set-up. A sting. Werner Strasser and Herman Grundig were two of the best cipher and code experts in the Third Reich..."

"Were?"

"Allow me to finish," he said, opening his eyes and staring into mine. "We had intended to kidnap them and their two friends – both skilled radio operators privy to classified information – and replace all four with our own operatives. These operatives were to board and subsequently commandeer *U-27*. They had the necessary password and signal sequences to do so. As you know they never had the opportunity."

I thought back to the four men I'd seen on the beach at Campobello. "Why seize the submarine if you've already got the Germans?"

"*U-27* carried a code machine known as the Enigma. It's been deemed Top Priority to get our hands on one."

"And?"

"Oh, some day."

"You mean to tell me you didn't have ships from the Portsmouth Naval Yard out in the Gulf of Maine waiting to intercept the U-boat in case your well-laid plans went awry?"

"Yes. And yes. But there wasn't any U-boat. That's where the 'were' comes in. *U-27* eluded us and sank with all hands somewhere off Georges Bank. Far too deep for us to recover. Or find."

I didn't know how to take the news. Or what to believe. My heart raced. I returned to where my coat lay on the floor. It was surrounded by cigarette butts. I took a fresh pack of Philip Morris out of the pocket, lit one, and just stood there in the dark. Stood there and somehow did not feel all that sorry. U-boats were known to sink ships.

"We found flotsam from Marvin Halliday's boat, the *Barbara Ellen*, near the final sonar reading. The depth thereabouts is approximately sixteen hundred and fifty fathoms," the Naval man added.

"Why tell me all this?" I asked, badly in need of a tumbler of Scotch.

"I suppose because we have a grudging admiration for your resourcefulness, not to mention your perseverance and sheer tenacity. Pertinacity. And, of course, we know you wouldn't want anything to happen to your friends. Some of them do have careers," the white-haired man said wearily.

"Why isn't Deputy Chief Hardfield's name on your list? Not honest enough?"

Once more the three of them laughed. A peculiar thing considering the seriousness of the proceedings. The Glengarry fellow consulted the others, then explained, "We have Hardfield in custody. The man no longer presents a problem. After you informed on him to the R.C.M.P. and he took flight, he made it as far as the Gaspe Peninsula. Hardfield's become unhinged. Rants and raves day and night about King and Country and Mata Hari dancing in the nude."

The Naval man concluded, "Suffice it to say, Hardfield's a guest of the Canadian government in one of its better padded cells. Your Chief Delaney will quietly see to his replacement."

"Mind if I go somewhere and have a drink to that?"

The white-haired man lit his second cigarette. "Not at all. Have one for me. Hardfield was a horse's ass. It's beyond me how he ever rose to the position he did."

I repeated what my father always said. "Cream isn't the only thing that rises to the top." More laughter. I put on my fedora and approached the table. I'd had a shutterbug friend of mine develop the film from Werner Strasser's Leica. I dropped five photographs and thirty-six negatives in front of them. With bloodshot eyes, the white-haired man looked up at me. He was younger than I'd estimated, maybe even my age. He fanned the photographs out like playing cards. Which was good because I thought of the film as my winning hand.

Moving the desk lamp closer, the three men huddled over the photographs. The first two were of Wilder Hunter and the white-haired man in Salon A of the Royal Hotel. The remainder showed the three men talking to one another by the canteen at the Lily Lake Pavilion. It looked like a perfect winter day. A little girl in a figure skating costume shielded her eyes from the glare off the ice and snow as she squinted toward the photographer.

"Five aces," I said, leaving the room. No one said good-bye.

I took my own sweet time descending the stairs. Upon scrutinizing the negatives they'd see me in various locations around Saint John and Lancaster. And a few of Sullivan with Hardfield. And a nice one of me and Roxanne in February at the bus stop by the Bank of Nova Scotia.

I stepped out onto the sidewalk. It was dark and cold, the streets in the business area deserted. I glanced over my shoulder as a man in a cinnamon overcoat walked past. Letting an interval tick by, I hurried to the corner of Church Street and ran up to Canterbury. The overcoat got into Delaney's car, shook the Chief awake, then they drove off toward the South End.

I scratched my head in wonder and went off in quest of that Scotch. I had secrets to drown and had to sink them deep.

CHAPTER SIXTY-THREE

MY CONSCIENCE GAVE me a lot of trouble for a couple of days. Then I sobered up and stopped feeling guilty. Or sorry for poor old Jack. The three nameless men who grilled me on Prince William Street were long gone, the office as empty as the day of the questioning. In spite of their benign appearance they employed methods almost as malignant as the forces they opposed. Maybe that's what it took. But it wasn't carved in stone that I had to like it. Or approve.

I showed my I.D. to the corporal at the guardhouse and drove into the Armoury yard. I parked the Pontiac in the shade of the main building and walked over to the parade grounds. The air over the Bay of Fundy was clear enough to see all the way to Nova Scotia, a dark blue line above the horizon. It was unseasonably warm for the last day of March. No one was fooled into thinking spring had actually arrived; nevertheless, it made winter-weary Saint Johners happy.

Chief Delaney beckoned from beneath the portico of the Armoury. "One last meeting," he had said, "and that's a promise." He was dressed for the weather in slacks, windbreaker, tweed cap, and a good mood.

We went inside. In the reception room Delaney consulted a directory mounted next to a display of regimental badges. I followed as he short-cut through the gymnasium to a staircase on the other side. Raw recruits, sweating through calisthenics, kept their eyes fixed on the drill instructor as we passed.

We went up the stairs and came out onto the raised track surrounding the gym. "I haven't been in here since I was in Sea Cadets," I said. Looking down, I felt a momentary pang for my lost youth.

"Twenty-five years for me, Jack," Chief Delaney said. "When I enlisted in 1914. It's scary. What I knew then you could fit onto a pinhead."

We entered a long corridor, floors polished to a brilliant shine, the smell of wax and cleansers overbearing in the tunnel-like confines. At the end, a spiral staircase led up to the top floor. Delaney knocked on a solid oak door stencilled with the number 410. Hearing movement inside, he said, "Ian, it's Gord."

The door swung open. A slender man with a thin face greeted us. "Hello. Do come in, please. Make yourselves comfortable."

His English accent was impeccable. And authentic. A cinnamon-brown overcoat and an umbrella with an ivory handle hung on a coat rack. This was the man I'd given the slip after he shadowed me to Gillespie's Poolhall. It was on the day I discovered a roomful of stolen goods in the flat below Sullivan's. I was sure he was also the same man who had anonymously overseen the Dictaphone interviews at the Admiral Beatty Hotel on St. Patrick's Day. And presumably, drew up the documents that I signed afterwards.

A kettle whistled in a room to the side. "Make yourselves comfortable," he repeated, indicating a pair of leather chairs.

He pushed a curtain aside and disappeared into a small kitchen. I looked around the room. There was a plain beige carpet on the floor, a rolltop desk, a bookcase crammed with military histories, and a day-bed draped with a Hudson Bay blanket. Spartan quarters for a man with expensive taste in clothes.

I lit a cigarette and got up to look out the window. Below, Vulcan Street ran directly to the harbour. From here there was a bird's eye view of Shorty Long's woodyard. And further out, the West Side piers were plainly visible. I picked up a pair of field glasses and watched the men at Shorty's bundle kindling and bag coal.

"Surveying your second station, Detective Ireland?" the Englishman said.

"That's not all that funny, Commander," Chief Delaney said only half-seriously.

"Or all that untrue," the fellow said smoothly. "One must find his trusted allies wherever he may."

He positioned a portable table on the carpet. It was loaded down with a teapot, three mugs, and a bottle of cream. Sitting on the day-bed, he put a cigarette into a holder and waited for me to take a seat.

"It is of paramount importance that what we are about to discuss remain secret," he said, tipping the tea into the mugs.

"Same rules as the Admiral Beatty Hotel?" I queried.

The epitome of composure, he smiled thinly and lit his cigarette. "Precisely."

Chief Delaney sipped. "Coffee? I figured tea, you being British and all."

"Tea? Appalling beverage, not fit for a man to drink. Can't stand the stuff."

"Is this going to be another instance of rank and service branch only? Or don't I deserve an introduction?" I said impatiently. Penny was to meet me at Pepper's Diner and I didn't want to keep her waiting.

Delaney raised an eyebrow and shook his head. "Sorry." The fellow offered his hand. "This is Commander Fleming, British Naval Intelligence."

"What brings you to our fair city?" I said. "Besides the opera and the superb dining."

"Jack," Chief Delaney warned. "Be nice."

"It's quite all right, Gordon. If anyone deserves an explanation, Ireland does."

"Oh, I like the first-name basis. You guys known one another long or are you just members of the same club?"

"Jack, don't go overboard. Commander Fleming is on our side. Okay? He's with us. Now, don't get hot under the collar. Relax and listen for a change."

"Thank you, Chief Delaney." Fleming went to the window and sat on the sill, blue sky outlining his tailored suit. "I'm with B.S.C. British Security Coordination. We'll soon have offices in Manhattan..."

I interrupted. "New York? Why's that?"

"In the eventuality that the Nazis invade Britain, we've thought it wise to have key intelligence services safely out of reach. Furthermore, we can more readily dovetail our efforts if the American espionage agencies are close at hand."

"Invasion? We're not at war yet and the Americans may not get involved in another European conflict."

Delaney cleared his throat. "I'm going to let you guys sort this out," he said. "Mind your manners, Jack." It was near noon hour and the Chief's stomach was rumbling. In a few minutes he'd be in some greasy spoon attacking a blue-plate special. Or two. He said his good-byes and seemed relieved to be out of the picture.

TERRY CRAWFORD

After the door closed, Fleming continued, "The Intelligence Community never sleeps. It has recognized the imminence of war for years. Particularly since '36 when Germany occupied the Rhineland. There will be war within the year. Hitler has a plan for the conquest of Europe." He paused to allow his statement to sink in.

"If you're looking for an argument, pick another subject," I said. "But the American Secret Service. Wilder Hunter's with them, isn't he?"

"Yes. The Americans sometimes have a tendency to handle some information with reckless disregard for consequences, but they are firmly against, as is Roosevelt, the rise of Hitlerism. F.D.R. fully supports the secret war."

"That's reassuring. But what do you need from me?"

I didn't mind Fleming; at least he was part of the British Empire. But the Americans operating on our soil did distress me. Even if they were after German agents, it was a matter of sovereignty. And they behaved as if they couldn't trust us to handle our own affairs.

Fleming got directly to the point. "You can be elusive, an in-one-door-and-out-the-other sort of chap. I lost you on the evening of March nineteenth and didn't see you again until the following night. Where were you and what happened?"

"I'll answer that. But first – you've been on my trail for awhile. How come?"

"Pure chance. I was keeping a watchful eye on Wilder Hunter. He successfully infiltrated the Nazi enclave aboard the *Bergensfjord* but it was all very hush-hush. Too hush-hush. We usually share intelligence information with the Americans, so naturally our suspicions were aroused. You vastly upset Hunter and his superiors. Indeed, to the extent they thought to muzzle you by having you swear to secrecy. However, they reconsidered and let you off with a verbal warning to halt your investigations, a warning which emanated from Hunter. The Americans felt that you would only accelerate your efforts to get to the bottom of things if called upon to sign on the dotted line. It was an astute judgement on their part. Especially considering how blind to jurisdiction you are. Doctor Cromarty was another matter. He was effectively silenced, and in a manner of speaking made an accomplice to the Sullivan cover-up by signing papers obliging him to secrecy."

"Was the paperwork Cromarty signed legitimate?"

"Yes, very much so. I should remind you that the documents you signed at the Admiral Beatty are also legally binding. Any transgression will be taken with the utmost seriousness. I hope you don't mind me emphasizing that fact – the utmost."

Fleming came away from the window and sat down in the chair Chief Delaney had left empty. He moved like a well-conditioned athlete, someone ready for action at the drop of a hat.

"To continue," he said. "After the Germans tried to intimidate you by forcing your Studebaker off the road, you persevered. In so doing you had them rather on edge. To say the very least. My reasons for following you were twofold – to try and determine what the Germans had up their collective sleeves – and watch your back. I'm sure it was only through the intercession of Wilder Hunter that you weren't killed or otherwise knocked out of the game. The Studebaker business was a rogue action not sanctioned by Hunter."

I drank another mug of coffee and smoked one of Fleming's English cigarettes. He didn't seem to mind the silence and patiently waited for me to begin. I told him about the photographs of Campobello Island and how I had caused the Nazis to scrap their plans and escape on the *U-27*. I gave him most of the details about my activities from the time Marvin and I left Saint John until our return. I didn't say anything about the loss of the *Barbara Ellen* or the U-boat.

The steam whistle at the sugar refinery shrieked out twelve o'clock. Fleming smiled. "Excuse me for a minute."

I got up and stretched while he rattled around behind the curtain in the little kitchen. He reappeared with a shaker and two cocktail glasses. He strained a drink into each glass. "I know it's early, Ireland, but it is after twelve. Join me in a vodka martini?"

"Don't mind. What's the occasion?"

"Well, in a way you've given yourself a seal of approval. Much to my great relief, I might add. Cheers."

"Cheers. How so?"

"I know about the loss of *U-27*. Your statement shows that we can trust you to keep a secret."

The vodka martini was something new to me but I could develop the habit. "So you know the three no-names. I spotted you after they questioned me."

TERRY CRAWFORD

"No, I don't know them but I have a feeling I soon shall. As for seeing me, that was intentional. As regards the *U-27*, the B.S.C. has its own sources."

"H'mm," I said. "Nice drink, Commander. Got the recipe?"

"Try *The Savoy Cocktail Book* for the ingredients. However, I believe these should be shaken, not stirred," Fleming said, pouring another into my glass. "This is genuine Russian vodka – *Stolichnaya*. Officially, you see, as far as the world is concerned, I'm in Moscow. Have been these last several weeks. *Nostrovia*."

I raised my glass. "Down the hatch."

"Please accept my apologies for the official secrecy, but publicity could expose clandestine operations and place some of our operatives in grave danger."

"I understand. At least you didn't threaten me with a list of my friend's names like those characters on Prince William Street did the other day."

"They did that to you? My word."

He contemplated something for a minute, then smiled. "You must admit, Ireland, that you do have quite a little network. Out here on Vulcan Street, for instance."

"Friendly forces." I thought back to Black's Harbour and the names in the guest book at the Bayview Cabins. I tore the page out of my notepad and handed it to Fleming. "I think I saw your name recently."

He studied the list. I explained where I'd gotten the names.

He read them aloud. "K. Philby, W. Stephenson, Harry Hensley, David Cornwall, I. Fleming. A joke in very poor taste, I'm afraid. If this is an example of Wilder Hunter's sense of humour then he will have to be severely reprimanded."

"That bad?"

"These are the names of active personnel in the Intelligence Community. Harry Hensley is practically a recluse. Our top code-breaker."

"In room forty of the Admiralty, no doubt."

"How do you know that? Not that I'm saying…"

"I read about room forty in a book about the Great War. Maybe you British *are* too traditional. Manhattan might be a worthwhile change of venue."

Fleming said, "Yes. We can be too traditional. Somewhat."

"More than somewhat." I set aside the martini glass. "Drinks were tops. Listen, I have to meet a lady friend. Are we finished?"

"Yes. This terminates the matter. I must say it's been interesting."

We shook hands at the door. "Yeah. You gave me lots to think about."

"But not talk," Fleming cautioned. "Thank you, Detective. I wish you well."

"Same on this end, Commander."

I left him standing at the opened door. He was still there when I reached the stairs. He gave a polite nod and was gone. It was the last I heard of Fleming until years and years later.

Outside, I sat behind the wheel of the Pontiac and watched the young soldiers legging it around the cinder track. I wondered how many of them knew they were ghosts already.

CHAPTER SIXTY-FOUR

PENNY LISTENED TO the radio and hardly spoke on the drive from Pepper's Diner in Lancaster to St. Stephen on the Maine border. She was a good driver, handling the Pontiac like a Montreal cabbie: fast on the take-off and swift on the road. The trip was never-ending. Woods, woods, and woods. Glad to have a chauffeur, I lit Penny's cigarettes and otherwise napped.

I was asleep when she screeched to a halt. Groggy and still half dreaming, I asked, "Are we there yet?"

A pair of irate men in business suits shook their fists at the car and moaned about women drivers. Penny got out, came round and opened the passenger door, then pulled me by the sleeve to the sidewalk. The men did an about face and scurried into a dry- goods shop where they pretended to admire the chintz.

"My strapping bodyguard," Penny smirked, leading me arm-in-arm down the street.

"You're a bad girl," I said.

There were cigarette ashes on her short coat and skirt. As I brushed them off with a clean handkerchief I noticed eyes watching, as they will in any small town. Finished, I gave her a large kiss.

"You don't know how bad," she said, walking on ahead.

I followed and caught her by the hand. "I'm willing to learn."

We strolled through St. Stephen toward the International Bridge. The sweet smell of chocolate wafted on the breeze from the Ganong's candy factory. "Don't let me forget to buy a five-pound box of chocolates for Shorty Long's party tomorrow," I said.

"Good show," Penny said. "What an odd assortment of people you count as friends. I don't know of anyone who celebrates April Fool's Day, with the exception of Shorty and that woodyard crew."

"It's one of Shorty's 'pagan festivals.' He observes May Day, Labour Day, and Halloween. And the Feast of the Lupercal instead of Christmas."

We wandered in and out of a few side streets, stopping to admire some of the splendid Victorian houses. For the time being there was no need to hurry, and that was nice. Eventually, we came to the bridge and crossed the St. Croix River to the United States.

A U.S. Customs officer directed me to a glassed-in booth where William Roberts, a man I had contacted the day before by telephone, sat with his feet up on a chair. He was reading a Zane Grey western and drinking black coffee out of a tin cup.

"Just like a real cowboy," I said.

A bulky, curly-haired man with a beaked nose, Roberts stood up slowly. "Does no harm to pretend. The wide open spaces are a long ways from Down-East. You must be Detective Ireland. I recognize your accent."

"*I've* got an accent?" I said, flashing my I.D. for the record.

"Dry as salt herring," Roberts said, shaking my hand with an iron fist.

He rooted around in a drawer and extracted a set of automobile keys. "That vehicle you inquired about is outside a garage about a block away. I'm on break. I'll walk you down."

We went out into the sunshine where the sight of an American flag made me stop for a second.

Massive in his uniform, Roberts limped painfully. "Gout," he explained. "Doctor says I eat too many lobsters. That's why I have to keep my feet raised. I says to the doctor, 'I can't eat enough lobsters.' What are you gonna do, you only live once, right?"

"As far as I know," I said.

Penny was on the other side of the street, keeping pace and window-shopping at the same time. The stars and stripes seemed to be displayed everywhere in the stores.

"Here she be," Roberts said.

Wilder Hunter's green Plymouth sat at the front of the lot. It was rubbing elbows with a row of used cars, mostly old Fords from the '20s and early '30s. I looked at the price tag. On the surface it was a steal.

"They're askin' too much," Roberts said.

A mechanic in greasy overalls ambled over at Roberts' call.

"This man's from New Brunswick, Saint John police. He's got a couple of questions for you regarding the Plymouth," Roberts said.

The mechanic didn't seem to want to bother. I offered him a cigarette, which he took, lighting it with a wooden match he scratched on his zipper.

"What's wrong with it?" I asked innocently.

"Some bugger sugared the gas tank, ruined the motor. Damn shame, it is."

"Yeah," I said, unable to hide a smile. "Tell me about when it came in."

"It was the twentieth. I remember 'cause I had a dentist's appointment. Pair of teeth yanked." The mechanic grinned, two bottom front teeth missing. "The car arrived coughin' and sputterin' like it had T.B. Fella driving was too pissed-off to talk. When I looked it over and give him the verdict he took out the luggage and set it onto the sidewalk. Darndest thing, all he says was, 'Damn Ireland'."

Roberts glanced at me without comment.

"The woman," I said. "What about her?"

"Lady with him was in a daze like she was sleepwalkin'. What a honey. Didn't say a word. Why should she? After he struck a bargain with me to get rid of the Plymouth, I heard this guy marched downtown and bought himself a brand new DeSoto. Cash on the barrelhead."

I showed both men a photograph I'd pinched from inside Deputy Chief Hardfield's desk at the station. They nodded.

"That's her," the mechanic said, "Right as rain."

It was Helena Ardith Grace, Mrs. Hardfield. The woman who liked to dance. Even if it was alone.

"Officer Roberts, could you open the trunk?"

I thought about Helena and the footprints in the ashes at Sullivan's. I was going to be the biggest fool at the April Fool's party.

"Empty," Roberts said. "I could've told you that."

I peeled back the floor mat, exposing the New Brunswick license plates. "I'd like to have these, if you don't mind." As an afterthought, I'd gone to Motor Vehicles and checked the numbers. The plates were registered in the name of Helena MacKenzie.

When Roberts balked, I said, "Evidence."

"Sure enough." He checked his watch. "I best be gettin' back."

"If you want to sell this heap," I said to the mechanic, "there's a clerk in the general store in Black's Harbour, son of the owner, told me he'd like to have it."

"I'll sure give him a try. Thanks, mister."

"Believe me, it's my pleasure," I said.

I waved to Penny. She removed her beret and took the pins out of her hair. Using a mirror in a furniture store window, she combed it out with her fingers, letting it drape loosely onto her shoulders. I liked it that way and she knew it.

"Hi, bright-eyes," I said. Unlike New Brunswick, which didn't have taverns and bars, Maine was awash. "Let's go for a drink."

We found a quiet bar and ordered Manhattans. There was a sea shanty on the juke-box, very faint. I inserted a handful of nickels and punched in a bunch of those sappy love songs Penny liked so much. A few of them actually contained music and weren't all that bad.

"Whose photograph did you show those men?" Penny asked, sipping her third cocktail.

"Mata Hari."

Tipsy with booze, and not upset, she said, "So don't tell me. I'm just a curious little cat, that's all."

I ate a bowl of pretzels then we went for a sight-seeing stroll around Calais. Penny bought a replica of the flag of the thirteen colonies and a wood carving of a black bear. I purchased two pints of Seagram's V.O. and put them in my pants pockets. At the border, Officer William Roberts gave us a salute and a come-back-soon.

We lingered for a while on the bridge and watched the flow of the St. Croix River. After a sobering walk up and down the streets of St. Stephen, we bought five pounds of chocolates at the Ganong's factory and returned to the Pontiac.

I got behind the wheel and drove the twenty-odd miles to St. Andrew's. Penny smiled when I parked in the lot reserved for guests at the Harbour Light Inn.

It was the slack season and we had the place almost to ourselves. I signed the register Mr. and Mrs. Edward K. Ellington and gave the clerk the suitcase for two I'd packed the night before. Taken by surprise, Penny fairly purred as we went back outside into the sunshine.

I scrounged a couple of deck chairs and arranged them on the lawn by the breakwater. The sun was strong and the salt air bracing. A fishing boat chugged out of the harbour. The scene was postcard picturesque.

I pulled my hat brim down and peered out to sea. Way out beyond the horizon, down deep, sixteen hundred fathoms or more…

"Jack, you've got that far-away look again," Penny said, nudging me.

I looked into her eyes and said, "I was somewhere else. Sorry."

THE END

Made in the USA
Middletown, DE
18 November 2017